Zoë Ferraris moved to Saudi Arabia in the aftermath of the first Gulf War to live with her then husband and his extended family of Saudi-Palestinian Bedouins. She has an MFA from Columbia University and is the author of two previous novels, *Night of the Mi'raj* and *City of Veils*. She lives in San Francisco.

Also by Zoë Ferraris

Night of the Mi'raj
City of Veils

Kingdom
of Strangers

Zoë Ferraris

Little, Brown

LITTLE, BROWN

First published in Great Britain in 2012 by Little, Brown

Copyright © Zoë Ferraris 2012

The moral right of the author has been asserted.

A CIP catalogue record for this book
is available from the British Library.

ISBN 978-1-4087-0365-6

Typeset in Caslon by M Rules
Printed and bound in Great Britain by
Clays Ltd, St Ives plc

Papers used by Little, Brown are from well-managed forests
and other responsible sources.

MIX
Paper from
responsible sources
FSC® C104740

Little, Brown
An imprint of
Little, Brown Book Group
100 Victoria Embankment
London EC4Y 0DY

An Hachette UK Company
www.hachette.co.uk

www.littlebrown.co.uk

Kingdom
of Strangers

I

The SUV hit the sand drift, skidded and stopped in the middle of the road. The Homicide team got out, four men in plain clothes, their shirts wrinkled, faces stung by the sun. Only one man had thought to bring a scarf for his head, the others made do with sunglasses.

The local police pulled up behind them. The Bedouin who had found the corpse could see at once, from the subtle way the men's bodies showed deference, who was in charge. Lieutenant Colonel Inspector Ibrahim Zahrani did not introduce himself. The Bedouin approached him, anxiously recounting how his truck had jacked off the road, throwing one of his sheep out of the flatbed and forcing him to stop. When he'd gone to retrieve the sheep, he'd found it. Everyone followed him over a rise in the sand.

It was hard to tell at first whether it was a man or a woman. Five sets of boots stopped in a semicircle around a mutilated face. The cheek and left eye had been ripped away – probably a bullet's exit wound – and the remaining skin was desiccated grey and coated with sand. From the tiniest sliver of black poking up from the collar, Ibrahim guessed she was female.

His first thought was that some desert boy had shot his sister through the head for a 'crime' that involved the family honour. Who else would bury someone way out here? Too far south to be Jeddah, this was a forgotten strip of sand sixteen miles inland from the main road, which was not even a proper highway itself. They'd got lost twice on the way here and had had to wait for the local police to come and get them.

He gave the face another look. It was not a desert face. Even with all the destruction you could see that it was Asian.

Ibrahim glanced at his watch: 1:30 p.m. If they were lucky, they could be done before the most infernal hours of the day. It was early autumn, really just an extension of summer. The heat was already clipping his thoughts like an impatient listener. The local officer, Hattab al-Anzi, didn't look like a man who worked a desert beat. Pasty-faced, squinting, covered in sweat. He hooted his horn and drove off, presumably to fetch the Coroner, or perhaps the forensics team, who were no doubt stuck circling the same three roads Ibrahim's men had just cursed to hell.

Behind them, the sheep were bleating in the truck bed. Half the road was covered in sand. Just a few metres ahead of where they'd stopped the SUV, the road was impassable. Such an isolated spot. The drift might have gone unnoticed for weeks.

'Any idea if this happened recently?' Ibrahim asked the Bedouin.

'Yeah, we had a windstorm last night. A bad one. Certainly bad enough to blow a dune over the roadway.'

When he said *dune*, he motioned in the direction of the body. All Ibrahim could see was a great vista of sand, broken here and there by outcroppings of rock. It took a loosening of perspective, some stiff stumbling back to the road, before he saw how the area around the body was slightly raised. There had been a dune there – not a very high one, probably a barchan, its back to the east-blowing wind.

He watched his men trample the crime scene and heard his junior officer, Waseem Daher, admonish them. 'Go back to the car! You're stepping on evidence!' No one listened, but they stood near him, turned to him when he spoke, always eager. Daher hadn't fully realised his power over other men.

The sun beat down on them like licks from a blowtorch. When the cars finally arrived, they came funerary style, a procession of Red Crescent ambulances, the Coroner's van, two Yukons with forensics teams. The local cop, Hattab, brought up the rear.

'Stupid guy,' someone said. 'Would someone tell him you're not supposed to lead from behind?'

'He's just making sure he can get out first, in case we have another windstorm.' This was Daher.

Within minutes, the scene was a maelstrom of men. The forensics team cordoned off the area around the body with long sticks and a swirl of blue tape. Ibrahim intervened; he wanted the whole dune sectioned off, so they expanded the area, pushing the men further back. Two younger officers had arrived with the Coroner, also named Ibrahim, but whom everybody called Abu-Musa, the father of Musa. He was actually the father of Kareem, and should have been called Abu-Kareem, but at a coffee shop one afternoon he had attempted to convince Chief Inspector Riyadh that *musa*, which was the name of the prophet Moses, was also the genus classification name for bananas. And they were so named because Moses's mother had stuffed a banana into the baby's mouth before placing him in a reed basket and pushing him down the Nile. The banana was nutritious but more crucially kept the baby quiet so that the Egyptians wouldn't kill him. Chief Riyadh, unused to following such convoluted intersections of history and myth, simply sucked on his hookah and grunted, 'You know this how, Abu-Musa?' The name had stuck.

Ibrahim had never worked with Abu-Musa before, but the man's temper was legendary, as was his overbearing righteousness. Right now he was waiting for forensics to finish excavating the torso. Two Red Crescent men moved in to help set up the vacuums that forensics would use to remove the sand, and Abu-Musa shouted at them: 'Get back from there! You don't touch her!'

'She's dead,' one of the RC responders replied.

'No one should touch her! Now get out of here.' Abu-Musa pushed the man aside. He wasn't worried that someone might disrupt the evidence; he was watching out for virtue crimes, a man touching a woman's body, defeating her honour even in death.

The familiar crackling of tyres on asphalt and a small explosion of dust announced the arrival of another SUV, this one carrying Detective Inspector Osama Ibrahim.

Osama got out, surveyed the scene, and went straight to Ibrahim. The two men shook hands and Osama offered an apology for not having welcomed him to the department before this.

Everyone was acting deferential. Ibrahim had been in the department for two weeks now, a transfer from Undercover. He had seniority only because, at forty-two, he was older than most of the other officers, because he had worked Homicide many years ago, and

3

because he had royal family connections. He was sure that, soon, the cracks would start to show.

'Local Bedouin found a woman's body in the sand,' he said. 'Have a look.'

Osama went off.

The Red Crescent responders were grumbling about Abu-Musa and discussing an incident that had been in the news. A female student at the Teachers' Education College in Qassim had fallen ill. The college had called the Red Crescent but when they arrived, the college authorities had forbidden the paramedics to touch her. They'd been afraid she would die, but apparently more afraid that, touched by strange men, she would lose her dignity. Amidst all the arguing, the girl had died. Fortunately, these two RC responders seemed appalled by the whole event and were wary of the same thing happening to them.

'The *fuck* he thinks we are – a pack of pimps?' one spat.

Osama came back looking shaken. Ibrahim recognised the look. You believed you were immune to death, having seen whole rooms splattered in human fluids – and then one woman's face struck you down again. 'Local trouble, you think?'

'Maybe.' Ibrahim studied the scene. 'Is your Coroner always so aggressive?'

'Yeah, but only when female victims are involved.'

'Naturally.'

There was a sudden crack. It was a small sound but it provoked a wave of curious silence. One of the Red Crescent men had stepped into a soft part of the sand and his foot had encountered something hard, which had splintered. Ibrahim went over, shouting: 'Nobody move!' Surprisingly, everyone obeyed.

The man had already lifted his foot out of the sand and Ibrahim could see from his face what he'd found.

'That sounded like bone.'

'It was.' The depression where the man's shoe had been was filling with sand. Ibrahim caught sight of what might have been another face.

They were five metres away from the original body.

'Everyone stay exactly where you are,' Ibrahim boomed. 'Except for you.' He pointed at the forensic photographer. 'Take photos of everyone, exactly where they are now.' The man scrambled into action. Then Ibrahim pointed to Daher. 'Get the local guy to radio in a request for some trackers. Murrah if you can get them, and as fast as possible.' Daher jogged to the police car, where Hattab was enjoying the air conditioning.

Ibrahim stood guard, his gaze challenging anyone to move so much as a millimetre. Like children in a game, they stood awkwardly frozen, their faces throwing off the burden of heat and now alive with expectation, the strange delight of being told what to do when it actually counted.

His men had trampled the area well, but by the third body they could still find no pattern.

The Murrah trackers who arrived – a grandfather and his nephews – spent hours going over the site, memorising boot prints, sandal prints, eliminating the men who were there with such deftness it seemed magical. They didn't even need to consult the photographs the forensic guy had taken. Then they started again, looking for the things that didn't belong. They probed the ground, bending over with hands on knees, squatting, kneeling, staring at the same spots in the sand for whole minutes at a time, following subtle trails. They found the next six bodies with hands like divining rods, feeling mysterious geometries in the air above the sand, and only then did a pattern of sorts begin to emerge.

The bodies were all female. They had all been buried at the back of what had been a crescent dune. There was an underlying rock formation that gave the area some stability; that made it possible, for example, for a murderer with a penchant for returning to the same burial site to actually find that site in the case of a sandstorm blowing his dune across the road. A slight depression leading down from the road meant that no matter how many windstorms came through, the sand would re-accumulate at this spot. Over the course of months it would rise up into a dune, blown by steady winds. In a storm, it would topple onto the road, like a slow-motion wave crashing onto the beach. The road would be cleared and eventually the sand would rise again.

As the body count grew, Ibrahim kept returning to a single thought: *Why here?*

They had to bring in water trucks, and a local restaurant (only thirty-two kilometres away) prepared huge plates of rice and lamb, wedding-style, which the men ate distractedly, if at all. The blasting waves of heat began their killing spree by stealing the men's appetites. Two men collapsed and had to be driven back to Jeddah in the back of a Red Crescent van.

He bent over body after body, the heat like hooks cutting into his back. Sweat dripped so freely that his shoes were wet. Even the Murrah began to look wilted.

The scene unfolded like an archaeological dig, sprawling out towards the desert, growing up over surfaces decorated with canvas blankets, stakes, lights brought in as the sun grew red and dipped to the edge of the earth's plain. Nineteen bodies in all. He dreaded the number when he heard the Coroner say it. Abu-Musa came to talk to him, the first time he'd done so all day. The sunset made his grizzled face almost pretty.

'Did you hear what I said? Nineteen bodies,' Abu-Musa said. 'Nineteen. You know what this means?'

'*And over it is nineteen?*' Ibrahim recited.

Abu-Musa nodded, looking quietly pleased. That verse from the Quran, mysterious out of context, had prompted men over the centuries to conjure wild fantasies about the importance of the number nineteen. The most recent incarnation came from America, in Tucson, Arizona, where an Egyptian biochemist, Rashad Khalifa, claimed that the archangel Gabriel had revealed to him in the text of the Quran a hidden mathematical code that could be unlocked using the number nineteen.

But the subsequent verse in the Quran was a simple explanation of it: *And we have set none but Angels as Guardians of the Fire, and we have fixed their number.*

It meant that there were nineteen angels guarding Hell.

'Could be a coincidence,' Ibrahim said.

'Are you sure about that?' Abu-Musa smiled, a cold gesture. 'I believe you won't find any more bodies out here. Whoever did this has his reason.'

'All the same,' Ibrahim said, 'maybe it just happens to be nineteen.'

2

Katya Hijazi was carrying the latest batch of files down to Inspector Zahrani's office when an explosive round of laughter from the situation room drew her attention. She crept down the corridor, wanting to know what was so funny at a Homicide meeting.

The crowd was dispersing, and she watched them through the doorway, the men talking, conversations erupting here and there, laughter, nods of agreement. No one looked her way, they were too busy staring at Waseem Daher, one of the junior detectives whom Katya had met twice and already counted as among the few people she would gladly shove into an industrial meat grinder. Last week, Daher had accused her of being a hot shot who fancied herself the centrepiece of every investigation, thanks to growing up watching *CSI* and believing that forensics officers actually did all of the investigative work. If he noticed her in the doorway, he didn't let on.

Pictures of the victims' faces filled most of the whiteboard at the front of the room. Katya had been so busy in the lab that she hadn't seen the bodies yet. Every time she went downstairs, the Examiner's office was crowded with senior officers and Ministry of Interior agents. They had never had so many bodies at once. In fact, they didn't have enough freezer space in the women's lab, so they had put the overflow in the men's side of the building and prayed that no one else in Jeddah died until they finished processing the evidence.

It had taken three days to remove the bodies from the site. They had even brought in an archaeologist in the desperate hope of establishing that they were historical. But from what forensics now knew, the most 'historical' of the bodies had died ten years ago.

Katya had spent the past four days bagging and labelling the clothing of the dead, and running blood and fibre samples like a drone, disconnected from any greater knowledge of what she was doing. Information about the murders had to be ferreted out through hasty conversations with Majdi, one of the male forensic pathologists, or by some old-fashioned investigating of her own: eavesdropping and 'borrowing' the reports that never managed to circulate to her desk. She had a few in her arms right now, but they'd turned out to be duds.

She did know that the investigators still hadn't identified any of the women. They were mostly immigrants: Filipinas, Sri Lankans, Indonesians, most in their early twenties. All of their faces had been torn apart, and there were no fingerprints. The facial reconstruction specialists had just produced some sketches and this was what Katya was after.

As the men started coming through the door, she drew to the side. She didn't want to go up to her lab and sit in front of a machine for the rest of the day. She wanted to interview people, scour the streets for a potential witness, do all of the things that would most contribute to the investigation and that these men were gearing up to do, or doing easily, without worrying about what it would mean for their virtue. But she couldn't interview anyone. Maybe they would find it improper to talk to a woman. She would have to have a male chaperone. She would have to have some authority to force them to talk. She could always shove her way through the door, but there were more subtle obstacles than a door. There were gateways in the mind, blind alleys and narrow passages, labyrinths that made up whole cities of thought, whole worlds from which people would never make an exit, surrounded as they were by heavy stone walls from the era of the Rashidun Caliphate.

She went to the end of the hallway, dropped the files in Zahrani's box and went straight downstairs to the Medical Examiner's office. There were two entrances to the lower floor of the building – one for men and one for women. She took the appropriate door and wound her way to the front of the building where she found Adara in the female autopsy room.

'Oh good, you're here,' Adara said. 'Put on some gloves and come over.'

Katya did as she was told and braced herself to look at the five bodies lined up on stretchers against the wall.

'They originally numbered the victims in the sequence in which they were found, but it turns out that was haphazard, and now they want to re-number them according to the chronology of their deaths, which makes this one the most recent.' Adara motioned with a needle to the chest she was currently stitching closed. 'They just brought her in this morning.'

'How long has she been dead?'

'It's difficult to say, but no more than six months.'

'I don't know anything about it,' Katya said. 'I've just been running blood samples and looking at the photos of their faces.'

'Well, their faces pretty much tell the whole story. Every one of them was shot through the back of the head at point-blank range. Bullet exit wounds damaged most of the faces, but it's still possible to see some facial characteristics.' She motioned to the woman on the table. 'What else I can tell you is that she was between twenty and twenty-five years old. There is a broken tibia, a broken femur, no evidence of rape. And then, of course, her hands.'

Katya looked at the woman's arms and nearly fell over. The hands were missing – both of them. That explained why there were no fingerprints.

'They're all like that,' Adara said.

'All?'

'Yes. Each one was cut off with a single stroke after the victim was killed.' Adara's hands were making rough work of the stitching. She threw down the needle, went to the sink and threw up.

'Sorry,' she muttered. 'Pregnant.'

'Oh. Congratulations.'

Adara wiped her mouth and rinsed it with some water before coming back to the table.

'Do they still have their feet?' Katya asked.

'Yes.'

'I know the investigators have just got some facial reconstruction sketches,' Katya said. 'They're planning on showing them to the consulates.'

'And you think ... ?'

'That that's going to take a few years. The consulates won't know anything. Look how bad they are with the living.'

'Well, yes,' Adara said. 'I think they're right to presume that most of these women were foreign labourers, probably housemaids.'

The biggest shock to the department was the possibility that one person had done this, that one person, over the course of many years, had been silently killing women and no one had noticed. Katya had already begun assembling missing person files, but it was likely that these women had never been reported missing. Their employers probably assumed that their housemaid had run off, like many of them did, in search of a better job or to get away from an abusive situation. The housemaid wouldn't want to be found – she might be sent to prison.

It was possible, too, that whoever killed these women had hired them as housemaids himself. That he kept them in seclusion, tortured them slowly, one at a time, before killing them. That from the very moment these women entered the country, no one but the killer knew they existed.

'What do you know about serial killers?' Adara asked.

Katya shook her head. 'Not much.'

'Well, I just heard that they're bringing in a man from the American FBI, someone who specialises in serial killers.'

'That seems excessive,' Katya said. 'I mean, we've had them before.'

Adara looked at the bodies lined against the wall. 'I guess they figure that this one is different. A new breed, perhaps. He's been working for at least ten years. Chief Riyadh is ashamed. Everyone is feeling humiliated. They didn't know this was happening. They're ten years late. It took the police four years to track down that serial killer in Yanbu. Riyadh's not going to let this case last that long.'

On her way back to the women's lab, Katya stopped at Majdi's office but he was on the phone and Ministry agents were milling about. She quickly ducked back into the corridor and took off down the hall. Just this week the religious establishment had issued a fatwa against female cashiers, saying it was sinful for women to work in public positions where they might come into contact with men. It might have become yet another ridiculous fatwa that Saudis would allow themselves to feel guilty about but would roundly ignore, except that the grand Mufti in charge of validating the fatwa actually extended its reach by banning women not only from cashier positions but from every other kind of job that would bring them into contact with men. The first line of battle on these things was in government positions, and especially those in law enforcement. She hoped the King's brothers or the King himself might do something to overturn it, but until then all the women in the lab were holding their breath.

3

It was only to be expected that at the worst possible moment, his son's life would implode. Zaki's marriage had been a disaster from the beginning. Ibrahim had watched the pressure build for three gruelling months. Even the shocking appearance of nineteen dead bodies was not enough to alter this inevitable motion towards the deep, dark, inward-sucking force of his failed family.

His favourite son, Zaki. Ibrahim sat in the courtroom and listened as the boy tried to explain himself to the judge once again. He had made a mistake. It was all too easy when you didn't know the bride before you married her. They – both of them – were just asking for a divorce.

The judge made no sign that he'd heard; but something in his eyes told Ibrahim that he wasn't buying it, that he heard men say this sort of thing all the time. But what was Zaki supposed to say? That he had never meant to marry a woman like Saffanah: righteous, religious, praying five times a day and asking him to take her to Mecca once a week? The judge would kick him out of the courtroom for his disrespect to Islam.

The way Zaki told it, when he woke in the morning, he'd find his robe, his *'iqal* and his *ghutra* neatly laid out on the bed. And socks – she always put a pair beside the robe, on the off chance that he was one of those idiots who actually wore them. In the kitchen, he'd find his breakfast on the table, his coffee poured and sugared, his bread fresh from the oven. After breakfast, he'd find his wallet and keys on the table by the front door. He would only see

Saffanah once he'd climbed into his car and looked back at the apartment. She'd be standing behind the half-shuttered window looking out at the street. At least he assumed it was her behind the burqa; there was no one else at home. He had no idea what she did all day. She was too pious to own a mobile phone. She said they were tools of moral ruination. When he came home in the evenings, his dinner was waiting for him. His prayer mat was laid out with a change of clothes. She did such a good job of taking care of him, while the whole time refusing to give him the one thing a husband expected. At night, in the bedroom, she wouldn't touch him. He had never seen her naked. He knew it was his right to demand it, but he didn't want to force her. In fact, he wasn't sure he wanted it at all.

Just a few days after the wedding, even before Zaki had started to complain about it, Ibrahim had sussed out the situation. Though Saffanah was never in his way, her distance, silence, and pitch-perfect obedience were going to start getting in the way.

'This,' Zaki had shouted one night, 'is why I hate religion!'

'Don't say that,' Ibrahim said, shocked. 'She is not Islam. She is not even a good version of Islam.'

They had already told the judge that they hadn't consummated the marriage, and that Saffanah was still a virgin. Delicately, Zaki had suggested that a doctor could confirm it. Saffanah's father Jibril had shot out of his chair, shouting in protest. The judge had quietened him with a wave of his hand and then turned to Zaki with a look of deep scepticism.

'But it's true!' Zaki said.

Jibril was quick to respond. He argued that it didn't matter what had happened in the bedroom. Saffanah had been married for three months now. No man was going to believe she was a virgin, even if she was. Ibrahim hated to admit that the bastard had a point. It was going to be difficult for Saffanah to remarry.

She was sitting on the other side of him. Not a single piece of skin was showing anywhere on her body; her burqa was an impenetrable slab of black, and she was wearing socks and gloves. But her posture said everything. She slunk down in her chair, arms curled around her torso, head bowed. Saffanah – pearl. She was awkward, clumsy, painfully self-conscious. Her face was misshapen, lumpy like bread dough. Nothing glimmering; Pearl-like only in that she had become the hidden wound in Zaki's soft interior.

The only time Ibrahim ever saw them interact was when she brought Zaki his dinner. She wouldn't eat with the men because she believed it was improper for a wife to eat with her husband. What would happen if she ate faster than him? She'd finish before him! She might even eat more than him! She would, in her own words, be 'acting like a husband', which was a capital crime. Ibrahim tried explaining that 'acting like a husband' was a legal euphemism for the crime of homosexuality, but when he said the word 'homo-sexuality' she covered her ears and started muttering prayers because the word was sinful. She prayed for Ibrahim's protection as well, since he was the offender who spoke the wicked word, and when he said no, don't be ridiculous, she spent the rest of the evening sprinkling the house with holy water – quietly, mind you – and submitting herself to Allah.

She made Zaki's mother look like a rare specimen of moderation.

Ibrahim knew that his biggest mistake had been not standing up to his wife, Jamila. She had pressured Zaki into marrying Saffanah, a spinster at twenty-two. She had lived in terror that she would never marry, because the Prophet had said that good Muslims should marry. She was desperate, and no one would have her. And Zaki, at nine-teen, was not terribly handsome, a younger son with a mediocre job, or so his mother liked to remind him. Ibrahim could have done more to stop this from happening. What was the rush? But he had learned to pick his battles with Jamila, and in this case, she had opened with a volley of bazookas and RPGs, followed by a mini-nuclear device, and he just hadn't had the strength to fight back. Now he was paying for it, having to shepherd Zaki and Saffanah through months of misery.

Ibrahim looked at the couple, both facing forward, ignoring one another. He wondered what would happen if Saffanah spoke up in her defence. *Their* defence. She would probably ruin it by telling the judge that her husband was an infidel. He smoked. He didn't pray five times a day. In fact, he didn't pray at all. And he listened to music. It struck Ibrahim suddenly as the saddest part of this whole fiasco that Zaki had once owned a guitar, had had ambitions to play it, had even formed a loose band, and then, because of his foolish and overbearing mother, had married a stranger when he should have been off plucking strings in someone's garage and enjoying the last of his young adulthood.

From the other table, Saffanah's father Jibril was gloating. The longer the silence dragged on, the more pleased Jibril seemed with himself. He had the law on his side, the bastard. The marriage contract stipulated very clearly that if Zaki should decide to ask for a divorce, he would have to pay fifteen million riyals – enough to support Saffanah comfortably for the rest of her life. As a divorced woman with no one to keep her, she'd have to beg off her parents for eternity. But of course no one in the family had that kind of money. Who would? He'd known plenty of men who'd divorced their wives and never paid a penny, or at least had never paid the millions they'd sworn to pay. So it should have been simple for the judge – Zaki and Saffanah wanted a divorce, and the Hadith said that all you needed to do was tell your wife 'I divorce you!' three times, and that was it. Done. Could it have been any easier? But her father refused to take her back.

It was annoying the judge, too. He sat there, exchanging the odd glance with Ibrahim, scratching his already over-scratched beard, staring at his water glass, the ceiling fans, the broken tiles on the floor, all in an effort to look studious when clearly he was at a terrific loss. Ibrahim could see his mind working. The good side was saying: *Let the kids have their divorce!* But the pompous side was grappling with the legality of breaking the contract.

When it was his turn to speak, Jibril stood up and told the judge that Zaki had ruined his daughter, and that until he could pay what the marriage contract stipulated, her family wasn't going to have her back. Clearly it was taking all of Zaki's self-control not to start shouting. Ibrahim felt the urge himself. He wanted to tell the judge that Jibril was the king of the pimps. That he'd divorced his first wife without paying so much as a halala, and that as a result Saffanah and her mother were wretchedly poor. That Jibril had seven ex-wives, and four current wives, every one of them pregnant, with twelve children between them already, and if he wasn't so prodigious in the bedroom he might actually have more generosity of spirit for his first child, the poor Pearl, and her tragic mother.

Jibril was still speaking. As much as he loved his daughter, he

15

simply couldn't take her back. Saffanah was already twenty-two; her chances of remarriage were practically zero. How would she support herself? Was she supposed to be a burden on her parents for the rest of her life? Were *they* going to pay for her meals, her lodging, her regular trips to Mecca? What would happen when he died? His daughter would be alone, with no children, no money, no husband, no future. Then it would be the job of the state to take care of her, would it not? And everybody knew what a wonderful job the state did of caring for its independent women! She'd wind up a prostitute, and everyone knew it.

Only he didn't actually say the word prostitute; he said 'indecent'. She'd wind up *indecent*. Yes, Saffanah – the woman who pulled crumpled prayer schedules out of the waste bin and ironed them flat – Saffanah would start turning tricks at the Corniche. Ibrahim watched as the judge silently churned that bit of cream. *Indecent*. It was precisely the sort of word he needed to focus his resolve. The problem had been complicated until that word arrived. Now it was simple: there was no way to justify condemning a woman to a life of dissolution, no matter how much she might want to escape her current woes.

The judge's face told him everything: *No divorce, kids, sorry.*

Ibrahim felt the veins in his temples throbbing. Just last week a man had divorced his wife in this courtroom because she'd been watching a male newscaster on TV all by herself. She'd been alone in a room with a strange man. Never mind that he was on a flat screen. *That* stupid husband could get a divorce, but Zaki couldn't?

Triumphant, Jibril took a seat and turned to his daughter. 'I love you, Saffanah,' he whispered, 'but it's the truth, and you and I both know it.' Then he looked at Zaki and actually smiled.

They stood outside the courtroom and watched Jibril drive away. Zaki helped Saffanah into the back of the car. She fumbled for the seat, banging her head on the doorframe. Ibrahim had seen this performance before. Zaki would tell her to put her seat belt on. More people died every year from not wearing a seat belt than from any other reason, did she know that? She'd shake her head – not 'no, I didn't know that', but 'no, I'm not buying it'. She'd cross her arms, the Saffanah seat belt, and sit that way until he started the car. There was no wearing seat belts where Saffanah was concerned, because the belt might outline her body, and any man in a passing car would be able to see her shape, and that was unacceptable.

After watching her bump her head on the doorframe, Zaki said: 'You should get a burqa with a slit for the eyes.'

She didn't reply.

Ibrahim went to climb in the passenger seat but Zaki stopped him. 'Baba, please drive. I'm going to walk.'

'What?' Ibrahim blurted. 'No. Just come home. It's too hot to walk.'

Zaki's face was pale with pent-up rage. 'If I get too hot, I'll take a taxi,' he said. He shot one final glare at Saffanah and walked away.

Ibrahim got into the car and looked at Saffanah in the rear-view mirror. She was facing forward, her head tilted in a defiant way. 'Put on your seat belt,' he said, just for good measure.

He started the car. He knew it was wrong to be angry at her, but he couldn't help it. Her hostile, guilt-charged silence was familiar. Jamila did it all the time, only without the religious overtones.

They were three streets from the courthouse when he heard a choking sound from the back seat. He spun round to find Saffanah pulling on the door handle. He stopped quickly. She pushed the door open, leaned over and vomited onto the street, but because she wouldn't raise her burqa, the vomit spilled onto the fabric of her veil and down the front of her cloak. Only a small splash of it reached the pavement.

Ibrahim leapt out and went running to her side, but by the time he got there, she was sitting upright again, her vomit-stained veil sticking to her chin. She would never take it off in public, even in the car, even covered in vomit.

'Wait here,' he said. He left the car double parked and jogged down the street until he reached a corner shop, where he bought tissues, bottled water and chewing gum. The shop owner, God bless him, was a generous man who rushed upstairs to his flat, nicked a face covering from his wife, and gave it to Ibrahim. When Ibrahim got back to the car, he laid the items on the back seat next to Saffanah. 'Here,' he said, 'something to clean you up. And a new burqa.' Then he got in and started driving.

He took the highway and was nearly home before he noticed Saffanah using the tissue to wipe her face. She bent over so that no one driving by could see the delicate operation, and she removed the stained veil and put on the new one. Then she put a stick of chewing gum in her mouth. A few minutes later she opened a bottle of water, slid it under her veil and took a sip.

Ibrahim breathed in relief and turned his attention back to the road. He'd driven past the turn-off for their neighbourhood and was now heading into the southern outskirts of the city. Traffic was thin here, he could already see desert ahead. On impulse, he decided to keep driving.

A few minutes later, Saffanah started watching the window. He wasn't sure how much she could see through her veil and the tinted windows, but clearly she realised they'd gone past their usual exit. He decided not to explain it. The air in the car smelled of vomit, so he cracked a window and turned up the air conditioning.

He took an exit for a housing complex that looked newly built. He drove past the empty homes, imagining how boring it would be to live out here, with strangers for neighbours. There were no shops here yet, just empty, palatial houses.

He could tell from her posture and the tilt of her head that she was alert, curious. Coming up on the right was a large field and a few camels behind a wire fence. There was a small house to one side. He stopped the car, parked on the side of the road, and went to the back door to help her out.

It surprised him that she didn't protest. She hadn't asked a single question or spoken one word since she'd got in the car. He'd been trying to think of her as a daughter – had been trying for a few months now – but he kept coming up against the knowledge that he would never let one of his own daughters act like this, he would never encourage this kind of pious isolation and flaunting of religion – a *variation* of religion, somebody else's version. But when he opened the car door and Saffanah got out, the kick in her step pleased him. Maybe this whole time she'd just needed to get out of the city.

A middle-aged Bedouin man came out of the house and started up a conversation with Ibrahim. Saffanah stood to the side, looking at the camels, three of whom had come to the fence and were now leaning over it, stretching their long necks to reach her. Nervously, she approached them, lifting her hand carefully to rub one behind the ear. The camel snorted and stuck his nose in her neck. *Doesn't he smell the vomit?* Ibrahim wondered. But apparently not, because the camel fixed his teeth around the bottom of her burqa. Saffanah twitched and pulled away, and with a rip the burqa came free. She quickly ducked to the side, hiding her face from the Bedouin, but she needn't have worried. The man was quicker than her. He turned to the camel immediately, shaking his head with a laugh and reaching for the burqa. But the camel was trotting away and the Bedouin had to chase him across the field.

It took Ibrahim a moment to notice that Saffanah was laughing. She straightened very slowly, the smile still in her eyes, and when she saw that the Bedouin had politely turned his back on her, she actually looked happy.

'Dirty bastard,' the Bedouin muttered to the camel. 'You're a dirty old man.'

Two other camels were still at the fence, sniffing interestedly at Saffanah's neck. Ibrahim watched her, half-listening to the Bedouin scold his camel. Suddenly Saffanah nuzzled her nose into one of the camels. It was a miraculously small gesture that conveyed something quite grand: neediness and sadness, the desire to give comfort as much as to receive it, and a kind of pleading quality that said: *Please forgive me.*

Maybe it was the gesture, maybe the vomiting, but a sharp thought cut straight through his mind. *She's pregnant.* It wasn't rational. Saffanah was too religious to have got herself into something like that. It didn't make sense. But fifteen years of police work had taught him to trust his intuition. *Pregnant!?* All of the blood in his arms seemed to come to the surface. He jammed his hands into his pockets and wrapped one around his mobile phone. His skin prickled. Saffanah?

He wasn't angry, exactly. He felt amazement and chagrin. When did she meet the man who had deflowered her? He felt certain it wasn't Zaki – his son complained far too much about her frigidity to leave much room for doubt. Zaki left the house as often as he could. God, she could have been meeting any number of men!

She had noticed the change in his demeanour and was now

petting the camel in a nervous way. As soon as the Bedouin was far enough away, Ibrahim moved towards her. He removed her hand from the camel's face and held it. It was the first time he'd touched her.

'Saffanah. Look at me.' He said it kindly, but she turned to him as if he were holding a whip. He squeezed her hand reassuringly. 'You're pregnant.'

She jerked back, a spasm of shocked denial.

'It wasn't a question,' he said, squeezing her hand harder now. 'How far along are you?'

'I am NOT—'

'I'm a policeman, Saffanah. I know when someone's lying. Just tell me. I won't tell anyone. I promise.'

She stared at him. She did a damn good job of pretending indignation. In fact, she'd done a damn good job of everything. And she was stubborn. There was no way she was going to admit to the truth, and bullying would only entrench her resistance. He sighed.

'All right,' he said, letting go of her hand. 'I just thought, with you throwing up back there ...'

She turned back to the camel pen. The camels kept nudging her, and she continued to pet them, but her hand worked mechanically.

He realised that they could never send her back now. If her father found out, he'd make Zaki pay for the child for ever. If he found out that it wasn't Zaki's kid, Jibril would have his daughter tried for adultery.

Ibrahim's arms were still tingling and he realised he was afraid for her now. 'Well,' he said, 'after what happened today, I think the best idea is to go home and have sex with Zaki.' At the word 'sex' her hand froze on the camel's ear, then slowly continued. 'After a while, you get pregnant and have a baby. If you want to do it differently, Zaki's going to realise that it's not his. Does my wife know?'

She gave him a look of outright disgust.

'Well, thank God for that,' he muttered.

Something was forged between them in that moment, the magnetism of shared secrets. She stopped petting the camels, curled her arms around her waist and stared at the fence. If this were his own daughter – one of the twins, say, because Farrah was hopeless – and if she weren't already pregnant, then he'd tell her she'd better get an education before ruining her lovely figure with pregnancies and the kind of slovenly overeating that comes from boredom and from being stuck at home like a good Saudi housewife. He'd tell her she'd better get a career in case her husband turned out to be a jackal and left her with kids to raise on her own. He'd try to forge some strength into her, the kind of fierce, dignified personal power that was, in his family at least, the most highly regarded quality in a woman. But he sensed that Saffanah would recoil at these sentiments.

The Bedouin brought back her burqa and Ibrahim thanked him. It was wet with camel spit, and torn at the edge, but Ibrahim insisted it was fine. Saffanah took it gratefully and put it on at once.

They walked back to the car, but Ibrahim forced her to sit in the front seat, and he wouldn't start the car until she put on her seat belt, which she did slowly, like a reluctant child. They didn't talk, but he could tell that she wanted to say something. Probably: *You don't really think I'm pregnant, do you?* He wasn't in the mood.

By the time they reached the main road, the sun was setting. It filled the sky with a dazzling pink and for a moment he felt cocooned in a spool of candy-floss. It reminded him of being a child and going to the funfairs in the evenings. He'd gone to those same funfairs with his own kids, but Jamila had always made it a torturous experience. And now what would happen to Zaki and Saffanah, going to funfairs openly hostile to one another, with a child that wasn't even theirs?

He reached into the door pocket and found his cigarettes, lit one and dropped the pack on the dash. He felt vaguely guilty for smoking around a pregnant woman, but lo, the surprises weren't over that day. Saffanah picked up the packet and took out a cigarette. He was too amazed to speak. Saffanah – smoking? She didn't even shoot a guilty look in his direction before lighting it, inhaling right through her veil.

In that moment, everything became clear. Saffanah, as he knew her, was a total lie. Her religiosity looked like a pretence now, a shield to keep Zaki away – perhaps because she was in love with someone else? Hell, she'd been trying to alienate the whole family. Who she genuinely was, he couldn't have said.

'You shouldn't smoke,' he said lamely. 'Not if you're pregnant.'

She didn't reply. Glancing over, he saw that her veil was sticking to her face, a wet trail was streaking down each cheek. She was crying.

'Oh, Saffanah.'

Ibrahim parked on the corner furthest from the house. He wanted to give her a chance to collect herself before facing the family, should any of them happen to be lurking outside. The street was empty. They sat quietly in the car, Saffanah facing the window and probably seeing nothing. It was dark, and he knew from experience that wearing a face veil in the dark made you as good as blind. He had actually tried it himself one night – he and his brother Omar had walked up and down the street with their wives' burqas on their faces, trying to settle an argument about whether Omar's wife, Rahaf, could possibly have walked into the neighbour's car accidentally, thus setting off the car alarm and infuriating the neighbour. Omar had insisted she'd done it on purpose, but Ibrahim argued that even if your burqa had eye holes, it was hard to see what you were doing. So Saffanah's being turned away from him seemed like a silent plea for privacy – or forgiveness, he couldn't say which.

Once he finished his last cigarette, they got out of the car, Saffanah fumbling in the dark. He came around to her side of the car and said, 'Walk beside me. I don't want you setting off any car alarms.' She obeyed and they made their slow way down the street, Ibrahim watching her every step to make sure she didn't trip. When he got her to the house, he heard his wife's voice coming down the staircase, a low grumble that was unintelligible but which he implicitly understood. She was complaining about something, probably Ibrahim's inability to get his son a divorce.

Saffanah refused to remove her veil until they reached the second-floor landing. (The downstairs neighbours were a constant threat to propriety.) So he walked her to her door. She gave him one last frightened look before she went inside.

Ten minutes later, he was driving back into the city. He took the Corniche road. Roundabouts and their statuary glittered in the lights – from traffic, street lamps, floodlights and apartment buildings, a flowing river of light at the edge of the dark Red Sea.

He parked in his usual space beneath Sabria's building, the space allocated to her apartment and which she might have used, had she been allowed to drive. If the neighbours paid any attention to him at all, they assumed he was her father. He looked old enough. (Although once a female neighbour had mistaken him for a driver and asked him for a ride.) In paranoid moments, he considered parking on the street so no one would suspect that Sabria had a male visitor, but parking was scarce here. It was a relief to have a dedicated slot, because it seemed the more he came here, the more urgent he was to see her. In the beginning, she had needed him more – for sexual fulfilment, for comfort, and even for simple things like going to the doctor. They weren't married, yet she had become, in essence, his second wife. Over the past two years, his need for her had grown greater than he had expected.

He saw a woman going into the lift, so he took the stairs. The neighbours were mostly foreigners – a doctor from India, a few Egyptian couples, not the kind of people who gave much thought to Sabria's marital status or to the man who visited her at night and left before dawn. All the same, he thought it prudent to avoid talking to them.

He took the stairs two at a time and wasn't even out of breath when he reached the fourth floor. He went straight to her door. When she didn't answer, his chest started to feel tight and he took a few breaths. His heart was pounding. He should have taken the lift. He knocked again. No answer.

Fishing in his pocket, he took out the key. She had given it to him a year ago, and he kept it on his keyring, dangling there as innocently as his own door key. But he had never used it. He wasn't even sure it would work. It slid into the lock, and the door opened.

The apartment was dark. The stillness made him nervous. She always had music playing, the television on, Al Jazeera flickering silently in the background. Food cooking on the stove. He stood in the quiet and launched a single question at the universe: *Where is she?*

Feeling oddly like an intruder, he sat on the sofa and tried to reach her on her mobile phone. It went to voice mail on the first ring, which meant that it was off.

He went directly to the neighbours. Iman and Asma were a blatantly lesbian couple who claimed they were sisters. They had a wall in common with Sabria's apartment and on quiet summer nights, when the noises from their bedroom strained through the wallboards, Ibrahim would often lie there wondering if the women would ever get caught, and who would miss them if they were executed. They seemed to exist in a world of their own.

They were the only neighbours who ever came to the apartment, who ever exchanged more than an occasional hello with Sabria. Asma opened the door and gazed at him with the diffidence she had demonstrated ever since Sabria told them he was a policeman.

'I'm just wondering if you've seen Sabria today?' he asked.

She shook her head. 'Not since yesterday.'

'Did you hear her go out?'

'No. Why? She's not there?' Even Asma seemed to find this odd. 'Maybe she went to the shop?'

'I thought she'd be here.'

Asma called to Iman, and the two women stood there, puzzling out the last time they'd seen Sabria. It had been two days, in fact, once all the details were straightened out, but Iman was certain that she'd heard noise coming from Sabria's apartment late this afternoon.

'It sounded like she was at home,' Iman said. 'I heard the television.'

'OK, thanks,' Ibrahim said. 'If you see her, tell her to call me.'

He went back to the apartment. He hadn't talked to Sabria since the night before, but she'd been just as ever. Happy to see him. Smiling. Plying him with chicken and rice and a bowl of *halawa* mixed with cream. Sliding into his arms as he sat in a post-dinner coma watching her, arousing him with the warmth of her hands, the power in her thighs as she climbed onto him.

He took another look around. No sign of forced entry on the door jamb, the handle. Windows locked. Nothing out of place. Only her handbag, keys and mobile phone missing. She had gone somewhere. *There's going to be a stupid explanation.* But he couldn't think of one. Every time he'd toss out an idea, he'd feel a skipping panic, little splashes of excitement before each notion sank. He was surprised that it could happen as easily as that – that the most important thing in your life could vanish so quickly and quietly.

4

The worst part was that there was no one to tell.

He lay awake, staring at the wooden window screen of the men's sitting room. Dawn hadn't broken, they hadn't even sounded the first call to prayer, but he'd woken up anyway, panicked about Sabria.

In the five years he'd known her, she'd never been on time for an appointment. Yet in the two years since they'd been together, she'd never missed a date. They hadn't had a date per se, but they saw each other three or four times a week. If only he could tell Omar what was happening, his brother would, by his very embodiment of authority, provide an answer. But what was Ibrahim going to say: *I've had a mistress for two years and now she's gone?*

It was tempting to blame his paranoia on the discovery of the bodies. He remembered this from before, working in Homicide in his late twenties. Every time there was a murder, he grew panicky if something went wrong at home. Now more than ever he needed the rest of his life to retain its delicate, secret structure.

Someone had to know where she was. She didn't have many friends. She worked during the day, in a women-only shopping mall. Her co-workers were as mysterious to him as any stranger in a *niqab*. Her family was in Indonesia, or maybe they'd moved back to the Philippines by now. She never talked about them, only about her mother, who was dead.

His mind tore through the possibilities, cutting intersections, ignoring pedestrians, hitting wide-open highways that circled him back around a whole metropolis of problems that hadn't existed before last night. Had she grown sick of him? Had she left for someone else? Why not a goodbye note? Had someone taken her? She was anonymous. Who even knew she was there?

He could think of a few people who might want to hurt her. Her old employer, the bastard who had raped her when she was working as his housemaid. But the bastard had fallen into dark history, was never mentioned any more. And why would he come after her? If there was a reason, or even the hint of a threat, she would have told Ibrahim first thing.

Maybe someone from one of her Undercover jobs might be looking for revenge. She had been hired for Undercover five years ago, which was how they had met. She'd done a number of assignments with Ubayy al-Warra before being transferred to Ibrahim. He'd been working a female shoplifting network and needed an infiltrator. It was hard enough finding a woman for such a task, let alone a proficient one. Sabria had been excellent.

She'd eventually decided that the job was too taxing for her. He knew all the cases she'd worked on with him, but there were dozens more she'd done in the two years with Warra that he knew very little about. She hadn't talked about them much, except to say that they were uninteresting.

The house began to stir. He leaned his head against the wall and checked his phone. No calls. Few people would have understood that he was sleeping with a woman he hadn't married, and those who would have understood were too close to his family. He couldn't trust that they wouldn't say something, and he didn't like people carrying dangerous secrets around. Only Sabria had ever had that privilege.

They weren't married because Sabria was already married. She'd been forced into it by her former employer, the same man who had raped her, neglected her, and who was no doubt brutalising some new young housemaid at this very moment. Mahmoud Halifi. He had disappeared over five years ago, shortly after Sabria had fled his house. It occurred to Ibrahim that if she ever saw Halifi again, she might do something rash. She carried pepper spray and was proficient at kung-fu, but Halifi was twice her size, all raw muscle and fury and animal brutality. He could easily overpower her.

Halifi had raped her multiple times, but it wasn't until Sabria became pregnant that he forced her to marry him. They conducted a two-minute ceremony in his living room, and the bastard had actually notified the records office, making it completely official. She had miscarried a week later. In order to divorce him, she would have to find him, and she hadn't put any energy into that over the past five years.

The fact that she and Ibrahim couldn't marry didn't bother her as much as it bothered him, but when he really thought it through, the conclusion ended somewhere with his wife having him killed quietly in his sleep, or arranging for him to be ostracised by his family and friends for the rest of his life.

He got up, got dressed and managed to leave the house without having to talk to Jamila, even though it meant missing breakfast with the twins, who were ten. He sent them each a text telling them he'd see them after dinner and would they please remember that it was Thursday – they had a date for ice cream? They both replied with happy emoticons.

He reached Sabria's apartment and did another sweep. Still empty. He went back to the neighbours, who said she hadn't come home the night before. So he returned to her apartment, sat at the kitchen table and began calling hospitals.

5

It was clear from the chatter that the department was quite proud of not having a specialist in serial killers on hand. It was, in fact, a matter of national pride that they didn't need one. And there was a certain hunger in the men's faces knowing that an American was going to enter the room to explain something only an American would know. And they would, ever so politely (Ibrahim could see them planning their deftness), berate America for importing its violence to this virgin country – not a country immune to violence, but certainly one that had never produced a Hannibal Lecter. (He felt certain there were men in the room who didn't realise he was fictional.) There was an eagerness, too, that said, very well, we may have produced Osama bin Laden, but you produced a kind of viral Jeffrey Dahmer that has spread around the world, and apparently only you have the vaccine?

He overheard someone whisper: 'Do you think he'll talk about Ed Bundy?'

'*Ted* Bundy!' Daher corrected sharply, slapping the officer on the back of the head.

It had been a long weekend. Ibrahim had spent the whole time worrying about Sabria, but now, watching the situation room fill up, he tried to put her to the back of his mind and focus on the case.

A few officers weren't there, and half of forensics was still out at the gravesites. They had finished removing the bodies, which had all been brought to the Examiner's, but in the past twenty-four hours forensics had uncovered something else: the killer had buried one of the severed hands near the body it belonged to. This had prompted the forensic and excavation teams to widen the area around each of the bodies in search of more artefacts. They had found another two hands buried near another body, but that was it.

Ibrahim was surprised that he was still in charge of the case. Riyadh had sent him to the desert because he'd been out of practice with Homicide cases for ten years. Now he suddenly found himself sitting on top of what might be the biggest case of the decade. He could probably expect to hold on to it for another hour at the most. At the back of the room, the department's other detectives were forming a group: Osama, Abu-Haitham, and the tall, bluff Yasser Mu'tazz, plus two others whose names he couldn't remember.

As soon as the American appeared, all expectation collapsed. Ibrahim could almost hear the 'Shit!' in mental unison, followed by an intake of breath as Dr Charlie Becker walked into the room. Her face was a clean porcelain, her button-down shirt almost a mockery of Saudi manhood: white and loose, but clinging in just the right places. She wasn't even wearing a head scarf, and her long auburn hair had a springy quality that made it seem alive whenever she moved her head.

She looked momentarily confused, as if she'd walked into the wrong room in the wrong country. She glanced back at her guide, Chief Riyadh, who strode forward, nodding paternally at her, before taking up position in front of his men with a careful sternness on his face.

'Gentlemen, I'd like to introduce you to our FBI specialist in serial killers, Dr Charlie Becker, who has so graciously flown in from a conference in Dubai.' It was clear from Riyadh's voice that he'd had no idea that Dr Becker was a woman until she'd arrived at his office. 'Dr Becker does not speak Arabic, but Officer Kazaz has offered to translate.' Everyone looked at Kazaz as if he were a newly anointed king.

Ibrahim caught sight of the old Murrah grandfather, Talib al-Shafi, who had been responsible for most of the tracking at the gravesites. He was standing by the door, a slight man, his thick grey hair plaited and tucked up beneath his head scarf. As Charlie Becker walked into the room, he studied her walk, looked at her feet, seemed to find them acceptable, then turned and left.

'Thank you so much for having me,' Charlie said, surprising

everyone. She could not have known that the crisp, high notes of her voice broke against walls that had not rebounded a female sound for years. She noticed the effect of her words on the men's faces and blushed ever so slightly before pressing on. 'I'm a psychiatrist by training but I got involved with the FBI as a specialist in certain kinds of deviant behaviour, and now I focus exclusively on serial killers. I understand you have one on your hands right now.'

A few men nodded, but the rest were dumbstruck by her manner, both vulnerable and confident, by the fact that her hair announced its presence by glittering in the fluorescent lights. Most men in the room had a good enough grasp of English to understand what she was saying. The translation was merely a back-up. Ibrahim stepped forward.

'Dr Becker,' he said, 'thank you for coming. I'm Inspector Ibrahim Zahrani and I'm in charge of this case. We do appear to have a serial killer and we'd appreciate anything you could tell us.'

'I understand you've never had one before?'

This triggered a discussion, once it had been translated. 'Of course we've had serial killers before,' Daher remarked in Arabic. 'Does she think that we're completely backwards?'

'Tell her about Yanbu,' someone else said.

'She already knows about that,' the translator replied. 'She's asking about this department specifically. Has anyone in this room ever dealt with a serial killer before?'

'Sure,' Osama said from the back of the room. 'The warehouse killer.'

Kazaz translated this.

'That's a spree killer,' Charlie said, promptly ending the discussion. 'Spree killers are different. They get carried away with bloodlust. A serial killer is someone much more thorough, and generally more careful.'

Ibrahim noticed Katya Hijazi slip into the room. She stood just inside the doorway and tried to look as if she belonged there. Charlie noticed, too, smiled at her, and fumbled whatever she was saying, causing the rest of the room to turn and stare at Katya. Finally Charlie gave up and said 'Hello' with a vague expression of pity on her face. Katya looked as if she wanted to slap her.

'Anyway,' Charlie went on, 'the most important step in these types of investigations is to identify what you're dealing with. And you're halfway there. You already know he's a serial killer. Until you start identifying some of the victims, there's not much anyone's going to be able to tell you about your killer specifically – such as where he might have met these women, what sort of neighbourhood he lives in, what sort of job or family or other public façade he might have. So I'll tell you what we know about serial killers and then I'll speak generally about yours, given what we do know about the patterns of his killings.'

Once the translator had finished, the only sound in the room was the low whirr of air coming through the air-conditioning vents.

'For most serial killers, it starts with a fantasy,' Charlie said. Someone had offered her a bottle of water, and she cracked it open, took a sip. 'Everyone has them, right? You fantasise about being the boss at work, about your wife loving you more than anyone else in the world. Whatever it is, it's probably normal.'

Somewhere beside him, Ibrahim heard a long, low whispered, '*Ayyyyyyyywa.*' Yeeeees. He suspected Daher.

'Most killers kill for obvious and intelligible reasons – greed, anger, revenge – but for a serial killer the reasons are personal, internal, and not fully comprehensible. They are more like compulsions. Their murders satisfy a deep inner need, the playing out of some fantasy that they've nurtured, usually for a very long time. Since childhood. Their fantasies are brutal. They commonly involve sadistic sexual violence and disfigurement. You've seen disfigurement here.' She glanced at the white board, where photos of the nineteen shattered faces hung in neat rows. 'But the important thing to know about the fantasies is that they're like addictions. I know you don't have a whole lot of gambling or alcohol – or even drugs here. But you do know about them, and I'm sure you've seen them.

'Typically, alcohol medicates a problem or a pain, and so does fantasy. So the killer is relying on his fantasies to make himself feel better. He'll nurture his fantasies for many years, and like all addictions, it gets to the point where he needs more in order to sustain the buzz. One beer doesn't get you drunk, so an alcoholic will start to need ten, or twenty. For the killer, he reaches a point where he needs to make his fantasy real.'

Charlie looked out over the room. She was more confident now, no traces of self-consciousness. She noticed Daher, something in his face, and said: 'You have a question?'

He shook his head.

'No, go ahead,' she said. 'Mr . . . ?'

'Daher.' He cleared his throat. 'Waseem Daher.' It was funny to see him so uncomfortable. 'I was just wondering. He's crazy, right? He thinks it's OK to kill someone for his sick fantasy. Why is that?'

'Good question. Psychologists call them psychopaths or sociopaths, depending on certain factors. But it's more common these days to think of them as having what we call Anti-Social Personality Disorder, or ASPD. Briefly it means that they don't have a conscience like you or me. They are often incapable of love, which means they don't develop lasting relationships unless there's an obvious cause for it, like sex or money. They are impulsive and aggressive. But the most defining aspect is really that they have absolutely no sense of guilt.'

'So they don't understand how to treat people?'

'We-e-e-ll,' she said, 'they don't feel what normal people feel, but they do understand people to an amazing degree. They are capable of deceiving even people who are close to them – family members, co-workers – and they can do that precisely because they understand them. They're usually very good liars. And highly intelligent.'

Daher nodded uncomfortably.

'Should we be looking at old criminal files for our killer?' Ibrahim asked.

'Yes,' Charlie said, 'you should absolutely check, but you may not find anything. In some cases serial killers have a history of violent crime, but it's more true to say that they're very, very good at not getting caught. And if you do look at criminals, look for pyromaniacs and stalkers. Those are the most common early crimes for this type of individual.'

Ibrahim nodded.

'Specialists talk about six phases of killing,' Charlie went on. 'These are psychological phases that were identified back in the eighties that most serial killers go through. The killer begins with a fantasy. Phase one. He withdraws into his inner world and develops the fantasy. Phase two begins when he starts actively looking for a victim. Most killers will start in a place that's familiar to them.

Somewhere they're comfortable: their favourite street, a neighbour-hood café. This could take weeks or months. The victim has to match the fantasy.

'The next few phases can happen very quickly. Phase three, the killer tries to win the victim's trust. Four, the killer captures the victim and reveals who he is. Five, he murders her. Six, he crashes from the high of living out his fantasy. So let's make up an example: a killer sits next to a woman at a bar.'

Daher shook his head with a frown.

'Oh right,' Charlie said, 'not a bar. You don't have them. Maybe a restaurant, then.'

Daher shook his head again.

'Yes, Mr Daher?'

'That's unlikely to happen here. Men and women sit in different parts of restaurants.'

Charlie nodded. 'OK. How could a man encounter a woman here? In public.'

The men looked at one another. Did this woman not understand anything about Saudi Arabia?

'He could talk to her on the street,' a voice said. It was Katya, still near the doorway. Everyone turned to look. 'But that doesn't mean she would talk back. She probably wouldn't.'

'Under what circumstances would she talk back?' Charlie asked.

'If she knew him.'

'Most likely, she wouldn't know him. The killer would want her to be a stranger.'

'OK,' Katya said. 'She wouldn't talk to him unless, perhaps, he needed her help.'

Daher, who had been watching this exchange with a dark look on his face, put in: 'Like Ted Bundy.'

'Good point,' Charlie said, still looking at Katya. 'So maybe he lured her with a false vulnerability. Where else could he find a woman?'

'Well, she could have been his housemaid,' Daher said.

'She probably wouldn't have been,' Charlie said, 'at least not con-sistently. In phase two, when he's trolling for the perfect victim, he's looking from afar. He's studying the victim for signs that she'll be like the woman in his fantasy – and the more you get to know someone, the less like fantasy they become. So they look for superficial things, usually physical characteristics. For example, Ted Bundy preferred women with their hair parted in the middle.'

'Well,' Daher said with a dry laugh, 'our killer won't be looking for a particular hair style.'

Charlie gave him a wry smile and turned back to Katya. 'Right. He might be looking for facial features, then?'

'Maybe,' Katya said. 'Or just . . . a shape.'

'Excellent. Maybe she's always petite. Or skinny.'

Riyadh, who had been standing to the side, said: 'All of the victims were between 1.8 and 1.9 metres tall. And all of them were immigrants, mostly from Asian countries.'

'How tall is 1.8 metres?' Charlie asked.

'Just under six feet,' Katya said.

'Oh, OK. So they're pretty tall.' Charlie turned back to the room, but not before giving Katya a secretive smile. 'It's not very common to find tall women among certain racial groups, so you already know one thing about him: he likes tall, Asian women. He's targeting an unusual type. One of your main problems is going to be determining how your killer found and captured his victims. How he won their trust.

'There's one more important classification about serial killers that you're going to want to look at, and that's organisation. How organised is he? Another way to think of this is: how elaborately does he plot and execute his fantasy? Planning a murder takes time and energy. Some murderers kill their victims right away. That's the disorganised type. They tend to be sloppy. They also tend to be excessively gory and violent. The organised types are different. They make the killing phase – that's phase five in the sequence – last for days or even weeks. They usually don't kill the victim right away, or even if they do, they don't dispose of the body right away. They want to keep enjoying the thrill of watching their victim being abused. They want the fantasy to last as long as it can. It only ends when they get sick of it. Our Behavioural Science Unit developed this classification and it extends to crime scenes as well. The disorganised killer will leave, well, a messy crime scene. But an organised killer is elaborate and has usually planned out exactly how to hide every trace of his crime. Except for one thing, the totem.'

34

'What's that?' This was Kazaz, the translator.

'A totem is something he's saved from the kill – usually a body part, but it could be anything. It's something like a trophy. It reminds him of the experience and he can go back to it with pleasure or pride.'

'The hands,' Ibrahim said.

Charlie looked at him, her attention like a spotlight. 'Yes, he removed the victims' hands. Both of them, right?'

'That's right,' Ibrahim replied. 'He cut off all of the women's hands, but just yesterday we found three of them buried by the bodies.'

'Only three?'

'Yes.'

Charlie was thoughtful for a moment. 'The hands are probably his trophies. It's definitely worth asking why he only buried three of them. There may be some evidence on those three that would lead you to understand why he chose to cut hands off in the first place. You may not be able to figure it out until you catch him, but if you understand it, it can be a very valuable clue.

'You're going to need to find out more, of course, but from what you have learned about this guy, I think you're dealing with a very organised killer. He took the time to dispose of the bodies. And given their state – the missing hands, the mutilated faces – and the isolation of the locale, he's obviously been working systematically. The most recent victim was three months dead?'

'No more than six,' Ibrahim said.

'Then I hate to say it, but he will probably kill again soon. He will be, right now, planning his next kill. The real question is: how is he getting access to these women? Where is he finding them and what do they have in common? You obviously have a lot of work to do in terms of identifying them. He's going to realise that you've found out where he buried his victims, and he will adapt his methods. He probably won't go to the same place to find his victims any more, but he may not be so willing to change his "type".'

This was followed by an uneasy silence.

'Well,' Daher remarked in Arabic, 'maybe we should start telling our women to stay indoors.'

Charlie looked to Kazaz for a translation but he frowned.

The room fell silent with everyone full from their meal. Ibrahim detected a slight shakiness, so many officers unused to taking directions from a woman.

'I think that's enough for now,' Chief Riyadh said. 'Dr Becker has kindly agreed to be available to answer questions over the next month, so we'll be able to talk with her in more depth once the Medical Examiner has finished his reports and we've heard from forensics.'

The group broke up slowly. Charlie and Riyadh stood at the front of the room chatting, and Daher made a man-pack with his friends. Katya slipped out of the room.

In the hallway, Ibrahim bumped into Talib, the Murrah tracker.

'You left early,' Ibrahim remarked.

'Well, I knew it wasn't her.' He tossed his chin in the direction of Dr Becker.

'Thank God for that. But you said you didn't have a footprint of the killer.'

'Oh, we had something,' Talib said. 'Not clear enough for a photograph, but good for our purposes. Enough to get a sense of him.'

'Why didn't you tell me this at the crime scene?'

'It took a long time to eliminate all the other men who were at the scene.'

'All right,' Ibrahim said. 'It's definitely a man, then?'

'Yes.'

'And where does he live, this killer?'

Talib smiled. 'What a funny question. What makes you think I can answer it?'

Ibrahim shrugged.

'He lives in the city. Nothing wrong with his back. He's much taller than me, probably heavier.' With a small pair of hands, Talib cupped a gesture around his gerbil-sized paunch.

'And are you going to tell me how you came to this?' Ibrahim asked.

'He uses his right foot differently than his left. And the way that he uses it differently means either he has an injury or he drives a car. The right is more flexible, all the way along the bottom of the foot and even the ankle – twists side to side a little when he walks. It's the stronger leg, too. He's probably right-handed.'

36

'And he's a man because?'

'Only men drive cars.'

Ibrahim smiled, then let out a laugh. 'Yes, sorry. Glad someone's using logic.'

The Bedouin waved his hand in a courtly gesture that said: *I'm quite certain you're better at logic than I am.*

Ibrahim unlocked his office door and said goodbye to Talib. He'd barely had time to switch on the lights before the other men came in, first one of the junior officers, Shaya, then Daher and his followers. He saw a flash of black in the hallway and wondered if Katya had been wanting to speak to him as well.

The office was small – two tables and a desk, the best the department could come up with for now. It was totally inadequate for meetings. The men sat on the stools, perched on his tables. They wanted direction, he realised. He sat down.

'Well, the American was helpful,' Daher said. 'Nothing like a woman's face to focus the mind.'

'It wasn't your mind being focused,' one of the others said.

'No, no,' Daher replied. 'I now have a very clear sense of what we should be doing. We should be sitting in a conference room staring at a white shirt.'

The men had been pushing the boundaries since Ibrahim started at Homicide. They had realised that he wouldn't take offence at their joking. In the car riding out to the desert, before they had found the bodies, Daher, who had been reading something on his mobile phone, boomed out: 'Gentlemen, it's time to move to Malaysia!'

'Oh, no.' Shaya had rolled his eyes.

'Oh, *yes!* And do you know why? Because Malaysia has taken the remarkable step of *banning bras*. Yes, indeed. They are – and I quote the sheikh who made the ruling – "devil's cushions". And no good Muslim woman should wear one, because they exaggerate the shape and curvature of the breast.' He tossed his phone on his lap with satisfaction. 'Imagine, please, a whole nation without bras!'

It had made Ibrahim laugh then, but now he was beginning to get fed up.

'We ought to be ashamed,' he said. 'This man has been killing for over a decade and we haven't found out about it until now.'

The room fell silent.

'I'm sure someone noticed these women were missing,' he went on, 'but whoever they were, they didn't nag us. No one's been showing up at our office for ten years running. That's because they probably live on the other side of the world and they *can't* show up. They don't have the means.'

He hoped he wasn't going too far – or revealing his own angst. They had to find a killer, he was supposed to coordinate these overgrown boys with intelligence and a knowledge he didn't really possess, and the only thing he could think of was Sabria. Nothing like a woman to focus the mind.

'So basically it's our job to find out every single thing that we can, because someday we're going to find all those people who noticed and we're going to have to tell them what happened.'

He looked around. They all knew the situation: the Homicide department had a 90 per cent success rate in capturing and prosecuting murderers. Never mind that the figure may have been a little bloated by those zealous officers who 'encouraged' confessions by any means possible. The fact remained that the department had a lot to live up to. And right now, Ibrahim was ten years out of practice.

'Do you think they'll keep us on this case?' Daher asked.

'Until I hear otherwise, it's our job to find the man who did this.'

He tried to conjure up protocols from long ago, but the decade between then and now had eroded most of his memory, and anyway the rules had changed. They had better forensics now. They had computers for everything. And the job of an investigator was to oversee the machinations of it all. But one thing hadn't changed: the dread.

'Why is it always the housemaids?' Shaya asked. He was the same age as the other men, but had none of their youthful energy, and more than his share of naivety.

'Look around, man,' Daher said. 'We have too many foreigners. Pakistanis, Indians, Africans. And with this many, you get the bad ones, too.'

'They're certainly responsible for more than their fair share of crime,' Shaya replied.

'That's because they're poor,' Daher said. 'Do you ever see a fat foreigner? No. Most of them don't make enough money to eat. Of course they're going to start stealing and killing each other—'

'They do commit crimes,' Ibrahim interrupted. 'But stealing and killing are two totally different things. And most of the time, it's their employers who commit the crimes. And those would be Saudis.'

No one replied.

'Now what's the latest word from forensics?'

'Nothing interesting yet,' Daher said.

Ibrahim looked at his men and thought of Sabria's hair, much thicker and shinier than Charlie Becker's. It had a weight to it. She would climb on him and drape it over his face and fill his nostrils with the smell of shampoo and sex.

'We know the heights, weights and presumed ages of our victims. We also have the sketch artist's impressions, so let's start with all of that. Daher and Ahmad, I want you two at the Filipino and Indonesian consulates today. Go over their records yourselves if you have to. Shaya, you're in charge of contacting Missing Persons. Same drill, do it yourself if you have to. The rest of you go down to Records and start looking through the computer files on missing persons. The national database.'

'What about profiling the killer?' Shaya asked.

Ibrahim rubbed his face and wondered if the boy had understood a single thing that Dr Becker had just said. 'That is what we're doing,' he replied.

Groans, sighs, some friendly slapping and shoving got them out. Ibrahim shut the door behind them, switched off the light, and sat down at his desk. Maybe Riyadh wasn't taking him off the case because he was too busy dealing with his higher-ups. It was only a matter of time before the Ministry's Special Investigations shouldered their way into it. There was no telling what would happen then. It might get taken out of police hands entirely.

More important to him now was finding Sabria. He needed his own plan. There was no battalion of men who would go charging forward on her behalf. She wasn't in any of the hospitals he had called, although it was possible she had been admitted anonymously. The only way to find out was to go to every clinic and show her picture around, but even then, a doctor could see a female patient without ever seeing her face. Checking them all would be a monumental task.

He looked at the phone, thought of dialling Missing Persons himself and reporting her, but he knew what they would do: protocols. Once they found out she'd worked in Undercover, Omar, Assistant Chief of Undercover, would be notified, and he would undoubtedly open an investigation, which meant that they would search her apartment with some of the finest forensic technology in the world. They'd find out about Ibrahim. He'd be an adulterer, at least until they took off his head. Undercover would close down the investigation. No sense wasting energy searching for a prostitute. And while all of that was going on, it could turn out that she'd been unconscious in a hospital the whole time. Or maybe she'd just run away. It wasn't worth the risk of reporting her yet. He had to find her himself.

6

Clutching her mobile phone, Amina al-Fouad stepped onto the third-floor balcony overlooking the street. It was bright, and out of habit she wrapped a plain scarf over her nose and mouth. She scanned the street for any sign of Jamal's GM but all she saw were the neighbour's children tearing into the alley and a few stray cats. She shut her eyes, listening for the giant rumble of the new SUV her husband had foolishly bought for their son, Jamal. At last she heard a familiar sound and watched expectantly as a truck turned onto the street. It wasn't his.

She flipped open her phone and tried calling him a second time. No answer. If she had bothered to listen to her daughter's instructions she would know how to text him, but it was too complicated. 10:40 a.m. She had to go to the grocer's, the florist's, the art supply shop, and she still had to pick up a birthday present for her niece. The party was at one o'clock. She had promised to bring fizzy drinks, napkins, streamers and balloons. She tried calling Jamal again and got the same response.

Now deeply annoyed, she watched two women making their way down the street. They had just stepped out of a taxi. If she hurried, she might be able to catch it. Grabbing her handbag and *abaaya* from a hook behind the door, she raced down the stairs.

The taxi had waited. It was parked on the corner like an animal catching its breath after a run. The driver had got out to buy cigarettes at the corner shop. When he saw Amina racing towards him, he swung open the back door and invited her in. She thanked him, told him to take her to the Jamjoom Centre, and they were off.

Rashid hated it when she took taxis. It was unsafe to get in a car with a strange man, especially a foreigner. It wasn't so bad if she was with friends, but she was absolutely never allowed to do it alone, and yet here she was, squirming in the back seat while the driver blew smoke into every corner of the car and refused to roll down the window because he didn't want the hot air coming in. The air conditioning wasn't strong enough in the back, so Amina was sweating, and every time she tried to open the window just an inch, the driver rolled it back up. She thought of Rashid finding out and decided simply that he wouldn't. She tried calling Jamal again and this time left a message: 'I'm in a cab going to the Jamjoom Centre, and you'd better meet me there in two hours or I'm going to tell your father and he'll take away your car.' Rashid would not take the car away. He had never punished the boy in his life. But Jamal might want to spare her from his father's anger, if he were to find out she'd taken a cab.

Two hours later, she stood on the pavement outside the Jamjoom Centre with three enormous shopping bags at her feet. She hadn't bought the drinks, but she'd found everything else, plus three gifts for her niece now wrapped in a floral paper with gold ribbon. She'd also found a dozen things she hadn't meant to buy, and decided she'd run the rest of her errands later. There was no sign of Jamal. She called twice and got no answer.

He has absolutely no understanding of things, she thought, glancing at the taxi queue. She wanted to take a cab – had put aside the money to do so, just in case – but Rashid was going to be at the party and she couldn't be sure he wouldn't see her getting out of a cab, or even coming through the door with all the shopping bags and Jamal nowhere in sight. He would know at once what she'd done. She tried calling her nephew. This was becoming an emergency. She had to be at her sister's house in ten minutes, and it would take thirty to get there. Her nephew didn't answer. What was it with these teenagers? They were the mobile generation. They used phones like a third hand. But if you called them, they never answered.

She tried again and again. She wasn't going to call her sister. Johara would be frantically preparing for the party so would delegate the problem to someone else and word would get back to Rashid.

Finally annoyed beyond belief, Amina tossed the phone in her handbag, picked up the shopping bags and headed for the queue.

7

Katya sat in a giant ottoman chair, trying not to slide too deeply into its recesses, while she waited for the bank manager to finish her conversation, then her phone call, then her studious typing at the computer. Katya had been watching her for twenty minutes from behind the glass partition. The manager was oblivious to the presence of the six long-suffering customers seated in her waiting area. When one of them got up to say she'd already been there for forty minutes, and she'd appreciate being seen sometime this century, the manager looked as if no one had ever before dared make such a brazen request.

'How should I know how long you've been sitting there?' she cried. 'I don't keep track of these things. You're just going to have to wait your turn!'

At the counter, customers were arguing about deposits, credit amounts, late payments. The privacy screens were pathetic; Katya could hear everything – even the bank clerk in the corner who hummed Nancy Ajram every time she counted notes. The front door opened with a whoosh of hot air, rustling the succulent leaves of the potted plants and swirling *abaayas* around bodies. A woman entered, her high heels clattering angrily on the polished marble floor. She walked straight into the manager's office and was greeted with cloying adulation. The manager rushed out to fetch coffee and dates. The new arrival dumped an obnoxiously large Dior handbag on the desk. A few of the women in the waiting area began to grumble, and one sighed loudly in exasperation.

Were men's banks so infernally slow and bureaucratic? Katya had only been into a man's bank on one occasion, when her mother (bless her), in a fit of outrage at the service in the women's bank, had marched across the street and pushed past the guards with the intention of speaking to the notorious 'man in charge' without whom apparently nothing could be decided in the women's section. She had brought a black pall of silence to the bank's vast interior. Fifty men had turned to stare at her, their faces cold with disapproval. Katya had scrambled after her, grabbing her arm and pulling her back outside, but her mother, then practically in the death throes of the cancer that had killed her, refused to budge until she had spoken to the manager.

Even if they wanted to, even if their husbands and fathers agreed to let them interact with strange men, even if they had drivers and ID cards and babysitters, Saudi women still struggled to find jobs. This grand country, which could import anything it needed, had also imported 90 per cent of its private sector workers. She had heard the anti-immigration cry from other countries – Europe wanting to send its Muslims home, America keen to close its doors to the Mexicans – but Saudi had let itself become a kingdom of strangers. It welcomed its immigrants because they lent the illusion that Saudis could afford hired help, because the immigrants did the jobs that most Saudis would never dream of doing – housekeeping, refuse collecting, taxi driving – and because without them, absolutely nothing would get done.

But these bankers were Saudi, part of a movement among more reformist companies to get Saudi women working (albeit, in women-only banks). If this was the 'Saudisation' of the work force, Katya reflected, then the country was heading for trouble.

She sat back in the ottoman and shut her eyes. She ought to give up and just go home, but this was the first time in a month she'd been alone and without any responsibilities. She hadn't wanted to face this moment until now, because what was waiting for her here was a marriage proposal and the man she hoped she loved, standing patiently at the edge of her life. Here also was her mind-numbing terror at losing her job.

If you don't get married, she thought, *you WILL lose your job*. She had lied and told them she was married, because in order to work in her department, she had to be. Only Osama had found out the truth. He

44

hadn't fired her yet, but the threat hung over her every day. It constituted the greater part of her antagonism towards Daher, who had seen her at work late one night and said: 'You don't *act* like a married woman.'

She knew he meant to say: *You're acting like a man*, but it chilled her anyway, and she found herself worrying about him most of all. Would he find out that she wasn't married? It would be as simple as heading down to the Records office and running a search.

But a marriage might just turn out to be a pretty, tree-lined avenue to the dead end of her dreams. She thought of Nayir and tried to remember the longing she felt for him, but fear had neutered her desire. Nayir wasn't the type to be comfortable with her working such long hours. And what if they started having children? How would she work and raise kids – and clean house and cook and tend lovingly to her husband's needs? He had proposed marriage a month ago. It was a painfully long time to make a man wait, and she still hadn't given him an answer.

She didn't have one.

It took her another hour to be seen, then another fifteen minutes of wrangling. They had accidentally closed her current account, into which she had recently deposited her pay cheque. The manager had no record of Katya's ever having been a patron of the bank. Even looking at the deposit slip Katya produced from her purse had no effect. The manager studied Katya, clearly wondering what sort of scam she was working. With typical efficiency, she drank another cup of coffee and fussed at her computer for ten useless minutes, then got up from her desk and went to talk to her boss, who was, apparently, the *real* manager of the bank. Half an hour later, she returned, reopened the account and reassured Katya that all was well. But nothing was well, not when one's livelihood was stored so tenuously in the memory of a machine, as if one's livelihood didn't already face a dozen more powerful forces bent on wiping it away.

He was talking to a neighbour. When he hauled the rope from the water, bent over, one knee on the ground and his head turned up at an odd angle like a man inspecting the underside of a camel, the fabric of his shirt was pulled tautly against his back. Even from five metres, she saw the muscles – a landscape of softly cut dunes, elegant, vast. She would normally have averted her gaze, but she let her eyes rest on his back for a moment. *I could touch it*, she thought, *if we were married. I could fall asleep with those great arms around me.* It was illusory, that form. As solid as it was, it would be subject to shifting winds all the same.

What surprised her was the relief she felt when he stood up and saw her and his face lit quietly with pleasure that even the neighbour noticed, and which caused the man to excuse himself. Nayir coiled the last of the rope and dropped it on the ground, a gesture that said firmly that he'd lay down anything for her, and for a very brief moment her own million grains of doubt were blown clear away.

Then she told herself not to be an idiot.

'*Sabah al-khayr*,' she said. Good morning.

He averted his gaze and greeted her with a simple 'Good morning'. She wasn't wearing a veil. She didn't wear one at work, so why should she pretend to be more devout here?

They had talked on the phone, but this was the first time she'd seen him since the night he proposed. He was wearing his favourite well-worn blue robe. He'd taken off his head scarf, and his short curly hair shone black in the sun. A slight redness on his cheeks, a coating of dust on his sandals, the confidence in his shoulders all told her that he'd recently been to the desert. He took families on desert excursions to help them get in touch with their Bedouin roots or simply to give them the experience of the wilderness. On occasion, he worked search and rescue.

'I hope I'm not coming at a bad time,' she said.

'Of course not.' He glanced over her shoulder, a gesture she understood at once to say: *Who escorted you here? And is it all right with him that we're talking?*

'My cousin Ayman gave me a ride,' she said. 'He's just gone to buy cigarettes.'

Nayir nodded, perhaps better able to accept the impropriety of the two of them being alone now that a marriage proposal was on the table. He started walking towards his boat. It was too hot to stand in the sun.

'I'm sorry I haven't called,' she said. 'I've been working overtime on a big case.'

'Oh,' he said. If he'd been worried about her lack of response to his proposal, he didn't show it. Rather, he seemed relaxed, and there was a poise in his manner that she had ascribed to time spent in the desert but which might just as easily have been religiously inspired.

He led her onto his boat and she saw, with some surprise, that he'd situated a large beach umbrella above the wooden bench on the top deck. She imagined that he'd planned for this: having Katya arrive at his boat and not wanting to lead her downstairs, where they'd be alone and out of sight. The neighbours might notice and begin talking. She sat beneath the umbrella, feeling oddly pleased, while Nayir bent to the corner and retrieved the next surprise: a small battery-powered fan. He switched it on and coolish air blew across her lap. She smiled.

'This is very thoughtful of you.'

He excused himself and climbed down the ladder below, emerging a minute later with a small cooler full of ice, bottled water and cans. She took a Pepsi. He sat across from her and turned slightly to the side so that he wouldn't stare directly at her face. She sipped the Pepsi.

'It sounds like you're busy at work,' he said.

Yes, she wanted to reply, *and I have no idea how I'm going to get married, and have children, and be a mother and a wife while I'm supposed to be at work twelve hours a day, sometimes more.* Beyond that, how could she explain that the tedious lab work had lost its appeal? That she was struggling to push herself up a notch by getting more directly involved in investigations? That she had even, last week, taken the bold step of applying to the female police academy? What would he say to *that*?

'I'm sorry,' she said, 'I've wanted to come sooner, but yes, I've been extremely busy.'

He nodded. 'Actually, your timing is perfect,' he said. 'I was in the desert. I just got back last night.'

'Were you working?'

'Yes. I took a family to the Empty Quarter.'

'I've never been out there,' she said.

'It's beautiful. And safe enough, if you're prepared for it.' He looked at her then, which she found quite bold. Then he returned his gaze to the sea. She realised that something had shifted in him, as if

47

a deeper tectonic instability had rumbled and tossed and was finally settling into place.

She was struck suddenly with panic. She was twenty-nine and she ought to feel urgent to get married, but instead she was terrified. She could see her father's disappointed face as vividly as if he were standing in front of her. If her mother were still alive, she would cry to see Katya unmarried at this age.

'Have you thought any more about my proposal?' he asked.

'Yes.' They had reached this point too quickly. She felt them skidding into a crash.

'Ah,' he said.

She was outside all thought. Her only conscious awareness was that if she said no, she would hurt him irreparably.

'I applied to the police academy,' she blurted.

He studied her for a moment, which she found disconcerting. Then he looked down at his hands, and she caught the flicker of a smile. 'That's a big step,' he said.

'Yes.'

He came to sit next to her. For a moment it seemed that he might take her hand, but he refrained. 'Are you sure about this?'

'Yes,' she said quickly. 'I'm sure.'

'You don't want to work in the lab any more?'

'No.'

'But how will you be a cop?' he asked.

'I don't know. I want to work in Homicide. I want to be a detective.'

He looked into her eyes, which brought on a terrific swell of panic. 'I've said this before, but I want you to know that whatever it is, we'll find a way to work it out.'

She took his hand, realised her own were shaking. He saw it, too, and squeezed her hands in his. His eyes didn't leave her face, and their expression said: *Just say yes, yes . . .*

'Yes,' she said.

'Yes, you'll marry me?'

She nodded. 'That's my answer – *yes*.'

He smiled in a way she'd never seen before, a big delighted grin. He ran a hand down his face to try to soften it, but it sprung back like a cowlick. She smiled at him.

Just then a neighbour came out of his boat. Nayir dropped her hand and quickly stood up. The neighbour scarcely noticed the two of them sitting there, but to Nayir he might have been God himself sitting in judgement on their public impropriety.

Deflated, Katya stood up. 'Well,' she said, 'I'd better get back to work.'

8

Now it was a refuge, sitting at her computer, straightening up the files. She determinedly refused to think about what she'd just done. She would not admit that she felt the beginnings of suffocation, sand heaping around her while she made no effort to push herself free.

She recognised Inspector Zahrani the moment he stepped into the lab. Behind her, three women quickly covered their faces, like a flock of hens startled by a large human leg, but Katya had decided not to give in to that impulse any more.

She didn't know very much about Zahrani, just enough to realise that he didn't give a damn if a woman's face was exposed. The first time she'd met him, he'd even extended his hand to shake hers and thanked her for processing evidence so quickly. There was a slight accent to his voice that suggested he was Levantine – probably Palestinian. But his face was classically Bedouin, dark skin, long nose, giant almond-shaped eyes. He was a recent addition to Homicide, had migrated from Undercover for reasons no one knew. He'd only worked on two cases in the past weeks, both of them pulled out of the department's record room of unsolved crimes. He hadn't managed to solve either of them. Now he was in charge of the serial killer case. Chief Riyadh was clearly willing to let Ibrahim do whatever he liked.

He didn't usually come into the lab, but that was because Katya preferred to bring her findings downstairs. It was part of her plan to stay visible, to get more involved.

'Miss Hijazi,' he said. He was holding half a dozen files.

'Good afternoon, Inspector Zahrani,' she replied. 'I see you got the files.'

'Yes,' he said, setting them on her desk. 'And please call me Ibrahim. There's one thing in your report I didn't quite understand...'

The women grew a little quieter at the back of the room.

'I'd be glad to look at it,' she said.

'You know...' He was flipping through the folders. 'It looks like I've left one file downstairs. Sorry. Do you mind?'

'No, of course not.' Katya was already logging out of her computer and getting to her feet. 'I'll come down with you.'

'Great.' He swept the files into his arms.

Once the door to the lab had shut behind them, he stopped and turned to her. The hallway was empty, but only momentarily. 'I have to ask you a favour,' he said. 'It's very important.'

The change in his demeanour startled her. 'Go ahead,' she said.

'In private,' he said, looking around. 'If you don't mind.'

He motioned her into the ladies' toilets. She hesitated. He could be setting her up, but his anxiety was palpable. She followed him inside and he locked the door behind them.

'A friend of mine has gone missing,' he said. 'I'm very worried about her.'

Katya waited for an answer to the obvious question: why was he telling her?

'I don't know many women,' he said, 'and certainly none I could trust with this information. Most people don't even know that I still know this woman.'

So that was it. He had a girlfriend. She was mildly surprised, but guessed it was probably more common than she thought. 'So you haven't reported her missing.'

'No. It could just be – she could have left.'

'I see,' Katya said. 'What do you need?'

'She works at a boutique at the Chamelle Centre. Do you know it? It's a women's shopping mall.'

'Yes, yes, the one at al-Hamra.'

'I can't go in there, obviously, and I need to know if she's shown up for work recently.'

'Have you tried calling them?'

51

'I've been trying for the past few days. You have to leave a message and sometimes they'll call you back if you're wealthy and you're planning on spending large sums of money, but normally they don't. They don't know about me either, and I'd like to keep it that way.'

'I see.' Katya tried not to look at their reflections in the mirror. Being locked in the toilets with a man at work would be enough to get her fired on the spot. She kept wondering how they were going to exit. 'So you want me to go to the Chamelle Centre and ask if she's been at work.'

'Yes, but it's tricky. I've never met her co-workers, but she told me that they're snobs. Also, the owner hadn't officially signed the paper-work yet, and her visa is expired, so you have to be really careful not to let them think you're checking up on visa infractions. It's best not to go in as a police officer. You're just looking for a friend.'

'All right,' she said. 'I'd be happy to do it, but it'll have to be later this evening. I don't leave work until six.'

'That would be perfect,' he said. He'd been leaning over her in a kind of pushy panic. Now he stood back and exhaled. 'It's probably nothing,' he said. 'But I have a bad feeling.'

Katya nodded. She wanted to ask if he'd tried calling friends, hospitals, but decided it would be condescending. 'I'll go straight after work.'

'I'll drive you,' he said. 'You're OK with that?'

'No, my cousin drives me. He'll think it's odd if I'm late, and I'd rather that this didn't get back to my father. My cousin will be glad to give me a ride to the mall.'

They exchanged numbers and she promised to call once she'd learned anything.

'I'll go out first,' he said, reaching for the door. 'If it's safe for you to come out, I'll knock once. If it's not safe, I'll distract them. You just keep the door locked.' He was sliding out of the door before she could protest. A second later, he knocked.

The brisk way he handled the exit both filled her with admiration and pissed her off. Men didn't lose their jobs for indiscretion as often as women did. And she doubted, what with all the fear in the lab of being caught for this or that, that women were half as indiscreet.

9

The first victim was named Amelia Cortez. She was one of the two women whose hands had been found at the gravesite. The Medical Examiner had determined that she had been the killer's first victim, dead now approximately ten years. Forensics had identified her through a fingerprint match.

Amelia had been twenty-four, and judging by the passport photo that came from the Philippine Embassy, she was lovely – high cheekbones; a clear complexion; innocent, light brown eyes. She had been recruited in Manila and promised work as a personal assistant to a high-powered female journalist. Amelia herself had ambitions to become a writer. But when she arrived in Jeddah, her 'sponsor', a man named Sonny Esposa, told her that the only work available was as a nanny. She had no choice in the matter. In order to leave the country, she needed Sonny's permission, and he took away her passport.

She had also signed a contract promising to pay him for his services. The headhunter's fee was much more than she could afford. She was going to give him a little each month and pay it off that way. Instead of working for 600 riyals a month, Amelia wound up working for 200, taking care of five children, all under the age of ten. It would take her six years to repay the headhunter. She couldn't go to the police; they would only enforce the contract. So Amelia ran away. The people who had hired her complained – they had paid for a year in advance – and Sonny disappeared. No one knew what had happened to Amelia, and no one cared enough to find her. Her family in the Philippines sent letters to the consulate to no avail.

Ibrahim himself went to interview the family who had employed Cortez. He took Daher and Shaya. They also interviewed the consular officials, who had kept their own notes on the case but had not filed a police report. The story was the same: the woman had run off. No matter what the employer told you, when a housemaid disappeared, she was usually looking for better work somewhere else or trying to escape an abusive situation. It was a common enough occurrence and, short of finding a dead body, the police had no way to prove foul play. They had no luck at all tracking down Cortez's headhunter, Sonny Esposa. He had disappeared long ago.

Ibrahim went through the motions – the interviews, the car rides, the edgy conversations with his men – in a half-state of panic. He saw Sabria in every living room, consular office and police meeting room. He conjured up clear mental pictures of Cortez walking down the street, perhaps running a quick errand for her employer – *Would you mind picking up some bread from the baker's, some milk from the corner shop?* – and then Sabria slid into the frame, cloaked and veiled, and it was Sabria stepping into the wrong taxi, being held at gunpoint, frozen with terror. It was Sabria being driven to the edge of the desert, being immobilised by chloroform, then beaten and dismembered and shot in the head.

He had no idea how the killer caught his victims, and he was still a little fuzzy on the horrors perpetrated on the women, but in Ibrahim's mind, it was as clear as reality. Chloroform. Hard plastic restraints. A semi-automatic with a silencer. A small sword for cutting off the hands. He knew it was wrong to build mental pictures laced with assumptions and personal horrors, so he let the images play out like silent movies and reminded himself that it was far too implausible that Sabria, a woman with a natural distrust of men, would be taken by anyone, even at gunpoint. Equally implausible that the killer would have noticed Ibrahim so quickly after they found the bodies, and then found out about his mistress. It was the ego's darkest delight to assume it was the centre of the universe.

*

54

Chamelle Plaza was a women-only shopping mall made up of the kind of designer boutiques and spas that made Katya feel like a poor Indonesian street sweeper collecting empty bottles at the edges of a royal palace. Fifteen minutes shy of the day's last prayer time, the place was bustling with Sri Lankan housemaids looking after whole flocks of children while mothers flitted between day spas and manicure salons, hurrying to conduct their business before the call to prayer closed all the shops. The air was cool and clean and Katya stood in the central courtyard, waiting for the sheen of sweat to dry from her face and for her cloak to stop sticking to her clothes.

Her first thought was that if Ibrahim's girlfriend worked here, then the chances were good that she had run away with a wealthy businessman or maybe even a prince. Not that she would have met him at the mall, but simply that she would have been the type to trade in one old handbag for a more flashy one when the time was right. Walking past the overpriced shops staffed with snooty-looking women in Armani did nothing to interfere with the stereotype.

Before leaving the lab, she had run a search on the missing woman. It was probably redundant – Ibrahim would have checked already – but just to be thorough. She discovered that Miss Sabria Gampon's visa was indeed expired. She hadn't been deported, at least not officially. Sometimes it took a few weeks for the paperwork to catch up. She also discovered that Sabria used to work in Undercover herself.

Katya found the boutique. La Mode Internationale. It was tucked between a jeweller's store and a bustling café. She pushed through the glass door and crossed an enormous white marble floor with a self-important stride that she hoped matched the haute couture elegance all around her. Little nooks on the wall were lit with red lights and each held a handbag that looked more like a child carrier with hardware. A woman approached and greeted her with a plastered-on smile and a perkiness that she would have been happy to have seen at the bank but which felt oppressive here.

'Good evening,' the woman said. She was a middle-aged Filipina woman with an unnaturally high, girlish voice and lipstick so red it was impossible to tear your eyes from. Her nametag said Chona. 'What can we do for you today?'

'I'm looking for a friend of mine,' Katya said. 'She's been telling me about this place for a long time, and I'm finally in the neighbourhood and thought I'd stop by to do some shopping.'

'Oh, that's wonderful,' Chona said. 'And who is your friend?'

'Her name is Sabria Gampon.'

Chona's whole face stiffened, and she made no effort to hide her disgust. 'Sabria no longer works here, I'm afraid.'

'Oh?' Katya looked chagrined. 'I thought she was here just last week.'

Chona shook her head. She glanced nervously at the two other women behind the cash register and said in a low voice: 'The owner asked Sabria to leave three months ago. We haven't seen her since then.'

'Oh dear,' Katya said. 'I'm sorry to hear that.'

'Yes,' Chona said. 'But since you're here, was there something else we could do for you?'

'No, no,' Katya said. 'Was Sabria . . . ? I hope it wasn't . . .'

'I'm sorry, I realise she's a friend of yours . . .'

'We didn't know each other that well,' Katya said. 'And apparently I didn't know her very well at all.'

Chona pursed her lips. 'We discovered that she was stealing handbags from our back room.'

'Oh, no!'

'Yes.' She shook her head. 'I knew there was a problem from the beginning. She was always late for work, and sometimes she didn't show up at all. When she was here, she spent a lot of her time in the toilet, claiming she was sick. She was here for six weeks before we discovered what was going on. People can really fool you.' One of the other women began walking in their direction and Chona quickly said: 'Could I interest you in one of our handbags?'

'No,' Katya said, 'but thank you.'

She left, sparing a last glance at some of the more ridiculous handbags near the front of the store. One of them was priced at half her monthly salary.

She couldn't call Ibrahim in the car or at home without being overheard by either her cousin or her father, so she sat on a bench in the crowded courtyard just as the call to prayer was ringing out. Some women moved slowly towards a praying area, but most sat on

56

benches and drank their coffees, oblivious to the forced meditation of *Maghreb*.

Ibrahim answered on the first ring. 'Katya,' he said breathlessly, 'Thanks for calling.' She heard street noises in the background. 'What did you find?'

'I'm not sure you'll want to hear this, but according to women at the boutique, Sabria hasn't worked there for over three months.' This was met by silence, the distant hooting of a car horn.

'Did you tell them you weren't there about her visa?' he asked.

'Not directly. I said I was a friend.'

'I knew this wouldn't work,' he said almost to himself. 'Her friends are protecting her.'

'They didn't seem like very good friends,' Katya said. 'They told me they didn't like her from the start. She was always late and she didn't do her job. Six weeks into it, she'd been caught stealing handbags from their stock. They didn't seem happy about her at all. My instincts are telling me that the woman I talked to wasn't making this up.'

'No,' he said. 'I often took her to work myself. She was going to that shopping mall.'

'Maybe she didn't tell you about what had happened at the boutique and she was going somewhere else in the mall? A different shop?'

'No,' he said more firmly. 'She wouldn't have lied. She said it was that shop.'

Katya felt sorry for him and wondered how Sabria had managed to deceive him so completely. It wouldn't have been that hard to lie about her job, but to sustain his trust, to lie to him so knowingly, that seemed much more difficult to pull off. She remembered that Sabria's last sponsor had been the Jeddah police. She had worked with Ibrahim in Undercover. She probably knew how to lie well enough, but to lie to Ibrahim? He must have been crazy about her, willing to overlook what his intuition might otherwise have warned him against.

'I know you think I'm deluded,' he said, 'but I know her. I know her better than anyone. And you're right. It's possible she was doing something else in the mall. I can't think what. It could be anything. But she would have told me about the stealing. I know it doesn't make sense, but you just have to trust me. *She* trusted me. And I know for a fact that she was going to the mall every day.'

'All right,' Katya said. 'Do you have a picture of her? I couldn't get one from the visa file.'

'You checked the visa?'

'Yes.'

'OK. Thanks. And yes, I'll get you a photo.'

Katya went outside to search for Ayman in the car park. She was shaken, and it surprised her. There was no reason to be shocked that a woman would lie to her lover. It probably happened all the time. But something in Ibrahim's voice was firm and knowing. He wasn't splintering from the blow of Sabria's disappearance, he was worried. He knew that something was wrong.

10

Jamila was standing at the *majlis* door. She was layered with fat in great solid hunks, her belly, her wide hips – all of it showing quite plainly thanks to the tightness of her dress. On the front, where a regular housedress would display a delicate trim of embroidery, this one sported a large, square mat of faux animal fur that sprang out at odd angles and was, in one corner, indecently long. He called it her gorilla dress.

It was too early in the morning for any of this. But clearly she'd been out. She was still wearing her black *abaaya* over the top of the dress. The cloak hung wide open. Her head scarf displayed a similar neglect. It was hanging halfway down the back of her head, showing all of her thin, scraggly hair, its colour bright purple and red, an ambitious combination of henna and *karkadé* dye from hibiscus. He wondered where she'd gone so early on a Monday morning.

'Show your father. Show your father what the sheikh has done.' She dragged their oldest daughter Farrah into the room, pushed her towards him. Farrah stumbled forward, a vague smile on her face.

'My back pain has gone,' she said.

Farrah's back pain had been going on for years. Four pregnancies had only aggravated the matter. While Zaki was getting married, this was the battle Ibrahim had been waging with Jamila. He wanted to take Farrah to Cairo for better treatment, but Jamila insisted that they had come to the end of what medical science could offer and that it was time to seek spiritual counsel. A hundred thousand riyals in doctors' bills was evidence enough that Farrah wasn't simply ill;

59

she had been possessed by a *djinni*. Until they called it out, Farrah would suffer.

'I can move,' Farrah said, holding out her arms and twirling around.

'And how is that?'

She turned her back and lifted the tail of her shirt. He held the shirt while she unpeeled the bandage, exposing a grotesquerie that nearly made him gag. The soft skin of her back had been maimed by a branding iron. A one-inch-deep welt, red on the edge, black at the centre, was suppurating just above her left hip bone.

'What the hell did they do?' he asked.

'This is how they removed the spirit,' she said, refastening the bandage. 'By adding outside pain, it takes away the inside pain. Do you know what I mean?'

'Do *you* know what you mean?'

'It worked,' she said simply. Then she turned back to her mother, to the protective aura she offered.

He fought the volcanic fury that was building in his forehead, dripping its black lava into his eyes so that all he could see was a muddled portion of the room.

'*That* is the real medicine,' Jamila said, pointing at Farrah's back as she escorted her out of the room.

He refused to react. He went to the bathroom for ablutions. Cold water. Warm tile floors. Hands hot with fury. His prayer rug was practically bald from years of kneeling. He faced the balcony door. Prayers spilled from him unconsciously, his mind absent, suppressing the real prayer building inside him, too painful to think about. *Please God, give me Sabria; give her back.*

Before he could finish, Jamila set herself up outside the sitting-room door. She was annoyed by his silence. She began to sweep the stairs. And the carping began. Something about the twins being left to do their homework all by themselves, and how they shouldn't have gone to the exorcist with her, because they might have caught a *djinni* themselves, but their father was never home so what choice did she have? But it didn't surprise *her*. He was obviously hiding things. He couldn't even see to it that his son got a divorce – something that should have taken a few seconds. How long does it take to say 'I divorce you' three times in front of two witnesses? If he couldn't

60

manage that one task for the week, how was he supposed to manage anything else?

He walked right past her and went down the stairs, out through the door onto the stifling street.

About twenty years ago, and for reasons totally obscure to him now, his brother Omar had withdrawn his entire savings in cash. Ibrahim remembered the bank. It was in a busy shopping mall with a large car park, permanently crowded because of a restaurant that used to sell the best curry in the neighbourhood. His brother had left 30,000 riyals in a plastic bag on the front seat of his car and gone into the curry joint. He'd come back half an hour later to find that he'd forgotten to roll up the windows and had left the doors unlocked. The money was still on the seat, notes hanging seductively out of the plastic bag. Not a single riyal was missing. Omar sometimes used that story as proof that the Saudi punishment of chopping off a hand was an effective deterrent to theft, but Ibrahim didn't agree. He believed that honesty came from the impulse to please others. Unfortunately, so did lying. And that day, his brother had just been lucky.

Omar's building was right next to Ibrahim's, identical to every other building on that side of the street: a flat concrete front, recessed balconies, and high upper walls surrounding an open roof. The joke – a dumb one, but surprisingly common – was that they had bought identical houses because they both worked in Undercover, and if someone came after one of them, it would be nearly impossible to tell them apart.

Omar came into the *majlis* looking dishevelled.

'Remember the time you left a bag of money on the seat of your car?' Ibrahim asked.

'Of course I do, why?'

'You were lucky then, but, brother—'

'Don't start with me. I don't want to hear it. I'm tired.'

'Your luck is running out,' Ibrahim said.

'Oh, is it?' Omar raised an eyebrow.

Ibrahim noticed the weariness in his brother's face. 'What's wrong?'

'Why is my luck running out?'

'I'm about to move into your spare bedroom.'

'Jamila again?'

Ibrahim nodded.

Omar made a noise deep in his throat, half chuckle, half grunt of disgust, and sat down next to his brother. 'Let's be honest, your luck with women ran out twenty-five years ago.'

'I don't complain.'

'You should.' Omar shook his head. The men fell silent. They were poised on the verge of a familiar conversation, one that had previously led them into a jungle whose very vibrancy seemed deadly – a discussion of second wives. Specifically: should they break their family's long-held tradition of never taking more than one wife? Ibrahim had once been in favour of breaking it and had even looked around (the internet made this so much easier). Omar was completely opposed to the idea, not just because of tradition but because it was indecent – and a horrible thing to do to your wife, no matter how much you disliked her. Their argument had ended badly, with Ibrahim accusing his brother of having become completely subservient to his shrew of a wife – a charge that Omar threw right back at him. They hadn't spoken for a week after that – an eternity in brother time.

It came down to a deeper issue they had long ago recognised and never discussed: both men were in miserable marriages, and while it was possible to hide such things from society at large, it was nearly impossible to hide them from your family.

'I have a favour to ask,' Ibrahim said.

'I hope this isn't about Jamila.'

'It's about work.'

That surprised Omar. Although they'd worked in the same department, they scrupulously avoided letting work interfere with their home relationship. Omar had transferred to Undercover when Ibrahim was already halfway up the ranks to Chief, and in the space of three years, Omar had surpassed him. Now he was Assistant Chief.

'You don't want to leave Homicide, do you?' Omar asked.

'No, no, I like Homicide. I'm just working on a case that I think may be connected to one of the older cases Warra did in Undercover. I was wondering if you could get me the files for Warra's old cases.'

'Why don't you just go through Records?'

'I can't raise any flags on this one. It would jeopardise our investigation.'

Omar grunted and sat back. Ibrahim knew he was going to say: *You're lying. What's really going on?* But he must have picked up on Ibrahim's panic because he said nothing.

'I think one of the files may be classified,' Ibrahim said.

Now Omar sat forward again, looked down at his hands. 'What's this about?'

'I wish I could talk about it, but I can't.' Ibrahim sat back. 'I really can't. You're just going to have to trust me.'

Omar studied him.

'I've never asked you for anything like this before.'

'That's why it's weird—'

'And I wouldn't do it now if it weren't important.'

Omar exhaled. 'All right. I'll see what I can do.'

That afternoon as he was pulling out of the parking garage at work, his phone rang. It was Katya.

'I took the photo you sent me to the mall during my lunch hour,' she said.

'I'm impressed.'

'Well,' she said, 'I wish I had some good news for you. I showed the photo in a bunch of shops but nobody recognised her, so I took a risk and went back to the place where she worked. They didn't recognise her either.'

'What?'

'The woman they know as Sabria Gampon looks nothing like the woman in the photo. Nothing. All three of the workers there said it wasn't her. Not even close.'

'I can't believe that.'

'I'm sorry. They pulled out her employment record for me too.'

'Did you tell them you were a police officer?' he asked.

'No, I told them I was a private investigator looking into some theft issues another business had had with her. I'm sorry, I probably shouldn't have said that, but it got them to be helpful. Anyway, they gave me a copy of her job application and I thought you'd want to look at it. Maybe you can identify the handwriting – or not.'

'Yes, good. Can you bring it to my office?'

'I've already left it in your in-tray,' she said.

'Thank you,' he said. 'I really appreciate your discretion on this.'

'Of course,' she said. 'And one more thing. I checked the job application against her previous visa information, and whoever filled out the application knew the correct ID number for the old visa.'

'OK,' he said, struggling to focus. 'So whoever was posing as Sabria had access to her immigration information.'

'Right.'

He sat in his car for twenty long minutes staring at the wheel. Sabria wasn't Sabria? Yes, she was. She had always been Sabria. They had vetted her thoroughly in Undercover before hiring her. Of course she'd posed as someone else on her assignments, but as far as he knew she'd never hired anyone else to pretend to be her – and that's what this had to be. Because his Sabria would never have taken a job at a boutique and stolen handbags and got herself fired within six weeks, and then failed to tell him about it. And Katya's new evidence supported this idea: no one at the boutique had recognised her picture. Surely Sabria knew about this other woman who was going to the job she was supposed to be going to, and doing the work she was supposed to be doing.

It was suddenly possible that Sabria hadn't run away at all, that she was part of an undercover operation of her own – so deep undercover that she was hiding it even from Ibrahim – and that for some reason, something had gone terribly wrong.

I I

They had scanned every missing persons database in the country and come up with one hit that matched their sketches of the remaining eighteen victims' faces. One hit wasn't bad. Maria Reyes. She had gone missing in Jeddah. Three years ago, she had come in on a Hajj visa and apparently overstayed the two-week limit, because they had no record of her leaving the country. She arrived on a guided Hajj tour made up exclusively of women from the Philippines. Tours like that were, for most Muslims coming from overseas, the only way they could do Hajj as women travelling alone. According to the tour guide, Reyes disappeared two days before the end of the tour. The tour company assumed that she'd run away to find illegal employment. No one had ever heard from her again.

Three years was a long time to go back. Ibrahim suspected that the tour company would have changed its staff by now, but the man who was in charge of the Hajj tours, Benigno Dimzon, remembered Reyes. It was unusual for a woman to disappear from one of his tours. The company, Dar el Hijaz, was diligent about keeping an eye on their single women, even walking each of them to her hotel room at night and posting a guard outside the entrance to their hotel to make sure that none of them left.

'Then how could she have run away?' Ibrahim asked.

They were sitting in Dimzon's office, a small, well-lit room that smelled like car deodorisers. It was Tuesday morning just after the second call to prayer. Bright sunlight slanted through the blinds onto the man's face. 'I am still not sure how it happened,' Dimzon said.

'There is one moment on the tour when we allow the women to do some basic shopping – for personal needs, of course. We escort them into the shopping centre and stay with them the entire time. We have never had a problem, not in seven years of doing this – except for Miss Reyes. Most of the women on the tours are not poor people. They're not coming here to find work. They are good Muslims and they come to do the Hajj and then they go home. We charge a lot of money, and we require them to put down a large deposit that they can get back once they return to the Philippines. So you see, we don't normally have a problem.'

'I'm sure you have an excellent record,' Ibrahim said. 'I'd just like to know exactly what happened when Miss Reyes disappeared.'

'Ah, well.' Dimzon sat back. He was a compact man with a lively face and bright eyes, which were shining now with an old frustration. 'The women at the shopping centre were all properly covered except for their faces. You see, we want to be able to identify them in public, so we ask them to please keep their faces showing. If they have a problem with that, then we can give them a little ribbon that they pin to their shoulder here.' He pointed to his left shoulder. 'That way we can identify who is in our group and who is not. Maria was wearing one of the pins. I was keeping an eye on her myself, and furthermore, she was standing very close to me. I turned to talk to one of the cashiers and when I turned back, she was gone.'

'And you noticed right away?'

'Yes. I thought she had moved into the crowd of women. They were all standing in line, waiting for the cashier. But I went down the line and she wasn't there. She must have taken off her ribbon and sneaked away. She must have been planning it.'

Ibrahim felt that he was telling the truth.

Dimzon went on. 'I immediately asked everyone: Have you seen Maria? Nobody had noticed her walk away. One woman said maybe she saw her heading for the back of the queue, but it could have been someone else, because Maria's face was covered. But the women were all talking, looking at the things in the checkout queue. Should they buy this? Isn't that cute? You know how it is. Nobody really noticed.'

'Was anyone else around? I mean, were there any strangers nearby? Anyone you remember who didn't belong to the group?'

'Nobody in particular. There were a lot of people at the mall. It was crowded.'

It was as easy as that. All she would have had to do was cover her face and her hands, the *abaaya* and head scarf would cover the rest. A woman cloaked in black could disappear like a shadow blending into the darkness of an alley. Even if Dimzon had spotted her, it would have been hard for him to chase her down. He might mistake someone else for her, and if anyone believed that he was harassing strange women in public, there would be a furore.

From the moment Maria Reyes left the mall, she became anonymous and free. Was it liberating? Did she seize it greedily? She could transform into any other Overseas Filipino Worker, albeit an illegal one. OFWs were in huge demand. Or was the sudden break fraught with fear and desperation? According to the Medical Examiner, Reyes had died roughly six to eight months after her disappearance. It didn't seem likely that she'd been kidnapped on the same day she'd disappeared, but it was possible. The killer could have nabbed her and held on to her for months before killing her. The mall itself was nowhere near the area where Cortez, the other IDed victim, had disappeared. Ibrahim knew it would be difficult to find a connection between the two cases. The only thing that was clear was that they needed more information.

12

Maybe because she had just agreed to marry Nayir, Katya felt absolutely paranoid getting into the SUV with Ibrahim. The fear had a different tang than before, when she'd climbed into taxis or in the rare instance when she'd been in a patrol car with Osama. It was no longer just 'What if my father finds out?' but now 'What if my fiancé finds out? What if he gets angry, or suspicious, and calls off the marriage?' And there was the added bonus of 'What if Ibrahim finds out that I'm not really married? Will he report me to Chief Riyadh? And will I lose my job like Faiza did last month?'

So she kept her veil down and got into the back seat before Ibrahim could protest. She would have considered that behaviour ridiculous a week before, not least because she was relegating herself to an inferior status and segregation of a sort. But now it was necessary. If anyone caught her, at least she could say she was in the back seat, properly covered.

Ibrahim looked surprised when he climbed into the car. He spun around and stared at her. 'I don't mind if you sit in the front,' he said.

'I'm fine, thanks.'

He motioned to the parking garage around them. 'No one's watching.'

'It's all right.'

She could tell that it upset him. It seemed ridiculous that she'd just pulled this stunt with the most liberal-minded man in the department. He started the car and pulled out of the garage.

'I worked with women in Undercover,' he said. 'Mostly it's hard to find women to hire in the first place. They need to have police experience, and most women who do also happen to have husbands who don't like the idea of their wives pretending to be someone else for a few months and putting themselves in danger. Plus, the husbands get stuck with the kids. We actually had to pull a woman out of an assignment one time because her husband couldn't handle taking his son to the doctor.'

Katya gave a soft snort. 'Is that how you met Sabria – in Undercover?'

'Yes.' He studied Katya in the rear-view mirror, stared straight into her eyes. 'We worked together. Our relationship developed later, after she left.'

Ibrahim had called Katya early that morning to ask if she would be willing to lift whatever forensic evidence she could find from Sabria's apartment. It was Wednesday, and he was eager to do it before Thursday, the weekend, when most of Sabria's neighbours would be at home.

She told herself she was going along because if something bad had happened to Sabria, she would feel terrible knowing that she'd done nothing to help. But she was really doing this because Ibrahim was in charge of the serial killer case, and if this was what it took to get in on the investigation, then she'd do it.

On the seat beside her was a duffel bag that held a mobile forensics kit. She'd tended to the black bag lovingly for weeks, filling it with new, stackable plastic containers, baggies, syringes, all the gear she could pilfer from the lab. She'd been anticipating using it for an urgent situation, when the department finally called her into the field. Instead, this morning was its debutante ball.

'Did you have a chance to look at Sabria's employment application? The one I left in your in-tray? she asked.

'Yes,' he said. 'It looks like her handwriting.'

'So she filled out the form,' Katya said, 'but someone else took the position?'

'That's my best guess,' he replied, 'although I couldn't tell you why.'

From the way he pulled into the spot beneath Sabria's building, Katya had the feeling he'd done it a thousand times before. He offered to carry the kit but she held onto it herself and they took the lift to the fourth floor.

'I still think you should report her missing,' Katya said. 'Anonymously, that is.'

'The police won't do anything I can't do.'

'Why not get some help with it then?'

'I am getting help,' he said.

Ibrahim let them in with his own key. Sabria's apartment was small, with bright white carpets and simple furnishings. The first thing Katya noticed was an almost complete lack of anything that seemed personal or nostalgic. No photos of family members or friends. No books or knick-knacks. Nothing but a pair of two-seater sofas and a television on a cabinet. Some empty cups littered the coffee table. Katya wandered into the kitchen, the bedroom and bathroom. That was the extent of the household, and aside from a few toiletries and the clothing in the wardrobe, there was nothing dis-tinct about the apartment at all. Anyone could have lived there.

'Didn't she have any photographs or personal items?' Katya asked.

They were standing in the kitchen. Ibrahim looked around, as if the absence of these items had only just occurred to him. 'She doesn't own a lot of things,' he said. 'She keeps all of her photos on her computer.'

'And where is that?'

He led Katya back to the living room and opened the doors on the cabinet beneath the television. There was a folded-up prayer rug, a bottle of perfume and some old videocassettes.

'It's gone.'

'Was it a laptop?'

'Yes.' He stood up, looking shaken.

Katya sat on the sofa and began dusting the coffee table for fin-gerprints.

'Sabria didn't come to Jeddah with a lot of stuff,' Ibrahim said. 'And everything she did have was lost when she left her first employer.'

'Who was that?'

'She worked as a housemaid for a year. It was an abusive situation, so she ran away.'

'But that was a few years ago, yes?'

'About five years ago.'

'She's had plenty of time to accumulate more stuff since then,' Katya said.

'She wasn't much of a shopper.'

'How was she paying for the apartment?'

'I pay for it,' Ibrahim said. 'I pay for everything. Including the phone and food and . . . whatever she wants, which isn't much.'

Katya nodded.

'What are you thinking?' he asked. 'Why was she working if I was taking care of her?'

'Something like that. The problem is, she wasn't working. At least not where she said she was. But you assumed it was true, so what did you think she was doing with the money she was supposedly making? She never spent it on anything. Didn't that make you wonder?'

He shrugged. 'I just assumed she was saving it.'

'Did you ever ask her about it?'

'Not really.' He went back into the kitchen. She dusted some of the cups on the coffee table for fingerprints and thought of her father, whose signature move when confronted with difficult questions was to retreat to the kitchen and find something to eat.

'There's still milk in the refrigerator,' he said, coming back into the room.

She looked up.

'A whole litre of it. She drank it every day. If she were planning on leaving, she wouldn't have bought milk.'

'Nobody in your family had any idea you were seeing her?' Katya asked.

She saw a flicker of hesitation. 'That's right.'

'Are you absolutely certain?'

'Yes.' Now he put on a look of paternal agitation. 'Believe me, if anyone knew about it, the rest of my life would have fallen apart by now.'

'What about friends or co-workers?'

'We were incredibly careful to hide this from everyone.' He gave her a dour look. 'It's not exactly legal, you know.'

'What about the neighbours?' Katya asked.

'They don't care in the least.'

71

'How long had you been seeing her?'

'Two years.'

'Why didn't you marry her?'

'Because she's already married, to a man who used to rape her and whom she never wants to see again.'

Katya nodded slowly.

Ibrahim sat down on the sofa. 'I know you're thinking: *What if she just walked away?*'

'You have to admit, it's possible, even with the milk. Sometimes people make spontaneous decisions.'

'Sure.' He couldn't seem to get comfortable on the couch, so he stood up and went to the front window. He stood at the very edge and peeked through the gap where the wooden screen didn't quite make it to the window frame. 'We never even opened the windows,' he said, motioning to the screen. 'We had these installed and they stayed shut all the time. We almost never went out to eat, but sometimes we'd go to a private beach. We tried not to phone each other too much, and we used aliases when we did. On my mobile, she's listed as "Mohammed". Not even a last name. We were *careful*.'

To Katya it sounded claustrophobic.

'So yes,' he went on, 'maybe she got sick of it. She never liked Saudi anyway. She used to say that when she came here, she couldn't understand why anyone did what they did. She was raised as a Muslim. She thought she was a good Muslim, until she came here. "This place has Mecca," she used to say, "but these people don't practise the same religion that I do." It upset her.'

Katya finished dusting and stood up. 'I'm going to check the bedroom.'

Ibrahim came over and stood in her way. 'I've thought about all of this. I've gone over it again and again. I was sure that something bad had happened. That's what my gut was telling me, and usually when my gut tells me something, that's it. I believe it. But now . . . I don't know.'

'There's one thing we haven't considered,' Katya said.

'Trust me, I've considered *everything*.'

'Then you've thought that this may be connected to the case?'

'The serial killer?'

'Yes.'

Ibrahim let out a harrumph. 'OK, yes, it crossed my mind.' He shook his head. She could see he was getting tired, half of his mind still back on 'What if she walked away?'

She checked the bedroom: it was as sparsely decorated as the rest of the apartment.

On the way out, she noticed a shiny object protruding from the hallway carpet outside the door to the apartment. It looked like a nail. She bent to inspect it and saw a smear of something. Quickly opening her kit, she took out a swab.

'It's blood,' she said. He knelt to take a look. The nail was stuck into the floor. Someone had stabbed their foot on it. Katya prised a small shred of plastic from the underside of the nail. It looked like material of flip-flops or cheap sandals. 'This has to belong to someone who came to her apartment,' she said. They were at the end of the hall; there were no other doors nearby.

'It's probably her blood,' he said.

'Did she wear sandals?'

'Yes. All the time.'

They stood up. 'Just in case,' she said, 'I'm going to need your DNA.'

He nodded and opened his mouth for a swab.

13

Ibrahim drove them south to the neighbourhood of Kandara and parked near the bottom of the Sitteen Street Bridge, a monstrous highway overpass that housed a busy bus station.

Beneath the bridge, on a wide concrete walkway, there was a shantytown of the kind Katya had only seen in news footage – and even then, only in impoverished, dejected places like the slums of Brazil, or lawless parts of Africa, where human life was treated as cheaper than that of an animal. But here, in one of Saudi's wealthiest cities?

Most of the people in Kandara were women, and judging from the faces – most of them unveiled – they were predominantly Indonesian or Filipina, although among them were Africans, other Asians and Indians. There were at least a thousand, probably more, stretching for blocks, most sitting with their backs against a concrete wall in the shady spots. Corrugated metal panels formed lean-tos in places. Some people had built shelters from old boxes, mostly to protect themselves from the sun. Mothers sat with children heaped on their laps, their men in front of them, lying on cardboard or old blankets.

The police did not keep statistics on different neighbourhoods, but it was well-known that this was one of the worst. Thanks to the presence of the Philippine Consulate a few streets from the underpass, the masses had begun gathering here years ago, waiting for permission to leave.

'They say most of the people here overstayed their Hajj visas,' Katya said.

'Sure, that's how some of them got into the country, but look at them as a group. What's the first thing you notice?'

'They're mostly women,' Katya said.

'Right ...'

'And it's difficult for women to come to Hajj alone.'

'Exactly. Most of those women are runaway housemaids,' Ibrahim said.

He was quiet for so long that Katya felt prompted to ask: 'How do you know they're housemaids?'

'This is where we found Sabria.'

'This place was here five years ago?' Katya asked.

'Yes, but not as bad.' They stared at the figures at the front of the crowd, women milling about in ratty black cloaks, their clothing plainly revealed.

It didn't take much to end up on the street. Housemaids, street sweepers, gardeners – many of those who had come hoping for a better life found instead a system of indentured servitude. A head-hunter would bring workers into the country for a fee – 10,000 riyals or more. A price high enough that, given the worker's wages, it might take a decade to repay the debt. So the employer paid the fee, and the housemaid was under obligation to him until the debt was repaid.

But what if you hated your job? What if your employer stopped feeding you? What if they refused to let you leave the house, or call your family, or even talk to the headhunter who had brought you there? What if you were being raped or abused? There were few laws in place to protect you – most laws protected the employer from losing his investment, having purchased you. Your only option was to flee, and you wound up at Sitteen, begging the consulate to give you a new passport, even a temporary certificate, and a plane ticket home. You stood in line for the three paltry buses that appeared at Sitteen a few times a week and which would take you to the Saudi-sponsored Passport Department to try to straighten out the mess.

You fought to get on the buses, and even if you couldn't get on, you fought anyway, because if the police thought you were a prob-lem, they'd want to send you home first. If you weren't enough of a problem, they'd simply fine you for overstaying your visa and throw you in a prison cell from which you would not be likely to emerge without royal intervention. And hope to God you didn't wind up in a consular detention centre, where you might be shoved into a room and left to rot. Five Ethiopians had died that way a few weeks ago, locked in a toilet cell without a window, asphyxiated by morning.

Thank God for the mosques that brought daily food and water to Kandara. You couldn't comfort yourself with the fact that the buses came back every few days. The population under the bridge was like water from a tap you couldn't turn off. No matter how many buckets you put beneath it, the water just kept flowing. As soon as the buses left, the place filled right back up again.

'You think she might be here?' Katya asked.

'No. This place is a rat hole. Twice in the past month, the police have busted a prostitution network. But what matters to us is that about fifty per cent of the missing persons in Jeddah either come here or go missing from here.' He lifted a folder from the floor of the front seat and slid out a handful of papers, handing a bunch to Katya. They were sketches of the victims from the desert. 'I thought this would be the best place to start to ID our remaining victims. You OK with doing that?'

'Yes, of course.'

Ibrahim got out of the car and Katya followed him across the street. The first thing she noticed was the smell, a putrid swamp odour of dirty bodies, rotten food and mounds of faeces lining a small trench that ran along the underpass, all of it ripening in the heat. She drew her veil across her nose and made an effort to breathe shallowly, but the stench was overwhelming, enough to make her eyes water. It was slightly cooler beneath the flyover, but it was an airless day and the stench stuck to everything.

They wandered through the crowd for two hours, an infinity of heat and sweat and disappointment. Ibrahim stayed in her line of sight, but she never managed to catch his eye. They were deep in a makeshift tent area when she came upon a woman who was bending over a small child.

'Excuse me; I'm looking for these women.'

The woman glanced at the pictures. 'Never seen them. Try Aunie.' She motioned to a woman at the pavement's periphery. Aunie was a petite Asian woman, her black hair cut in a bowl. She was lying on her side on a half-rotted brown wicker chair, the nicest, perhaps only piece of furniture in the whole place. She wore a defiant short-sleeved shirt and a pair of loose trousers cut off at the knee. On her feet were plastic flip-flops.

She didn't sit up as Katya approached.

'Excuse me,' Katya said; 'I'm looking for these women.' She held out the sketches and, slowly, Aunie sat up.

'You're police?'

'Homicide.'

The woman nodded. 'So they're dead.'

'Do you know them?'

The woman didn't say anything. She reached into a worn plastic sack at her feet and began rummaging. Katya watched her extract a dirty piece of cloth, which she used to wipe the sweat from her face and neck.

'You going to arrest me?' she asked.

'Not unless you want me to.'

Aunie gave her a smile that looked more taunting than amused. 'I've never seen them,' she said, and lay back down.

'Maybe a cup of coffee would stir your memory?'

The woman eyed her.

'Or lunch?'

After some thought, Aunie sat up. 'No,' she said. 'I already ate today. But I'll need money for lunch tomorrow.'

Katya nodded. 'Tell me their names.'

The woman squinted and reached for the middle sketch. She frowned while studying it. 'Looks like Mahal.'

'Does Mahal have a last name?'

Aunie shook her head. 'Can't remember. She's Filipina.' She shoved the sketch back toward Katya, but Katya didn't take it.

'Do you know if she had a job?'

'No.' Aunie gave a derisive snort. 'No job. *Here*? What do you think, this is a hotel?'

'Before she came to the bridge,' Katya said somewhat impatiently. 'Do you know what she did?'

'No.'

'How about money for lunch the day after tomorrow?'

Aunie snorted again. 'All right, maybe she was a housemaid. I can't remember. Some brutal family.' She waved her hand.

'And why was she here at the bridge? Did they abuse her?'

'*Of course* they abused her,' the woman said, although for the first time her words sounded false. 'She ran away from them. From all of them!'

Katya nodded and took the sketch back. 'And you?' she asked. 'Why are you here?'

Aunie shut her eyes and sat back in the chair. It wobbled unsteadily. 'Most people here have the same problem.'

'No passport?' Katya asked.

'No!' Aunie sat up and opened her eyes. 'They have passports. Their employers didn't give them permission to leave. They need permission. And if they ran away, then they're not going to get it. So that's the *Saudis* creating the problem! You can't buy a plane ticket unless you have a recommendation letter from your employer. You need your employer's permission to leave? What kind of screwed-up country is that?'

'So Mahal didn't have her employer's permission to leave?'

'No, she didn't. If someone killed her, it was her employer. I guarantee it.'

'And you don't know who that was?'

'Can't remember. There are too many names. How am I supposed to remember?'

Katya reached into her purse and took out a twenty-riyal note. She folded it and slid it into Aunie's bag.

Katya was exhausted. Ibrahim had had no luck identifying the women, and there wasn't much they could do with the name 'Mahal' except inform the junior officers who were responsible for getting IDs from the consulates.

Back near the office, they stopped for fruit juice at an octagonal kiosk that was decorated with bright blue Pepsi logos. Ibrahim bought the drinks while Katya waited in the car, still utterly paranoid that someone would see her. She got as close as she could to the back seat's only air-conditioning vent and let it blow straight across her burqa. When Ibrahim returned, he was carrying two bottles of juice and two small plastic tubs of cut fruit, and he handed one of each to Katya.

'Thank you.' *Father*, she wanted to add. He was beginning to remind her of her father's friends – the two or three who ever spoke to her directly, and whom she actually liked. They had a way of diffusing any possible sexual tension with a casual paternalism that always made her feel formal and awkward.

Instead of heading to the office, he swung over to the Corniche. She thought they might be going back to Sabria's apartment, but instead he drove south until he found a beach car park that was relatively empty. He pulled up, facing the sea, and left the engine idling so that the air conditioning continued to make a dent in the heat. He opened his fruit box and began eating.

Katya opened hers and slid a slice of watermelon beneath her burqa.

'Maybe you're right,' Ibrahim said. 'I should report her missing.'

'I think you should.'

'But first I'd have to remove any trace of myself from her apartment,' he said. 'What do you think my chances are of doing that?'

'You'd have to hire someone to do it. A professional, I mean. It would be a lot of work.'

They continued eating. She knew they were both thinking the same thing: that by reporting her missing, they'd be condemning Ibrahim to charges of adultery. That is, if the police took it seriously enough to send a forensics team to her house. Sabria used to work for the police, so the chances were good they'd investigate thoroughly.

'I'll look into hiring a cleaner,' he said. He collected the plastic containers and the empty bottles, threw everything out the window. He put the car into gear.

'Thank you for letting me assist on this case,' she said. 'The serial killer, I mean. I want to be working on it.' She hoped that hit the right note, not sounding too desperate.

He nodded. 'I'll give you some more work if I can, but right now I have a responsibility to keep up appearances at the station. I've got to keep my team organised – at least until the Chief takes me off the case, which I still think he might do. Obviously I'm being distracted by this whole thing with Sabria. And that's what really counts for me right now. Catching a killer can take a long time. Finding a missing person is much more urgent. I can't tell anyone that, and it may be selfish, but it's the truth.' He shut his eyes for a moment, then opened them and looked at her. 'I'm sorry. I know you want to be a part of this, and I think you should be. But there's a lot to consider.'

'Sure,' she said, hoping it sounded normal. 'I understand.'

'I really appreciate your help.'

14

The Thursday–Friday weekend passed with painful slowness. Ibrahim arrived at work on Saturday morning just after *Fajr* prayer, when the building was still nearly empty. He was intent on tackling the pile of paperwork on his desk. He found that Omar had sent Warra's files from Undercover. They must have arrived after he'd left the office on Wednesday. They were wrapped in paper, stuffed into a plastic delivery bag labelled 'Closed Cases' and 'Homicide' to make them look innocent. Ibrahim tore them open and spent the whole morning reading through them.

There was a joke in Undercover that if you went into a situation and didn't bump into somebody whose third cousin recognised you from your neighbour's uncle's wedding, then you were probably spending all your time jacking off in the desert. They'd had so many covers blown that for a while they could only hire men from other cities, and even then a few operations went south because no matter how big Jeddah became, their men couldn't seem to get away from familiar faces.

Ibrahim tended to take a dim view of these things, and he suspected that most cases were just unlucky. The sense of persecution that comes with a terrific streak of bad luck had driven him a little crazy for a while, crazy enough to come up with an absurd idea for an operation which, he suspected, would never be successful even if they could get it by the Undercover Chief. They would infiltrate a female shoplifting ring.

Ibrahim and two of the junior officers in Undercover certainly had trouble explaining it to the Chief. Even once they were able to convince him that there was indeed a network of wealthy women working together to steal high-priced luxury items from upscale department stores (diamond bracelets were a favourite), they spent weeks working out what a successful operation would entail. They would infiltrate the ring, gather enough evidence, and what? Throw a dozen wealthy mothers in jail? A good half of them were pregnant at any given time. None of them had fewer than four kids. Most of them were married to upper-middle-class donkeys, guys who imagined that all those new clothes and jewels their wives were sporting were of course paid for by the master money-maker himself, whose ministry wages easily stretched all the way to the runways of Milan. They didn't realise that their wives weren't stealing because they were poor, they were stealing because they were angry and powerless and probably compulsive.

When Ibrahim first made the suggestion to the Chief, the Chief became very quiet. Then he looked at Ibrahim like he'd just laid an enormous horse turd on his desk and tried to pass it off as a Bedouin ritual of welcome. And instantly Ibrahim knew what he was thinking: *No way are we arresting a bunch of wealthy mothers.*

Someone quickly pointed out that they could always arrest the husbands in lieu of their wives. Nobody would bat an eyelid if they held the men accountable for their wives' conduct. The tension in the room broke for a minute. Someone else started joking that they'd be saving those poor women from their idiot spouses. They'd be like those 'domestic violence' units they have in other countries and that Jeddah was trying to have, and sort of pretended it had, if the politicians were to be believed.

At first the Chief didn't want anything to do with the ring. 'Back to drugs with the lot of you!' But they worked on him, choosing vulnerable moments, because they were sick to death of drugs. And they would never have admitted this, but they liked the challenge. *Infiltrate a closed group of women.*

Eventually the Chief acquiesced. Even he had been impressed by the 300,000 riyal, broad-daylight diamond heist at the al-Tahlia Jewellery Centre. The women had clearly done surveillance of the jeweller's security. They knew how to distract the female security guards, and how to get into the jewellery display cases. And they did

82

it all without the slightest regard for the battalion of video cameras that operated nonstop, even when the shop was closed. Why? Because their faces were covered, their bodies shrouded in shapeless black cloaks.

One of the techs had suggested they try a new software program – unDress – which could digitally strip the clothes from a person's body and which was sometimes able to put a face to a shapeless burqa. But no sooner had he suggested it than the program was outlawed by a senior officer who was appalled that his men were undressing women via computer and calling it law enforcement.

They believed there were six women in the group, but it was hard to know for certain since they always wore burqas. And it was nearly impossible to arrest a woman for shoplifting unless her husband was present and willing to let her be searched. The only way they could convict these women was by gathering proof of their crimes from other women – friends or family. What they needed was a way to get into the women's homes, into their lives and secrets, and the only way he could envisage doing that was by planting a housemaid. They had women on the force, but very few Asians and immigrants – the ethnic groups that could reasonably pass as housemaids. The only person available at the time was Sabria.

The files Omar had sent were from her years working in Undercover before she busted the shoplifting network. And everything she had told Ibrahim about them had been right: there was nothing unusual. And certainly nothing that he could connect to the disappearance.

With the shoplifting case, she had been undercover for four months, had been such an excellent housemaid and had become such good friends with the family that even after the mother, Salima, was taken into custody and told how she had been set up, she refused to speak poorly of Sabria. Miss Gampon, she said with a spark of grudging respect, was a professional to the bone. Ibrahim wasn't sure at the time whether that was a good thing. He gave Sabria three months off. She had come back a week later, asking if they had a new assignment for her. He said no, she needed some time to recover, get back to her life. She left his office obediently, but three months later she was back, ready for her next assignment, looking exactly as she had before. So he gave her a new assignment, and then another. And each one seemed to leave her unscathed. She did her work with a kind of completeness that frightened him now. She put all of herself into it. Everyone believed her. She could convince anyone that her intentions were genuine.

He shoved the files back into the bag and caught sight of Sabria's job application for the Chamelle Centre boutique. It was still lying on his desk covered in treasonous handwriting. In all the time they'd worked together, he hadn't known her at all. He had handled her with the robotic skill of a boss who could lose his job if he acted inappropriately with a female co-worker. It was only later, after she left, that he came to know who she truly was. And he thought very resolutely about that person now. The real Sabria would only send someone undercover, posing as her, if it meant serving a greater good. If it meant helping someone. But he still had no explanation for why the real Sabria hadn't told him all about it.

It was after noon prayers when Ibrahim stopped the car at the end of the alley. He and Daher got out. Already six police cars were crowding the scene. The duty officers had shut down the street for two streets in both directions and chased the last of the pedestrians from the pavements.

Ibrahim tried to force himself to walk a little more slowly. He wanted to run. He passed the street sweeper who'd made the discovery, heard Daher say, 'Boss, this is the guy ...' before he rounded the dumpster and saw the crime scene tape. He slid under it and went straight to the tangled mass of fabric that lay on the pavement. It was a woman's cloak. Empty. And lying beside it was a dismembered hand.

Subhan'allah. Bism'allah, ar-rahman, ar-rahim. His mind spiralled into prayer, he shut his eyes. The relief was so fierce it hurt.

He climbed back under the tape. 'You said this was a body?'

'It's not a body?' Daher stood anxiously beside him, trying to look useful and telling the duty officers to get on the other side of the crime scene tape.

'No, it's a hand.' *Should never have left Undercover.* He moved to the shade beneath the shop awning and squatted on the ground, resting his head in his hands.

'They found this right next to it.' Daher was standing above him, holding out a woman's handbag. Ibrahim took it and looked inside. There was a purse with an ID card in it. *Amina al-Fouad.*

'Make sure forensics gets this,' Ibrahim said. He barely had the presence of mind to consider that Falasteen Street in broad daylight without cars or shoppers was surreal. Aside from uniformed policemen and a few business owners, the only figure on the street was the scrawny street sweeper. He was leaning against a dumpster, looking nervous and perplexed, not like a man who had just discovered a dismembered hand.

Ibrahim got up and approached the man. 'Was it in the dumpster?' he asked.

'No,' the sweeper said, 'it was there. Just where you see it now. Some sinner's hand . . . ' He waved his hand and looked to the heavens.

'Did you see anyone near it?'

'No.'

It took fifteen minutes to establish what, generously speaking, could be called a crime scene. Two dozen officers were moving around. Shoppers were coming out of stores and stopping to gape. Abu-Musa arrived and pronounced the hand dead. Forensics arrived a few minutes later with an additional surprise: Katya stepped out of the van with her mobile kit and followed Majdi to the scene. Daher saw her and did a double take but kept his mouth shut.

Ibrahim's thoughts slowly shifted into the rational. He had been expecting Sabria to be lying there.

Katya looked appalled as she knelt near the hand.

'Yes, Miss Hijazi?' Ibrahim asked.

'I'm having trouble imagining someone planting this here,' she said. 'How did nobody notice?'

Daher snorted, as if the answer were obvious.

'This isn't that far from the street,' Katya went on. 'And this street is normally very crowded. Whoever put it here must have done it very recently. I'm sure it wouldn't go unnoticed for very long.'

Daher sniffed and looked away, fully intent on ignoring her remarks.

'I don't know,' Ibrahim said. 'You'd be surprised what people fail to notice. We've got men talking to the shop owners nearby. Maybe someone saw something.'

'It would be good to get a description of our killer,' Daher said.

'You're already assuming this is connected to the serial killer case?' Katya asked.

Daher looked at her sharply. Her previous bafflement, although irritating, was at least understandable. But how dare she criticise him?

Katya ignored him, a calculated bait. 'Our serial killer never left a hand on a street before,' she said. 'He buried them in a secret gravesite.'

'Of course it's him!' Daher said. 'He's telling us to screw off! This is an angry shout from our man.' He motioned to the hand. 'He's saying he's in control, and that he can do whatever he likes, and there's nothing we can do to stop him. I'm surprised. That message should be obvious.'

Katya zipped her duffel with an angry yank. 'This could be the hand of someone who was punished for theft.'

Daher snorted.

'It could also be a copycat crime,' Katya said.

'Sure,' Daher said, 'except that no one knows about the bodies in the desert except us.'

'Why couldn't it be one of us?' Katya asked.

Daher guffawed. 'Yes, of course! And I vote for the American. She came here with her own angels of death to wreak vengeance on the terrorists.' One of the junior officers who'd been listening gave a wan smile.

'What?' Daher asked.

'Nothing.'

'You know what I'm going to say, right?' Daher asked.

'Something about Charlie's Angels?' the junior officer said.

Daher froze. 'Man, how can you make jokes at a time like this?'

'It's not a joke. It's just what they're saying.'

'I was going to say that the first rule about serial killers – one that Dr Charlie forgot to mention – is that they're *American*. White males in their thirties. Normal-looking guys.'

'He's probably not American,' Katya said, standing up.

'Oh?'

'Someone would have noticed an American.'

'Not if he was in an *abaaya*,' Daher shot back.

She barely glanced at him as she followed Majdi out of the alley. Ibrahim motioned Daher out. He was flushed, but at least he'd managed to get in the last word.

Stopping at the van, Katya turned to Ibrahim. 'In order to establish a connection to the serial killer case,' she said, 'we're going to have to figure out a couple of things. First, whether this hand was severed *post mortem*. All of the hands at the gravesite were cut off after the victims were dead. It looks like a female hand, but we have to be sure. Also, we'll have to find out when the woman ...' She looked into the handbag. '... Amina al-Fouad, went missing – if she is missing. It could be her hand, but that needs to be checked.'

Ibrahim was about to reply when Daher cut in with what he felt was a lame attempt at grabbing his attention.

'Boss,' he said, 'we checked the consulates for that name you gave us. The woman's name?'

'Mahal,' Katya said.

Daher was startled and looked at Ibrahim as if to say: *How does she know?*

'She was at Sitteen with me,' Ibrahim said.

Daher didn't respond, but Ibrahim saw the look of betrayal in his eyes. Why had he taken Katya and not Daher to Sitteen?

'Did you learn anything at the consulate?' he asked Daher.

'There were no missing persons named Mahal,' Daher said in a brittle voice.

Ibrahim saw no gloating in Katya's face as she walked away, but he worried anyway about the feelings between her and Daher and where those particular agonies might lead.

'He's simply *not qualified*,' said the voice of Yasser Mu'tazz.

Ibrahim was standing in the hallway outside the office of Chief Riyadh, hoping to give him a briefing on the crime scene. He'd been just about to go inside when he heard the sharp tones, felt the prickly sense that Mu'tazz was talking about him.

'Inspector Zahrani is a senior officer with over ten years' experience in one of the roughest divisions in Jeddah.' Riyadh was standing up for him. That was a surprise. 'I realise he's never worked a serial killer case before, but neither has anyone else in this department.'

'I just don't think he's cut out for it.' Mu'tazz made no effort to soften his tone, or even tack a polite 'sir' onto the sentiment. He was clearly furious. Ibrahim knew why. Mu'tazz had worked in Homicide the longest, and he had more experience than anyone else, but he had no connections. His father was a peasant labourer from Yemen who had made a bit of money developing a textile business in Jeddah – but not enough money to be invited to the homes of the elite. Ibrahim's family, although not wealthy, were Bedouin, with friends in the Ministry and a particularly close friendship with Princess Maddawi, one of the elder cousins of the King. When he'd decided to transfer out of Undercover, he had done the legwork, but Maddawi had secured him the position.

'I'm keeping an eye on him,' Riyadh said.

'I saw him leave the parking garage yesterday with one of the female lab techs.'

Ibrahim's chest constricted.

'I know,' Riyadh said thinly. He hadn't liked the idea at the time, and apparently he liked it even less now. 'I sanctioned that because it was necessary.'

'Where were they going?'

'To follow some leads on the case that required a woman's presence.'

'And he couldn't take one of the female officers along?'

'No one was available that day.'

'One of the male officers, then?'

'I try to avoid sending a male officer to interview a woman,' Riyadh said drily, 'to avoid contradicting our virtue policy.'

There was a rustle as Riyadh stood up, probably hoping to bring the conversation to an end. Ibrahim turned down the hall.

15

Fingerprint and DNA analysis indicated that the severed hand belonged to Amina al-Fouad, the woman whose handbag had been found at the scene. They also determined that the hand had been cut off while she was alive.

Amina didn't fit the profile: she was a Saudi housewife, aged thirty-nine, who lived in the Corniche district with her husband and six children. She had never had a job outside the home, and although the family was wealthy enough to have two housemaids, Amina wasn't much of a shopper, the favoured pastime of other women like herself. She only left the house with her husband's explicit permission.

'She would not have gone to Jamjoom by herself,' her husband said angrily, for the fifth time.

Ibrahim was sitting across from Mr al-Fouad in the family's *majlis*. The sofa felt as if it had never been sat on before. Everything he had seen of the house so far gave him the idea that it was a showroom for Pottery Barn. He thought of his own house, its ragged furniture and decades-old décor, and decided that he preferred his own way.

Al-Fouad was clearly upset. He had reported his wife missing seven days ago, the same day she had disappeared. Now he was struggling with the kind of shock and amazement that would have been extremely difficult to fake. Ibrahim hadn't mentioned the serial killer. They couldn't establish the connection for certain yet, so why make the husband worry more? What bothered Ibrahim was al-Fouad's insistent sense of honour, which had been growing more pompous by the minute. The son, Jamal, had already told Daher that his mother had taken a taxi by herself to Jamjoom. He said he'd had a voicemail message from her, but he'd deleted it. Jamal was supposed to have picked her up at Jamjoom, but he didn't make it on time. He suspected she'd left Jamjoom in a taxi as well.

'Mr al-Fouad,' Ibrahim said, 'in order to do everything we can to find your wife, it's essential that we know exactly where she was and what she was doing there. In cases like this, it's important to put one's honour aside, because the fate of your loved one may hinge entirely on the smallest, most uncomfortable detail. You have to trust us to be discreet, and we have to trust you to tell us the absolute truth.'

Al-Fouad wasn't having it. He shook his head stubbornly and said once again, 'She would not have gone—'

To ensure that he didn't explode, Ibrahim pretended to make a note on his paper pad. He wrote: *Husband is a pompous donkey's arse.*

'OK,' Ibrahim said. He was angrier than he should have been and he knew his professionalism was slipping, but he didn't care. 'We also need a photograph of your wife.'

'I'm going to tell you what I've already told the police – I don't want her face all over the nightly news!' al-Fouad cried, his voice rising sharply.

Who was this man? This throw-back to barbarianism? How could he not do absolutely *everything* in his power to ensure that his missing wife was brought home safely? Ibrahim's fury was boiling over. What filthy scum let his honour stand in the way of a woman's life?

'Unfortunately,' Ibrahim snapped, 'the best chance we have of finding your wife right now involves showing her face to as many people as possible. Someone will have seen her. And that person will call us. And thanks to the kindness of our fellow Muslims, it might be possible to bring your wife back alive. But only if we can get a photograph of her.'

Al-Fouad looked as if he were going to leap off the sofa.

Ibrahim's next words came tumbling out with an anger much more savage than al-Fouad's. 'We also need a full-body shot of your wife.'

'What?'

'We need to see her whole body, preferably in a cloak, because when women are in public, sometimes they don't show their faces, and all people see is the figure. I'll give you five minutes to come up with these photographs or I'm going to arrest you myself.'

Al-Fouad's face was grey and trembling. He stood up from the sofa and marched out of the room.

Five minutes later, Ibrahim was standing outside the al-Fouads' front door, handing two photographs to Daher.

'Get these to the press,' he said. 'Don't mention the serial killer or the severed hand; just say that this woman has gone missing.'

'Aren't you going to clear this with Riyadh?' Daher asked.

'Just do it.'

Daher looked scared as he walked away. Ibrahim felt shaken. He sat down on the top stair and tried very desperately not to think about Sabria and all the things he should be doing right now to find her, but it was no use pretending that his anger was all about al-Fouad.

16

The next few days were rough. The serial killer case – or what had come to be referred to as the Angel case – had top priority, which meant that every significant piece of evidence, every important interview and crucial meeting, was handled by the men, and that Katya, consigned to an upstairs lab, was made to do the lowest of grunt work, once again without understanding its relationship to the case at hand. It was merely 'get me the DNA results on this blood' and 'tell me what kind of fibre this is', while the clothing itself remained in Majdi's lab downstairs, and the bodies that once held the blood in question remained in the overcrowded freezer room.

She felt like one of the grunts who built the Pyramids, shoving a gigantic stone across the desert, never seeing the great structure it was meant to build. No one had the time to stop and explain anything, least of all to a woman who worked in forensics. She had heard, indirectly from a very frazzled Majdi, that the officers were investigating every taxi company in town. They had an idea that the killer might be a cab driver, although why, she could only guess. Her tenuous connection to the developments of the case was Ibrahim, but he was too busy.

She put aside a bit of time every day to process the evidence from Sabria's apartment. This was harder than it sounded because she had to disguise it as a fictional case. At the same time, she had to appear to be working diligently on the Angel case, the only one they were allowed to be handling at the moment, and so she found herself juggling unmarked files, vigilantly watching over the lab's machines, and even openly lying to the other lab techs, who seemed to sense that she was hiding things. In all of the evidence she'd collected at Sabria's apartment, nothing significant had emerged. She was still waiting for the DNA results from the blood swipe she'd taken from the nail in the hallway.

She would have given anything to have an excuse to go down to Ibrahim's office, and once or twice she had walked past simply hoping to appear casual, but he was never there, and she didn't want to call him until she had some news. A previous Katya might have marshalled the nerve and gone down anyway, but now there were the dual hurdles of Daher having a reaction every time he saw her and this being an enormously important case – one that was still drawing envoys from the mayor's office and the Ministry itself. On top of that, getting engaged to Nayir had begun to make her paranoid about the smallest things. She wasn't sure if it was simply that she was afraid of Nayir's finding out just how much she interacted with strange men, or if there were more going on inside her, some reflexive fear of the whole situation, marrying a man who was still something of a mystery, and not in a good way.

Her father had been overjoyed when she'd told him she'd accepted the proposal. He'd gone straight out to crow about it to his friends, and before long she was receiving gifts. He would bring them home after his long nights at the café. A delicate gold bracelet from Qasim. A bag of gourmet Indian tea with a real British teapot from Awad Mawjid. An elegant, leather-bound copy of the Quran from Imam Munif. The gifts pleased her father more than anyone else, and he went around generally beaming with pride and being generous with his nephew, Ayman, by letting him have the car whenever he liked. It was fine to be around Abu when he was in this state, but more and more she found herself worrying about it at work. What if she and Nayir were unable to reconcile their different ways? What if Nayir, so struck with love for her, didn't really mean what he said: that they'd find a way to work things out? What if he turned into a 'beard', some old ayatollah who would never truly change his rigid ideas about the proper behaviour of women? And how would all of this affect her elderly father?

In the middle of these worries, she stumbled suddenly on the answer to her Ibrahim dilemma. She called his mobile but he didn't answer so she left a message explaining that she needed a full-body picture of Sabria, preferably in a cloak. He could email it to her, or leave it on her desk. His phone cut her off before she could explain why she needed the picture, and she was afraid to call back in case he thought she was pestering him.

Annoyed, she threw the phone back in her bag.

It was something of a relief when Charlie Becker came into the lab, her auburn hair swinging like a flirty giggle. The other women stared at her, but Katya, whose work station was closest to the door, stood up and said hello.

Charlie greeted her, came up to her desk and leaned in for a conspiratorial whisper. 'I'm here for most of the day answering questions, but it's lunchtime and I was wondering if you could tell me where I could find a safe place to eat.'

'A safe place?' Katya said. Her English, such as it was, came from college courses and, more recently, her cousin's large stash of banned movies. She could understand what Charlie said, even if she tended to take everything literally.

'You know,' Charlie said, 'somewhere the men won't watch me eat.'

'Ahh.' Katya nodded and stood up, grabbed her bag from the counter and motioned Charlie to the door. 'I know a safe place.'

It was a thrill to leave the building, even if it was with the clumsy American who had made Katya feel both pathetically repressed and self-consciously exposed when they'd first met in the situation room. Now Katya was worried that her English would sound like something from a B movie.

They wound up at Cilantro's near Le Chateau. Charlie found it disconcerting that they had to go in through the back entrance for women, and that they had to crowd into a tiny lift to reach the second-floor 'family' section, where women were allowed to dine alone. Once they'd taken their seats at a quiet corner table near an ugly but modern-looking brown slate wall, Charlie let out a shivery sigh and sat back. Katya realised with some surprise that she was upset.

'I'm sorry I don't speak Arabic,' Charlie said. 'There's a lot I wish I could tell you right now.'

'You can tell me in English,' Katya fumbled out.

'OK, well, I hope this doesn't offend you, but how can you stand working in that place? The men are like animals!'

Katya smiled politely. 'It's because you're not wearing a veil.'

'I know!' Charlie sat forward. 'That's what bothers me, frankly. I've seen other Western women on the streets here, and they're not wearing veils.'

Katya shrugged, wanting to point out that perhaps those other women had the same problem.

'The men at the office keep asking me out,' Charlie said. 'I mean, I thought this was a country preoccupied with virtue. The blatant come-ons surprise me. It's hard to get any work done when you've got to field the sex stuff all the damn time. I'm sorry, I don't mean to criticise. I'm just – I'm getting sick of it already.'

The waiter arrived and they ordered Reuben sandwiches. Katya was beginning to wonder if she could survive a whole meal listening to this woman complain in English. She was already feeling defensive.

'Just say "no",' Katya said. 'They will leave you alone.'

'Yeah,' Charlie said with a sigh. 'Thank God they're so busy hunting down the cabbie.'

'The cabbie?'

'The cab driver – you know they're looking into the cab companies?'

Katya nodded uncertainly.

'Have they not told you? Good Lord.' Charlie took a sip of her water. 'Well, first of all, the Bedouin tracker guy told Inspector Zahrani two weeks ago that the killer used his right foot more than his left and that he probably drove a car, maybe for a living. I mean, most men drive cars, but apparently this was a significant difference. So they thought the killer may be a cab driver, and they started investigating. Then it turns out that Amina al-Fouad probably got into a cab when she disappeared. Now they've amped up the investigation of cab drivers.'

Katya was delighted. She found herself understanding most of what Charlie said, and of course Charlie would know everything about the case. It occurred to her that she had Charlie all to herself for at least another hour.

95

'It's possible that it could be a cab driver,' Charlie said. 'That seems to be the only way a man can get access to a woman around here.'

Katya nodded. 'It is known to happen,' she said.

'What do you mean?'

'Women in cabs get kidnapped,' she said. She wanted to tell her about the man who had come into the station last month because his wife had been abducted. He and his wife had been in a taxi and the driver complained that the car wasn't working. The driver asked the man to get out and help him push, and when he did, the driver leaped back in and drove away with the wife like some Bedouin raider from a time that should have passed into oblivion. As far as Katya knew, the wife was still missing.

Charlie looked horrified. 'How do you get around, if you can't trust cab drivers?'

'My cousin drives me,' Katya said. 'And a friend of my father's sometimes, too.'

They were silent for a moment.

'Can I ask you about the case?' Katya asked.

'Go ahead!' Charlie said.

'This totem that you talk about. We think it is the hands.'

'Right. The severed hands.'

'What do you think it means?' Katya asked. 'He keeps only some of them?'

Charlie seemed to relax and gave her a quirky smile. 'You know, nobody has asked me that yet. I mean, they've asked for a dozen explanations of totems, but they haven't wanted my opinion. I've been thinking about it, too. In general, the totem is a tangible reminder of the kill. It's like a memento, except the killer can choose any memento. I don't know why he only buried those three by the gravesite. The real question, I think, is: why does he cut them off? What is the significance of the hand?'

Katya shrugged, not certain how to explain her ideas in English.

'Based on past experience,' Charlie went on, 'I would guess that the hand is somehow related to a trauma. One of the psychological theories about fantasy is that all fantasy – any kind, but especially the sexual kind – is actually a person's way of dealing with the effects of a trauma. Are you following?'

'Yes.'

'For example, one time I had a psychiatric patient who, as a child, hated his best friend's mother. She was always mean to him – seemed to think he was too poor and too stupid to play with her son. Eventually, she forced the friendship to an end. At the time, it was horribly painful for my patient. Years later, he became obsessed – now, he had a clinical disorder, so this is a bit extreme – he became obsessed with a sexual fantasy in which he was sleeping with a man who looked and acted very much like the father of his friend from childhood. And the fantasy always involved the mother walking in on them and discovering that her husband was gay and becoming angry, or getting drawn into the sexual encounter as a submissive. I'm sorry, I can see you're not totally following.'

'No, I understand,' Katya said. 'Fantasy is to heal the pain of something bad, maybe from when you were a child.'

'Exactly. So part of this killer's fantasy involves removing these women's hands. The hands are especially important to him, so there will be a reason why. Maybe he lost a hand. Maybe someone who abused him had an injured hand. It could be anything like that. I suggested to Inspector Zahrani that he do a medical records search for criminals with injured hands. It's a long shot, but in my experience, catching a serial killer can take months, even years. The more you do, the better your chances are of catching the guy. I can tell you want to say something.'

'Yes,' Katya said. Their sandwiches had arrived and they both began eating. 'In Saudi Arabia, when you chop off a hand, it means that the person was a thief.'

Charlie paused with food in her mouth, a look of amazement making its way onto her face. 'You know, I knew that, I just didn't— God, I'm an idiot. Of course. It's the punishment for theft. So maybe this killer feels the need to punish his victims. Maybe he thinks of them as thieves.'

'And more,' Katya said.

'What do you mean?'

'In Saudi, when you execute a woman, you don't cut off her head. You shoot her in the back of the head.'

'Is that right?'

'Yes. If they chopped off the head, it might roll and the burqa might come off, and you would see her face. So they shoot her instead. They sometimes give her the choice.'

'My God.' Charlie put her sandwich down. 'So this could all connect to an executioner fantasy.'

'Perhaps,' Katya said, 'the killer thinks he is like … an executioner. But how does that help us find him?'

'Well,' Charlie said, 'maybe one of his relatives or someone he loved was executed unfairly. It might be worth looking at execution records. Do you keep those?'

'We can get them,' Katya said, feeling pleased. 'But the hand on Falasteen Street, from Amina al-Fouad. It's not like the others. Do you think it is also the Angel killer?'

'What did you call him?'

'The Angel killer.' Now Katya was surprised. Why would Charlie know everything but that? She explained what she could about the nineteen bodies and the significance of the number nineteen in the Quran.

Charlie had stopped eating and was listening intently. 'So based solely on the fact that you find nineteen bodies, you think this killer imagines himself an Angel of Vengeance – one of the Angels who guards over Hell. And he's punishing those who should go to Hell?'

'Yes,' Katya said, 'something like that.'

'Well, it fits in with the execution fantasy. Religious ideas do drive some serial killers. Maybe you're looking for a fundamentalist.'

'That should narrow it down,' Katya said. Charlie laughed, but Katya hadn't intended it to be funny. Charlie seemed to realise this and stopped laughing.

'Most serial killers don't look crazy from the outside,' Charlie said. 'In fact, they look just like everyone else, maybe even a little better. They spend a lot of time trying to blend in.' She picked up her sandwich again. 'To answer your question: yes, I think the dismembered hand is connected to the Angel killer.'

'But he has never cut off a woman's hand while she was alive. And he has never left a hand in the city before. And clearly he also left her handbag there so we would identify her.'

'Right. This one was different. Probably something triggered it, and I imagine it was that you guys found and removed the bodies from the site. In a way, those were his trophies, too.

'If you think of it in terms of fantasy,' Charlie went on, 'the hand on Falasteen Street could also be an evolution of his technique. Most killers' techniques evolve. They become so good at it they can do it perfectly. They know just how to capture someone, how to keep them alive, how to prolong the torture. They know how to *not get caught*. That's what makes them so damned dangerous. But they can also get sick of doing something so well, and maybe they want something more challenging. So they change their style.'

'Do you think he will kill Amina?' Katya asked.

Charlie's face tightened. 'Yes. He's become bold enough to leave her hand in a public place and risk being noticed. But now you have one advantage. For an organised killer like him, it was a sloppy thing to do. He may have left some evidence behind. Have you found anything?'

'I don't know,' Katya said. 'I just run samples. They don't tell me what it means.'

Charlie studied her. 'I'll try to find out.'

Katya smiled.

'In the meantime,' Charlie said, 'look for patterns. With an organised killer like this one, there will be patterns.'

On the way back to the office, Katya checked her phone and saw with pleasure that Ibrahim had sent three full-body shots of Sabria dressed in a cloak, along with a note that said 'Thank you'. She said goodbye to Charlie at the entrance to the building and caught a taxi at once to the mall. Before getting in the cab, she inspected the driver carefully and saw what she was certain was only a cheerful, paunchy, middle-aged Pakistani who graciously opened the door for her and turned down the music when she got in the car.

17

'We do not touch women.' This was Abu-Musa, the Chief Medical Examiner, standing in the morgue with Officer Mu'tazz. Abu-Musa of the swampy brown eyes and cold silences. The odd, guerrilla-warfare trousers, one cargo pocket bent out of shape from years of holding a travel Quran. A great pair of shoulders and hands, the strangling kind.

'So you've only got one woman working on nineteen bodies?' Ibrahim asked, deliberately provoking, trying to snap them out of the reverie that they could afford to be virtuous.

'She's doing her job.' Abu-Musa said this menacingly, as a man defends his wife.

'This man is killing women,' Ibrahim snapped back. 'You can't expect that we'll catch this guy without knowing all the facts. And the faster we get that information, the better we'll be able to stop him from killing again.'

'Then start looking for the foreigners who might have killed these women.'

Ibrahim was disgusted.

'You haven't even tried that, have you?' Abu-Musa said. 'But goodness, why would a foreigner be killing here? Maybe because the past three serial killers have been foreigners?'

'We have to identify the bodies,' Ibrahim said coldly. 'That is our *best* chance of finding this man.'

'You have your sketches of their faces.'

'We need all the forensic evidence we can get from the bodies. And we need it now.'

'You will get it when it's done.'

And here comes the pomposity, Ibrahim thought.

'If your values don't hold up in a crisis,' Abu-Musa said, 'then they aren't worth shit.'

Maybe they're not worth shit, Ibrahim wanted to reply, but he saw plainly what he was up against. Here were two men who had already begun to suspect him of indecency, and it would only be made worse by this conversation.

He went back to the situation room. It was empty, the end of the day. A cool Wednesday night. Tomorrow was the weekend. Everyone would be out with friends, picnicking with their families on the Corniche, perhaps pretending there was no killer stalking the labyrinth. He went to the whiteboard and began taking down the photographs, not out of the distorted sense of propriety that would belong to Abu-Musa but because he didn't want to stare at them any more. The brutalised faces contained remnants of Sabria. An eye. A cheekbone. His mind knew it was just the angle but the adrenalin proved to him that his body did not.

He went back to her apartment as he had every night since she'd disappeared, crazily half-expecting that she'd be there. Before the disappointment could truly stab him, he left again quickly and drove around the city, welcoming the evening gridlock, trying not to stare at every woman on the pavement.

He had often had the experience with Sabria that when he took her somewhere he knew well and attempted to share what he knew about the area, she grew tense and distant. It had come out at some point that she felt intimidated by his knowledge of the city. It had taken even longer for her to admit that she was angry about it. Not at him, but at the situation. The only reason she didn't have that knowledge herself was because she didn't have the free access to places that he did. Even doing undercover work, she'd spent most of her time posing as a housemaid, trying as hard as she could to blend seamlessly with the world around her, which meant acting as most women did.

He'd started taking her to the same few places over and over. Safe places, like the floating mosque and a private beach down the coast where no one would see them. How badly he'd wanted to take her to so many other sights in the city! The al-Tayibat City Museum and Rayhanat al-Jazeera Street to see the city's sprawling history crammed into three hundred rooms. Or to Khayyam al-Rabie for her sweet tooth. Or to Yildizlar for the hopelessly romantic dinner he had always wanted to buy her. But the fear of being recognised was greater than desire.

That was the idea behind Katya's request, he supposed: a full-body picture of Sabria in a cloak and scarf. Maybe no one at the women's shopping mall had recognised Sabria's photo because they hadn't paid much attention to her face. But they might recognise her shape.

He wanted to tell Katya that he knew exactly what she was doing. It was something he had practised since he was a child, small and scared and running through the souqs and shopping malls, always terrified of losing his mother, his burqa-clad, not-very-affectionate mother. She was shaped like a lot of women, he realised rather quickly, and she always covered her whole face, always wore a robe that cloaked her ankles and shoes, which left him little to go on. She moved quickly through the crowds, as if afraid of being seen, afraid of getting stuck somewhere. Omar was always comfortable running off. If he couldn't find his mother, he didn't panic. He was as independent and quick-moving as she was. But Ibrahim had nightmares for years about losing her in the market. He came to recognise the smallest things. At seven, he had already worked out how the curve of her shoulders was different from other women's – she had a strangely sloping back, and funny rounded shoulders that were just a tad too thin. It was probably where Farrah got her back problems. He learned the shape of her head, the details of the pins in her head scarf – always worn the same way, simple black safety pins around the crown of her head. He knew her walk, the quick little jolts, the energy of it. He came to know her form so well that sometimes when she met him after school, he could pick her out of a crowd from fifty yards.

He was heading home, finally, when Katya called.

'I'm glad you phoned,' he said. 'It's late and I wasn't sure it was appropriate to bother you.'

'I did discover something interesting,' she said. 'Although I'm not sure what to make of it.'

'Go ahead.'

'One of the women who works at the mall café recognised her immediately from the photos. She said that Sabria used to sit at the café and she would meet other women there. They would talk for a while, and then the friend would leave.'

'Was it always the same friend?'

'No, a few different women. She also said that Sabria was always going to the toilet. At first she assumed she was just drinking too much coffee, but after a while she noticed that the friends would go with her and they'd be in there for a long time – longer than normal, anyway.'

'Did she have any idea what they were talking about?' he asked.

'No, but she said it seemed important. They never seemed to be having fun. And aside from buying coffee, Sabria never did any shopping.'

'So it was obvious that something strange was going on,' he said. 'When did the barista notice all of this?'

'She said it took her a while. Sabria usually covered her face, and the barista only recognised her by her shape. She caught glimpses of her face once or twice. Sabria kept her burqa down, and since she seemed like the super-modest type who didn't want people looking at her, the barista didn't stare.'

'And she's sure that it's her?'

'I showed her the picture of Sabria's face, and she felt quite convinced that it was the same person.'

'OK,' Ibrahim said, thinking. 'So she *was* going to the mall.'

'Apparently, yes.'

'And meeting with women.'

'Some of them were Filipina. The barista said they looked poorer than the average shopper, and that Sabria always paid for their coffees.'

'Housemaids.'

'Did you know any of her friends?'

'No,' he said. 'Except for the neighbours. She didn't—' *tell me any of this.*

So Sabria had lied about what she was doing at the mall, but she'd been at the mall anyway, meeting with friends she never talked about. It didn't have to be as nefarious as it seemed. Maybe she was helping them.

'There's something else,' Katya said, 'but it's not about Sabria. It's about the Angel case.'

'Go ahead.'

She launched into an explanation about the significance of the severed hands and the shot to the back of the victims' heads, and the idea of an Angel of Vengeance. *Nineteen.* This was the inevitability that he'd dreaded from the day they found the bodies. Abu-Musa's smug smile came back to him as truth.

'That's a very astute connection,' he said. 'I'll make sure we follow up on it.'

'I take it you'll be looking into amputation records,' she said, 'of people who were punished for theft?'

'Well, yes, I think that's the place to start.'

'I know it's not my place to say this,' Katya said, 'but it might be useful to look at the execution records for Jeddah over the past thirty years as well.'

'You think the killer might be an executioner?'

'No. Dr Becker gave me this idea, actually, but it's possible that the killer lost a relative or someone he was close to, and that this person was executed.'

'You're assuming that the execution records would give information about family members left behind,' he said. 'I don't think they do.'

She sighed. 'Then we'll have to find the families ourselves. I just think that we need as much information as we can get in order to build a profile of this killer.'

'Yes, you're right. But that's going to take an awful lot of work.'

'I'd be glad to go over the case files myself. The lab doesn't need me standing by the machines all the time.'

'I'll see what I can do. And I'm glad you think it's your place to say all of this, Miss Hijazi,' he said. 'You're doing excellent work.'

She was quiet on the other end. He couldn't quite work her out. She was bold enough to call him late on a Wednesday night and tell him how to run his investigation, but proper enough to sit in the back seat with her face covered like a cowering Saffanah. Perhaps, just like Saffanah, she was no Saffanah.

'I'll arrange for those records to be pulled,' he said. 'Is there someone else in the lab who can help you look through them?'

'Yes, I'm sure I can find someone.'

'Good.'

He thanked Katya and hung up but was suddenly drained. Every time he forced himself to focus on the killer, he felt the same sense of dread. The whole case was expanding outward like a cell infected by a virus. Any moment now it was going to explode and send its replicated contents into the whole organism.

As he drove the final mile to the house, he stopped staring at the female pedestrians and wondered about all the places Sabria had gone without him.

18

The desert gravesite was all but abandoned. Two officers sat guard at the turning where the county road made a sharp right onto the stretch where they'd found the bodies. The road was even more overrun with sand than it had been. Crime scene tape marked the perimeter of the graves and two guards patrolled a newly worn path around the edges.

Katya showed her ID badge to the officers and they let her pass. Nayir was driving. She was in the front seat, feeling the heat of the sun on her cheeks despite the Land Rover's air conditioning. Behind them, the Murrah trackers, Talib al-Shafi and his two nephews, were crammed into the front of a Toyota flatbed truck that appeared to be older than her.

She had been too flustered to ask Ibrahim for permission to do this. During their phone conversation, she'd felt she'd already been bold enough to suggest opening the execution files. Then she'd run out of steam – or sensed he had run out. She considered this trip of lesser consequence, somehow, and had arranged it with Majdi's help instead. He'd given her the Murrah tracker's phone number, and, graciously, Nayir had called on her behalf.

It was Thursday, the first day of the weekend. Nayir had been excited to have a justification for making a desert trip with her, but she had killed it on the way out by telling him about the Angel murders. He'd listened fully, his only reaction a quiet horror. It still patterned his face as they drove up to the site.

They weren't interested in the gravesites but in the area around them. Far enough around them that, for example, a killer could arrive there without being noticed by the police guards. Because he had been back here. He knew the bodies had been removed.

They drove up to the crime scene tape, which glistened like a pale ribbon in the over-bright sun, and got out of their vehicles to have a look around. After some careful study, the men decided that it would be best to head west, where the terrain was somewhat hillier and where it would be easier for a killer to see the site without himself being seen.

They drove back to the county road and drove west at a pace that felt slower than the collapse of a civilisation. The Murrah's truck was in front, the two nephews now kneeling in the truck bed, one on each side, gazing down at the marks on the roadway. They even did tyre tracks, those bloodhounds. Nayir and Katya watched in suspense.

Finally, they stopped and one of the men jumped over the bumper and prowled the hard shoulder. They'd found something. He motioned to Nayir to back up and take a right into the desert.

Nayir drove the Land Rover onto the sand and rolled down his window.

'There are tracks here,' the Murrah nephew said, pointing to where the Toyota had stopped. 'Someone swept them over but they're still here.'

'They swept them over?' Nayir asked. 'With what?'

'A piece of cardboard. We'll leave the truck here and lead you on foot so we can keep an eye on the trail.' He glanced very briefly at Katya, a gesture that said: *We wouldn't want to disturb the privacy of your woman, either.* Nayir nodded gratefully. Katya felt herself slipping into that nod, into the version of the world where she would expect to be left alone in a car. Then she reminded herself that this whole trip was her idea – thanks in part to an American woman who didn't even own a veil – and that in a few short minutes she'd be out in the sand sweating nails like the men.

They followed the Murrah about three-quarters of a mile south. The Land Rover's tyres made popping noises against the gravel littered here and there. Finally, the Murrah raised his hand and Nayir stopped the car.

Katya got out and slipped her burqa over her nose and mouth, tucking it into her head scarf. She did this partially to put the Murrah at ease but mostly because the sun hit her face with an intensity that suggested it might liquefy her soft tissue. She slid on a pair of sunglasses and followed Nayir, literally stepped into his footprints. One of the Murrah noticed and said to Nayir: 'She doesn't have to do that. We know what her prints look like already.'

'It's good to be careful,' Nayir replied.

They stood there, waiting for the grandfather, Talib, who was taking his time reading the tyre tracks that led up from the road. When he finally reached the group, he said: 'He drove a GMC and his right front tyre is low. What else have we got?'

It didn't take long to see the footprints.

Talib didn't speak for a long time; he simply studied the ground, moving around and nodding as if listening to the wind tell a story.

He motioned Nayir closer, pointed to a smudged area on the ground and began to explain. 'The car stopped here. He got out and went over there, came back to the truck. He was probably upset, the prints are angry coming back.'

That might have been when he discovered that the bodies were missing, Katya thought.

Everyone followed the prints to the edge of a gently curved dune. From there it was easy to see the gravesites. 'He stops here,' Talib said. 'This is the lookout.'

Katya took a dozen photos. 'Do you have any idea when he might have come out here?' she asked.

'I'd say these prints are about five or six days old,' he said.

'The police were still here,' Katya said, 'and forensics, too. The place would have been full of people.'

'If he came in the mid-morning,' Nayir said, 'they might not have noticed him here. The sun would have been behind him.'

Talib nodded.

'But how did he get past the police cars on the road?'

'From the south.' Talib pointed. 'There's another road leading around the site, and his tyre tracks turned in from the opposite direction to ours.'

'He may have had a habit of coming here,' Katya said. 'Maybe he always checked the site from afar before driving closer.' She thought back five to six days. That was when they'd found Amina's hand on

Falasteen Street. It was possible that the killer had come here to check on his site. His discovery that the bodies had been found could have triggered a rage that prompted him to cut off Amina's hand before he had originally planned to do it. Yet if Amina was indeed one of his victims, there was still the question of why she didn't resemble his previous type.

Katya continued taking photos. The other men moved away, except for Talib. He stood looking out at the graves, studiously avoiding her gaze.

'You don't need to do that,' he said. 'I'll remember the prints.' As he turned away, he said over his shoulder: 'And don't worry, it will hold up in court.'

Her friends had long ago stopped asking her when she was going to get married. She was twenty-nine now, far too old to catch a good husband. It became impolite to ask. Her few good friends had tried for years to find a husband for her. She was always on the top of their guest lists for weddings, since that was where most matchmaking occurred. But after her failed engagement to Othman, even her good friends had stopped talking about marriage, perhaps thinking that she needed some time to recover, or perhaps believing that she never would. As this silence ensorcelled her, she had grown cynical about her own prospects without even realising it.

Nayir's proposal should have broken the spell. Instead, it had cast a new spell of its own.

The drive back was tense. She compared Nayir to her cousin. Ayman had grown up in Lebanon and spent an unnatural amount of time watching satellite television, so had a great deal of knowledge about the world. He'd known exactly what a serial killer was and had even conjured instant trivia from his memory. Did she know that John Gacy had raped thirty-two men and buried them in his basement? And that Jeffrey Dahmer had been trying to turn his victims into zombies? (And that scientists had saved Dahmer's brain for their own studies?) She had found Ayman's easy recollection of facts disturbing, but not more so than Nayir's gravitas.

'We've never had one before,' he said. 'This type of *shaytan*. He exists in other countries, but not here.'

'Maybe not,' she said. 'Or maybe we've just never noticed. It took them years to find out about this one.'

It seemed to make him angry. 'How do so many people go missing and nobody notices?'

'They were foreign workers,' Katya said. 'Probably they'd run away, and nobody knew where they were to begin with.'

'And now the killer knows that the police have found the bodies,' he said. 'What do you think he'll do next?'

'I think he already has his next victim.' She was tired. The heat had sapped her and the discoveries of the day had only made the whole situation more disturbing. She wanted him to tell her how strong she was, how brave.

'There is a chance he could find out about you,' he said. 'About who is working on this case.'

'There's always a chance of that.'

She could feel him trying to be careful in his reply, but in the end nothing came out and they spent the rest of the ride home in uneasy silence.

19

Thursday morning, the first day of the weekend, Ibrahim went in to work anyway. He couldn't face another day sitting at home, worrying helplessly about Sabria.

He was surprised to find Majdi and Daher in the forensics lab. Daher was wearing jeans and a T-shirt, not his usual black suit. He was sitting at the desk beside Majdi, texting someone.

Ibrahim's phone vibrated and he took it out of his trousers. Daher had been texting him. The message read: *Majdi found something.*

'That was fast!' Daher said when he saw Ibrahim. He got up, looking vaguely embarrassed to be seen in his street clothes. It reminded Ibrahim how young he was.

'What did you find?' he asked.

Majdi stood up and motioned to the computer screen. 'We've identified the other victim whose hands were found at the gravesite,' he said. 'Her name was May Lozano. She was twenty-five years old. She went missing over a year ago.'

'Excellent,' Ibrahim said. 'Why did this take longer than the ID on Cortez?'

'I had to do it the old-fashioned way, compare her prints manually to a bunch of files we received from the consulate for missing housemaids.'

'That had to have been a lot of work,' Daher said.

'I was able to narrow it down based on Adara's report that May Lozano died about a year ago. She was the second to last victim, and the only one for whom we found both hands.'

'Very good,' Ibrahim said. 'Was she here as a housemaid?'

'Yes. She lived with a family in Jeddah. It's in the report.'

Ibrahim went to talk to Lozano's employers. Like Cortez, Lozano had been recruited in Manila, but she had worked in Jeddah as a housemaid for five years. When she went missing, her employers filed a missing persons report, and the police followed up. According to the report, friends of hers said that although Lozano missed her family in the Philippines, she'd been happy in Jeddah. The family who employed her had paid off the headhunter fee and she received a decent wage. They treated her well.

According to the family, she hadn't run away from them; she loved them almost like her own family. They had been distraught when she disappeared. It had happened on her birthday – they were planning to take her to Jollibee, her favourite restaurant – and they suspected foul play, although they had no idea who would have kidnapped her. She had no enemies, not even in the Philippines. They reported her disappearance to the police and the embassy, but no one could find her.

Ibrahim did find out that Lozano had been noticed missing almost immediately. She had left the house at 5:15 p.m. to head to Jollibee to meet a friend. It was a six-block walk from her employer's house to the restaurant on al-Khalidiya. She was supposed to have met her friend Mary at 5:30. They were going to talk for a while before the family came to join them at about six o'clock. But when the family reached the restaurant, they found that Lozano wasn't there. Her friend was sitting at a table, waiting.

Ibrahim and Daher walked the six blocks themselves.

'I guess she didn't take a taxi,' Daher said.

The restaurant was brightly coloured, a variation of McDonald's with a large plastic bee and bowl of honey out front.

None of the workers in the building had been there longer than a few months, but the manager, Arnel, remembered May's disappearance. He was a clean-cut, thirty-something Asian man in a pale blue shirt and black trousers. A red lanyard around his neck carried an ID tag. If he'd taken off the blue baseball cap that seemed to be part of the uniform, he could have been mistaken for a medical intern or some other young professional.

'Yeah,' he said, looking upset at the memory. 'The family came in looking for her. Her friend was here, waiting. We knew May. She came here with her family a lot. That was horrible. She wasn't the type to run away.'

'You thought she ran away?' Ibrahim asked.

'That's what they always say. These women, sometimes they get abused.'

'Did she look abused?'

He shook his head.

'Tell me, did you notice anything unusual that night? Anything outside, or in the street? Any odd people?'

'Yeah, one thing. I told the police about it back then, but they didn't seem to think it was important. There was a woman across the street who collapsed. She got carried away in a Red Crescent van. The police said they'd check it out but I never heard back about it.'

'Could that woman have been May?'

Arnel shrugged. 'It's hard to see out of the front windows sometimes, and it was down the road. One of my workers was outside and he saw it. I didn't get a good look at the woman. I went outside and saw the man putting her into the back of the van. The van drove away pretty quickly after that.'

They thanked him and walked out to the street.

'It's going to take some time to hunt down this friend of hers,' Daher said, flipping open his notepad. 'They said she left the country.'

Ibrahim stared down the street, trying to imagine an ambulance there. It would have double parked, stopping traffic in one direction.

'What are you thinking?' Daher asked.

'Our killer could have used a taxi to kidnap his women, but he could also have used an ambulance.'

Daher blew out his cheeks. 'Yeah, I guess. But then he's only getting women who've been injured?'

'Maybe he injures them himself,' Ibrahim said. 'It wouldn't be impossible. He comes up behind them, kind of like a mugger. Sticks a gun in their backs, tells them if they make a noise, he'll shoot. He injects them with something that knocks them out. They collapse into his arms, and he carries them to his van. By the time anybody notices – which is probably when the woman collapses – they don't

113

think there's anything wrong with a paramedic carrying a woman to his ambulance. Maybe they're worried about her, but they're going to be looking at her, not the killer.'

Daher nodded. 'Yeah, that makes sense.'

'But you're not convinced.'

'Well ...'

'Go on.'

'I just think it would be so much easier if he was posing as a taxi driver. He wouldn't have to risk one of the women screaming for help, or somebody noticing him.'

Ibrahim nodded. 'Maybe you're right, but I think we'd better keep the paramedic angle in mind.'

20

Friday morning, the building was empty. Everyone would be back to work on Saturday, filling the polished hallways with voices, laughter, the smack of Daher's hand meeting a younger man's head. Now the only noise to break the silence was the *clunk* of the central air conditioning kicking into gear, and in a few hours, the call to prayer. It always clanged through the local mosque's loudspeakers with a jolt.

Ibrahim slid into the building, clutching a cup of coffee and feeling dead. He had spent the rest of Thursday arranging for copies of the execution files as well as the amputation-for-theft files showing the cutting off of hands and feet. Daher had offered to deliver them this morning, even though it was the day of rest, even though his job didn't pay him nearly enough to encourage such loyalty. Ibrahim wondered idly if Daher's home life was as miserable as his.

Farrah was still at the house, waiting for her husband to return. She was a welcome presence in that she and the twins kept Jamila busy, and that kept Jamila's nagging at a minimum. The problem now was that they were in a concocting mood. Bored, with no more medical drama, they were poised to become the agents of someone's undoing. Ever since Farrah had visited the exorcist, the household had an underlying hint of lunacy to it.

At his office, he discovered that Daher had already delivered half of the files, probably the night before. He had arranged the boxes in a neat row on the table. Ibrahim set his coffee on the desk, pulled up a chair and cracked open the first file.

He wasn't sure what he was looking for, but he went through the files anyway, trying to avoid reading too much detail. A man was found guilty of killing his wife and children. A woman was found guilty of killing her mother. Another man – murder of a stranger in a convenience store. He went through most of the files for 2003 and found nothing but murder. That was a little surprising.

He moved up to 2007. There was a bit more diversity. Most of the executions were for murder, but those that weren't usually involved multiple crimes. A man from Chad had been sentenced for child abduction, rape, theft and drug use. He was only twenty-one. There were more executions for drug dealing, and even one for homosexuality.

He heard the slam of a door down the hall, footsteps squeaking on the linoleum. Daher came in carrying two more boxes. Sweat was dripping down his cheek.

'*Salaam aleikum*,' he grunted, setting the boxes on the floor by the table. 'This is the last of them.'

'Good. Thanks for bringing them in.'

Daher stood by the door, debating with himself. Then he pulled up a chair.

'You don't have to stay,' Ibrahim said.

'Of course I'll stay!' Daher said. 'We should all be working overtime. This is an important case.' He sat down somewhat awkwardly beside his boss and pulled out a file. 'What are we looking for?'

Ibrahim explained what Katya had told him on the phone, being careful to credit the psychologist as well, lest Daher's envy find its focus solely on Katya. Surprisingly, Daher was all business. He even interrupted and said, 'And of course this is why he buried nineteen bodies. He fancies himself an agent of Allah.'

'It would appear so.'

'So what exactly are we looking for?' Daher asked again.

'It would be great if we could find someone who was punished for theft and who also had a relative die on the executioner's block, but seeing as that might be impossible ... ' Ibrahim shrugged. 'Just tell me if anything stands out.'

Daher seemed to sense the futility of the work, but he plunged in anyway. They read in silence for a while.

'What do you think about the "nineteen" thing?' Daher asked. 'Do you think there's a hidden pattern anywhere in the Quran?'

He was referring to the spectacle of Islamic scholars letting themselves get carried away with conspiracy theories about numbers and the Quran. It was known, for example, that the word 'prayer' appeared in the Quran five times (echoing the fact that Islam has five compulsory prayer times each day), and that the word 'month' appeared exactly twelve times, and the word 'day' exactly 365 times. But that did not mean that everything was part of a mysterious pattern.

Theories about the importance of the number nineteen seemed to dominate the conspiracy thinking. Nineteen was the number of verses that the archangel Gabriel gave to the Prophet Mohammed in his first two visits to the cave. Nineteen was also the number of letters in the first verse of the first chapter of the Quran, a verse that was repeated fifty-four times throughout the holy book. To compound matters, the only chapter where the word 'nineteen' appeared was entitled 'The Hidden Secret'.

'I think there's no special significance to the number nineteen,' Ibrahim replied, 'except maybe to our killer.'

They read. Daher became serious and quiet in a way Ibrahim had never seen before. For a moment, Ibrahim could imagine him becoming Chief someday.

'Maybe Dr Becker's idea is right,' Daher said. 'Who has experience of cutting off hands? An executioner, right? Has anyone thought that maybe he's our guy?'

'As far as I know, you've just originated the theory.'

'Whatever this guy is, he's getting a thrill from doing this. At least that's the word from Charlie Angel.'

'I find it disturbing that Dr Becker has unwittingly taken on the nickname "Angel" just like our psychopathic killer.'

'Well,' Daher replied, 'he's not an angel, he's an angel *killer*.'

'Ah.'

'And they're both American,' Daher added.

'You're going to have to toss that idea out of your head. I've read through five years of executions already, and do you know what I see? A whole bunch of Saudi killers. If killing is a virus, then we're overdue for a mutation.'

Daher gave this idea the polite room it deserved, then said: 'Honestly, I think it's fitting that we've got two angels in this case. One is good, one is bad.'

'Very well,' Ibrahim said. 'And you're right, the executioner would have the tools for the job, including possibly enjoying it.'

'But you've seen the executions,' Daher said. 'You see how the minute he cuts off a head, the police pull the executioner away. They're standing there waiting to pull him away because they're afraid he'll get the bloodlust and start hurting other people. Right there in the square! In front of hundreds of people! But bloodlust is real. They always have to pull him away.'

Ibrahim had seen executions as an officer, right up close. 'That's true, but it's also the tradition. Does he ever look like he needs to be pulled away?'

'Sometimes, yes!'

Ibrahim tried to square the image that was forming in his mind of their serial killer with his impression of the one executioner he'd met. On many counts, Daher was right, but Ibrahim's gut was already organising a protest.

'I talked to an executioner once,' Ibrahim said. 'You know what he said about his job? He was *raising awareness.*'

Daher let out a laugh.

'That's just how he described it,' Ibrahim went on. 'Raising awareness of the horror of murder, and trying to encourage people not to make mistakes in five minutes of rage that will ruin their whole lives.'

Daher was grinning. 'That's funny. I guess he thinks that most killers have no self-control. Is that true?'

Ibrahim shrugged. 'Most people who kill lose their self-control, if only for a moment.'

'But not the Angel killer,' Daher said. 'He's *planning* this stuff.'

They heard footsteps in the hall and Daher sprang from his chair. In the split second before his body launched towards the doorway, his right arm swung to his hip. He was reaching for a gun he didn't carry on Fridays to an empty office building. Ibrahim was startled by this.

Daher spun round with a look of disgust. 'Miss Hijazi is here,' he said.

Katya stopped at the office door. She was holding two files.

'*Ahlan,*' Ibrahim said, standing. 'This is a nice surprise, Miss Hijazi. Please come in.'

'*Ahlan biik*,' she replied. 'I was just here picking up some files.'

'Why are you working?' Daher asked with barely concealed disapproval. 'It's Friday!'

'It's not Friday for you, too?' she asked, walking past him into the office. To Ibrahim she said: 'I took a trip to the desert yesterday. I went out to the site.'

'You went by yourself?' Daher asked.

'No, I went with the Murrah. Talib al-Shafi and his nephews accompanied me and my husband.'

'Did you have permission to do this?' Daher asked, looking at Ibrahim. 'I didn't hear anything about it.'

'We didn't spend much time at the site.' She was still speaking directly to Ibrahim. 'We went west and were able to find the place that we believe the killer went back to. I guessed he had to have gone back, otherwise how did he know that we'd found the bodies? And we're assuming that he knows that, because of Amina's hand.'

'Good thinking,' Ibrahim said, feeling flustered. 'So you think you found the spot where he went?'

'Yes. Talib said that a man arrived in a GMC truck and walked to a lookout where he could see the gravesites. He also said the footprints indicated that he was upset.'

'But you're not at all sure that this is the *actual* killer,' Daher said.

'Talib was certain that the footprints at the lookout site matched the footprints from the gravesite.'

'I thought the footprints from the gravesite weren't especially clear,' Daher said.

'They had enough to go on.'

'So let me get this straight, some blind old Bedouin tracker is going to tell us this is our murderer? Those footprints could belong to anyone!'

Ibrahim saw Katya's face stiffen. 'It's a very remote site,' she said. 'There were no other footprints out there.'

'That doesn't mean that there was *nobody* else out there.'

'The point is that Talib believes the footprints match,' Katya said. 'So if it was our killer at the gravesite, then he went to the lookout site six or seven days ago.'

'Next time,' Daher said, 'something like that has to be *cleared* with the detective in charge of the case – that's Zahrani – and it needs to be cleared with Chief Riyadh. You could have messed up the crime scene!'

'I work in forensics.'

'Yes, but you do forensics in the lab, not out in the field. How often have you gone to an actual crime scene? Once? Twice? There are *rules*, and just because you've been to a crime scene doesn't mean you know how to handle it. Technically, you being there alone means that we can't use that evidence in court!'

'*I wasn't alone.*'

'Fine, the Murrah was there, and that *may* be admissible in court, but it could have ruined everything.'

Ibrahim was, once again, immobilised by these two. If he defended Katya, he risked alienating his best officer, if he didn't defend her, he risked losing the one person who was in his closest confidence about Sabria – and the person who was approaching the Angel case most creatively.

'And how was *your* Thursday?' Katya asked Daher.

He jerked back, looking offended. '*We* identified one of the other victims.'

Katya turned for the door.

'Do you have a driver?' Ibrahim asked.

'Yes.'

'Good. I'll walk you to the garage.'

'That's not necessary,' Katya said.

'None of us should be here alone, especially when it's empty like this. If the killer knows about the gravesite, he knows about us.'

Katya nodded reluctantly.

Once they were out of earshot, Katya said, 'Actually, I hoped to find you here. I have the results from the blood sample we found on the carpet outside Sabria's apartment door.'

'Go ahead.'

She hesitated. 'The DNA isn't yours, but it is from someone related to you.'

'What?' He stopped walking.

'Yes,' she said. 'And it's male.'

A rush of terror and fury and sharp disbelief. 'Are you sure about this?'

'Yes, I double-checked it. That's what took me so long.'

'OK.' He noticed his breath was short. 'OK, I'll take care of this.'

'You know who it is then?'

'I think so,' he said.

'Do you want to get some DNA from this person?' she asked, pulling a swab out of her pocket.

He shook his head. 'No. I'll just ask.'

'All right.' She seemed uncertain. 'I thought you said no one in your family knew about her.'

'Obviously I was wrong.'

Jamila met him at the door with a look of wild excitement. Apparently, they'd already concocted their drama. It came out, as he moved past her into the living room, that she'd pulled off a phenomenal stunt, one not likely to be replicated for another ten years: she had managed to arrange a husband for Hanan, the older of the twins.

'She's only ten,' Ibrahim said. He glanced in the bedroom, saw it was empty. He was looking for his oldest son, Aqmar. Aqmar's wife Constance had answered the door downstairs and said he was up here.

'It doesn't matter if she's ten!' Jamila cried. Farrah stood to the side, looking awkward. 'She won't marry until she's sixteen anyway. But I've arranged it! It only needs your approval.'

'Who is this man?' He pushed past her and went into the women's sitting room. It was empty too. 'Where is Aqmar?'

'The man is named Taha al-Brehm, he's the son of my cousin Abdullatif in Riyadh.'

'Have you ever met him?'

'He owns a textile factory and three mobile phone shops, and his father has more money than anyone in the whole family.' Jamila clapped her hands.

'Have you told Hanan about this?'

'Not yet.'

'Where is Aqmar?' he asked again.

'I don't know. What do you think? He'll make an excellent match for her. He's very traditional. He likes to ride horses and train falcons, think of that!'

He turned to Farrah. 'Have you seen your brother?'

'He's on the roof,' she said, glancing guiltily at her mother.

'He's not on the roof,' Jamila said with irritation, blocking Ibrahim's passage to the front door. 'Now what do you *think*?'

'I think you must be crazy to believe I'll approve letting anyone marry Hanan without her permission, I don't care if he has more money than the King.' He pushed past her and made for the door before the barrage could start. But indeed the noise followed him up the stairs.

He couldn't believe she would even try it. He had only agreed to Zaki's wedding because *Zaki* had agreed – and you would think after that fiasco, she might have shown a little restraint.

Aqmar was sitting on a carpet on the roof, looking like a grim *mujahideen*. He was wearing khaki trousers and an old army green T-shirt that he hadn't worn in years. Ibrahim often thought that if he hadn't put his foot down and refused to let his son run off to Iraq to fight *jihad* against the West, Aqmar would be dead now. The phase of wanting to be a hero had passed as quickly as it had come, but in a father's heart, such things never die. The coals on the hookah pipe beside him were nearly expired, and the fragrance of *shisha* still hung between the walls.

Ibrahim and Sabria had been coming back from the private beach one evening a few months before when she had needed to call in at the grocery shop. They had stopped. Getting out of the car, he had spotted Aqmar and Constance strolling along the pavement, window shopping. Ibrahim had hastily ducked into the car and prevented Sabria from getting out. He had driven off at once. He couldn't be sure, but he felt that his son had seen him. They never spoke about it. Aqmar's behaviour towards him hadn't changed, so Ibrahim told himself he was imagining the worst.

Now, on the roof, Aqmar saw his father and raised his hand, which was clutching a mobile phone.

'Zaki just called to say he's camping with some friends in the desert this weekend. He wants me to make sure Saffanah has everything she needs. Can you believe this guy?'

Ibrahim sat beside him, leaned his back against the wall and tried to relax. 'Any *shisha* left?'

'No.' Aqmar looked guilty and made to get up. 'I'll make some more.'

'Don't worry, just sit.'

Aqmar leaned back and threw his phone on the carpet. 'I don't understand why he married her. He knew it was a bad idea. And now he wants to throw the whole problem on us.' By 'us' he meant the two of them.

'Did he tell you about the divorce court?'

'Are you kidding? He wouldn't shut up about it.'

Ibrahim pressed his back into the wall and tried to breathe. He wanted to take some time, weave his way like a boxer who doesn't mean to strike a blow, who doesn't want to be struck, but who's stuck in the ring nonetheless. But any minute Jamila would come trudging up the stairs, or perhaps one of the grandkids.

'Let's go to the mosque,' he said finally. Aqmar looked resistant, so he added, 'It's Friday.'

The night air was a cool pleasure once they were moving through it. They didn't talk much, but decided to walk all the way to the big mosque on Makkah Street, not to the smaller one they usually went to. The big mosque was a modern structure, square and blunt, its only flourish the minaret, which was ornate with tile work. The inside was so crowded that they had to squeeze into the back with barely enough room to tip their heads in prostration. After prayers, they left before getting sucked into conversations. They stopped for ice cream at a *boofiya*. It was a tiny one-room establishment with a pair of white plastic chairs by the door. Two men were sitting there, one sipping tea and reading the paper, the other eating what looked like a *Sambooli* sandwich. It wasn't until they were heading home that Ibrahim dared to start the conversation.

'An associate of mine from Undercover went missing last week.'

Aqmar looked confused, obviously wondering what this had to do with him.

'Her name was Sabria Gampon.'

His son's face, unaccustomed to deceit, revealed shock and shame and anxiety in that order, which Ibrahim took to mean that Aqmar knew just who she was, that he was embarrassed about it.

'What happened?' Aqmar asked.

'We're not sure, but they found someone's DNA on a nail in the carpet just outside her front door. Someone cut their foot there.'

Aqmar flushed painfully. 'I went to your work one day and saw you

123

leaving the building. I thought I'd catch you in traffic but I couldn't and then I saw you parking . . . '

It was a truism that police wisdom – the ability to spot liars, to see emotions in a glance, to tease out vulnerability and thus the most deeply buried secrets – disappeared when the subject was someone you loved. It panicked him to realise that he couldn't tell if his son was lying.

'So you were there?' Ibrahim asked.

Aqmar nodded. He lifted up the strap of his sandal to show where the cut had been. It was smoothing over but still red.

'. . . I guessed you were visiting a friend.' Aqmar's voice was pinched. *I thought I found you cheating. Tell me she was a friend.*

Ibrahim saw his entire life as a father opening up into a giant precipice at his feet, and he stood perfectly poised between the impulse to tell the absolute truth and the knowledge that the truth can be the most destructive force in any relationship.

'We were finishing up a final assignment,' he said. 'Did it surprise you that we have women in Undercover?'

He hated himself.

'No. You've said that before.' Aqmar still looked embarrassed. 'You said one time that most of the theft in Jeddah was committed by women.'

'Or men dressed like women.'

A dozen questions were driving nails against the inside of his skull. *Did you knock? Did she answer? Was I in the shower? Did you stand there, listening?* He tried to remember if Sabria had seemed different. If she'd known Aqmar had come, if she'd answered the door.

'Do you remember where you were Wednesday two weeks ago?'

Aqmar gave a grim half-smile. 'Am I being interrogated?' When Ibrahim didn't reply, he said, 'I work every Wednesday night until ten. You know. That's my fourteen-hour shift. You can call my boss.'

'When were you at the apartment?' Ibrahim asked.

'About three weeks ago.'

'Do you remember which day exactly?'

'Um, yeah . . . it was a Sunday. I wasn't working that day.' Aqmar slowed to cross the street. 'I probably should have knocked, but I thought you were working and I didn't want to interrupt.'

And there it was, the real punishment for his lying: his son could have been lying right back. Maybe what Aqmar wanted to say was: *I guessed you had a mistress and I was horrified and I ran away and stubbed my foot on a nail.*

Ibrahim saw him struggling with darker things: anger on behalf of his mother, disappointment at his father's lying, a conflicting desire for his father's happiness and an understanding of why he might have chosen this route to it, a feeling of shame at the whole situation.

'We have women in Homicide, too,' Ibrahim said, 'but we barely see them.'

Aqmar nodded. 'I hope your friend is OK.'

They walked the rest of the way home in silence.

Back at the house, Aqmar said goodnight and went into his apartment, where a very patient wife had been waiting for three hours. Ibrahim heard Jamila upstairs on the phone, complaining loudly to a friend about his irrational behaviour – not letting Hanan get engaged to a wealthy cousin! It was his cue to give a soft tap on Zaki's door, just across the hall from Aqmar's.

Saffanah answered with only one eye exposed. It was red and bloodshot. She stood back and let him in.

He walked into the hallway where she stood clutching her waist, looking miserable.

'How are you feeling?'

She shrugged.

'How is it with Zaki?'

She shook her head. 'He won't,' she said, clutching herself even more tightly. He could tell from the way her shoulders trembled that she was trying not to cry. It was a fight she lost almost immediately.

'Let's go out,' he said. He couldn't stand to see her cry. 'Do you need groceries?'

She nodded.

They went to a medium-sized supermarket. She made him wait at the entrance until the only other shopper – a man – had finished his purchases and left. The shop was just closing but the owner waited graciously while Saffanah patrolled the aisles with her basket, keeping a vigilant eye on the door in case another man should come in and cut her shopping short. She still didn't lift her burqa, and this time he guessed it was because her eyes were red and swollen. Maybe they had been all along.

When she came back to the counter, Ibrahim paid for the groceries and helped the owner bag them. As soon as they were back in the car, he said: 'Zaki went out of town this weekend, and I know you don't like to spend evenings with my wife, so why don't we go and sit with Aqmar and Constance and bake those brownies?'

She looked down into the shopping bag and shook her head.

Once he'd carried the groceries inside, he crept upstairs to his own apartment. Jamila was still on the telephone but fortunately the front door was shut so her complaints were only a muffled noise. He ducked into the men's sitting room, grabbed a few pillows and carried them to the roof. There he laid a little bed for himself near the hookah pipe and fell asleep gazing up at the starlight, wondering what his son was thinking of him now.

21

She was up and out earlier than usual that morning. The city was on its knees, its backside shimmering in the pinkish light of morning, its head buried in prostration. The muezzin's song rang through the streets. Every mosque's loudspeaker caught its own small section of the world. Men were praying in rows on the pavements, strangers brought together. A time to prepare for the day. Katya had never prayed on a pavement in her life, but sometimes on quiet mornings like these, she longed for it.

She had only just got out of the car in front of the station when Majdi texted her the words: *Crime scene – now*, along with an address. She got back in the car with Ayman and they drove to the location.

When they reached the address, she gasped.

'What is it?' Ayman turned to her.

'Nothing,' she said. 'I thought it was something else.'

Clearly, he didn't believe her, but she thanked him and got out of the car, trying her hardest not to look panicked. She was standing in front of Sabria's apartment building.

She took the lift and emerged onto the fourth floor. The door to Sabria's apartment was open and two men from forensics were standing there. They moved to let her in.

She found Majdi in the living room. He looked harried. 'You said you wanted to do live crime scenes.'

'What happened?' She could barely get the words out.

Majdi raised his hands. 'It's not a murder, don't worry. A woman has gone missing. Someone reported it this morning.'

'Since when do we do missing persons like this?' She was struggling to control her panic.

'We don't, but this woman used to work for Undercover and they sent a special request for forensics. Chief Riyadh called me this morning and asked if I'd be willing to do this before coming in to work. I would have texted you then but it was a little too early.'

Katya felt the heat rushing to her cheeks. 'How long have you been here?'

'Over an hour. We've still got to do the bedroom and bathroom.'

It took all of her self-control not to dash into the hallway to call Ibrahim. She had to stay here and get her hands on as much evidence as she could. Frantic thoughts were rushing through her: Can I destroy the evidence? Alter it? Can I even get hold of it? Have they already sent it back to the lab, or are they sending it to Undercover to have them process it at a different lab? How long will it take them to find out that Ibrahim has been here?

'Did she live alone?' Katya asked.

'Yes, but she was married. They haven't been able to track down her husband yet.' Majdi gave her a grim look. 'In cases like this, it's usually the husband.'

'What do you mean, "cases like this"?'

'I just mean when a woman goes missing.'

Majdi was worried about the way she was reacting. If she didn't pull it together, he'd never invite her to a crime scene again.

'I've got to get back to the lab,' he said. 'Are you OK here?'

'Yes, I'm fine.' On his way out, she called to him: 'Majdi, thanks.'

He nodded and left.

She decided it was crucial to focus on the things that could implicate Ibrahim sexually with Sabria. She went straight into the bedroom and got to work. She had just flipped back the bed sheets when a thought struck her: Ibrahim had to know immediately. He had to come here. If he were here now, finding his DNA here wouldn't matter.

She whipped out her mobile phone and called him. He didn't answer. She took a breath and tried again. The third time she left a message. 'Come to Sabria's apartment immediately. Someone just reported her missing and forensics is here already. Just trust me, you have to come.'

She hung up and prayed to God that he'd get the message before it was too late.

'I overheard the older guys saying that we've had serial killers before,' Daher said.

Ibrahim and Daher were in the hallway outside the situation room. The door was shut but from the sounds inside, the room was already full. Ibrahim reached for the door, but Daher stopped him. 'They say they were just never able to prove it,' he said. 'Why? Because nobody thinks we have these killers. The only serial killer crimes that have been reported by the news were committed by foreigners, did you notice?'

'This is really bothering you,' Ibrahim said, 'that he might be a Saudi.'

'*Have* we had a Saudi serial killer before?'

'I don't know. Ten years ago in Homicide we had a few cases where a man would kill repeatedly, but it was never like this. Never this systematic; and certainly never this well-planned.'

Daher seemed somewhat relieved. Ibrahim opened the door.

The Bedouin tracker al-Shafi had suggested they look for a cabbie two weeks ago, but they didn't have a decent profile of their killer. They had simply sent the most junior officers to collect information from the taxi companies about their drivers' criminal records. This turned out to be disappointing, since most companies didn't keep such records. Those companies that did were happy to provide the information, but, like the execution and amputation records, it was useless until they had a better profile of their killer.

The cab idea had begun to frustrate them all. It wasn't surprising that they couldn't find the killer among the fifty thousand taxi drivers in Jeddah. The problem was, once you set a hope in motion, it was hard to stop it from blowing through the investigation and leaving all kinds of discouragement in its wake.

Now he was going to tell them that their killer might have posed as a Red Crescent driver.

He got up in front of the crowd and saw frustration and anger all over the room. At the rear, Mu'tazz was sitting with his back to the wall, watching Ibrahim through a pair of lazy lizard eyes.

He told them about May Lozano and the ambulance on the night of her disappearance, leading gracefully into his theory that the killer could have used an ambulance or Red Crescent van to kidnap his victims. But even as he was talking, he could see the men mulling over the truth: they didn't really have anything to go on. The killer had just left a bloody stump on the street, an act that said, *I am killing women, and you can't do anything about it.*

'We are assuming, for the time being, that the desert killer is the same man who has kidnapped and dismembered Amina al-Fouad,' Ibrahim said. 'Now the previous victims had their hands severed *post mortem*, but Amina's hand was severed while she was still alive. The appearance of Amina's hand came very shortly after our discovery of the gravesite, so we believe the killer acted in a rage after he realised that we had found the bodies in the desert.' He briefed the men on the footprints Talib had found in the desert, feeling a twinge of guilt for not revealing that Katya had been the author and executor of the idea. Mu'tazz needed no more fuel for his war machine against Ibrahim.

'So he wants us to know that he's kidnapped Amina and that he's going to kill her. But I want to emphasise to you all that Amina al-Fouad may still be alive, and I don't think I have to tell you that the search for our killer is more urgent now than it was when we found the bodies.'

This was met by a moment of silence before Mu'tazz spoke up.

'She's probably dead,' he said. A few men turned to look at him.

'Yes, Lieutenant Colonel,' Ibrahim said, making an effort to control his voice. 'What makes you say that?'

'She lost a hand. Unless the killer has a medical degree, he's going to have a hard time stopping the bleeding.'

'Failing a doctor's careful monitoring,' Ibrahim replied, 'he could do what they did in the Middle Ages and dip the limb in tar.'

'I doubt very much that he cares to stop the bleeding,' Mu'tazz said.

The room seemed to grow even quieter.

'OK.' Ibrahim did his best to appear cool. 'And what do you suggest?'

'Since she's probably dead,' Mu'tazz said, 'it's more important to find out why he chose al-Fouad, because it might help us understand who he will choose next. The only way we're going to work that out is to understand his reasons.'

'In other words, profiling,' Ibrahim said, glancing at Dr Becker. 'If that's something you'd like to be a part of, Lieutenant Colonel, I'd be glad to assign you to work with Dr Becker.'

Got you. Mu'tazz had trouble concealing his disapproval.

Ibrahim turned his attention back to the rest of the room. 'It's never a good idea to assume that a missing person is dead. It is our job to find her. I want to focus our energy right now on getting al-Fouad back alive and the only way we're going to do that is to find our killer. Mu'tazz is right, the way to find him is to understand what he's already done. Dr Becker has provided me this morning with the most up-to-date profile of our man, and I'm going to make sure you all get a copy. I want everyone on board and knowing what we're looking for.

'I'm sending four men – you know who you are – undercover to the Sitteen Street Bridge,' he went on. 'It's very possible that's where our killer found his previous victims.' Here he stumbled, felt himself losing focus. *Don't be ridiculous*, he thought. *Sabria hasn't been taken by a killer. He didn't have enough time to plan it. It doesn't fit.* 'So the men I'm sending to Sitteen, your focus is going to be on IDing the victims. We're trying to establish a link between them, and so far we have nothing other than ethnic type. Dr Becker has said that the killer usually picks his victims from a familiar place, so they all may have some connection to the bridge. Also, you men who are looking through records, I want you to focus in particular on anyone who has a connection to the Kandara area. Inspector Osama Ibrahim has agreed to work exclusively on the al-Fouad case.'

He divvied up the rest of the assignments quickly. When he was done, Osama came forward to collect his men and take them to a different office for briefing. The men who had been chosen for the Sitteen operation came to the front of the room. Ibrahim was relieved that the crowd was dispersing. It left Mu'tazz on the outside. He didn't belong to a team. He was stuck doing desk work. And yet he remained at the back of the room, watchful.

22

The Operations Room of the Jeddah police was more like a day spa than a dispatch room. Large potted palms, plush carpets, the kind of neutral décor and quiet efficiency of a five-star hotel. The whole thing was a giant raised fist to the idea of a dispatch room. There was no crackling static or shouting, only calm workers speaking in concierge tones. They were determined to uphold the seven-minute rule: that it would take no longer than that for police to respond to any call. They even assisted people who requested wake-up calls, since the emergency number '9-9-9' was unfortunately similar to that of the main desk for most hotels, '9-9'.

Major Hamid always seemed more like a tour guide than the head of Operations. He led Ibrahim to a bank of computers at the side of the room and excused himself. When he returned – Ibrahim clocked it at six and a half minutes – he brought the recording of the man who had reported Sabria missing. Ibrahim took a seat at the counter and listened through a pair of headphones to the conversation.

'Yes,' the man's voice said, 'I'd like to report my neighbour missing.'

'Very good, sir, I'm going to transfer you to Missing Persons.'

'No, I don't have time for that. I just want to give her name and address.' He spooled off the information as if he were reading it from a card, leaving the dispatcher no time to protest. 'She hasn't come in or out of her apartment for seventeen days.'

'All right, sir,' the dispatcher said. 'Thank you—'

The man hung up before the dispatcher could finish.

Ibrahim listened again and again. He didn't recognise the voice. At first it had sounded hurried and annoyed, but the more he listened, the more expressionless it seemed. He couldn't hear the impatience, he was simply assuming it. *I don't have time for that.* But the voice itself was even and calm.

Who was this man? *I don't have time.* He only said that because he didn't want to talk to Missing Persons. He didn't want to answer anyone's questions. (Who are you? Why are you keeping an eye on a woman's apartment? Does she live alone? Where is her *mehram*?) Anonymous callers were common enough, but Ibrahim feared he was listening to the voice of a kidnapper.

Katya had already left Sabria's apartment by the time he got there, and then it was too late. He'd called her immediately. She said she wasn't sure if she'd got everything. They might have sent some evidence to Undercover already. Homicide had told them that they were back-logged with the evidence from the Angel case.

He had spent the next hour beating back panic, his mind in a death-defying acrobatic swing. Would they find out that he'd been her lover? Or would they simply assume the DNA was her 'husband's'? When would the call come from Omar? (He had to have put it together already – why else would Ibrahim have asked for those files?) Or would Omar tell himself that it was work-related, and never speak of the matter again?

Strangely, nothing had happened. The building had hollowed out for lunch. The Angel case had consumed the rest of them. The few men who weren't in the field were reviewing files. Ibrahim had gone to forensics and talked to an over-stressed Majdi about the Angel case. When he'd tried to discover if they were working on any other evidence, such as whatever they'd collected from Sabria's apartment, Majdi had simply waved it off. They were too busy to think of anything else but the Angel case.

He replayed the tape. *She hasn't come in or out of her apartment for seventeen days.* It was far too precise. The kidnapper knew exactly how long ago he'd nabbed her. But why on earth did he want the police to find out?

'Here's the trace.' Major Hamid handed him a slip of paper. 'It was a disposable phone. Looks like the call came from the vicinity of the Red Sea Mall.'

'That's the really big one?' Ibrahim asked.

'Yes, eighteen entrances and four thousand parking spaces. You need a tram to get around there. But we've got him pinned here near the entrance to Danube when he made the call.'

'That's probably the busiest entrance,' Ibrahim said.

'Yes. Sorry.'

'Can we work out where he bought the mobile phone?'

'Yes, but it'll take about a week.' In a world of seven minutes, a week was almost not worth thinking about.

'Let me know what you find,' Ibrahim said. He thanked the Major and left.

The house was empty. Everyone had gone to a neighbour's wedding and he was supposed to be there himself, but the groom, the son of a man who had never had a kind word for Ibrahim, Omar or any Zahrani in a twenty-mile radius, was just as much a donkey as his father, and Ibrahim decided he would feel no guilt for staying at home.

He stood in the kitchen, brewing tea and waiting for his hookah coals to heat. The kitchen was a boxy room that always felt too dark and large. Women never congregated joyfully here. They took their chopping and peeling to the living room just outside the door. A half-dead potted mint sat on the window, leaves curling in the heat.

He wandered into the living room. Through the bathroom door he caught sight of his granddaughter's Barbie dolls having a Jacuzzi session in the bidet. The bedroom was overflowing with dirty laundry.

He went into the sewing room, a forbidden space. Jamila had claimed it like he'd claimed the men's sitting room. Here was her sewing machine – a black monster with a treadle – and her over-flowing wardrobe. It contained a mind-boggling array of outfits, each ill-fitted to her present bulk. She attended to the clothes regularly, they were cherished symbols of the women she would never be but had wanted to become: artist, businesswoman, traveller. She would sit at the sewing machine for hours, adjusting seams to perfection, but in the end, she always put on the gorilla dress.

The building was choking him. It was dark and steamy, and the desert crept in, blowing sand beneath the doors and filtering sunlight through cracks in the walls. He had thought for years that they should get a nicer place, but Omar was next door, his cousin Essam lived at the end of the street, and it just didn't seem worth it to move everyone away for the sake of a nicer living room, a better view.

He took the tea and coals to the roof, but there was still no escaping Jamila. Over the past twenty-four years, she had lodged in every crack in the concrete walls. They had married at eighteen by parental arrangement, just like Zaki. Through the latter part of secondary school he'd been in love with someone else. Maidan. She was a Filipina girl whom he'd met on the street as they were walking home from school one day. He could never remember exactly how it had happened, but after a while he was borrowing Omar's car to pick her up from school. How he had managed to pose as her brother made no sense to him now. They couldn't have been more different. He had his family's classic Bedouin features – the long nose, swarthy skin, and deep brown, almond-shaped eyes, passed down from his mother's side. Maidan was short, pale and round, all soft curves. They had spent their afternoons at the beach, at funfairs, and simply driving through the desert. He had wanted to kiss her but never had the nerve to make the first move. She had asked him to once, and he had done it, but it scared them and they never did it again. They had plans to marry.

For six months they saw each other most days but the weekends, when his family demanded that he stay at home. And then one day he'd gone to pick her up from school and the headmistress had come out to speak to him. She'd stood by the metal gate at the school's entrance and called over to his car. 'Maidan has left Saudi Arabia. As her brother, I expect that you might know that already.' She'd given him a final glare, turned around and gone back into the girls' academy. The gates had shut and he had never seen Maidan again.

He had never met her family. He didn't even know which apartment she lived in, just the building. He went there, desperate, and a downstairs neighbour confirmed that the Filipino family had moved out.

He spent months reliving their relationship. Every word, every gesture, every offhand remark took on new meaning as he prised back the delicate skin of appearance in search of the core. Why hadn't she told him she was moving? Had she planned to leave him from the start? She had lied, he saw now, but how much? And when?

And at the bottom of it all: had she ever really loved him?

In the end, he'd come to see that she was a coward, and that what he wanted in a woman was a strength like the best women always had, the ability to tell you just where to shove it. That's what he'd told his mother, when she brought up the subject of arranging his marriage.

'I want a woman who can stand up to me.'

He had no idea what he was saying at the time. He only knew the dark heart of it: *I want a woman who would never leave me without an explanation.*

Half of his mother's face curled into a sly grin, the other half eyed him suspiciously. 'Only a strong man says something like that,' she said with a certain pride. 'But I'll tell you honestly, Jamila is the strongest woman I know.'

Upon later reflection, he had to admit that she was right. Jamila was strong, but only on the outside.

At the time he had shot off the sofa and stormed into the living room shouting, 'For the last and final time, I will not marry Jamila al-Brehm, God-dammit!' He'd slid into his sandals and left the house, slamming the door behind him.

Two months later, they were married.

The real problem was that they'd been promised to each other since birth. Their mothers were best friends. It was a little unusual that such promises should be made among friends instead of family, but the women had had a lifelong bond. For eighteen years they'd kept their promise alive. The marriage between their children would make the two women legitimate family to one another, as if their magnificent bond needed further cementing.

And, just like Zaki, he had taken three months to realise that he'd made a horrible mistake. By then, however, Jamila was pregnant with Aqmar, and there was nothing to be done.

He laid the pipe down. Smoking alone made him miserable. He had hoped being at home would keep him from fixating on Sabria, but he'd only fallen into older memories instead. It was all leading up to the single idea, not particularly original, that Sabria had been the best woman he'd ever known. Not Jamila, not Maidan. She was the woman he'd chosen, and one who would never simply disappear.

He dumped the rest of the tea on the coals and left the house.

23

Katya's mother had taught her about the three kinds of dreams. *Nafsani*, dreams which came from fear and desire. *Rahmani*, truthful dreams that came from God and that would often bring you visions of the future. And *shaytani*, dreams inspired by the devil.

As a child she had asked her mother if it was blasphemous to have dreams of prophecy, and her mother replied that interpreting dreams was not the same as prophecy. It was not against Islam. Hadn't Joseph, son of Jacob, successfully interpreted the dreams of the nameless King? And what was Katya's dream, she asked, the one that was making her so unhappy?

Katya said that the Hadith instructed that it was important not to speak about your bad dreams, in case they came from the devil. But her mother replied with a counter Hadith that said that you should only tell one person, the person you were closest to and whom you trusted the most. Katya thought this sounded better than her own Hadith.

So they sat down and determined that Katya's recurring dream about losing her tooth was in fact a bad omen. Teeth represented the family, 'all of them packed in a neat little mouth', as her mother said, and when one falls out, it means that someone will leave, or die.

'Was it a scary dream?' her mother asked.

'No, I wasn't scared. It was just disgusting.'

'And which tooth was it?'

'The back one.'

Sure enough, a few weeks later, her uncle Ramzi died in Lebanon, and the dreams stopped.

Over the years, Katya had forgotten about it. It stood alone among her dreams as a successful prediction. Or perhaps, with her mother gone, she no longer knew how to interpret things.

She was at home, sitting at the kitchen table, an old Formica-topped thing on metal legs, leftover from her childhood. The television, on but muted, was on the counter in front of her. It was Saturday, and Abu had finally left to go to evening prayers with his friends. The minute he'd shut the door, she'd pulled the folder from her rucksack and slid out the pictures.

Just before leaving the office, she had worked up the nerve to sneak into Majdi's lab and make copies of the gravesite photos. They were Xeroxed, but good enough. She had also made copies of the map that showed where each of the bodies had been found at the site. Now she cleared the kitchen table and laid the photos out as they might have appeared from a bird's-eye view in the desert.

The table wasn't big enough. She was going to need five times the amount of space. Ideally, she would have liked to hang them on the wall. She would have done it in the lab, but there was not enough space there, either – too many shelves and air-conditioning vents. Her bedroom had a similar problem. There was a huge wall in the living room but she didn't want to display the bodies when there was the chance that her father would bring his friends back from the mosque. They had never had a women's sitting room, just the kitchen, which was too small and cluttered.

What was the difference between a fantasy and a dream? When Charlie talked about the killer's fantasy, she meant it almost as if it were a dream – a *shaytani*, of course. Katya had had plenty of those herself. But Charlie described it as something much bigger, a kind of epic, recurring *shaytani* that existed in waking life as well, the different parts of which were heavy with individual meaning. *Look for patterns*, Charlie had said to her at lunch. *With an organised killer like this one, there will be patterns.*

Katya continued to lay out the photos. She had no other idea how to begin a search for patterns but guessed the first step was understanding the mind of the killer, and for that, she wanted a map.

Ayman came into the kitchen looking sleepy. He took the teapot from the sink and began filling it with water.

'I thought you were supposed to go shopping,' he said.

Katya shot out of her chair. '*Allah*, I forgot!' She shoved the pictures back into their folder and looked at her watch. She was supposed to have met Nayir half an hour ago. 'Oh God, I'm so late!'

'Do you need a ride?'

'Yes!'

Ayman put down the teapot and headed for the door.

The news report was appalling. Everyone watched in frozen disbelief. Not that they hadn't seen violence before, or seen a woman's smashed and burned and beaten face. It got to everyone, of course, but what really disturbed them was the neat little interview with the woman who was accused of committing the crime. She was sitting in a quiet, sunlit room with her two sons on either side of her, looking for all the world like the perfect Saudi housewife with her *niqab* draped elegantly over her face, dark eyes lowered from the invasive camera. In a soft voice she explained that she would never hurt her housemaid. The woman had been like a sister to her. The housemaid – that smashed and burned and beaten woman who would never look like a whole human again – that housemaid had done those things to *herself.*

Katya was standing in the changing room of the bridal shop in a gown of pale ivory. Two Filipina women had been fussing at her back, and another – the shop owner, whose name was Jo – was holding the train.

'You disgusting whore,' Jo muttered to the TV. The women had already taken Katya into their confidence, but one of the younger girls glanced at her, worried that she might be offended by the cursing.

'Pin this on.' Jo shoved the train at one of the girls and marched out of the room.

The atmosphere relaxed somewhat, and the girls' hands stayed busy. Katya hadn't watched the news in days. Between investigating Sabria and the Angel killer, work had been taking up every waking thought, probably because she'd been avoiding thinking about the wedding. Even the time she and Nayir had spent in the Land Rover driving out to the desert had been filled with talk about her job.

If this were a real Saudi wedding, she thought, the first thing they'd do was find the banquet halls. One for the men, and a bigger one for the women. Hers would be lavish: a stage and catwalk, tables for a thousand people. There'd be pink carpets, gold chandeliers, massive white bouquets on every surface. She had no idea what the men's hall would look like – she'd never actually seen one – but assumed it would be a duplicate of the women's. She had met her first fiancé at a wedding. Othman had told her all about the Bedouin warriors dancing with their swords, the prodigious amounts of incense and coffee and dates, and the way the groom sat on his throne, a bit stuffy, receiving the same blessing from every mouth: 'From you comes the money, from her the children.'

The women's section was less formal. Everyone greeted the bride, but the mothers and older women swept through the hall inspecting the single girls. Their sons weren't allowed to see these women before marriage, but the mothers were, and they were going to conduct a thorough study and hopefully find a good match for their sons – or, truthfully, a good match for themselves. If the house-hold was segregated, the women would spend more time with one another than with their husbands. Katya never passed these inspections. She was too quiet and plain. She was never interested in the sumptuous ball gowns and she didn't have the time or desire to spend a whole day grooming. She didn't own enough make-up to fill a shoe.

She and Nayir had agreed to a small, unadorned wedding. Neither one of them had the enormous families it would take to fill a banquet hall. Nayir preferred to arrange the locations anyway. Katya's main job was to choose the dress.

If this were a real Saudi wedding, she thought, *my family would be here right now. Mothers, sisters, cousins. They'd be helping me choose what to wear for the biggest day of my life.*

Five minutes later Jo came back into the room. To Katya she said, 'I'm sorry. I just can't stand this.' She motioned to the television. 'It never stops.'

140

'It's horrible.' Katya didn't want to tell her that there were even worse things than beatings. That among the police records, nearly sixty per cent of unidentified murder victims were female housemaids. And that they had just found another nineteen.

'This colour looks beautiful on you,' Jo said. 'Have a look.'

Katya spun to the mirror again. 'I like the colour,' she said, 'but the bodice is too frilly.'

Jo nodded and went back to the spare fitting room, where she'd hung another dozen dresses.

In between gowns numbers four and five, Katya sneaked to the front window, which was blocked from the street by heavy black curtains. She drew the curtain aside and peered out.

It was dark and the shopping area outside was lit with hundreds of golden string lights and a giant star-shaped lantern. Standing directly beneath the lantern, Nayir and Ayman were sipping juice and talking. Ayman said something that made Nayir throw his head back and let out a belly laugh. *Mash'allah*, he was the best cousin she could hope for.

As she dropped the curtain and drew back into the shop, she felt a sting of . . . envy? Sadness? She would never be able to make Nayir laugh like that. With her, he was always delicate, protected.

It took an hour, switching in and out of different dresses. Katya might have enjoyed it, but Jo's anger clipped her movements. The girls had gone silent. Katya gave in to the mood and listened as Jo began to relieve herself of tormented thoughts. Earlier that year, it seemed suicide was the thing. One housemaid had tried to hang herself, another swallowed detergent, a third jumped from the roof of her building. Not nearly as bad as the woman whose employer hammered twenty-four hot nails into her face, hands and arms. (That was a year ago in August.) Or the girl in Abha whose employer beat, burned and stabbed her, then cut off her lips. (November.) Not to mention two unidentified bodies found the next month (well, the two that made the news.)

In January, the story was a little different – and gave Jo cause for some hope, late though it was. A Saudi woman had been sentenced to three years in prison for the violations on the November girl. Thanks to new laws that had been passed, this was finally possible.

But only a few weeks later, a housemaid was arrested for using 'sorcery' against her employer and his family – or so the employer claimed. (February.) Then a girl jumped from a third-floor balcony to escape her employers and was found to have been brutally beaten and burned. (March.) She ticked off the remaining months, rushing right up to this evening's instalment: October.

Katya had never known an unhappy housemaid. Overworked and frazzled, yes. Annoyed by loud children, definitely. But abused? No. And yet today, every housemaid she encountered was dead or badly mutilated or both. She told herself that this was because she worked for the police.

Slowly, Jo's vitriol began to spread outward; not content to list crimes, she began to blame the entire country.

'You people let your men tell their women every little thing they can and cannot do. It's the same with employers. They're allowed to tell a housemaid anything, and she has to do it. Even sex!'

Katya realised her silence was now being mistaken for complicity. She wanted to leave. She didn't want to buy a dress any more – there weren't any good ones here anyway.

She looked at her watch. 'Oh no, I've got to go! My cousin will be angry.'

The three women looked at her with disappointment. Was she, too, simply a woman on a lead?

Katya got dressed and slid into her *abaaya*. 'Thank you so much for your time,' she said and scurried out of the door.

Nayir was walking as slowly as possible to enjoy every single moment he could catch with her. Her cousin Ayman had wandered off, talking on his mobile phone, and for now Nayir had her to himself. The best parts of their relationship so far had occurred during walks like this on the Corniche. He had even proposed marriage in a restaurant not far from here.

It was evening, and as far as Jeddawis were concerned, the day was properly beginning. It was finally cool enough to be outside. For Nayir, the darkness added an extra layer of privacy. No sun to shine through a woman's cloak and outline her figure. No stark illumination of the exposed faces that women seemed to prefer more and more. And those women who forsook head scarves completely – from a distance it seemed that each one's hair was a veil. It was more common now to see families picnicking on the pavements with their teenage daughters romping freely, wearing jeans and T-shirts and looking as mannish as their brothers – some even with short hair. The feeling that suffused him in the presence of it all was one of inexplicable sadness and loss.

With a sigh he let it go and it wound like a single, frail cloud into the dark sky. He was going to be married to this beautiful woman walking beside him. Soon he was going to do what his body had wanted to do since the first time he saw her: scoop her up like the small thing she was and kiss her face a hundred times and curl his body around her, naked and full of bliss. Walking beside her, smelling the warmth of her hair and neck, every particle inside him that was capable of feeling was lit up like a star.

So much of his life seemed foreign to him now. After she had agreed to marry him that day on his boat, he'd gone below and the interior of the yacht, which he'd lived in for years, seemed different – small and dank, full of artefacts from dreams that had died long ago. Maps and navigation manuals left over from his fantasy of sailing the world alone. Business cards from men at the camel market – a reminder that he had once wanted to buy camels and spend long months in the desert with the Bedouin. It surprised him how easily he had accepted the death of these dreams. And now he was eager to move into what was new. To sign the marriage document. To make it real. This urgency was also driven by the memory of what had happened with Fatimah, who had ripped him up by the roots and thrown him aside. He was terrified that this engagement would end the same way: suddenly and with helpless fury. Only this would be more brutal. He had so much more invested. The fear thrummed deep in his chest, racing like hummingbird wings, and he swallowed it hard, clawed it back. *Get away from the bloom in my heart.*

The thing was, all that was good was more dazzling than ever, but all that was bad came with a terrific shock. He had never known jealousy so charged. It could stop his heart. When Katya talked about her job, he tried to take comfort from the good she was doing for society, but at times he nearly died with the thought of every man she talked to, the men who saw her face, who spent entire days having access to her that he couldn't. On his knees at the mosque, he'd lost whole *du'as* being distracted by disgust for his fellow men. He thought of them all: men who leaped out of their cars to harass single women walking down the street. Men who sneaked into women's shopping malls dressed like women so they could prey on young girls. Men who Bluetoothed naked photos of themselves to anyone in a sixty-foot radius: pompous pectorals that appeared on his mobile phone, the peacock feathers of the modern teenage boy. He was determined to control this fury. When he came back to his senses, he prayed for forgiveness, prayed that no matter what vulgar temptations got thrown in her path, Katya would love him with her own single-minded passion.

'I need a wall,' she said.

'Pardon me?'

'A big, blank wall.' She sighed, and he stole a glance at her face. It wore preoccupation, defiance. 'I managed to get copies of all the photographs of the dead bodies. There are nineteen of them, remember? I need somewhere to hang them all in the positions in which they were found.'

He wanted to ask why the investigators hadn't done that already. But of course they wouldn't want pictures of women's naked bodies displayed on their walls unless it were absolutely necessary. And perhaps it wasn't.

'Majdi – you remember him? The head of forensics. You met him that one time. He's already created a computer model of the site that's true to geographical detail,' she said. 'But it's kind of flat and meaningless. I think it's best to do this the old-fashioned way.'

He tried to understand. Who better to look at photographs of women's bodies than a woman? 'I have a wall for you,' he said.

She immediately shook her head. 'Your boat is far too small.'

'I was thinking of my uncle's house.'

'Oh, that's very sweet, but we couldn't. They're graphic photos of dead women. You probably won't want to look at them yourself.'

'It won't bother me or my uncle,' he said. 'We won't look at the photos, if that's what you want.'

'No, no, it's not that—'

'We have a wall.'

*

An hour later, they were standing in Samir's basement.

Katya had never met Samir before. Although he was Nayir's only family, she had not heard that much about him except that he had raised Nayir by himself, without a woman's help. Perhaps for that reason he'd seemed mysterious. Had he cooked? Changed nappies? Sung lullabies and read stories and held Nayir on his lap when he cried? She imagined a chubby, effeminate man who watched soaps every day, sitting on a tatty sofa in the same dressing gown he'd worn for thirty years.

The real Samir was stocky but graceful. He wore a pair of shiny leather loafers, a suit with a waistcoat and a dark green cravat tucked into his collar. It was nearly nine o'clock when they arrived at his door, and he answered looking very much like a butler, his grey hair glimmering in the golden light of his hallway.

He smiled at Katya in a way that was understated but beaming somehow with an inner excitement. He welcomed the three of them and sent Nayir to prepare tea and dates while he escorted their guests to the empty wall.

Samir was a chemist like her father, but where Abu had spent his life working in factories and universities, Samir had remained independent. He worked out of his basement, doing freelance projects for archaeologists and the occasional historian, conducting his own research into anything that interested him, the details of which he assured her were boring. He kept his equipment in a basement laboratory. Katya and Ayman were standing there now. It was brightly lit and spacious, and the cool air was a relief. Ayman grinned.

'Will this be enough space for your photographs?' Samir motioned to the wall at the back of the house.

'More than enough,' she said. 'However, perhaps I should do this myself. The images are graphic.'

'Yes, yes, I've seen crime scene photos before. I've even unearthed dead bodies myself at archaeological digs. I know what to expect. Unless you'd prefer us to leave?'

'No, you're welcome to stay. I just wanted to warn you.'

'Well, don't worry. I won't be offended, and I'd be glad to assist. The more eyes the better.' Samir glanced at Ayman, who shrugged affably, trying to look adult. He was hoping that Katya wouldn't force him to leave. He was only nineteen and inclined to get grilled by Katya's father about her whereabouts.

She took the photos from her bag and began to hang them up. Samir oversaw the operation, guiding her from the map. They had just finished the last photo when Nayir entered with a tea tray. The look of quiet dismay on his face made her feel ashamed.

'I'm sorry,' she said. 'I should have warned you we were hanging them now.'

'It's all right,' he replied, setting the tray on a work bench. At least he hadn't said, 'I'll keep my gaze pure.' How many times had she heard that ridiculous phrase? It meant that a man could look at something scandalous – a woman's naked arm, her hair, her neck – and choose not to see it, because his mind was pure.

Once the photos were up, Katya felt ridiculous. Now what?

She had already noticed from the map that the bodies had been buried in a circular formation, with twelve bodies on the outer edge and seven filling up the middle.

'Well, it's a circle,' Ayman said.

'Technically, it's a hexagon,' Samir replied. 'In fact, a very carefully shaped hexagon.'

'Does it mean anything?' Ayman asked.

'I don't know,' Samir said. 'What do you think?'

Katya glanced at Nayir. He was staring at the photos with a look of quiet horror.

'It's the shape of a honeycomb?' Ayman said.

'Hmm, yes.'

They fell quiet. Katya realised that she hadn't really needed a wall as much as she needed a crime team who was familiar with the case.

'What are these crosses on the map?' Samir asked.

'Those mark the spots where they found the hands,' Katya said. 'The victims' hands were cut off.'

'Only three of them?' Samir asked.

'No, all of the victims' hands were cut off, but they only found three of them buried at the site.'

'And the other hands, where are they?'

'We have no idea.'

Samir took a marker from a jar on the desk and placed a small cross on each of the photos to show where they had found the hands.

'But how peculiar that only three should be buried!' Samir said, still looking at the map.

They fell into an even more maudlin silence. Nayir, who had poured everyone a cup of tea, was the only one who had actually picked up his cup. He leaned against the desk and sipped his tea.

'The bodies,' he said. Everyone turned. It was a surprise to hear him speak. 'They're oddly positioned.'

'It looks like the killer just dumped them there,' Katya said.

'So this killer takes a great deal of time plotting out a hexagonal burial pattern, and then he simply tosses the bodies into their graves?' Nayir asked. 'They're all buried in haphazard positions.'

'You're right,' Samir said. 'That is odd.' He turned to the wall and Nayir stood up, both seeming to come to something at the same moment. 'Can it be?' Samir said.

Nayir set his cup on the desk, took the pen from Samir and went to the wall. 'There is a pattern. Do you see it?'

She was staring frantically at the photos. 'No. What?'

He started at the uppermost right-hand corner. Beneath the body, he drew a simple shape.

It was the letter 'B'. It was also the shape the body was positioned in, with the head and feet slightly turned upward. The point beneath the stroke was where the hand had been buried.

'*Allah*,' Katya whispered. 'It can't be.'

Nayir continued drawing. On the next photo to the left, he wrote 'S'.

He wrote it without the left-hand tail, because it was meant to connect to the following letter, 'M'.

From a bird's-eye view, the body had been buried with the torso bent to the right, arms curled to the chest to resemble an 'M'. He wrote the entire photo collection out in letters, but they had already figured out the phrase. It was as familiar to them as breathing.

Bism'allah, ar-rahman, ar-rahim.

'In the name of Allah, most gracious, most merciful.' The beginning of every prayer.

Katya had to sit down. Samir, who looked rather pale himself, brought her a cup of tea and sat beside her. She had a fleeting moment of regret that this should be their first meeting. She took an unsteady sip.

'Monstrous,' Samir whispered.

Nayir set down the marker and came to his uncle's side. Ayman was unable to move, his eyes fixed on the wall with a look of amazement.

'I didn't realise that this is what you did at work,' he said.

'Drink your tea, young man,' Samir said. 'This is nothing to marvel at. It is evil, and when you see it, you should turn away.'

Surprisingly, Ayman obeyed. He sat down next to Katya and drank his tea. 'But just because you've worked out his mad genius, so what?' Ayman said. 'It doesn't mean anything. He said something we all say every day. I mean, it would have been nice if he'd left his address or something.'

This won no smiles.

'I'm sorry about this,' Katya said. 'I shouldn't have brought these here.'

'Don't apologise, my dear,' Samir replied, patting her on the arm. 'Nayir has solved a puzzle for you. It is also remarkable to see first hand what sort of challenges you face in your work. Now we will have an even higher respect for what you do. And no one here,' he looked around, 'lacks the stomach for it, least of all yourself.'

She gave him a half-smile and refrained from pointing out that Ayman was right, it all meant nothing. They had simply pulled back the rock and looked down at the teeming insect colony of a psychopathic mind.

On the way back to Ayman's car, Nayir said, 'When I struggle with things, especially things I can't understand, I find it's best to search for the answer in a dream.' He gazed at her face, a phenomenon rare enough to make her feel flustered. '*Istiqara*,' he said. 'Ask for an answer and Allah will oblige.'

She smiled. She had forgotten that there was a fourth type of dreaming – *istiqara*. 'Maybe I'll try that.'

'I'll email you the prayers.'

She thanked him and climbed into the car beside Ayman.

24

Oh Allah! I ask guidance from Your knowledge
And power from your might
And I ask for your great blessings.
You are capable, and I am not.
You know, and I do not.
You know the unseen.
Oh Allah! If you know that this information
Is good for me in my present and later needs
Then make it easy for me to get
And bless me in it.
And if you know that this information is harmful for me
Then keep it away from me
And ordain for me whatever is good for me
And make me satisfied with it.

This was her earnest petition just before bed. It led to an agonised darkness of heat and sweat and bed sheets twisted around her feet like chains. It led to hellish caverns of al-Balad where half-human creatures from the age before man were born of the blood of murdered women. They sprang, fully formed, from a touch of fire into the stunted forms of *efreet*, their skin blackened, crisp and peeling from the flames, their eyes yellow and malevolent and all-seeing. They chased her into alleys and set her clothes on fire. They were born of the blood of women, and they craved her. They surrounded her in the alley on Falasteen where Amina's hand had been found, and they dragged her screaming down the pavement, their swords chopping off first her feet, then her hands, her body bouncing helplessly over the corpses of countless other women. All the women of Jeddah were lying there, dead. Daher was there, too, and Ibrahim. They were talking. She screamed, but they couldn't hear.

And then the dream changed. She was in a world of hills and rain, grey skies and green fields. She was being dragged across the ground, over thorny bushes. Then the *efreet* were shoving her into the earth, a cold, black, fertile, insect-laden earth from an ancient imagining. It had crossed continents to reach them, this fairy tale of black earth. They shoved her in, filling her mouth with it, forcing fistfuls of dirt down her throat, and she woke with a horrified gasp and rolled out of bed and cried.

'In the Tale of the Porter and the Princess,' Katya said, 'the princess kills the *efreet*, am I right?'

'Yeees.' Her father was giving her a dour look. 'Why do you ask?'

'I had a dream last night that a bunch of *efreet* shoved me underground. It makes me think of that story.'

'I don't remember what happens,' he said, 'except that the *efreet* attacked the princess because the porter sneaked into the underground lair to rescue her, and the two lovers wound up kissing. The *efreet* are jealous creatures.'

'She kills them all, in the story,' Katya said. 'She burns them to cinders.'

But it made her feel no better about the dream.

'Are you all right?' he asked. 'You look very pale.'

She went to work feeling persecuted, unable to shake off the last remnants of the night. She had prayed to Allah, and the Devil had answered instead.

Modern-day devils are not hard to spot. They pose as the most righteous. They live in fear of being found out for what they really are.

This was Katya's first, ungenerous thought when she passed Abu-Musa in the hallway on the way to Ibrahim's office. He scowled at the

151

floor as she went by. He might have scowled at her face but that would have been improper.

One of the reasons she hated him was because he looked almost exactly like a sales clerk at IKEA to whom she had once given her address and phone number for the delivery of a desk and a set of shelves. He had then called her every day for a month, first leaving messages asking politely if she would meet him for dinner, then, when he realised she wouldn't call him back, leaving hateful messages, accusations that she was a whore, that only a whore would give a strange man her number, and that he was certain she ought to be properly treated with a cock shoved violently between her wet thighs. She had had to get a new telephone number, and for months she had been afraid to go in or out of her apartment on her own.

She stopped at Ibrahim's office door. He was standing behind his desk, frowning at the stacks of papers piled there.

'Yes, Miss Hijazi,' he said when he saw her.

She stepped inside and laid a folder on his desk. 'I'm sorry to add to your piles of paperwork,' she said, 'but this is very important. I discovered it last night.'

'What is it?'

Abu-Musa appeared in the doorway behind her. He was still scowling. 'Is it proper for you to be here, Miss Hijazi?'

She was taken aback. In all the months she'd worked here, she'd never actually been told that she was acting out of place. It was usually communicated via a gesture or glance, a whispered warning from her boss Zainab.

'Miss Hijazi has just delivered a very important case file,' Ibrahim said. 'Can I help you?'

'Technically, Miss Hijazi should not even be in the building,' Abu-Musa replied.

Katya thanked Ibrahim and left the room.

She didn't work that morning. She sat in front of her computer, one hand on her mouse, and stared at the screen. If someone passed behind her, she clicked the mouse to make it seem that she was busy, but her mind was the only thing in true motion.

At eleven o'clock she left the building for an early lunch break. She had brought a packed lunch but she wasn't hungry; she just wanted to be outside.

She headed away from the water, deeper into the city, and walked as if she had a purpose, even if it was only to be walking. She passed mothers shepherding children, young men leaning from car windows laughing, their music vibrating in her ribcage. Old men stood in front of their shops, smoking cigarettes and talking. In front of a *boofiya*, men were perched on plastic chairs, watching a television that was plugged into a generator, their only shade a feeble tree. Two young girls were sitting on a wooden fence, eating fruit and whispering over a shared mobile phone. When a young man approached them, one girl threw a grape at him and hissed, and he turned away, flushing.

The sunlight hit her face, and the heat enveloped her while the comforting sounds of traffic and laughing voices finally shook the last of the dream from her psyche. There was no death here, no blood and no *efreet*. But there was something else scratching at the edge of her consciousness. Amina al-Fouad. The alley. The dismembered hand. And she saw something plainly. It was irrational, fleeting. She stopped walking, grasped it, and quickly turned back towards the station. She began to hurry. It all became clear because she did not believe that God would let the Devil answer her unless the Devil had something to say.

One of the reasons he'd left Undercover was that he hated working in a department where nothing ever seemed to get done. In a flurry of activity, you prepared your agents, then you sent them to their assignments and you waited. For weeks. Months. Pushed papers around your desk and kept an eye on situations. But you were the shepherd whose sheep had run off to play with wolves and so you sang a lonely ballad by your campfire and told yourself everything was under control. You knew nothing, saw nothing, but every once in a while news would trickle back, and you'd celebrate or cry. In the end, it was as depressing as his family.

There were no shepherds in Homicide, only good old-fashioned Bedouin who banded together, formed alliances, and swore to protect one another against the unspeakable harshness of the world. Of course there were rivalries, but death was so close here, and all the paths you followed were designed to stave it off. Cover yourself. Move slowly. Follow the habits of the fathers, the men who died learning so that you could be wise.

Only now he was beginning to feel that there was something stifling in the camaraderie. That it encouraged closeness but not innovation. That the person who was accomplishing most on this case was a woman who stood outside the campfire circle, gazing in with a longing that, if fulfilled, would probably stifle her too.

The crime team was energised. He had only to send out word that they were meeting and the rumours began to fly. There had been a breakthrough on the case! They could stop their drudgery and do something important! Maybe one of them would even get a shot at nabbing the killer! Dr Becker could tell them a dozen times that it might take years to catch this one, but no one believed her.

Once again Mu'tazz stood at the back of the room, arms crossed, a sour expression on his face. Ibrahim hated to admit that Mu'tazz made him nervous. Despite feeling that he'd gained the upper hand at the last meeting, every disapproving twitch in the man's face spoke as loudly to him as someone shouting through a megaphone.

Dr Becker showed up wearing a black *abaaya* over her clothing but still no head scarf. They were cowing her slowly. Ibrahim was relieved that she was still there, although she didn't look happy.

The whiteboard hadn't been big enough, so the photographs of the nineteen victims were hanging on the wall. Majdi had put them up with Katya assisting. She stood now in her favoured position by the doorway. Waiting to make an exit, he thought.

Once all the noise had died down, Ibrahim pointed to the photos and said, 'I would like you to tell me what you see.'

Everyone turned to the left, or to one another, with confused looks on their faces.

'Go ahead, just tell me,' Ibrahim said. 'What do you see?'

'Dead bodies.'

'Yes. And something else? Something hidden, perhaps?'

After a long silence, the men began guessing. A pattern in the circle? A sextant? A hexagon?

'There is a pattern,' Ibrahim finally said. He went to the wall and began to write on the photographs. First 'B' then 'S' then 'M'. He had barely started the second row when the men recognised what was happening. Wild talking broke out.

'*Bism'allah, ar-rahman, ar-rahim,*' Shaya said.

Silence fell. Daher's mouth hung open.

'Miss Hijazi noticed the pattern last night,' Ibrahim motioned towards her. She remained unflustered under the gazes of twenty envious men. 'Thank you, Miss Hijazi.'

Another silence fell, a continuation of the previous wave of shock. Mu'tazz looked disgusted, but whether this was because of the message or because Miss Hijazi had found it, Ibrahim couldn't tell.

'Well, he's a Muslim,' someone said gravely.

'He may know Islam,' Daher replied, 'but he's not a Muslim.'

Ibrahim stepped in before the argument could become annoying. 'I'm sure you're all wondering how this is going to help us.' He turned to Katya. 'Miss Hijazi, why don't you come up and explain your theory?'

Katya stayed by the doorway. Everyone turned to her again except the few men in the room who couldn't bring themselves to look.

'I think it's possible he has repeated this pattern somewhere else,' she said, motioning to the wall. 'We suspect that he's taken Amina al-Fouad, and her hand was posed as well – perhaps as a full stop marking the end of a sentence.'

Ibrahim motioned to the whiteboard behind him, which held a photograph of the hand. As he did this, he noticed Mu'tazz glowering at Katya.

'It's possible,' Katya went on, 'that she will be the first victim in a new series of attacks, and that the killer has altered his style of killing because he's angry that we found his desert site. But I think it's equally likely that al-Fouad could be the latest in a series that has been going on without us noticing. Part of a sentence we haven't read yet.' She seemed to notice Mu'tazz staring at her; and her cheeks darkened.

'You mean, this killer hasn't just been burying them in the desert,' Shaya said, 'he's been killing all over the place?'

His tone suggested all of the affronted pride and scepticism that the department was feeling. *What do you mean we didn't notice?*

Dr Becker looked up. 'It's actually quite normal,' she said. 'Police departments all over the world don't usually notice a serial killer until he has been killing for quite some time. That's because most serial killers don't leave a signature, as we call it, and they generally don't stick to one location. Jeddah is a huge city with many different precincts, so it's entirely possible he could have been operating within Jeddah all this time.'

'Except,' Daher said, 'I think that we might have noticed women being murdered, and having their hands cut off, long before now, don't you think?'

'Your man's signature is the cutting off of hands,' Dr Becker replied evenly, 'but it's also the posing of the bodies and the shooting through the head. It could be that he's been killing in the city using any of those signatures – or perhaps none. He's already proven that he can kill in large numbers. There could be more. The signatures may have developed over time. There could have been victims before that you don't know about and won't be able to connect to the case through a signature alone.

'It might be best,' she went on, 'to go back to your unsolved cases. He may not have cut off their hands or shot them. Maybe he just posed the bodies. Maybe he just shot them. Look for any points of similarity.'

'That's going to take forever,' Daher said, looking angry now.

'Well, as I understand it,' Dr Becker replied without the slightest hint of sarcasm, 'the Jeddah police have a ninety per cent success rate in capturing murderers, so there shouldn't be that many files to go through.'

Daher smiled. 'With respect, Dr Becker, you don't know Arabic. Any of our letters could look like a human body. We could review a hundred old murders and find a whole novel written on the streets! It doesn't mean there's a connection.'

'You're right,' Ibrahim said. 'It's going to mean a lot of work, and some educated guessing, but I think it's a viable lead and I'm going to assign that work to Miss Hijazi.'

No one protested, not even Daher. Ibrahim had been hoping for that. Once they realised that the most tedious grunt work would be done by a woman, they lost the urge to complain.

'I've already spoken to Chief Riyadh and we're going to cordon off the back section of this room so that Miss Hijazi and some of the female investigators can set up an office space for all the files they're going to look through. I would ask you all to please give them their privacy.'

'Don't the women have a bigger room upstairs?' Shaya asked.

Ibrahim explained that Miss Hijazi had already offered to look through the execution and amputation records. The boxes were taking up a conspicuous amount of space in the women's lab. Now with dozens, possibly hundreds, of unsolved case files to go through, she faced being crowded out of her office altogether.

Everyone seemed to accept this except for Mu'tazz, who shook his head theatrically and marched out of the room. No doubt he was heading straight to Chief Riyadh to complain.

As the rest of the men left, Ibrahim caught sight of Daher's face and saw that he was angry. So angry, in fact, that Ibrahim thought it wise to keep an eye on him.

'The problem is,' Katya said in a low whisper, 'that a lot of old cases weren't ... done right.'

She and Charlie were sitting in the women's section of Pizza Hut. When Charlie had seen the familiar logo out front, she'd laughed, grabbed Katya's arm, and said, 'My God, you know the way to my heart!'

'Really?'

'I miss home right now. This is perfect.'

Now they were sitting over a large *halal* pizza with tomatoes and cheese.

'What do you mean they weren't done right?' Charlie asked.

'The police need a confession from a killer. Without it, they can't sentence him.'

'So the confessions were faked?'

Katya sighed. 'Sometimes, the suspect is pressured.'

'Torture?'

'Yes, maybe. It depends.'

'So that's why you have a ninety per cent success rate?' Charlie asked.

'Yes, perhaps.'

'I see. So you need to get all of the cases, not just the unsolved ones.'

'Yes. But by asking for those I am saying that the police did not do their jobs.'

Charlie narrowed her eyes. 'Did they give you the files?'

'No, not yet. Inspector Zahrani is trying. It might take some time.'

'Jesus.'

They ate in silence for a while. Katya's thoughts turned back to the killer.

'It still bothers me,' she said, 'that the killer did not treat Amina like the others. She was still alive when he cut off her hand.'

'Yes,' Charlie said. 'And I agree with what you said: it's likely that his new behaviour is a reaction to this investigation. Also, Amina is not like his other type. So maybe he only cut off her hand to let you – the police – know that it was him. Otherwise, you might not have made the connection.'

'But why would he do that?' Katya asked in bafflement. 'Does he *want* us to catch him?'

'Sure. It could be that he wants recognition for his crimes. He may even be proud of them. Until now he has gotten access to women and no one has noticed they're missing. The thing is, Amina went missing almost a week before the killer went back to the gravesite, so he had already kidnapped her before finding out that the police had discovered the graves. He must have known the moment he kidnapped her that someone would be more likely to notice her missing. She's a Saudi, not a housemaid.'

'Maybe she was wearing a veil and he didn't realise she was a Saudi?' Katya asked.

Charlie shook her head. 'As far as we know, he's never picked a non-Asian woman before. I think he knows how to figure out what a woman looks like. I really believe he's taunting you.' Charlie set her pizza down. 'As you said, Amina may be the first or the last in a series of city victims. No matter what, I think we have to assume the killer is not done. And we have to find the pattern before he kills Amina, if she isn't already dead.'

25

'Remember the paedophile?' Shaya asked.

They were in Ibrahim's office with Lieutenants Daher, Abdullatif and Zunedh. Ibrahim was sitting at his desk. He hadn't called them in; they had spilled in after the meeting, agitated.

'Which one?' Daher asked disparagingly.

'The one they beheaded. I think it was last year. They caught him in Hail.'

'Yes, yes, I remember.' Daher stood and leaned against the wall.

'Well, I was thinking,' Shaya said. 'He was raping young boys and then leaving them out in the desert. He was a serial killer just like our guy. And he was a Saudi.'

No one replied.

'He was young, that guy,' Shaya went on. 'Twenty-two, I think. And one of the foreign papers said he had a psychiatric disorder, but we executed him anyway.'

'And we should have,' Daher said. 'So what if he had a disorder? He was killing people. Children! Think about it, man.'

'Think about what?' Abdullatif said. 'He wasn't in control of his own actions. He was crazy. Shaya's right. They should have worked that out and shown a little mercy.'

'What about the families?' Daher asked. 'Their children are dead.'

'Killing the madman isn't going to bring them back,' Abdullatif said flatly, ending the discussion. They turned to Ibrahim, in case he wanted to weigh in. He would have liked to tell them that of course the country had its own serial killers, that all their bellyaching about it only revealed their youth and naivety, and that there was no good answer to the question of capital punishment.

'So now we know our killer is clever,' Ibrahim said. 'He fancies himself a very clever man. Writing messages with dead bodies.'

'And what a message,' Shaya said. 'It's completely sick.'

'But he's not a total madman,' Daher said. 'If he was, he'd be as easy to catch as the Hail killer.'

'That took four years, by the way,' Ibrahim put in.

'Dr Becker said that killers tend to pick victims from their own ethnic type,' Daher said.

'*Tend to* is not a law,' Ibrahim said.

'I know,' Daher replied. 'And it's not that I'm upset about it. Shaya's right. We have our own killers. But we're trying to profile this guy, right? We ought to be able to figure out where he's from.'

'Of course,' Ibrahim said, 'but in the absence of evidence we have to keep our minds open.'

'I wonder if they called in an FBI profiler for the Hail case?' Zunedh asked. He was the quieter of the officers, painfully shy. It was a surprise when he spoke. He immediately flushed in embarrassment.

'Yeah, good point,' Daher remarked. 'Why do we need one now?'

So that was it – the real source of agitation. *Why are women working on this case?* Ibrahim had suspected it but had hoped he was wrong.

'Stop moaning,' he said. 'We're lucky to have Dr Becker here, and we're lucky that Miss Hijazi noticed the pattern. I expect the same kind of brilliance from all of my team.'

Daher's anger rose again. He turned pale.

As Ibrahim watched them leave on their assignments, he began to worry. It was only a matter of time before Daher's wounded ego drove him into the orbit of Abu-Musa and Mu'tazz, men who believed that women should be prohibited from doing police work except where they were absolutely necessary to maintain the standards of segregation: autopsying female corpses, processing female biological samples, and occasionally interrogating female witnesses. Once Daher migrated, the other men would, too. Ibrahim thought suddenly of Katya setting up her own campfire in the situation room.

Had he been reckless proposing it? Why not let her conduct the work up in her lab? He suspected his own ego at work. He was dragging her into the fight.

Chief Riyadh was sitting at his desk, flanked by large potted ferns and a pair of framed photographs, one of King Abdullah, the other of the Minister of the Interior, the King's brother Nayef. The air was cool enough to be painful, although Riyadh, in his magnificent bulk, was sweating anyway, crevices of darkness staining his shirt at the armpits and the folds of his belly.

Across from him, two men were sitting in the heavy wooden chairs. A third chair had been left for Ibrahim. A uniformed officer stood by the door. The moment he walked in, Ibrahim recognised them all from Undercover. He saw his future in a flash: jail sentence, humiliation, death.

Riyadh's face was relaxed, only his waxy, protuberant mouth looked annoyed.

'You know Inspector Ubaid from Undercover,' he said. Ibrahim nodded and shook Ubaid's hand.

'They're here about a missing person who used to work for you in Undercover. I realise you're busy with a murder investigation, but I told them you'd be glad to answer their questions.'

Ibrahim sat. 'Of course.'

'A woman who used to work with you – her name is Sabria Gampon,' Ubaid said.

'Sure. I remember Sabria.'

'She was reported missing yesterday.'

'She no longer works for Undercover,' Ibrahim said, feigning slight confusion.

'In fact, no,' Ubaid said, 'but we feel it necessary to investigate anyway. Her neighbours called to report the disappearance.'

'Her neighbours?'

'Yes. Well, the brother of one of them. According to dispatch – they were the ones who traced the call – his name was Mr Saleh Harbi. The neighbours – two females – were concerned, and Mr Harbi works for law enforcement, so they turned to him.' So Asma and Iman had grown too worried about Sabria's disappearance. Ibrahim should have talked to them, come up with an explanation. Now it was too late.

'But of course you know we like to take care of our workers.' Ubaid said this with a chummy smile that made Ibrahim think instantly of how quickly and horribly Undercover had offered the position of Assistant Chief to Omar, because he was the older brother.

'Yes, of course,' he replied.

'And we tend to investigate these things, since there is always the chance that this kind of disappearance could be related to the work she used to do for us.' The way he said *us* managed to exclude Ibrahim.

'What leads do you have?'

'We've been looking for her husband,' Ubaid said. 'Unfortunately, we haven't been able to find him.'

Ibrahim shot a glance at Riyadh, who had put on a charming mask of hospitality and concern.

'As far as I remember,' Ibrahim said carefully, 'she was married by force. She hadn't seen her husband for a few months when she came to work for us, and that was, what – five years ago?'

'Yes.' Ubaid looked prissy when he pursed his lips. 'However, she remains married to this man – and not for visa purposes. Her visa has expired.'

'I see. So how can I help?'

'Did you ever meet her husband?' Ubaid asked.

Ibrahim shook his head. 'No. I believe they were completely estranged.'

Ubaid looked as if he might remark on the inappropriateness of hiring single women. 'Well, apparently Miss Gampon was not working. Her neighbours have confirmed this.'

Ibrahim realised that the neighbours had been trying to protect her. They knew her visa had expired. What they didn't know was that any investigation into a missing woman, no matter how earnest, was always going to come down to the woman's virtue.

'Yet she lived in a nice apartment,' Ubaid continued. 'We spoke with the landlord, who confirmed that she had never missed a rent payment.'

Mash'allah, al'hamdulillah, and triple thanks to God that he had never paid the rent himself, that he had insisted on giving her cash every month, that he had never let himself be seen by the land-lord.

'... and we wondered how she was paying for it, so we looked into her banking records and discovered unusual amounts of money.'

'How unusual?'

'Tens of thousands of riyals being deposited – and then with-drawn – every month.'

Ibrahim could not have been more baffled.

'That is an unusually large sum of money for an immigrant woman who has no job,' Ubaid said.

'Yes, so you think this money ...' Ibrahim waved his hand, but Ubaid didn't fill in the rest. 'Well, what?'

Ubaid's fussiness, the little uptilt of his frowning face telegraphed instantly that he was going to make a case out of this, that he had enough evidence to convict Sabria, in absentia, of virtue crimes, and that he was going to do it, was even excited about it, because some-thing like this would make his cock stand up as hard as granite for the rest of his life.

'We found evidence of multiple men at her apartment.'

'You suspect prostitution?' Ibrahim's voice sounded far away to him now. *They have the evidence from her apartment.*

'The deposits to her account were large,' Ubaid said. 'And they were relatively consistent.'

Ibrahim wanted to tell them that Sabria had come to Undercover after a year of rape, torture and abuse, that by some perverse law of human evolution, this had given her the cunning, bullheadedness and fury she needed to perform undercover work, and that in that work she had found a way to rescue herself. He wanted to grab skinny little Ubaid by his neck and make sure he understood that women who went through such an experience had only one thing to be afraid of: men like him who sat on their dainty little arses intel-lectualising virtue.

'Where did the money come from?' Ibrahim asked.

'We don't know. It was always deposited as cash. The withdrawals, too, were taken out as cash.'

'Did she make a large withdrawal before she went missing?'

'No. In fact, she did not make any withdrawals this month.'

Ibrahim nodded. 'So she probably didn't run away.'

'No.'

Ibrahim glanced at Riyadh again. The Chief wore a look of polite regret that Undercover should have hired such an amoral woman, and found out about it in such a scandalous way.

He had to proceed with caution. They were already looking for a way to implicate him in this. A woman doesn't become a prostitute overnight. And wasn't he the one who'd fought so hard to keep her on the force? Did he know back then that she was a whore?

'I'm sorry to hear this,' Ibrahim said. 'All I can tell you about her is that she was an excellent worker. She helped us take down a shoplifting network that we'd been after for a long time. She went into some very risky situations and managed to gather enough evidence for us to implicate a number of high-value criminals. We were sorry when she left.'

Ubaid hadn't been listening, only waiting politely for Ibrahim to finish. He already knew his position on the virtue of Sabria Gampon.

'Prostitution is a serious crime,' he said, his expression perfectly communicating his intentions: *We plan to prosecute this*. 'We suspect that her husband was acting as her pimp, but if what you say is true and she hadn't seen this husband for many years, then perhaps she had someone else. We intend to find out.'

Ah, the double crime of prostitution *and* adultery. No wonder Ubaid was looking so smug.

'Let me know if there's anything else I can do,' Ibrahim said, nodding.

The men rose and shook hands, and Ibrahim surprised himself by walking out of there without fainting.

'I pulled the nail out of the floor before I left,' Katya said, 'so there were no blood traces.'

'*Al-hamdulillah*,' Ibrahim snapped.

He was pacing. They were in the third-floor toilets, whispering by the sink. It was late and the building was nearly empty. Katya was frightened anyway – that he would explode, that he would draw someone's attention and they'd get caught and things would look even worse than they were.

164

'I know you think my son did it,' he said. 'He was there. I saw the cut on his foot.'

'Oh,' she said. 'Why was he there?'

'He followed me from work one day. But he didn't talk to her. He was working on the day she went missing. I double-checked with his boss. My son had absolutely nothing to do with her disappearance, I can guarantee it.' He gave her a wild look. 'Someone is setting her up.'

'All right,' Katya said slowly. 'But she was hiding something.'

'I know. Dammit!'

'They must have sent evidence to Undercover before I got there,' Katya said for the third time. 'I took all the evidence I collected to my house. I did that immediately. My cousin picked me up and I took it straight home. Later, I switched the evidence. I stole hairs and fibres from other cases, relabelled them and put them into Sabria's file, so now it should look like the only other people at her house were women.'

'It doesn't matter. Undercover already has its damning proof. I think they were lying when they said they found evidence of multiple men at her house. That can't be true.'

'Do you think they would go that far in setting her up?' Katya asked.

'Why not? It would be the easiest part. Plant some hairs in her bedroom. The question is why are they doing this?'

Katya was silent.

'They know something about her. They want to stop something. It's still going on, whatever it is. Or they wouldn't feel the need to do this.'

'What about her banking records?' Katya asked.

'They didn't say how much, just that she made big deposits every month. Tens of thousands. And then she took the money out again later in cash.'

'Do you think they falsified that evidence as well?'

'No. I don't know. It would be a lot harder to do.'

'It makes no sense,' Katya said. 'Why would she deposit money and then take it out again? Why not just keep the money hidden somewhere?'

'I have no idea,' he said. 'I'm convinced that something bad has happened to her, and whatever it is, the answer is at the Chamelle

Centre. Those women she was meeting: something was being transacted. And I can't go there myself. Dammit!' His fist hit the wall. The mirror rattled.

'I'll go back there,' Katya said, 'and find out what I can.'

He stopped pacing. 'Thank you, Katya. I'm sorry I'm so angry. I appreciate your help. And please be discreet. These people aren't playing around. Undercover may have found out about the mall and they may have someone there already. Don't let them see you.'

'I'll be careful.'

'I have to make a phone call.'

'All right,' she said.

He was out of the door before she could duck out of sight. She heard his footsteps march halfway down the hallway before he realised he'd forgotten to knock to let her know it was safe to come out. He came running back, knocked, and dashed back towards the stairs.

Discovering that you are not unique is a charm that only works in certain situations. You're rejected for a job or you're hurt by a friend. Don't worry, it happens to everyone. Outside the appropriate context, it's shattering. *I am not the only man she loved. I am not the only man who shared her bed.*

He wasn't shattered by it yet because he didn't believe it, but there was a growing crack in the glass.

He called Fawzi, his contact at the Ministry, to ask whether he had found an address for Sabria's ex-employer. (He refused to think of him as her 'husband'.) With an insouciance that was infuriating, Fawzi said, 'Yes, as a matter of fact. Here you go.'

Ibrahim copied down the address. Fawzi had probably been sitting on it for days, too lazy to pass it on. Ibrahim couldn't explain how important it was. He was already taking an enormous risk just asking for it.

'Thanks for keeping this quiet,' Ibrahim said.

'Sure. Is this part of that serial killer case you've got?'

'No. It's an old case.'

'I won't say anything.'

Ibrahim wasn't sure he believed it but thanked Fawzi anyway.

The address was in Karantina, which wasn't that far from its sister neighbourhood, Kandara. The slum area got its bastardised English name from the fact that it had been a quarantine zone for a few hundred years when periodic epidemics swept through the city. It used to be far enough from the city centre to be considered safe. Today it was closer, linked by an ugly highway. The overpass cut a slash through the neighbourhood and provided the only separation from a giant oil refinery that spewed petro-filth into air already miserable with mosquitoes and the smell of raw sewage.

Beneath the highway were shantytowns of the kind that made Kandara's Sitteen Street look upscale. Most of the residents were Africans, men and their multiple wives, their innumerable children who ran naked and blighted through the trash-choked streets. They were men who had burned their passports when they got here so as not to be sent back to even worse places. At least here there was a market for drugs and prostitution. At least here the police would turn a blind eye. At least here the government would leave them alone, even if they had been abandoned under a flyover where the infestation of mosquitoes led to outbreaks of malaria and dengue, and rampant prostitution brought hospitals new cases of AIDS every day. The modern quarantine was government neglect.

Who says that the government doesn't understand justice? Ibrahim thought bitterly as he drove through the streets. The government knew just how to handle Karantina. They ignored the scale as one side of it tipped lower and lower – heavy with theft, illegal substances, brothels, and the kind of ruined morality that accounted for Jeddah's highest murder rate. When the law sought justice, it would balance the scale with a sudden, vicious down-stroke like the swing of an executioner's blade. That was how they had taken down the flourishing 'Friday markets' on Yazeed Ibn Naeem Street where the locals dealt in food, clothing, furniture and home appliances – all of it stolen. The police had rounded up 3,500 thieves in a single operation. Ibrahim knew it was only the pretence of justice. There was nothing worse than an abrupt smack from an otherwise absent father's angry hand.

It didn't surprise him that Halifi would end up here, in the city's graveyard of hope, but it made him uneasy. Every time Sabria had talked about him, she had given the impression of a man who went

167

to great lengths to appear wealthy, stable and respectable. He ran an import company that was clean all the way down the figures on its books, but on the side Halifi imported women, luring them with the promise of well-paid jobs as housemaids and then selling them to wealthy clients who wanted discreet sex – the kind that lived in your house and also did the cooking and cleaning. In some cases, Halifi would sell women to escort services, or even to independent pimps. He seldom turned down an offer if the price was high enough, and there were plenty of unsuspecting women coming from abroad.

Ibrahim might have tracked down Halifi years ago except that Sabria hadn't wanted it. She didn't want to try to unwind herself legally from this man because it would only bring back the past. In the first few months that she and Ibrahim began seeing one another, she talked about Halifi only three times before casting him into the void of non-existence.

The apartment building didn't have a posted street number, but nearby buildings did, so he was able to determine that he'd found the right place. It was an old concrete structure, dirty and plain. In a normal neighbourhood, two families might have lived there. In Karantina, it was probably a drug den.

He had the feeling that Halifi wouldn't be there, or that he was about to walk in on some lesser office of Halifi's operations. Ibrahim was so full of rage that he had to sit in the car for five minutes and remind himself that he was only there to find Sabria, and not to do anything foolish.

The front door was off its hinges. When he pushed it, it fell against the wall behind it and he had to step over the lower half to get into the foyer. It was dark, a long passageway with two doors at the end, both of them open. There were noises inside, but nothing to indicate that the residents had heard an intruder.

He entered the apartment on the right. The first room held only a sofa and a TV. The sofa had been gutted. In the second room he found Halifi. He was sitting cross-legged on an old mattress in the corner. A young woman was sitting on a cinderblock beside him, taking a hit from a crack pipe. She was naked, her backside and lower back marked with red welts.

'Mahmoud Halifi,' Ibrahim said.

168

The woman turned. She was a migrant, probably Filipina. She blinked and looked back at Halifi, handed him the pipe and stood up. She left the room just as a modest Muslim housewife might leave once her husband's guests had arrived. As she went past Ibrahim at the doorway, she grabbed her left breast with one hand and jiggled it happily in his direction.

Ibrahim had planned all kinds of clever tactics to get Halifi to talk, but seeing the man's state of consciousness, he knew they were useless.

'I need to find Sabria Gampon,' he said.

Halifi didn't look alarmed, not even when Ibrahim dragged him to his feet and threw him against the wall. When Ibrahim asked, 'Where is she?' Halifi let out a surprised laugh, a choked guffaw that said, *Oh yes, I remember her, that long-ago whore*. Ibrahim delivered a punch that broke Halifi's nose and sent him crashing into the wall, but he still didn't seem to understand the severity of it. He simply rolled onto his stomach, climbed to his knees, and watched the blood dribble from his mouth to the cement floor. He looked up at Ibrahim.

'Where is Sabria?' Ibrahim growled, although his gut was already telegraphing that this had been a mistake, that he was wasting his time.

'How should I know?' Halifi drooled another clump of blood and sat down on his haunches. 'Haven't seen her in *years*.'

Ibrahim wanted to kill him. Even now, after all the silence that Sabria had used to bury the man, Ibrahim's disgust and hatred were still right there. It would have been easy. Take one of the empty syringes lying on the floor and inject an air bubble the size of a halala into his neck. Even if the police decided to investigate the death of yet another Karantina junkie, they wouldn't get further down the suspect list than all the other junkies on the block. But he couldn't risk it. There must be nothing to tie him to this man or this place.

'If she's gone,' Halifi said, 'then she ran away. That's what she always did.'

Ibrahim kicked him to the floor and left.

26

On Monday, Katya spent her whole lunch break at the Chamelle Centre's café. Ibrahim couldn't risk driving her there himself, so he'd offered her money for a taxi. Instead, she'd called Ayman, who was glad to pick her up.

She ordered a latte and sat at a table with a newspaper open in front of her. She was drawing a bit of attention sitting there alone – most women came here with friends – but that was the idea. She wanted someone to notice her. Someone to think she was odd and look at her twice, maybe pause for a good study. And she wanted that person to know something about Sabria.

It began to feel idiotic, so she got up to talk to the barista, the same young woman who had identified Sabria from the full-body shot. Her name was Amar and she recognised Katya.

'Have you found her yet?' Amar asked.

'No, I haven't,' Katya said. 'You remember seeing her with other women, right?'

'Yes.'

'Would you recognise any of the women if you saw them again?'

'Yes. In fact, one of them keeps coming in here. She sits at that table in the corner and waits, but your friend doesn't show up. She seems disappointed.'

'Do you know her name?'

'No. But I would know her if I saw her.'

'When did you see her last?'

'This morning. She comes around ten o'clock. Maybe she'll come tomorrow.'

'Would you tell her I have something for her?' Katya said. 'It's important.'

Katya had half of the files for the department's unsolved murders. They were sitting in boxes on the floor behind her. Records had promised her the rest when she was ready for them. She also had all of the files for the current case – the photographs, sketches and thin reports on the nineteen victims by various officers working under Ibrahim, plus the file for Amina al-Fouad. She'd spent so much time over the past week finagling to get her hands on these files, it was funny now to think that they had been the easiest ones to acquire.

She was unable to get access to any of the solved murder cases. Katya imagined that they were locked in file cabinets in the Records room. What she didn't have to imagine – what was made plain to her from a conversation with Ibrahim – was that the real obstacle to reaching those files would be convincing Chief Riyadh that they were vital to the case. Ibrahim had briefed him on Katya's discovery, and Riyadh had approved the temporary change in her work duties, but he had said nothing about releasing the files. Perhaps he wasn't convinced that Katya's theory was correct.

Then there was the technical problem: there were more solved cases than unsolved ones, and Katya and Ibrahim would have to come up with some system for selecting the ones that were most relevant. That is, if Riyadh agreed to release them. Katya knew very little about the Chief, but a hunch told her he wouldn't be offended by the suggestion that some of those old murder cases had been wrongly prosecuted. However, he might feel that all the extra work involved in assembling and sorting the files was a complete waste of time.

By Tuesday, they had set up the office space downstairs, and she plunged into the files on her desk. Every time she thought of 'her desk', she made an effort not to smile. It wasn't actually a desk, just a large Formica table with folding legs. Around it were six standard-issue metal police chairs with ripped leather cushions, usually occupied by one or two female officers. The whole set-up was surrounded with heavy black curtains, but they had two table lamps and part of one window, so there was enough light. The curtains simply blocked them from seeing anything of the room around them. It could have been a stool and a cardboard box and she would have sat there with the same quiet pride of a falcon.

That morning, two female officers came to help read through the cases. They worked earnestly at first but had not noticed any patterns, so they had gossiped away for a few hours. Katya had previously been in awe of these women – trained officers from the police academy. She had to marshal the nerve to tell them to read the files again, and then again, however many times it took before they noticed something.

Once the women left, no one came into the purdah except Ibrahim. He was delivering a few stray files. He rapped lightly on one of the metal poles that held up the black fabric screens, a cue for whoever was inside to prepare for his entrance. Katya knew that sooner or later she would begin to feel that she had only managed to move her confinement downstairs. But there was no dampening her satisfaction yet. She had even allowed herself to fantasise about becoming a detective and having her own office – God protect her and forgive her vanity.

She spent the rest of the morning reading files, but found nothing of interest. She was sitting alone in the purdah when she heard a light tap on the metal pole. The curtain parted to reveal Dr Becker. She was carrying a box, which she set on the table.

'One shipment of solved murder files,' she said happily. 'As requested.'

'How did you get these?' Katya asked, standing up.

'I convinced Chief Riyadh that I wanted to do some work comparing murders in America with your murders here.'

Katya was amazed. However, it turned out that the box contained thirty-eight case files from the late 1980s. Not as useful as she would have wished.

'I thought I'd sit with you a while and do what I can,' Charlie said.

'I'm sorry.' Katya motioned to the papers on the table. 'None of it is in English.'

'I can always look at pictures,' Charlie said.

Indeed she could. Katya drew a graph of the letters of the Arabic alphabet and asked Charlie to put aside any of the files where the position of a victim's body resembled any of the letters. Charlie dug into her box and set to work eagerly, but ten minutes later, she stopped in exasperation.

'None of these files have photos,' she said.

'What?'

Charlie motioned to the ones she'd just riffled through. 'No photographs in any of them. I'm getting a bad feeling about the rest.'

There were only three files with photographs, and those were partials showing a foot, a bloody arm. Katya was baffled. The department had used forensic photographers since the very advent of cameras. Why were these cases missing photographs?

'Someone took the pictures out,' she said. 'We always take photographs of the victims.'

'Even of women?' Charlie asked.

'Ye-es,' Katya said uncertainly. 'Even of women.' That was true now, but had it been true twenty-five years ago? She was more inclined to think that someone had nabbed the photographs in the name of decency.

Katya leafed through the files herself. Charlie was right: the crime scene photos had been carefully neutered. They showed only a single body part, or shots of the objects that were found at the scene. A gun. A bloody hammer. There were no full-body shots of the victims.

'Could this be a virtue thing?' Charlie asked.

'Maybe,' Katya replied. It certainly could have been a virtue concern. Someone like Abu-Musa could have got access to the Records room, gone through all of the female murder victims and destroyed the photographs that showed a whole body, a face, an indecent amount of skin. In the strictest version of Islam it was forbidden for a person even to appear in a photograph. Exposing the *awrah*, the intimate parts of the body that required covering, was even more taboo.

But Katya had a cold prickling at the back of her neck. There were darker reasons for someone to excise a photograph from a case file.

*

'I just kept asking myself, what do we really know about this guy?' Daher was repeating himself, to reassure them both that his thinking was sound. 'We know nothing. But what can we reasonably presume to know? Two things for sure. One, he's got a religious hang-up. And two, he's a nut case. So if you put that together in the most obvious way, then of course he's going to wind up at an exorcist sooner or later. Right?'

Ibrahim nodded. 'It makes sense.'

'Then why do none of these quacks have anything useful?'

'We've got some names.'

They got out of the car. They were in Kandara, just a few streets from the Sitteen Street Bridge, about to visit their fifth exorcist of the day. Daher was probably right – and even though it didn't look like the idea was going to turn into a viable lead, he was clever to have put it together.

Ibrahim couldn't stop thinking of the welt on Farrah's back, of Jamila's smug pride. It still angered him. Even if Farrah never had another back pain in her life, he refused to accept that some quack exorcist had pulled a *djinni* from her body. He had simply delivered a placebo effect with a very ugly scar and the potential for infection. As long as the remedy remained effective, they had every reason to be grateful, except that he didn't like his children buying into that crap, especially when it was connected to religion.

They made their way into the narrow alleys. Jeddah had a dozen big-name exorcists, and probably hundreds more who performed in their basements or living rooms and whose fame was local to a neighbourhood or even a street. The important thing was that the practitioners only performed *ar-ruqyah ash-shar'eeya* – Sharia incantations based on Islamic prayers. Anything else would get them a death sentence and a public beheading.

'Did you tell this guy we were coming?' Ibrahim asked.

'Yes. I made an appointment. And I told him we were police.'

The house was modest on the outside, a simple wooden door with wooden shutters on the windows on both sides. They rang the bell and a servant let them in, leading them into a small courtyard. Thanks to a fountain and some overhanging plants, the air was cool. They sat on a pair of wooden chairs to wait. It was certainly nicer than anywhere else they'd been that day. At least the exorcist was well-mannered enough to let his guests wait in the shade, even if he didn't offer them anything to drink.

'Something's been bothering me,' Daher said. He still had that nervous look on his face. 'If you consider all of the religious stuff going on in these murders, our killer obviously has to be some kind of religious figure.'

'And you're thinking: What if he's an imam?'

'Yeah, something like that.'

'It bothers me, too,' Ibrahim said. 'He's twisted something sacred, which puts him about as far from an imam as you can get.'

'I have trouble imagining it,' Daher said. 'I think back on all the imams and scholars I've ever known, and I can't see any of them committing murder. So I can't see our killer as an imam, no matter how hard I try.'

Ibrahim wasn't sure how far he could go with this conversation, but he decided, since they were on a good footing right now, to take a risk.

'Most imams are not perverts,' he said, 'but whenever you take anything too far, you spoil it. Think about these imams who are completely preoccupied by virtue, so much that they can find a crime in anything. The guys who issued fatwas outlawing women eating ice-cream cones in public, because of the "connotation". Or the sheikh who said that it was unacceptable for a man to sit on a chair that a woman had recently vacated, because her residual warmth on the seat might be arousing. Even if something like that were to happen, does the sheikh really think that pointing it out, making everyone aware of it, is going to control it or make it go away?'

'Everyone knows those guys are nuts.'

'Everyone? Really?'

'OK, but you know what I mean.'

'People buy into that crap all the time,' Ibrahim said with a little too much heat. 'I'm just saying that there are sheikhs who have become so obsessed with virtue that they've turned into perverts themselves. They see sexual innuendoes in the most innocent things.'

Daher was quiet, thinking.

'Maybe there's something bigger that we have to stomach here,'

Ibrahim said. 'Our killer is an extreme person, but as we're thinking about who he might be, we find we can see him in other people. Innocent people. He's making perverts out of us.'

'Yeah. That's exactly what it feels like.'

Just then, the servant returned with two glasses of water.

Charlie sat with her for the rest of the afternoon. As usual, Katya ate a packed lunch, which today she shared with Charlie. A hummus sandwich, some pretzels, cheese sticks, carrots, and a Diet Coke from the refrigerator in the lab. The apple, which they couldn't figure how to split evenly, sat on the desk in front of them.

They hadn't finished with the files in the boxes on the floor. So far only six of them contained crime scene photos showing full-body shots of the victims, and none of the six bodies looked unnaturally posed.

'Here's something,' Charlie said. 'Maybe.'

She passed Katya a photograph of a severed hand. Katya read the report and discovered that it was not a murder case. Twenty-one years ago, a homeless man had found a severed hand in a drainage ditch near the Kandara overpass. He had called the police, who had opened an investigation. Forensics had discovered that the victim had been alive when the hand was severed. They were uncertain, though, whether the hand had been legitimately severed.

When people were punished for theft, their hands were cut off by the city executioner, who used a smaller sword than the one he used to sever heads. The hands were then buried properly under the auspices of the Jeddah police. Occasionally, a person was given a lighter sentence in which he or she was allowed to have a doctor surgically remove the hand using anaesthesia. According to the report, it was possible that the doctors did not always dispose of the hands correctly, and that one of the hands found its way into the city's drainage system. The case itself – which someone had ridiculously labelled *Salem-i-dek*, or 'God bless your hand', a common phrase used to praise a fine cook – seemed to be one of those files that didn't have anywhere else to go. It wasn't a homicide case, but it was unsolved.

The officer in charge, Lieutenant Yasser Mu'tazz, had been

thorough enough to investigate the route of the drainage pipes and to interview all the doctors whose offices might have had some connection to the pipe system. He'd found nothing unusual at any of the clinics, and none of the doctors had ever amputated a hand. He had also talked to the officers in charge of the disposal of severed hands and found their procedures exemplary. The fingerprints from the hand matched nothing in the national database anyway, and the case had been in limbo ever since.

It was odd that Mu'tazz had gone to such lengths when the hand had been found in what was essentially a run-off ditch for those two times a year when it actually rained in Jeddah. Looking at the photograph, Katya could tell that it hadn't rained in a while. The ditch was bone dry and covered in a thick layer of sand.

'This is odd,' Katya said. 'This case is over twenty years old. What's it doing in the recent case files?'

When Katya looked up again, Charlie's face was grave. 'I've found something else,' she said. She had been holding all of the photographs from the case, and she passed another one to Katya. It showed the same severed hand from a different angle. The photographer must have got down into the drainage ditch to take the shot. The ditch itself was about a metre wide. It looked as if the hand were crawling towards the camera.

'Look on the wall behind the hand,' Charlie said, 'or rather, the side of the ditch.'

There was a blood smear there, blackened by the sun.

'Doesn't that look like a letter to you?' she asked.

'Yes,' Katya said. It was definitely not splatter. The edges of the smear were too uniform, as if they had been painted. 'But it's impossible to tell which letter. It could be half of an F or a Q.' The camera's scope wasn't wide enough to capture the whole thing. She flipped the photograph over. There was a faded name and address stamped on the bottom-right corner in an elegant script. *Hussain Sa'ud*.

They studied the rest of the photographs but none of the others showed the blood at all. And for all Katya knew, it could have been a smear of something else. She read through the file again. Mu'tazz made no mention of the blood at the scene. Had they taken a sample of it? Tested it for a blood-type match to the hand? Katya's frustration competed with her distrust. It seemed odd that Mu'tazz would assume that the hand had come sailing down the ditch when it clearly hadn't rained in a while. Odder still that there may have been blood evidence at the scene and they hadn't collected it – at least not according to the report. She saw Charlie watching her, and explained what she could about the case and Mu'tazz's behaviour.

'Maybe he was a rookie?' Charlie asked.

'What's that?'

'A beginner.'

'Ah, perhaps,' Katya said. 'But he was a lieutenant. I wonder why he hasn't said anything about this now.'

'The case *is* twenty-odd years old,' Charlie pointed out. Seeing the look on Katya's face, she added, 'But I know what you're going to say: it's not every day you find a severed hand.'

Imam Abdullah Arsheedy looked like the most normal imam in the world. He had a plain face surrounded by what must have been the religious insiders' secretly-agreed-upon respectable proportion of beard, hair and head scarf. Only his eyes brought the face any distinction. They were slightly too small and sunken, almost ugly, but shining with curiosity.

The men sat in his office, a dark, cool room stuffed with religious textbooks. The air was heavy with dust and the smell of incense. Over tea, they exchanged pleasantries and discussed trivial things, winding their lazy way to the vital parts of the conversation. It was only when they veered into the subject of exorcism that the sheikh revealed what Ibrahim considered to be a touch of madness.

'Magic is real,' Arsheedy said plainly. 'The Prophet himself – peace be upon him – said "the evil is a true reality". He was referring to the evil eye. It is accepted in the Quran that magic exists and that it has its own powers, and that those are real. What the Quran does not accept is the *use* of magic. That is forbidden.'

'And how is what you do any different than magic?' Ibrahim asked. He already knew the standard answer to the question; he just wanted to hear Arsheedy's response.

'With the permissible methods of the Quran and Sunnah it is possible to extract magic from a person after the magic has occurred.'

The sheikh seemed to recognise that Ibrahim was sceptical. He spoke to Ibrahim alone, ignoring Daher completely, and he used the tone that a father reserves for a child when explaining common sense.

'The thing to remember,' Arsheedy went on, 'is that magic only affects a person by Allah's will. It is wrong to believe that something can happen to you and that there is some force greater than Allah, and which He cannot control. Therefore, when someone is afflicted with evil magic, it makes sense that the only refuge from it is with Allah. What I do has no benefit in itself, all of its power comes from Allah.'

Ibrahim had to admit that the sheikh seemed rational enough, except for the small matter of his believing in magic. But arguing about the words of the Quran with a sheikh was never a good idea, especially if you wanted information from him.

'That's very interesting,' Ibrahim said. 'So you must see a number of people who have been afflicted by various types of magic. They may seem, on the outside, to exhibit the characteristics of schizophrenia, for example, or some other psychosis. Do you ever refer them to medical clinics?'

'Yes, occasionally,' he replied. 'Although most of the supplicants come to me after medical science has failed them. They have already tried Western drugs and therapies and those have been ineffective, so they seek direct help from Allah instead. One of the other requirements for *ar-ruqyah ash-shar'eeya* is that the supplicant be a believer, and that he or she believe, as I do, that everything they are asking for is coming directly from Allah Himself.'

'That makes sense as well,' Ibrahim said. 'So would you say that most of your supplicants are especially devout?'

'There are varying levels.' Arsheedy always seemed to be speaking frankly and openly, no matter what he was saying. 'I think that mental disturbances can make people much more receptive to faith. They are in a state of higher need, you might say, and so faith is especially important for them. It is a way of healing the suffering they experience.'

'And what if the supplicant is not, say, possessed by a *djinni*,' Ibrahim said. 'What if he has schizophrenia?'

'All suffering is a kind of evil,' the sheikh replied calmly. 'And

Allah is available to cure all suffering. Perhaps the cure works best in conjunction with medical science, but there are certainly cases where medicine cannot do anything, and an exorcism alone has the power to relieve the spirit of its pain.' He set his teacup back on the tray, crossed his hands on his lap and studied his guests. 'Am I wrong to assume that you are here on police business?'

'No, that is correct,' Ibrahim said. He glanced at Daher, who looked the very picture of an earnest schoolboy. 'We are trying to understand the pathology of a particular criminal we've encountered. He's been killing women, and there are religious references in the way he is killing them.'

The sheikh nodded sternly. 'I am afraid I cannot help you with pathology per se, but I can testify that when a man is truly stricken by evil – either by *djinni* or by the evil eye – he becomes capable of the most depraved acts you can imagine.'

'Yes, I'm sure,' Ibrahim said. 'Presumably even if those acts defile the very name of religion?'

'Especially then,' Arsheedy said. 'I sometimes think that it's the only way evil can truly express itself – that is, by distorting religion. It doesn't surprise me that your killer is using Islam in his perversions. Evil tries to destroy that which is most sacred – and it always fails.'

There was something cold in the man's unwavering belief. 'This may seem a very odd question,' Ibrahim said, 'but do you happen to have any supplicants – either now or in the past – who have lost a hand? Or who were affected by someone who lost a hand?'

Arsheedy considered this and slowly shook his head. 'Nothing comes to mind,' he said. 'I do have supplicants who have lost a hand, but they do not come to me for exorcism.'

'I'd like a list of those supplicants, if you don't mind.'

The sheikh frowned. 'I'm afraid I can't simply give away names,' he said. 'You understand.'

'I'm afraid I can't simply turn the other cheek when a man practises magic in an Islamic society,' Ibrahim replied casually. The sheikh opened his mouth – no doubt to defend himself – then seemed to think better of it. He reached into his desk drawer and took out a sheet of paper and a pen.

180

'Do you ever get scared?' This was Daher. Despite his previous silence, his words provoked no surprise from their host.

'Yes,' Arsheedy said, glancing at Ibrahim, 'it is difficult not to when confronted with evil.'

'So you think of that evil as something separate from the person himself,' Daher went on. 'It must be hard to make that distinction when you've got someone in your office who is losing his mind, who maybe becomes violent.'

'Funnily enough,' the sheikh admitted, 'the violent ones don't scare me. Usually physical violence is the purging of something, or the body's attempt to rid itself of something wicked. The ones who truly frighten me are quiet, austere, but you can see the vast hatred in their eyes. You can feel it, even if they do nothing. You can sense it the moment they walk into the room. Those are the ones who frighten me. It's almost as if they have made an effort to take control of the evil themselves, and in doing so, they have bonded with it.'

Daher sat back, looking uncomfortable. Ibrahim sensed that the sheikh had something else to give them.

'There was a man once who frightened me more than the others,' Arsheedy said, setting down his pen. 'He came into my office with a clinical history of anxiety and depression. His family had always treated him as if he were normal, but his parents were dead and he hadn't married. His siblings lived in Najran, but he worked in Jeddah. I think he felt very alone. He had a job as a Red Crescent responder and he told me that he had been in the back of an ambulance one day with a person who was possessed by a *djinni*. He believed that his problems started that day, that somehow the *djinni* had passed from the first victim into him. He came to me and requested an exorcism. He didn't seem possessed by a *djinni*, but I trusted his word, and I gave him an exorcism. It was a strangely calm affair. But the whole time I had the darkest feelings about the man. I felt that everything he told me was a lie. I can't tell you why, it was simply a feeling. I prayed about it for months, asking for forgiveness, clarity and mercy, but I had nightmares on and off for weeks. The man came back a few weeks later to assure me that I had successfully exorcised the spirit, but I didn't believe him. It still bothers me now, I think, because I don't understand it.'

'What was this man's name?' Ibrahim asked.

'Sheikh Rami Hajar.'

The Records clerk looked about fifteen years old. He greeted Katya with a nervous nod and glanced twice at the ID tag hanging from her neck. The photo on the tag showed the same black head scarf and face he saw before him, but he seemed disbelieving anyway.

'Can I help you?'

'Yes, I'd like to speak to the Records manager,' she said. 'I believe evidence is missing from some of the files I've received.'

The boy swallowed, got up and left the small room. Katya stood at the window, staring out at a waiting room notable for its emptiness. No tables or shelves. Two chairs in a far corner. The records were stored somewhere behind the locked door to her left.

Finally the manager appeared.

'What can I do for you?' he asked.

She handed him two of the solved case files. 'These files were requested for the Angel case for the specific purpose of comparing full-body shots of the victims with the current case. Unfortunately, there are no full-body shots in the files. Could these be copies of the originals?'

The manager frowned and flipped through the files. 'No, they're not copies.'

'The forensic photographers would have taken full-body shots of these victims back in nineteen eighty-nine, would they not?' she asked.

'Yes, they would have. And you're right, they're not here.' He shut the files and passed them back to her. His face hardened. 'You'll have to request a review.'

'A review?'

'Yes. Specifically, your boss has to approve and request a review and send the forms down to our office. Once we receive the forms, we'll look into the matter.'

'How long will that take?'

'We'll get to it as soon as we can.'

'And how long is that?'

'I'm afraid I can't say.'

'You realise this is an urgent matter,' she said, making an effort to soften her tone.

'I understand,' he replied. 'The sooner you can get me those forms, the faster this gets done.'

Aggravated, she turned and left.

Ibrahim found Mu'tazz in his office. It was late afternoon, still sunny outside, but the office had no windows and the lamp was glowing at his desk. Mu'tazz was focused so intently on his reading that he didn't notice Ibrahim in the doorway, and when he did, he shut the folder.

'*Masa' al-khayr*,' Ibrahim said. Mu'tazz didn't reply. Ibrahim laid a file on the desk and explained about the case of the dismembered hand, which Katya had found earlier that day.

Mu'tazz opened the file, took a quick look and shut it again. 'We've had body part cases,' he said. 'What's the problem?'

'How many have you had?'

'I don't keep count.'

'But you've had others?'

'Yes. A leg once. An arm.'

'I never heard about any of them,' Ibrahim said.

'That's because you didn't work here.'

'They may be relevant to our serial killer investigation,' Ibrahim said. 'So I'll tell you what. You pull the files for those cases and put them on my desk by tomorrow morning, and I won't report you for obstructing my investigation.'

Mu'tazz stared at him like a dumb animal.

Ibrahim turned to leave but stopped in the doorway. 'By the way, I've authorised a review of all the case files from nineteen eighty-eight and 'eighty-nine. It seems that none of them contain full-body shots of the victims. It would appear that the photographs were removed from the files.'

'Well, that tends to happen,' Mu'tazz said. 'It's called decency.'

'Destroying evidence is about as indecent as you can get in a records room.'

'Not if the case has been solved,' Mu'tazz replied.

Ibrahim left before he could lose his temper. He went back to his office, poured a hot cup of tea from the electric boiler and tried to forget about Mu'tazz, but it was too late. He'd been caught in the man's orbit. Resentful, inept, using religion as a passport to gain respect from the higher-ups, even as the higher-ups saw the falsity of it. He had heard whispers that Mu'tazz had never been accepted by his peers because he was odd. That was enough. Men always needed weaklings to remind them of their power. There was indeed something pathetic about the man – and, like all things that looked innocent and weak, he could be dangerous. At what point did a man give up his dream of fitting in and begin to plot against those who rejected him?

Ibrahim opened the folder on his desk, the one he'd bribed Chief Riyadh's secretary to procure. It was the work history of Lieutenant Colonel Yasser Mu'tazz.

It was no surprise that Mu'tazz's work history was mediocre. He was thorough and persistent only when it was required and – as best as Ibrahim could judge from the reports – he wasn't the sort to trust his instincts, if he even had them. His reports were about as conventional as they could get.

It was also no surprise that Mu'tazz remained the least respected of the officers in the department. The reviews his superiors had written about him over the years pointed delicately to the fact that he had never made much of an effort to fit in and that the other men found him difficult to relate to. As a result, he had been passed over for promotion four times. None of this had had any apparent effect on Mu'tazz's performance. He continued to work quietly and half-heartedly, no doubt still blindly hoping that someday someone would give him his due.

There was no indication in the files that the man was excessively devout, or that he was the type who would dare to break into the Records room and systematically censor all of the department's solved murder cases that involved pictures of naked women. Ibrahim hoped to catch some subtle whiff of Mu'tazz's personality, at least enough to judge whether Mu'tazz was devious and perverted enough to do something like that. Instead, the thing that stood out in the files was the pure beauty of Mu'tazz's penmanship. It was humbling to compare it to his own scrambled writing. Could you hate a man whose hand wrote such consistently elegant and symmetrical letters? The calligraphy pointed to something much finer in Mu'tazz than he had realised, a striving for purity beneath the laziness that was fouling his work life.

27

After a quick stop at the Chamelle Centre, where for the second time Katya failed to meet Sabria's friend, they were in the car again, shooting down the highway's fast lane. Nayir was watching closely for the hazards there – drivers cutting in without signalling, bored young men pulling whatever stunts they could think of, hanging from car doors, their feet skimming asphalt. The worst, in Katya's opinion, were the cars of young men who pulled so close beside you that they'd take off your side mirrors if you weren't quick enough. They only did it when there was a woman in the car, her window was open, and it looked like they might have a chance to toss onto her lap a weighted slip of paper containing the vital ingredient to any man's future: a mobile phone number where the woman could reach him, should she find him attractive at 120 kph from the chest up. Katya had been hit by these nuggets before. With Nayir, she kept the windows shut.

Nayir, who didn't believe in using the air conditioning, probably for reasons of borrowed Bedouin purity, obligingly turned it up when she was in the car, almost to the point of freezing. During the last month she'd been in his car twice and both times had to ask him to turn it down. She imagined her nipples protruding exuberantly through the thin fabrics of her shirt and cloak – a horror, should he notice. Nayir's gaze was well-managed, but that didn't stop the eye from seeing.

It wasn't getting any easier to be alone with him. They should be eagerly discussing their wedding plans, but they had already agreed to the details. Now the quiet in the car was heavy with worry and awkward glances. Katya's thoughts were consuming her. She worked ten to twelve hours a day, even weekends, with barely enough time to do the shopping, cooking or laundry that her father still couldn't be bothered to do, so much did it offend his manhood. The house was a mess. Ayman would do the dishes once a month, if forced, but for the most part he cleverly avoided Katya's father, who was the only one capable of putting him to work.

What free time she had had mostly been spent hunting down Sabria, processing evidence from her apartment, and scrambling to hide the evidence that might implicate Ibrahim. She was still concerned with tracking down Sabria's friend at Chamelle. And although she was grateful that she was working on the Angel case from the comfort of her mews in the situation room, she had not been relieved of her other responsibilities in the lab. She was still in charge of coordinating the work of the four female technicians, who were, by a generous estimation, suffering from the incompetence and lack of motivation that went hand-in-hand with a job that promised no advancement.

While this mental cacophony was reaching its crescendo, Katya heard the lone strains of self-doubt crying from the distance. She was not fit to be a wife and mother. She and Nayir had already discussed that they would live with her father until they found a suitable apartment of their own – his boat being too small for the two of them. So the marriage was effectively adding the burden of another person to her already frazzled home life. Even once the chaos died down at work, she would still be putting in nine-hour shifts every day. She would probably be sleeping less at night. She might even become pregnant. She tried not to believe that this would ruin her career, but sometimes the thought terrified her.

A series of wedding stores had brought her face-to-face with young brides – pretty, sweet, cherubic things made even more beautiful by the electric mix of fear and excitement in their faces. They gave off the promise that they'd do anything for their husbands. They didn't have jobs. They'd hardly finished school. They were children who were ready to plunge into lives where their husbands' needs came first and nothing else mattered. By comparison, Katya felt like an outlier, one of those women she'd read about in the occasional newspaper article glorifying the Saudi woman's push for independence by showcasing a successful businesswoman or a philanthropist. *Look at this rare specimen who has enough energy to be married, have six kids and a full-time career.* She had often thought that her outlier status might be acceptable to a liberal man – apparently there were some – but was uniquely unsuited to a traditional man like Nayir. And it was only a matter of time before he found that out.

She had admitted to herself, just the night before, that she might have made a mistake in saying yes to this marriage proposal. It was a crushing realisation. At least she still had the chance to stop it before it got any further. Yet of all the horrors she could imagine perpetrating, disappointing Nayir ranked among the highest. It was now a matter of choosing which disappointment would hurt him less. Last night, she had sat by the phone and pondered her options. End it now, a gunshot wound of disappointment. Don't end it now and bleed him slowly for the next few years. And find yourself boxed in, overworked, dreams slipping through the cracks of a fractured life.

Instead, she had called and asked for a ride.

Now they arrived at the home of Hussain Sa'ud, the name that was stamped on the back of the photograph of the dismembered hand. They got out and stood facing an ugly house. It was modelled on a Bavarian castle with sunken windows, brick turrets, and a front door that looked more like a drawbridge. The house itself was too small to capture any of a castle's grandeur. The whole building was painted a blinding white, offset with light blue roof tiles. It reminded Katya of the notoriously tacky Disneyland castle house on Iskandareya Street.

Nayir knocked. A few minutes later a girl no older than six answered the door. Katya introduced herself and asked to speak to Hussain, and the girl went tearing off into the darkened house, shouting for her grandfather. Two young boys poked their heads out from a room where a television was flickering, the sounds of a video game blaring. A woman dashed across the hallway holding a scarf over her head. They waited while cool air billowed out of the doorway.

An eternity seemed to pass before Hussain came to the door. He was a tall man, old but energetic, with a thinning yet still handsome face. He shouted at someone to refresh his tea in the garden then turned his attention to Nayir and Katya. As he came into the light, Katya saw that his eyes were green.

'Can I help you?' he asked.

Pre-empting Nayir, Katya introduced herself. 'I was hoping to talk to you about a photograph.'

'A photograph?' he asked.

She fished it from her shoulder bag and handed it to him. He took it and smiled. 'Ah, yes. This is from one of my unsolved cases.' He flipped the photograph over and saw his stamp in the corner. He smiled wistfully. 'I used to stamp everything,' he said. 'This was before people became terrified of their addresses being known. Back when the city felt safe.'

'You said this was one of your cases,' Katya said. 'You're an investigator?'

He looked taken aback. 'Yes, I was an investigator. This was my case. Where did you get this?'

'From the Chief Inspector at the Central Precinct. The file stated that the investigator in charge of the case was Detective Yasser Mu'tazz.'

'Oh, Mu'tazz was just a small piece of the puzzle,' Sa'ud said, smiling. 'Come in, come in. We'll get you some tea.'

Retired Colonel Sa'ud led them through a sequence of rooms that grew more and more untidy as they progressed to the garden at the back of the house. Here was an arbour of grape vines providing shade, a sitting room of sorts on a concrete patio littered with ornate floor cushions and small settees. The air was cool. Three large pipes led from the house and draped over the arbour, blowing cold air down into the space. Outdoor air conditioning. The ripe smell of *shisha* wafted around them. They were invited to sit. Hussain lowered himself slowly and slid back into his spot, a series of cushions that looked to have permanently moulded to his preferred position, lying on his left side, within arm's reach of the tea set, the hookah rope and a face-down leather-bound book.

Katya sat beside Nayir on one of the cushions and wondered how long it would take Sa'ud to realise that she had no importance in the department, that Nayir was not a policeman, that Sa'ud didn't have to tell them anything.

But even before the tea was served, Sa'ud made it clear that he considered them a welcome audience. 'You didn't know I was in Homicide for fifteen years,' he mused. 'I am seventy-five now, if my mother is to be believed. They didn't always do birth certificates back then. I'm from Mecca, but my work brought me to Jeddah and I've always preferred it here, Allah forgive me.'

Tea arrived with a plate of dates arranged in a flower pattern. Sa'ud began to talk about his life and they found it impossible to interrupt. He had situated them on this strangely quiet patio with no evidence of the modern world in sight, only felt from the air ducts above their heads. It was easy here to slip back to 1934, when his father had bought his first wife at the slave market in Mecca. It was easy to visualise the pirate gang who had raided a small village in eastern Saudi Arabia and brought back the most beautiful woman they could find. Oubaya, Sa'ud's mother, who was all of thirteen when she gave birth to him. He pulled them even further back, to his grandparents, who were Turkish, tall and blond (his green eyes were some mutation of their own sapphire ones), and who had made their fortunes transporting spices across the desert on caravans.

Katya, who normally had no patience for the dragging conversations that were a necessary precursor to doing business with anyone over the age of sixty, found herself perversely lulled into a wonder-world of history. It was Nayir who brought them back to the present.

'Times have changed,' he said with a hint of regret. 'But the hospitality of men has not.'

'No, no,' Sa'ud chuckled, 'and neither has their brutality. What was it you wanted to ask about the photograph, my friends?'

'I was wondering if you might have saved the negatives,' Katya said. 'I would like to see a wider view of the drainage ditch where they found the hand.'

'Oh?' Sa'ud set down his cup. 'And why is that?'

'I believe there may be something written on the side of the ditch.'

'Yes?'

'A single letter, written in blood.'

Sa'ud was quiet for a moment, his face unreadable. Katya felt a twinge of fear, worried that she had offended him.

'No,' he said. 'That is not a letter.' Those strange green eyes flooded with interest. 'It was just a smear of some paint or something. I am curious what makes you think this about a partial stain?'

'We have another case,' she said, 'in which we found a dismembered hand.'

'Are you working on that case?'

'Yes,' she said. 'Under Inspector Ibrahim Zahrani.'

Sa'ud studied her a moment longer and seemed to come to a conclusion. 'Well, then I guess I'd better tell you. The dismembered hand you see here was part of a bigger case. As I mentioned, it was one of my unsolved cases. I am not proud to admit the number of unsolved cases I still have, but in fifteen years in Homicide, I suppose that's to be expected. I used to call this one the Osiris case.'

'Osiris?' Nayir asked. 'The Egyptian god?'

'Yes. If you recall, Osiris was dismembered by Set, the god of the desert. He was cut into fourteen pieces and scattered over Egypt. His devoted lover, Isis, went looking, found the pieces, and reconstructed them for a proper burial. Only one part was missing.' Sa'ud gave a smirk, from which Katya gathered that the missing part would be indelicate to mention.

'The Osiris case began in late nineteen eighty-eight. I was about to retire from police work. I'd spent most of my time doing traffic patrols and working a desk job. I'd had a good career, but I was reluctant to give it up completely because I wasn't sure what I was going to do with myself. I felt I had missed something, some opportunity to be excellent at my job.

'My boss recommended that I take part in a community service project to help young men who were trying to mend their ways. The police had a programme where we took these boys fishing. They were various young criminals who'd been jailed for one reason or another but who were too young to give up on. Most of them were teenagers. The idea was to give them something constructive to do, to get them out of the city to appreciate nature and all that. So a friend of mine, Jameel, and I used to take them fishing every weekend.

'They were a very rough bunch, I have to say, but generally we had no problems on the boat. They liked fishing and sailing. Sometimes we even did a little snorkelling. I really believe that it was good for them, that it kept them out of trouble and gave them a basis for being good men.

190

'Anyway, one weekend we were out on the sea and we were using nets to catch fish. We'd made the nets ourselves, and we threw one out and brought up a whole school of wrasse. We pulled in the net and threw half of the fish back into the sea – we weren't going to eat that many. We sailed for a while and threw the net out again, only this time it got stuck on something. We had a hell of a time dragging it up, and when we did, we found a large wooden box. The bottom of the net was tangled around it. We hauled the box onto the deck. It was very heavy. We had even damaged the net in pulling it up. When we opened the box, we found something horrible. A dead body. It was a smaller person, probably a woman, judging from the robe that had also been put into the box. She had been cut into pieces.

'Naturally, we were horrified. We sailed straight back to shore and called the police immediately. This was before mobile phones. We had to wait quite a while for the officers and the forensics team to arrive. We set the box in the shade of a warehouse right by the marina. It was a big, open warehouse, and all of us were standing around, tired and in shock. We must have waited for two hours before the police arrived.

'In that time, one of the boys fell ill. He'd been slightly unwell when we left the dock that morning, but the combination of sun exposure, heat and activity had made his condition worse, and he collapsed. I saw that he'd become dehydrated. We carried him into the marina's office, where they gave him water and called for an ambulance. While all of that was going on, the police arrived to inspect the box. But when they got to the warehouse, the box was gone.'

'Someone stole it?' Nayir asked.

'Yes, apparently. Although we could never be sure when. With all the drama going on with this boy, nobody had noticed the box. We assumed that's when it had disappeared. The thing was, it was a heavy box. It's possible but not likely that one man could have carried it away, but he would have had to carry it to a car or truck. Twenty people searched the warehouse for the rest of the evening and all the next day, and the box was not there. It had left the premises.

'Over the next few days, the police interrogated every one of the eight boys who'd been on the boat. Each of them had a criminal record, of course, but all of them had an alibi. None had gone missing. None had access to a vehicle with which they could have driven the box away. It occurred to us as well to search the harbour. Perhaps someone had thrown the box back in the sea. It took a few days to get the equipment together to do that, but the box was not there either. Eventually, the police dropped the entire matter.'

'But you found a hand,' Katya prompted, pointing to the photograph.

'Six months later,' Sa'ud said. 'The hand showed up in a drainage ditch in Kandara. Then another hand showed up a short distance away. Mu'tazz was involved in the case at that point. Now Mu'tazz was no expert, but he was young and eager and trying to be thorough. The best evidence of that is that he managed to find me. He discovered that I'd had a similar case, and he contacted me. We linked the body parts, and I took control of the Kandara investigation from Mu'tazz. I explained the story to him. It appeared that whoever had stolen the parts had spread them throughout Jeddah. We found the right foot in al-Balad, a part of the lower torso in al-Aziziya, and so on. Over the next few weeks, we began finding other parts in different places. We didn't recover all of the missing parts. In fact, we only found thirteen of the original nineteen pieces that had been in the box. At that point, everyone began calling it the Osiris case, because of the number thirteen, although I always pointed out that Osiris's body was not complete. Still, the name stuck.'

'Were there any letters attached to any of the body parts?' Katya asked.

'No, but there was a message written at the very end. It was written in ink near the left foot. It quoted the Quran: *We have created all things in order.*'

'Did you test the ink it was written in?'

'Yes, it was standard calligraphy ink, the kind you can buy at any art supply shop.'

'Did the police ever come up with any other suspects?' Katya asked.

'Well, I'm sure you can see the complexity of the situation. On the one hand, they were looking for a thief who had stolen a box full of body parts and directly interfered with a murder investigation. On the other hand, they were looking for a murderer. They did find a thief, or so they believed. There were fourteen boys in the group, but only eight went out on the boat that day. Some officer decided that it *had* to have been one of them, primarily because nobody else knew about the box. I argued unsuccessfully that it couldn't have been one of the boys, because they couldn't have taken the box without me, Jameel or one of the other boys noticing. And the warehouse was open, so anyone could have walked through and seen the box and decided to steal away with it. We could have an opportunistic thief on our hands, a total stranger.

'But the head of Homicide at the time, Colonel Ghamdi, came up with their only working theory, which was that one of the boys had dumped the box into the harbour and then come back the next day with a net to dredge it up and take it home for himself. And indeed, the net we had made for the fishing trip had gone missing the next day.' Sa'ud leaned back and sighed. The cool air from the pipes washed over his face and he shut his eyes.

'So on that basis, the police arrested one of the boys who had been on the boat with us that afternoon. His name was Ali Dossari. The police said they had evidence against him, but I think it was scanty. They claimed they'd found a partial fingerprint on a watch that was found with the dead body. They matched this fingerprint to Dossari's. But I always believed that the fingerprint could have got there before the box was stolen, when we first opened it on the boat. Dossari was right next to me when we opened it.

'All the police really had was a confession,' he went on. 'I say that loosely. You know how it goes. Anyway, they charged him with stealing the box and spreading the body parts over the city.'

'And you think he was innocent?'

'I'm not sure what to think. But he was eventually found innocent and let go.'

'What do you think really happened?' Katya asked.

'I think one of the boys at the marina that night decided to be a nuisance and steal the box. I can't tell you who it was. The sad fact is that we'll never know what happened to the box after that. It was never recovered. Maybe the boy dispersed the body parts, maybe someone else did. It could have been anyone, really. In any case, it ruined our investigation.'

'Did you ever find out who the victim was?'

'No. We were missing the head, so we had no facial reconstruction to go on. We tried matching the victim's fingerprints to some of the missing persons cases at the time but we came up with nothing. I always knew that it would be a hard case to solve, but with the evidence corrupted like it was, it became much harder. It bothers me still, this one. I feel responsible for not safeguarding the evidence as well as I should have. But I also feel frustrated. I've gone back to this case many times and found nothing. The only good thing to have come out of it was that I felt so responsible, and was so annoyed by the actions of the Homicide team, that I started working on the investigation myself. It was the whole reason I got into Homicide in the first place. I spent another fifteen years working in the service, and I can safely say it was the best part of my career.'

Katya digested this quietly. 'Did you stamp all of your photographs?'

'Yes.' Sa'ud smiled. 'You think it's odd now, but we were responsible for all of our work. I liked to keep everything labelled and organised.'

'Do you happen to have any other photographs from the Osiris case?' she asked. 'This is similar to a case we're working on now.'

'Yes, I do have the photos. But if you're thinking that one of those boys may be connected to the crime, you're a few steps behind. I gave the photographs in question to one of the detectives at Central.'

'Oh,' Katya said. 'Who was that?'

'Inspector Mu'tazz. He came to me a little over a week ago.' Seeing Katya's surprise, he added: 'Fortunately, I do keep extra copies of all my photos and files. He didn't need the file – he keeps copies of some of his own unsolved cases. But he wanted photographs. They must have been missing from the file. Help me up.'

They assisted and followed him into the house, through the kitchen where a young woman scrambled to cover her face, and up a long flight of stairs to the second floor.

Katya was still reeling from the news that Mu'tazz had come to see Sa'ud and apparently not told Ibrahim about it. Surely, he must have learned something from the old man. And if Ibrahim knew about this, he would have told her. Wouldn't he?

They entered a clean, well-lit room. The metal desk and chairs, some filing cabinets and a pair of city maps hanging on the wall were its only furnishings. Sa'ud opened the lower drawer of one of the cabinets and withdrew a thick file. Inside were photographs of all the body parts from the Osiris case, and he laid these on the desk. While Katya studied them, Sa'ud went to the map and, with Nayir reading the locations from an old list, placed pins in the spots where each of the parts had been found.

'How much did Mu'tazz tell you about the case?' Katya asked.

'Not much,' Sa'ud said. 'Only that they'd found a woman's dismembered hand on Falasteen Street.'

'We also found a burial site in the desert with women's bodies posed as letters that spelled a message,' Katya said. She told him the message.

He stared, disbelieving. 'You found nineteen bodies in the desert?'

'Yes. And the women were all missing hands.'

'And what was the shape of the site?'

'They were buried in a hexagonal pattern similar to that one.' She pointed to the map. 'Except you only found thirteen parts.'

'That bastard Mu'tazz,' Sa'ud said. 'He never told me anything. You know, I think it bothered him that I took his case, and he's never forgiven me for it. What an old donkey. I take it he's not in charge of this hand case, either?'

'Is that what he said?' Katya asked.

'Yes.'

'No, he's not in charge. And I'm fairly certain he hasn't told the officer who is in charge anything about his visit here.'

Sa'ud gave a hard laugh.

He gave them a copy of the Osiris case file. He didn't want to part with his last Osiris photographs, and he'd already given the spare set to Mu'tazz, so he made photocopies for her. The file itself contained fingerprint analyses from the two hands and reports on the other eleven body parts found. Katya had a feeling that the case file she'd come across at the office had been a copy of Mu'tazz's original from before he'd made the connection to the Osiris case.

'You'll keep me apprised on the developments, of course?' Sa'ud asked.

'Yes,' Katya said, 'I will. But let me ask you one more thing. The boys who were on the boat that day, has anyone—'

'Oh, Mu'tazz said he was going to interview them, but I haven't heard back from him yet.'

*

195

Once they were back in the car, Katya burst out talking. 'I can't believe Mu'tazz didn't tell Zahrani. This may be really important to our case and he's hiding information!'

'That's suspicious, don't you think?'

'Yes, very. I mean, I don't think he's the killer. It's more likely that he just wants to solve the case himself.'

'You know him well?'

The question was posed naturally, but she knew there was a trip wire beneath it. 'I don't know him at all – I've never spoken to him, in fact. But I hear things from the other workers, and apparently he's one of these men who've been passed over for promotion more times than anyone can count, and he's bitter about it. Maybe he thinks that this is his chance to solve a big case, because he knows about the old one. He may even assume that he has a right to it.'

Silence fell. Nayir was struggling with traffic. This time, the only hazard was a man riding closely on their right and attempting to position his car so that Katya could see the placard stuck to his back window. On the placard was a telephone number in large print and the words: *My name is Khaled, call me if you like me!* When Khaled winked at her in his wing mirror, she ignored him. Nayir hooted and the man drove away.

'Perhaps Mu'tazz told Zahrani about all of this, and Zahrani just hasn't told you?' Nayir asked.

'I'm pretty sure if he knew, Zahrani would have told me.'

'You talk to him often, then.'

What could she say? Yes, we meet alone in the third-floor toilets, where he tells me about his adulterous affair?

'Inspector Zahrani has been supportive of women working in the crime team,' she said. 'And it's a good thing. Remember, I was the one who worked out the relevance of the positioning of the bodies.'

'Ah.'

'Thanks to your falcon's eye,' she added.

He nodded to acknowledge the compliment.

'I know you want to do more to solve cases,' he said, 'but it seems to me that the people who solve those cases are mostly men.'

'Yes.'

'And so, to become part of that, you're going to be in closer contact with these men.'

196

'Yes.'

'There are no Homicide teams made up solely of women?'

'No. Just men, with women assisting.'

He fell silent. She looked at him again, hoping to register a flash of affection, something that would soften this feeling between them and remind her why she was marrying him, but his face was dark and frowning.

28

Ibrahim and Daher were in the hallway talking to Chief Riyadh when Shaya came striding up, looking energised.

'I've found something about that name you got from the exorcist,' he said.

'Yes?'

'We have a list of employees from different taxi companies. All the men on the list have a criminal record *and* they live or work near Sitteen. Sheikh Hajar is on the list.'

'Our guy may be a *sheikh*?' Riyadh asked.

'Well, as far as I can tell, he's never worked as a sheikh,' Shaya said. 'But get this – before working for the taxi company, he was an emergency responder for the Red Crescent.'

Chief Riyadh raised a hand and Ibrahim knew he was preparing to say 'Go bring this guy in', but Shaya went blundering on. 'There's more,' he said excitedly. 'Sheikh Hajar's father was imprisoned for stabbing his wife.'

'How did you get that?'

'The precinct that arrested him sent over a file. There's something in the report about Hajar's early home life. His father was totally abusive, used to hang him from the rafters of the house and whip him. The father died in jail. Hajar was raised alone by his grandmother here in Jeddah. Apparently, after the father was imprisoned, the mother ran off and killed herself. A few weeks later, they found her body in Muscat – that's where she was from. I'm still checking the story, but so far I've managed to get a confirmation of the mother's death, the father's prison sentence and his death in prison.'

'What about Hajar's grandmother? Is she still alive?' Ibrahim asked.

'I'm looking into it,' Shaya said.

Chief Riyadh turned to Ibrahim. 'I want this man brought in.'

Ibrahim heard the subtext: *I'm keeping you on this case because you obey me, and if you don't, I'll find someone else.*

'Do we have anything linking him to the crimes?' Ibrahim asked Shaya.

'Bring him in anyway,' Riyadh said. 'I just want you to talk to him. Find out what he has to say about his record. Find out everything you can. He's not under arrest, this is just you asking questions, understand?'

Ibrahim decided not to argue.

Katya knocked and Daher opened the door. She could see past his shoulder that files were strewn all over the office.

'I need to speak to Inspector Zahrani,' she said.

Daher looked annoyed. 'He's busy.'

'It's important,' she said. 'It's about the Angel case.'

Daher went back inside and a minute later, Ibrahim came out.

'I'm sorry to interrupt,' she said. 'This afternoon I went to visit Retired Colonel Hussain Sa'ud. He was the one who took over the case of the dismembered hand that Dr Becker and I found in the old case files yesterday.'

'OK.'

'Back in nineteen eighty-nine, Colonel Sa'ud found thirteen body parts – minus a head – all belonging to the same woman. They were scattered around Jeddah. There's a much longer story behind it, which I won't go into now. It was called the Osiris case. Here's the file.' She handed him a copy.

'And you think this is related to the Angel case?'

'It's possible,' she said. 'The body parts were scattered throughout Jeddah in a shape similar to the one we saw in the desert. But there's one more thing.'

'What?'

'Originally, the dismembered hand case was run by Inspector Mu'tazz. Apparently, Mu'tazz went to visit Colonel Sa'ud last week and got a copy of this file. It includes reports and photographs of each of the body parts. Mu'tazz told Sa'ud that he was going to interview the old suspects from the Osiris case. Did he say anything to you about it?'

Ibrahim simply glowered at her.

'I just wanted you to know,' she said.

29

Sheikh Rami Hajar, the client the exorcist had told them about, was not a sheikh, as Ibrahim had assumed. He was simply a man whose mother had decided to name him 'Sheikh'. Ibrahim had cousins who had all been named for the days of the week, and he knew a boy in school whose siblings had all been named Mohammed, so why not Sheikh? Never mind that it was an insult to the popular under-standing that when a man was called Sheikh, he was either a Bedouin elder or a religious official. Or perhaps he had studied Islam so earnestly as to deserve the honorific.

Mr Sheikh Hajar seemed to be devoting his life to harassing women. He had been reported six times to the Committee for the Protection of Virtue and Prevention of Vice for the crime of 'inappropriate touching'. Having worked as a paramedic, he claimed that he had only touched women when it was necessary to save their lives, but that was not the story the women's families told. One young man – who was, in fact, an actual sheikh – claimed that his mother had been molested by Hajar, who had stuck his hands between her legs and 'put his finger inside her' in the back of an ambulance. Unfortunately, in a traditional court, a woman's word counts for only half of a man's, and since the son had not witnessed the act himself, he was unable to support its veracity. The claim had been dismissed, as had every other one. But one man at the Committee had stayed on top of the trend and eventually filed a report with the Jeddah police, stating that Hajar was up to no good and should be watched. The police were far too busy to bother with an inappropriate toucher, but they obligingly created their first file for Hajar.

A phone call to the Red Crescent revealed that he had been fired the year before for 'inappropriate behaviour'. They declined to specify the behaviour, saying only that Hajar seemed better suited to a profession that did not involve interacting with strange women. To that end, Hajar's superior had promptly recommended him for a job as a taxi driver. The absurdity of this was not lost on the Red Crescent officer, who told Ibrahim, 'Let us say that at least he has a talent for driving.'

Hajar, who had been born and raised in Oman, had moved to Jeddah at the age of fifteen to live with his grandmother. He retained his Omani citizenship but carried an '*iqama*, a Saudi residence permit, so it was easy to find his work history. He had dropped out of medical school and gone to work as a paramedic. After leaving the Red Crescent, he had found a job with the city's white taxi service, which was slightly more upscale than the yellow cab service, but his car was an older Toyota Camry and had no meter installed, so it was impossible to track his movements through the city. Or so the taxi company claimed. He had a mobile phone, of course, and a permit to operate, but no one knew where he went from day to day. According to a dispatch manager at the company's head office, Hajar had a clean driving licence and was considered a good worker.

The second police file on Hajar had one arrest, which had occurred at a Western precinct. Hajar had been charged with assaulting an officer and with 'unbecoming public behaviour'. Apparently an officer had seen him following a woman down the street, shouting at her, standing in her way, doing everything he could to stop her without actually touching her. When the officer tried to restrain him, Hajar had attacked the man, breaking his arm. Hajar claimed that the woman, like a certain number of women tended to do, had hired him for a fare and then revealed, once they'd reached their destination, that she had no money to pay him. It was simple for her, at that point, to get out of the taxi and walk away. It took a certain boldness to go after a woman, especially in a conservative neighbourhood like that one, where the chances of getting caught by the religious police were higher than average. But Hajar had not been willing to let it pass, so he had followed her. Even after being thrown in jail, Hajar remained furious that women should 'get away with such crimes'. Naturally, the woman's name was not on file, but Hajar had told the officer that he often picked up fares at Jamjoom.

On the surface, Hajar seemed like a minor nuisance on the streets of Jeddah, but Ibrahim remembered the strength of Imam Arsheedy's unease about him. Minor crimes sometimes indicated deeper currents. Not to mention that Hajar was a taxi driver who worked near Jamjoom. Looking at the mug shot, Ibrahim saw what Arsheedy had been talking about. Hajar's face was undistinguished, even normal, but there was something off about it. There was a blankness in the eyes, a void deeper than the typical hate-filled mug shot look. It was an animal gaze and belonged to someone unintelligent, not a man who had entered medical school. The police report indicated that he carried drugs on his person. *Chlorpromazine.* Hajar refused to say anything about the medication but his doctor had verified that the prescription was legitimate. A quick internet search revealed that chlorpromazine was an anti-psychotic.

Unfortunately, they had no address for Hajar. Certain neighbourhoods of Jeddah had no postal service, street names or numbers. According to his boss, Hajar lived in one of those. So Ibrahim and Daher sat in an unmarked car across from the dispatch office of the white cab company. Dispatch had called Hajar, asking him to come into the office to pick up a pay-cheque bonus, but clearly Hajar hadn't fallen for the bait because they'd already waited for two hours. Ibrahim knew it was ridiculous that they were doing such lowly work. It was also the weekend, which made it feel even more pathetic. But he was determined to do something.

Daher reached his third cup of coffee before complaining. 'Seems we could get the younger men to do this.'

'We could.' Ibrahim had put all of his attention on the taxis and had kept it there relentlessly. 'But I don't want to leave this one to chance.'

The truth was he was trying to control his anxiety. Most missing persons were found within the first forty-eight hours, or not at all. He should have bowed out of the responsibility for the Angel case – handed it to Mu'tazz, who probably deserved it – and focused his attention on finding Sabria, even if it meant taking time off work. He had no idea how he could have explained that to his family, especially to his brother who would have found out about it. But he should have tried.

He kept telling himself that it wasn't going to do Sabria any good if he got thrown in prison for adultery. If his entire home life got wrecked because his family found out he'd been seeing her. If he lost his job – and thereby his ability to stay informed about the search for her. And yet in quiet moments the truth was unavoidable: he had made cowardly decisions to protect himself, his career and a marriage that had died twenty years ago.

It was killing him that aside from the tenuous link to a strange woman at the Chamelle Centre, he had no leads whatsoever. He should be doing something – anything. Katya called him every day with another disappointing update. He was completely dependent on her, so he forced himself to trust her. Meanwhile here he was, sitting in a car, sipping coffee and doing mindless police work while there was still a chance that she was out there, maybe in somebody's basement prison or storage shed or desert shack, dying if not already dead. Undercover was after her now, too, and Ibrahim could only pray that Ubaid didn't find her first.

'Why did you leave Undercover?' Daher asked.

Ibrahim turned to him. 'They let me go.'

'Why?'

'I didn't follow the rules.'

'What rules?'

Ibrahim sighed. 'I thought it was OK to hire women. I pushed to keep them on the force. I fought with my boss about it all the time. And there were just too many other people in the department who didn't like it and who thought I was improper.'

Daher looked sceptical, as if he knew there was more to it than that.

'It's ridiculous,' Ibrahim went on. 'All this arguing about what women can and can't do is a waste of time.'

Daher nodded. 'Yeah, I just don't think it's entirely comfortable for women to be working so closely with men. It's not that I mind it so much, it's just—'

Ibrahim raised his hand. 'I don't care what anyone's personal feelings are about women, and you shouldn't either. If a preoccupation with virtue starts to get in the way of you doing your job, then something is wrong. And trust me, even in this city, something is always wrong.'

'Nayir has a lot of family,' Samir was saying. 'For example, my cousins and their families will be here for a few months visiting, not to mention friends. And there is Imam Hadi's family to think of. I do feel that it would be rather unpleasant, considering the fact that Nayir is their favourite and he's never been married before, to exclude them from the ceremonies.'

So that was it, Katya thought. The reason she found herself eating an endless dinner at Uncle Samir's house with Nayir and Ayman on a quiet Friday evening. Her father was at home fighting off a cold.

They had finished the meal an hour before and now sat on the patio overlooking a large garden of lemon trees and potted palms. Three of them sat in a row and Samir sat opposite like a judge holding court, albeit a casual, backyard one. He was leaning back, a cup of tea in one hand, a hookah rope in the other.

'I am sure that you have family and friends of your own who would be delighted to come. So I took the liberty of speaking to your father, who assured me that he has plenty of friends who would deeply disapprove if you two were to have a private wedding, without even a reception at which they could celebrate your success.'

Katya was beginning to think that her father had developed a 'cold' to avoid facing this conversation. He knew Katya would be angry that he and Samir had been scheming behind her back. Beside her, Nayir and Ayman sat frozen.

'And of course, your friends from work,' Samir went on, 'will want to share in the happy occasion.'

'Of course,' Katya blurted, hoping not to look terrified at the very thought. The people at work were the last ones who could ever find out about her wedding. She was afraid to look at Nayir, who knew all about the situation.

'We're going to have a small wedding,' Nayir said firmly. 'But you are right that a modest reception afterwards would be a good idea. For the sake of our family and close friends. I'll consider it.'

His tone was meant to end the conversation, but Samir, unaffected by his nephew's stern manner, said cheerfully, 'Well, Katya's father and I have already discussed details, and it is all agreed. We will pay for the banquet and Katya's father will take care of the invitations and phone calls.' Katya knew immediately that this meant *she* would take care of these things. 'We have drawn up a preliminary list of invitees and only need to know if anyone is missing from the list, which is something you must tell us.'

'How many people are on the list?' Nayir asked, looking more ragged now.

'Two hundred twenty-one.'

'*What?*'

'We didn't want to leave anyone out,' Samir said. 'You can make an enemy for life by forgetting a wedding invitation, remember that.'

Nayir looked exasperated and glanced guiltily at Katya. Ayman looked amused. 'I know a good rock band if you want one,' he said. 'Some friends of mine have a band called Silk Slave. They're here in Jeddah.'

Nayir shook his head.

'Don't you worry,' Samir said, 'we've already arranged the music. All you have to do is sit back and relax.'

Katya went home, took a cold shower, and tried to kick her mind into gear. She was numb and exhausted. She climbed into bed and stared at the ceiling with the realisation that she'd just committed to marriage. Not just to Nayir. This was much more complete. She'd committed to two hundred-odd people. And somehow that sealed it.

She drifted into a dream of swimming in the sea. The lightness. The floating. She swam among the bright coral and fish and admired the beauty of the water, the light pouring down, the smoothness of her skin. It thrilled her to be naked. Naked and outdoors. She thought of all the things she admired about herself: the lovely curve of her lower hip, the protrusion of her backside, the biceps that were both firm and delicate. It felt as if all her life she had wanted to be seen in her entirety, wearing skin-tight clothing or nothing at all, every curve of her not just showing, but *seen*, admired. It was the worst of sins, this vain pride, but she allowed herself to revel in every moment of it. She woke up happy and embarrassed.

30

She ran the fingerprints of the Osiris victim without any hope of finding a match. Indeed, there were no hits. More than anything, she would have liked to be able to go down to Mu'tazz's office and ask him what he'd learned in all his interviews with the boys from the fishing trip. Surely something, no matter how frail, would come up in that sort of investigation, some tiny lead worth pursuing. But she was absolutely certain that an impenetrable barrier existed between Inspector Mu'tazz and herself, a lowly lab worker. A woman trying to nose her way into a man's case.

She had given Ibrahim a copy of the Osiris file and kept Sa'ud's copy for herself. The file contained the names of all the boys who'd been on the boat when the box had been dredged up. It occurred to her that she could interview them herself, but there were eight names on the list. A task like that seemed too big. She would have to devote all her free time to it, assuming the men even agreed to talk to her, and was it worth it when Mu'tazz had done it already?

She sat in the lab for three hours before an urgency to leave the building finally got the better of her. Using the cab fare Ibrahim had given her, she went back to the Chamelle Centre, convinced that she would come to another dead end. It surprised her, then, that the barista, Amal, came around the counter to greet Katya and point her to a corner table where a woman was sitting completely cloaked and veiled, holding her shoulders in a dejected way with a cup of coffee in front of her.

'That's the girl,' Amal whispered. 'She came back this morning.'

Katya went immediately to the table. 'Excuse me,' she said. 'Do you mind if I ask you a question?'

The woman looked up at her, a pair of eyes barely visible in the shadows of her veil. She didn't speak.

Katya sat down. The woman tensed.

'I'm here about Sabria,' Katya said.

The woman sat up. Her eyes showed alarm. 'Why isn't she here?'

'I don't know. I'm looking for her.'

'You know her?'

'No,' Katya said. 'I'm doing this for a friend.'

'What friend?'

Katya sighed. 'Someone she loved.'

The girl's eyes showed scepticism. 'What do you want?' she asked.

'I'm looking for Sabria,' Katya said. 'She went missing from her apartment.'

'Are you with the police?'

'I told you, I'm working with a friend. Why were you meeting her here?'

The girl didn't reply.

'Was she giving you something?' Katya asked.

The girl looked as if she might get up.

'Look,' Katya said, 'this may be the only way we can find out what happened to her.'

'I don't know where she is,' the girl said.

'I know.' Katya was feeling exasperated now. 'But if you can tell me what she was doing here, it might help us find her.'

The girl stood up, put her fingertips on the table. Her hand was shaking. 'You people put an innocent girl in jail,' she said. 'Her name is Carmelita Rizal. If you want more information, go and talk to her.' She strode off. Katya got up and followed her.

'Who is Carmelita Rizal?' she asked.

The woman spun on her and screamed, 'Don't touch me!' Nearby shoppers turned to stare at Katya, and she backed away. The girl ran off, disappearing into the crowd.

A quick database search revealed that a woman named Carmelita Rizal was currently being held at the Briman Women's Prison in

Jeddah. Katya went back to Ibrahim's office but the door was locked and the light was off. She didn't even see Daher at his usual spot near the coffeemaker in the hall.

She was ready to go to the women's prison right now. She felt the same urgency she'd had all day, but Ayman wasn't answering his phone, and she didn't have enough money left for a taxi. Besides, she wasn't even sure that she could get into the prison. She needed to talk to Ibrahim. He was the only person who could facilitate the meeting discreetly.

Annoyed, she went back upstairs to the lab.

31

Two plainclothes officers had finally caught Hajar on Saturday morning, when he came to the dispatch office to pick up his 'bonus'.

In person, Hajar was even more disturbing than his photograph suggested. During Ibrahim's previous stint in Homicide, a senior officer had once told him that you could always spot a psychopath because they had too much white showing in the upper part of their eyes. It wasn't an affectation, more of a permanent, even genetic trait. If that was true, Ibrahim reflected, it was probably because psychopaths spent so much time staring aggressively at other people. Sitting across the table from Hajar, that stare made him feel as if he were being eaten.

They'd brought Hajar into the station while the police searched his apartment. He said he rented a small basement room in a building in Kandara, not far from the Sitteen Street Bridge.

Ibrahim began speaking to him.

'How long have you lived in Kandara?' Ibrahim asked.

Hajar didn't blink.

'Is that where you prefer to pick your women up?' Ibrahim waited.

Hajar didn't move.

'You might as well answer. We've got you for murder.'

'It's not right to kill people.' Although the tone had a careful neutrality, he kept that unblinking, shark-like gaze locked on Ibrahim, and he appeared to be harbouring a quiet, deadly rage. Ibrahim understood why Imam Arsheedy had been so unsettled by the man.

He opened a folder and took out two photographs of May Lozano, one showing her alive, the other dead. He laid another photo beneath that. It showed Amina al-Fouad.

'May Lozano,' he said, pointing to the photo, 'was kidnapped by a man driving a Red Crescent emergency vehicle. Exactly like the one parked in front of your apartment building. We found the keys to it in your living room. I find it very odd that you even own a van like that.'

Hajar looked unimpressed.

'Amina al-Fouad,' Ibrahim went on, 'was kidnapped in a taxi in front of the Jamjoom Centre. We know you drive a regular route to Jamjoom.'

Then Ibrahim laid a photo of Maria Reyes on the table. Watching Hajar for a reaction, he was disturbed to see none. 'All of these women were kidnapped from the area around the Sitteen Street Bridge, which is not very far from your apartment.' This wasn't true, but he wanted to see how Hajar responded. Again, there was nothing. 'And, of course, there's this.' He pushed another folder across the table, flipped it open. Hajar's criminal record was inside. 'You have a history of assaulting women.'

Hajar didn't bother glancing at the folder.

'Where were you three weeks ago on Sunday afternoon?' Ibrahim asked.

'I don't know. Probably working.' Hajar's voice was monotone.

'Do you remember any of your fares? Could anyone vouch for your whereabouts?'

When Hajar didn't reply, Ibrahim went on, 'So you don't have an alibi either?'

A light rap on the door and Majdi came in, holding another folder. He bent and whispered something to Ibrahim before leaving. Ibrahim opened the new folder.

'It looks like forensics has already found blood and hair in the back of your van.'

For the first time, Hajar looked smug. 'It's a Red Crescent van.'

'They found it on the inside wall in the back of the van,' Ibrahim said. 'Most victims get put into vans on a stretcher. This blood was nowhere near the stretcher, but it was in the place you might expect to find blood if you bashed a woman's face against the van's wall. It was close to the roof, so she was probably standing. Maybe even fighting back.'

He felt it then, the first tremor of fear coming from Hajar.

There was another noise outside the door. This time Chief Riyadh came in. Ibrahim saw immediately that something was wrong. When Ubaid and two men from Undercover showed their faces in the hallway behind Riyadh, Ibrahim went numb.

With a tilt of his chin, Riyadh motioned him out the door. Ibrahim got up.

In the hallway, Chief Riyadh said, 'Why don't we go up to my office.' It wasn't a question. They followed him silently. Two long minutes of dread formed a strange parallel of disbelief and acceptance around Ibrahim. He knew they'd come for him, that they'd found something. He knew, from the expression on Chief Riyadh's face, that he was no longer in charge of the Angel case. But he couldn't believe it. It seemed ludicrous when they all sat across from Riyadh's desk and Ubaid said, in his delicate, almost seductive voice, 'We've found evidence, Inspector Zahrani, that your relations with Miss Sabria Gampon were much more intimate than you described in our previous conversation.'

'I'm not sure what you mean,' Ibrahim replied. His voice sounded a thousand miles away.

'Well, I'd rather not be specific, but we found ample biological evidence that you were in her apartment within the past month, and that you were, in fact, sharing her bed.' Ubaid seemed angry when he said it, as if having to make a statement like this – even in the privacy of an office – was an offence that Ibrahim should have spared him. *Sharing her bed*. If he weren't so numb, so helpless in his own shock, Ibrahim might have said, 'Actually, I shared more than her bed,' just to see what it would do to Ubaid's grotesque face.

Riyadh's expression showed disappointment and a touch of its own anger. Riyadh was justified in that, at least. He was about to lose the chief investigator of his most important case.

'I think that, as a police officer,' Ubaid went on, 'you understand that it is incumbent upon us to uphold standards of decency – perhaps even more so than other citizens, for we are the law.

'I've arranged for these officers to bring you into custody. Discreetly, of course. And in the name of discretion, we'll be taking you to one of the private facilities near the central office to answer some questions.'

They were trying to avoid putting him in the same building as his brother. Clearly Omar didn't know about this yet.

Riyadh looked as if he might protest, but what would he have said? I need this man – he's the only one who can solve the Angel case? There were other men, probably more suitable than him, if less pliable. A stronger Chief might have slammed down his fist and said with great passion that virtue crimes don't matter when the greater danger to this city was the fact that a serial killer was on the loose. In God's name, could they not wait? But Riyadh was not that man. And who could blame him? What he would have had to go up against was too big for a single person to tackle.

Ubaid stood quickly and motioned to his men. They circled Ibrahim, who stood politely. He considered, very briefly, making a run for it, but the idea seemed ludicrous. He'd been running this whole time, from his wife, from Undercover and its restrictions, from his brother's prestige and what it had done to his career, and finally from the responsibility of finding Sabria. As the men led him out the door, he realised that he wasn't tired of running; it was just that his gut, his trusted instincts, were telling him that the game was up.

32

Sunday morning, Katya walked into the situation room and saw that her desk was gone. The black curtains had been taken down and the poles leaned against the wall. The numerous file boxes and all of the materials she'd arranged on the desk had disappeared completely. She stared in shock.

Gathering herself, she went back into the hall, feeling flushed and vulnerable and angry. She saw a few officers outside Ibrahim's door, but behind her someone called her name. It was Adara.

'I have something in the lab for you,' she said.

'Oh,' Katya replied. 'I'll be down in a moment.'

'Why don't you come down now?'

Mindlessly, she followed Adara to the lift. When they were inside and the door had closed, Adara said, 'Ibrahim Zahrani was arrested last night. He's being charged with adultery.' Katya felt dizzy. 'Apparently he was sleeping with one of his former workers from Undercover, a woman who has since gone missing. Chief Riyadh turned the Angel investigation over to Mu'tazz.'

'I can't—' Katya was almost speechless. '*What?*'

The lift doors opened and they walked out. As they passed by the men's autopsy room, Katya saw Abu-Musa sitting quietly at his desk, reading a book and enjoying a cup of tea.

'Who did this?' she whispered.

'Some men from Undercover,' Adara replied.

'Are you sure it wasn't someone in Homicide?'

Adara didn't reply until they'd entered the women's autopsy room and shut the door.

'Abu-Musa has no reason to turn him in, if that's what you mean,' Adara said.

'Abu-Musa hasn't done any work on this case, has he?'

'No, he hasn't,' Adara said. 'All of the bodies were women and of course he won't touch them. He stands guard to make sure that nobody else touches them either, so I suppose we should be grateful.'

Katya sat down in the room's only chair. 'I just can't believe it.'

'You mean about Zahrani?'

'Yes. He's in charge of this investigation!'

'I know.' Adara leaned against the counter.

'Damn it!' Katya felt herself choking up. 'So that's why they removed my workspace in the situation room. Mu'tazz doesn't want a woman on the case.' She looked up at Adara expecting to see strength in her expression, the kind of look her mother used to give her when she felt sorry for herself. Instead, she saw sympathy.

'I know about Zahrani's girlfriend and that she went missing,' Katya said. 'He had nothing to do with it. He was looking for her, and I was helping him.'

Adara didn't look surprised, just curious.

'We still don't know what happened to her. I managed to track down a woman she was meeting at the Chamelle shopping mall and the woman gave me the name of another woman who is currently in prison, saying *she* could explain everything. I was waiting for Zahrani to help me get into the prison. I still haven't told him about this other woman.'

'Well, you can't tell him now. He's in an interrogation facility somewhere.'

'What going to happen?' Katya asked.

'Apparently they have enough evidence to convict him of adultery. Majdi heard from Osama that the men who are charging him are ultra-religious types who are on a crusade. They're looking for someone to make an example of. He knew them in Undercover and apparently there's some bad blood there.'

'Will they really take him to court?'

'That's what everyone thinks.'

'This is crazy!' Katya put her head in her hands. '*Allah*, I'm not sure I can do this any more. I've been pulling ten-hour shifts, taking files home with me. I know I'm not supposed to, but it's the only way I can get all the work done. I'm trying to take care of the house, my father and my cousin ... I get about four hours' sleep a night. And on top of it all—' She looked up at Adara. 'On top of all that, I'm getting married next month. I know I haven't told you this, and I'm sorry, it's just ... I still haven't found a dress.'

She began to cry. It was so mortifying that she buried her face in her hands. Adara squeezed her shoulder.

'*La hawla walla kuwata illa billa,*' Adara said. *There is no strength nor power but Allah.*

Katya nodded, too overcome to speak.

'And you have His strength.' Adara released her. 'I'm glad you were helping Zahrani.'

Katya forced a smile. 'I'm sorry about this. I shouldn't be crying.'

'Don't worry.'

'You won't tell anyone?'

'Of course not,' Adara said. 'But I do expect an invitation to the wedding.'

Katya smiled. 'It's done.'

Adara handed her a tissue. She wiped her eyes.

'I have to get to the Briman Women's Prison,' she said. 'I know that this woman knows something about Sabria. It might be important for Zahrani that I find out. I just don't know how to get in there.'

'I'm sure you'll need clearance,' Adara said. She turned to the counter and began unpacking a box of supplies. 'I can think of one person who would be willing to give you that right now. But you'd have to tell him what you know.'

'Who?'

'Waseem Daher.'

'You must be joking.' Katya stood up. 'He'd report me as an adulteress just for *talking* to him. What do you think he would do to Zahrani?'

Adara gave her a reprimanding look. 'What do you know about Waseem Daher?'

'He's a jerk.'

'When Daher was six years old, his father died in a car accident because Daher was in the back seat making too much noise.' She grimaced. 'I think the lieutenant would be willing to make a phone call on your behalf, especially if it meant doing something that might help exonerate his favourite father figure.'

Katya sat back down. This didn't remove the sting of her anger. She could already see the smug look on Daher's face when he learned that she'd been booted out of the situation room.

'Did you really have something to show me?' she asked.

'Inspector Zahrani wasn't enough?'

The interrogation room was cold, which would have been a luxury if he hadn't felt so cold himself. A coldness to match the stone defiance in his heart. He wasn't going to tell them anything. And frankly it would be an insult for them to ask. Adultery suspects never confessed. They all knew the state needed four witnesses to prove anything. Four witnesses who actually saw the act. Even now, with photographs and DNA evidence, a judge wasn't going to sentence him without witnesses. That's what *Sharia* said. He could probably weasel his way out of the rest.

At first it was inconceivable that this could actually go to court, but as the hours crept by and the room grew colder, Ibrahim began to realise that they weren't going to question him because they already had everything they needed. They must have bribed or threatened the other tenants of Sabria's building to testify against him. Because Ubaid was determined.

That evening, the guards took him to a holding cell where he was fed a warm meal and given a copy of the Quran and a remote handset that would control the air conditioning. He grew angry then. They had promised him an interrogation. Where the hell were they? The next morning, the guards came back at the first call to prayer to offer him a prayer mat and water for ablutions, which he took. Afterwards, they led him back to the interrogation room, where he waited alone.

The fears grew magnificent; he couldn't seem to control them. He knew they'd found Sabria. She was dead. Strangled, beaten, shot. And they believed he had killed her. They were now assembling the case against him. They would say he'd known about her liaisons with other men. That he stumbled upon her in bed with a john, and that he'd killed her in a jealous rage, then hid the body. Afterwards, he'd lied to the police and, most crucially, failed to report her disappearance. Surely they could see that he didn't report her missing because he was afraid of being accused of adultery?

It would all be making perfect sense to them right now. If you were an adulterer, then why not a murderer as well? His imaginings became so vast that it surprised him to realise, shortly after lunch, that he had absolutely no proof Sabria was dead. That was the problem with fear – it clouded everything. He could never tell if it was the result of something he knew in his gut, or if it was simply paranoia, lodging in the same place from which his instincts spoke. He shut his eyes, tried to relax. Impossible. Was she dead, or was he just in a panic?

He smoked two whole packets of cigarettes and was just gearing up to request a third when the door opened. A guard stood in the hallway. Voices were hushed.

His sister Hamida walked in. He had never seen her at a police station before, which now struck him as odd. She was the type who would go anywhere as boldly as she liked.

She was older by twelve years and more like a mother than his own mother had ever been. She spent her winters in Saudi, usually arriving in October and staying until March. Hamida had married a Palestinian man, who had fathered six children before running off with a younger woman, leaving her to rely on the generosity of her family. So she did, migrating every winter among two dozen homes, staying in each for a week and minding her own business. By imposing herself in short, innocuous doses she had managed to vaccinate everyone against her presence and extend the family's charity for nearly twenty years.

Whenever Hamida stayed at Ibrahim's house, Jamila found something to complain about. But Ibrahim loved her. She was the only woman he knew who didn't give a crap about men or burqas or prayer times or propriety. 'I don't care which direction Mecca is in,' she would say. 'We live on a globe. No matter where I put my head, I'm facing Mecca!'

He stood to greet her, too emotional to speak.

She looked at him with a hint of scorn and said: 'They're letting you go home. You'll be under house arrest, but at least you won't be stuck here. Omar arranged it.'

He knew that, no matter what happened, Hamida was the one

person in the world who would always be on his side. He felt tears in his eyes.

'I told them I'd drive you home,' she said.

He choked out a laugh and hugged her so that she wouldn't see him cry.

The guard came in and made him sign for his belongings, which were only his phone and his wallet. They'd taken away his badge back at the station. The guard escorted them out by the route least likely to bring them into contact with anyone else.

Hamida pretended not to notice his tears.

'I thought you were in Gaza,' he said.

'I just got back today.'

'You're staying with us, yes?'

'Omar first,' she said. 'You know how he gets.'

It hadn't surprised him that Omar had arranged his release, but a knot of dread was forming. He couldn't see how Omar would remain unaffected by all of this. In fact, it seemed possible that the scandal would cost him his job – or at least his position in Undercover. Balancing loyalty to his brother with the need to uphold the standards of virtue in a department increasingly controlled by men like Ubaid would be nearly impossible.

An unmarked patrol car was waiting by the kerb at the front of the building. They climbed into the back. Two uniformed officers sat in the front and refused to look at him.

'Take us to Kilo Seven,' Hamida said haughtily. He almost kissed her.

He didn't dare think of what was waiting for him at home, he simply thanked God for his sister. When her husband left her, she had embarked on the nomad's liberated life. It was sloppy and unstable, but enormously satisfying for everyone in the family. If they ran out of things to talk about, there was always Hamida. Who was she staying with now? Did they give her and the children beds or mats? Were they feeding her? Why on earth did she go back to Palestine? She had a cottage in Gaza on a sprawling orchard, although when they asked her about it, she said she never actually slept in the house. She preferred to unroll a mat beneath the lemon trees. It was safer that way. ('Whoever heard of an Israeli bombing a tree?')

The house was a large part of Hamida's mystique. Any woman who could retain a home in Palestine and manage to live there was automatically ennobled. Every time she went back to Gaza, the women's chatter went wild: Allah, she'll die! She'll get shot and die! They'll be bombing trees next, you just watch! Pity and concern were the perfect balms to the inadmissible fact that they envied her like hell. That Hamida, they'd say, always moving about. Rootless! And now that her sons are grown, she doesn't even have a man in the house, *mash'allah*, she must be lonely! Yet the life pleased Hamida most of all. Ibrahim could think of no better shield to protect him from his family than her shining, thunderous dignity escorting him back to the house.

Daher was not in the situation room. He didn't have an office, only an informal desk in one of the side rooms behind the whiteboards. The desk was empty when Katya peeked in. It was nine in the morning, the place should have been teeming with meetings and rearrangements now that Mu'tazz had taken charge, but only two young officers sat in a cubicle, toying with their mobile phones and looking glum. They ignored her.

She went back to the lab and found Charlie Becker waiting outside the door.

'I heard all about what happened,' Charlie said. 'Chief Riyadh just pulled me into his office and explained that Mu'tazz is in charge of the investigation now.'

'I need to speak to Daher,' Katya said. 'Have you seen him? It's about Inspector Zahrani.'

'No,' Charlie said. 'But I'll help you find him.'

Charlie led her back downstairs to Chief Riyadh's office. She poked her head round the door and the Chief looked up from his desk. 'Yes, Dr Becker.' His voice sounded pinched.

'I'm looking for Lieutenant Daher,' she said. 'He had some information for me.'

'I believe he hasn't come in yet.'

They went back to the main hallway. Charlie headed for the front entrance. There was a security door there that most people used to enter the building. They stood behind it and waited.

Men came in, casting curious glances at them but politely looking away from Charlie's uncovered hair. Fifteen minutes later, Daher arrived with two officers.

'Lieutenant Daher,' Charlie said, 'we need to speak to you.'

He was surprised. The other men left awkwardly as Charlie touched Daher's arm. He cast a disparaging glance at her.

'We need your help,' Charlie said. 'It's about Inspector Zahrani.'

'What about him?'

Charlie motioned to Katya to explain in Arabic.

'Zahrani was arrested last night,' Katya said. 'He's being charged with adultery.'

'I know.' Daher's face went pale. 'What do you want?'

Katya waited for two men to step out of earshot. 'I need to get access to the Briman Women's Prison,' she whispered. 'I need to speak to one of the inmates there. She knows something very important about what happened to the woman Zahrani was supposedly seeing.'

'What?' he said fiercely, stepping a little closer. 'How do you know anything about this?'

'Zahrani knew this woman was missing. They worked together in Undercover. He asked me to do some investigating, because she worked in a women's mall and he couldn't go there himself.' She realised suddenly how feeble this sounded. Ibrahim was conducting a secret investigation? While the Angel case was going on? And he hadn't told his most trusted officer?

'He never said anything about this to me,' Daher said.

'Can you help me get into Briman Prison or not?'

'No,' he said. 'And if you're smart, you'll go upstairs to your lab and get back to work before Mu'tazz finds you wasting your time down here – or he may just decide to fire you.'

Giving Charlie a stiff nod, he walked away.

The police car pulled up in front of Ibrahim's building. None of the neighbours were out, but a few veiled women were talking down the street.

He spotted his brother-in-law's car parked by the front door: a large white 4×4 with red trim and a dented back bumper. Jamila's brother

Rahman was a miserable soul whose single purpose in life was upholding the honour of his family – and that included his sister. The sight of the car made Ibrahim realise how stupid he had been to agree to come back here. This was a prize Rahman would treasure: the wicked sinner returning home in disgrace to face his scorned wife. He would probably have been safer staying at the station.

He had no idea what his family had been told. He wanted to ask Hamida but would have been mortified to hear the truth in front of the other men.

Once they'd all climbed out of the car, Hamida put her arm in his and they went into the building. At least the police hadn't handcuffed him. The officers followed quietly. He wasn't sure what he was going to find, but halfway up the stairs, his legs began shaking. Hamida stopped beside him.

He couldn't focus. All he could think was a single phrase, far too painful to articulate. *Do they know?* He glanced at Hamida but she was still looking condescendingly at the officers who had stopped a few steps beneath them.

Of course they know, he thought. *How could they not?*

One of the doors opened on the landing above and Aqmar came out. When he saw Ibrahim, his expression said everything.

You've disappointed us.

'Auntie,' Aqmar said, giving a smile. '*Ahlan wa'sahlan.*'

She left Ibrahim then, moved past him to greet Aqmar and give him a meaningful look. Two runners passing a torch. She continued upstairs to Jamila's lair.

Aqmar couldn't meet his father's gaze. 'You'll stay with me,' he said.

'I'd better go up and speak to your mother,' Ibrahim replied.

'Uncle Rahman's up there,' Aqmar said.

'Then I'll talk to him, too.'

'They're talking about chopping off your head.'

Their eyes met, and Ibrahim saw his son's fear.

'All right,' he said, motioning Aqmar into the apartment. 'Then we wait.'

33

Verily, We have created all things in proportion.

According to Colonel Sa'ud that was what the delinquent had written in blood back in 1989. It had been bothering Nayir. Sa'ud had quoted the phrase as being, 'We have created all things in order'. But he should have said 'proportion', because that was what was written in the Quran. Once they'd left the colonel's house, Nayir had looked at the photographs from the file the colonel had given them. And indeed, the killer had written 'order' He had misquoted the Quran, not to mention perverted Islam in general, but he had also shown something crucial about himself.

Order.

Nayir had been having strangely unorthodox thoughts. He told himself that this was no doubt normal for a man deeply stressed by an upcoming wedding. He was thinking about God's will. The Quran was clear, again and again, that nothing happens that is not a part of God's will. The obvious question always followed: how could you explain evil? Why would God let a serial killer occur?

In whatever form He will, doth He put thee together.

And the answer most imams would give you was that God had chosen to let some people stray from the path of good.

We broke them up into sections on this earth ... some that are righteous and some that are the opposite.

But that wasn't really an answer. It was simply a logical extension of the idea that God was all-powerful. *Why* had He chosen to let some people stray? The only answer Nayir could come up with these days was that God had never been interested in creating a perfect world because he preferred its imperfections. It was much more interesting. But how could he let something like this come into being? Why, for that matter, did God put up with the Devil?

And yet this killer, who could take pleasure in ripping away a person's safety, honour and finally her life in the most grotesque way, he was preoccupied with order.

He pulled to the kerb in front of the station and saw Katya standing in a thin slice of shade made by the building's concrete awning. Her face was showing. It looked pained.

She got into the Land Rover. 'Thanks for coming,' she said.

'It's no problem. Where are we going?'

'You're not going to like it,' she said. 'I need to go to the Briman Women's Prison. I can show you how to get there.'

Prison? he thought. Some part of him still insisted on believing that she could be a police officer who sat at a desk, wrote reports, and had coffee with other female officers without ever leaving the station. He didn't like the other images that crashed the party: Katya riding in a car with a male officer all day, Katya putting on body armour and loading a gun, Katya sitting across from a brutal killer in an interrogation room. Katya facing down the Devil by herself.

Relax, he told himself. They didn't let female officers own guns or drive cars or even ride bicycles, so what kind of trouble was she really going to get into?

'Is this about the serial killer case?' he asked.

'No,' she said. 'It's about something else.'

He waited, but she was fishing in her handbag.

'You look a little stressed,' he said. She stopped fishing. 'Would you like to stop for some coffee?'

She looked at him wearily. 'No, thanks.'

Was he being paranoid? Every time he'd seen her, she'd been more and more anxious, and he couldn't help thinking that it was about the wedding. That perhaps she was having second thoughts.

'How are things going on the case?' he asked.

'They've got one suspect in custody.' She looked as if she were going to say more but stopped herself.

'Did you find out if Mu'tazz was really hiding the information from the chief investigator?'

'Yes, he was.'

Her clipped answers were making him more nervous by the second. 'And . . . ?'

She sighed. 'It's hard to explain.'

A few minutes later they arrived at the prison. 'Would you mind waiting here?' she asked.

'Of course not.'

'Thanks.' And with that, she was out the door.

'You'll have to forgive me; we're redecorating some of the rooms.' The prison head was a woman named Latifah Matar. She was short, compact, all swift movement, self-assurance, and a sensible, confident manner. She reminded Katya of long-ago primary school teachers, women as comfortable being punitive as they were exposing their tender sides. There was a large splash of grey paint on Matar's forearm, which had smeared onto her cloak and which she was now attempting to scrub clean with a wet paper towel.

'Good enough,' she said, rolling down her sleeve and motioning Katya briskly out the door. 'Come with me.'

Once Katya had explained that she worked in Homicide and was there about a minor forensics matter on one of their old cases, she had had no trouble getting permission to speak to one of the prisoners. In fact, Matar had welcomed the opportunity for a prisoner to interact with a woman 'who had her life together'. At a security station they encountered a female prison guard whose nametag read 'Warda'. She was over six feet tall and built square enough to pass as a man. She nodded phlegmatically as Matar led Katya through the gate.

The corridor was full of wonders. On the left was a giant studio littered with easels, palettes and dirty smocks, walled in by large paintings of flowers, machinery and strange human-like forms. There was a reading room there, with books and tables where women could write. On the right they encountered a beauty studio. Through the window in the door Katya saw a row of empty hairdryers and six women painting nails and cutting hair.

'I didn't know you had a salon,' she said.

Matar seemed to find her reactions vaguely childish. 'Yes,' she said.

'We believe it's important to give the women skills they can use when they get released.'

Katya was now doubly impressed.

'I tell the Ministry all the time that you can't put a woman back into society unless she can take care of herself,' Matar said. 'Most of these women need rehabilitation. They've been neglected. They have no education. And, frankly, work keeps them out of all kinds of trouble. Aside from the salon, and the literacy and art classes, we run a whole nurses' training school here as well.'

Suddenly the wail of a baby broke through the air.

'And, of course, there's the nursery.' They had stopped at a windowless door. 'This is where we'll find Miss Rizal. I'm going to ask you to wait here.'

Katya nodded mutely.

She wondered if whoever organised this place hadn't read the sign outside stating that this was a prison.

Shortly, the door opened and Matar came back out. 'Miss Rizal will be happy to talk to you,' she said.

'Oh,' Katya said. 'Well, that's very nice of her.'

'Miss Hijazi,' Matar said sharply, 'we like to give our women a sense of responsibility. Most of these women have made moral mistakes. They're not defective, and there's nothing inherently wrong with them. If they believe that about themselves, then it's only because someone else made a mess of their heads. So we try to teach them to respect themselves and others.'

'Yes, *sa'eeda*,' she said sheepishly. She hadn't meant the comment to be sarcastic.

'Very good. Now let me take you to the interview room.'

Mu'tazz would have giggled gleefully to see it: Ibrahim locked in his son's sitting room with the sounds of his wife's wailing coming through the ceiling. The imprisonment was just as strict as it had been at the interrogation facility. Here he was not allowed to use a mobile phone. Anyone who came into the house was searched. Poor Constance was so intimidated by the guards at her front and back doors that she refused to leave the apartment. Aqmar, on the other hand, had left and not returned. Ibrahim felt ruined.

It was just before *Dhuhr* prayer. He was sitting on the sofa, list-lessly watching Al-Jazeera, when he heard a noise outside the front door. The guard was saying something. Ibrahim looked through the peephole and saw Saffanah in the hallway. She was standing a mere foot from the guard, her head tilted slightly down and to the left, like an animal indicating its intention to move in one direction.

'No one is allowed in or out unless they've been searched,' the guard said for what must have been the third time, judging from the strains of annoyance in his voice. Yet Saffanah inched closer. The guard was trying to make it plain that she was not allowed inside because there was no way he was going to pat down a woman, and Saffanah was making it equally plain that she was heading into Aqmar's apartment, and that there was absolutely no way she would let a strange man touch her. She wouldn't even speak to the man. A pat-down would be unthinkable.

Ibrahim opened the door. The guard turned. And Saffanah darted into the apartment.

'Hey!' the guard shouted.

Ibrahim raised his hands. 'She's my daughter-in-law. She's a bit eccentric.'

The guard was furious. 'I'm going to have to report this.'

Ibrahim shut the door as the man was reaching for his phone. The guard stuck his foot in the door and kicked it open. He stood in the doorframe, phone to his ear, glaring at Ibrahim and Saffanah. 'She'd better not have a mobile,' he said.

'Don't worry, she doesn't believe in mobile phones.'

The guard moved his conversation into the hall and Ibrahim shut the door. The guard must have been living in the lining of Ubaid's sphincter. Ibrahim couldn't imagine a normal duty officer acting so rigidly about something like this. Then again, he had never been a prisoner before.

Saffanah was standing in the corner of the room by the sliding glass door that led to the balcony.

'What's going on?' Ibrahim asked. He'd just spent a few hours moping about and saturating every cell in his body with enough caffeine and nicotine to make him radioactive. He wasn't sure he had time for this little drama.

'I'm sick of being in the apartment alone,' she said.

227

She went to one corner of the sofa and sat. After a while, he took the other corner, put his feet on the coffee table and lit another cigarette. When Constance ambled in a while later, she greeted them and looked like she might offer tea, but then seemed to decide it was a bad idea. Ibrahim felt pathetic. Eventually Constance left them in silence, two broken-hearted people propped up on a couch.

On closer inspection, the building wasn't so glamorous. The visiting room was small and reeked of industrial detergent and floor wax. Carmelita Rizal was sitting on a sofa. Her son – probably two or three years old – was settling back into sleep beside her, his head on her knees. Rizal had a model's face – high cheekbones, full lips and big almond-shaped eyes. She was Asian, Katya guessed Filipina. She wore a long black cloak and a head scarf. Her son was wearing a pair of khaki trousers and a white shirt. Something about the outfit suggested government-issue. Katya found it depressing.

Katya sat in a metal chair. On the coffee table between them was a women's magazine and a small basket of faded plastic flowers.

'Miss Rizal,' Katya said, 'thank you for seeing me. If you don't mind, I'd like to ask you some questions.'

Rizal was making an effort to appear brave. 'What's this about?'

'I'd like to ask you about a woman named Sabria Gampon.'

Rizal tensed and gave her son's shoulder a squeeze.

·'Do you know her?'

'Hmm.' She nodded. 'We used to work together.'

'Where was this?'

'We worked in the same house.'

Katya shook her head. 'Can you explain that a little?'

Rizal gave a nervous exhalation. She began rocking her knees. 'Well, we both came here thinking we'd been hired as housemaids. Our employer was a man named Mahmoud Halifi. He is actually a criminal who brings women to Saudi and then sells them as domestic workers to rich men who want sex. For some reason he decided to keep Sabria and me in his own house. I guess he liked us.' The disgust showed plainly on her face. 'In a situation like that, you rely on each other. We became very close.'

Sabria was beautiful as well, and Katya could imagine how a

scumbag like Halifi would want to exploit the women's stunning looks.

'We lost touch for a while,' Rizal went on. 'She disappeared one day. I never knew what happened to her. Halifi told me he'd sent her back to the Philippines. I didn't believe him, but I had no way to find her. I began to think she'd really gone back.' She gave a sad, self-deprecating laugh. 'It turned out she had run away. Halifi moved to a different house. She said later that she came back to find me, but we'd already gone.'

'How did you find her then?'

'I ran away. I did what Sabria did. I went to Kandara. I was living under one of the bridges there, asking everyone about her, but nobody knew who she was. Then I got thrown in jail.'

'And may I ask,' Katya said, 'what are you here for?'

'Stealing and assault,' she said plainly. 'I couldn't find a job. I couldn't get a visa to leave the country, so I was stuck here. I had no family. All my family is in the Philippines. I was living on a pavement. We had to eat.' Her son stirred and she rubbed his head gently. 'Someone caught me stealing and I stabbed him.'

'How long have you been here?'

'Three years,' Rizal said without much bitterness. 'This is my last month.'

'How old is your son?'

'Three. He was born just before I came here.'

It was breaking Katya's heart to think that the boy had only ever known the inside of a prison. 'So how did you find Sabria?' she asked.

'She found me. One day, she came here. Someone who had heard me talk about her at the bridge finally found her and told her about me. It was amazing. I was so happy to see her I cried the whole time.' She laughed at the memory. 'Has something happened to her?'

'She's gone missing,' Katya said.

Rizal nodded. The smile disappeared. 'I knew something was wrong.'

'Why is that?'

'I haven't seen her in a month. That's a pretty long time, even for her.'

Katya explained about the accusations being levelled against

Sabria by Undercover. 'I met a woman at the Chamelle Centre who said that you might be able to explain some of the activity in her bank account. It might help exonerate her from these charges.'

Rizal laughed, and then she became steely. 'How do I know that's true? Maybe Sabria is in prison right now, and you're asking me to say something that's going to be used against her.'

'That's not why I'm here,' Katya said. 'The man she loves has just been arrested for adultery. If we can't prove that Sabria isn't a prostitute, then Ibrahim is going to be charged with being her pimp. If that happens, then the man your friend really loves is going to have his head cut off and we'll still be no closer to finding Sabria.'

'He wasn't her pimp,' Rizal said, sounding offended at the suggestion. 'Halifi was a pimp. Why don't they chop off *his* head?'

'If you can tell me what Sabria was really doing, it would help to clear her name.'

Rizal sat back, a look of dismay stealing across her face. 'Maybe not.'

'OK, even if she was doing something illegal,' Katya said, 'I bet it wasn't worse than prostitution – at least, not in the eyes of the law. And believe me, I will try to protect her in every way I can.'

Rizal didn't reply.

'I know this might get her in trouble,' Katya went on, 'but it may be the only way to find her. At the very least, it will help clear Ibrahim's name, and I think that's what Sabria would want.'

Rizal pondered this for a few more minutes and then nodded. 'All right,' she said. 'There are women at Kandara, see. Filipina girls, some Indonesian girls, who are like me. They've been raped. They've been beaten up. They've been treated so badly that sometimes they try to kill themselves, you know?'

Katya nodded.

'Every once in a while, somebody gets smart. They find out where this abuse is happening and they catch it on video. And then maybe they use the video to force the employer to let the woman go free – and pay for her to live by herself, so she doesn't have to worry about money any more.'

'Are you saying that Sabria was blackmailing an employer?' Katya asked.

'I'm not saying anything,' Rizal said. Her son began stirring. He rolled onto his back and his head slid off her lap. 'She was smart about money. And she cared about other people more than herself.'

'And the woman at the mall,' Katya said, 'she was getting money from this?'

Rizal tilted her head. 'I don't know who that was. But yes, Sabria was meeting women at the mall, and they knew about this.'

'Did Sabria keep the videos of the rapes?'

Rizal narrowed her eyes at her. 'There are back-ups,' she said. 'In case something happened to her.'

'I need to see the videos,' Katya said. 'They may be able to tell us who kidnapped Sabria.'

Rizal debated a moment longer then said, 'Do you have a pen? Write down this number.' Katya scrabbled in her bag for a pen and wrote the number on her hand. 'That's an IP address,' Rizal said. 'The tapes are stored online. Here is the log-in code.' Katya scribbled more numbers. 'Look at the site. You can see for yourself what horrible things these people have done.'

Nayir had never spent so much time quietly dying anywhere. The fact that it was happening in the sitting room of Katya's apartment only made it worse. It stirred all the memories of the last time he'd been there, when he'd waited for Katya's father (a man he hadn't met until then) so that he could ask for her hand in marriage. This new agony was no weaker. Fear was spilling over its barriers, heated by invisible toxins, preparing to contaminate everything.

Finally, the door opened and Katya came in.

'I'm wondering if you could give me another ride.' She shook her head helplessly. 'My cousin is still out.'

The highway's rhythm was soothing. She must have sensed that he was getting tired of being her chauffeur because she'd been squirming for the past fifteen minutes, chewing her fingernails and biting her lip. His more cynical friends had warned him about this. That getting married was conscripting yourself to servitude. You thought you were signing up for love and sex, but you were also signing up for giving them rides, for waiting in the food courts of shopping malls, in the sitting rooms of doctors' offices, in the queues at restaurants where they were not allowed to sit. You were signing up to spend a majority of your income on feeding, housing, clothing and pleasing the woman you married. In other countries, the financial burden could sometimes be shared. In other countries, women could drive themselves places. But here, well, you did everything for your wife.

'Nayir,' she said, her voice cracking a little, 'I don't think this is going to work.'

He surprised himself by pulling gracefully in to the slow lane and onto the road's hard shoulder. Only once the car had stopped did he feel the shaking deep in his spine. All the energy in his body vibrating from the sharp, sideways blows that lovers administer with the most delicate brutality.

The car's interior was dim, but he could see that she was upset, eyes filling with tears.

'What's wrong?' he whispered.

'There are all these things that I can't tell you about, because I'm afraid you'll disapprove.'

'Like what?'

'Things at work.'

'Tell me.'

She was quiet for a very long time.

It suddenly seemed ridiculous. They were going to end this because of her job? What could she possibly tell him? He felt he could forgive anything except the abrupt, inexplicable death of their plans.

'Just tell me,' he said gently. 'I'll try to understand. Because you're right. This won't work if we can't be honest with each other.'

She nodded reluctantly and began to explain about her behaviour at work: sneaking around, stealing files, surreptitiously copying photographs. She told him how difficult it was to go into the situation room when the men were meeting there, but how she forced herself to be brave so she could get information. She described the way she had presented her theory about the Angel killer working in the city, and she told him about the cloister they'd set up for her in the situation room, and about how that was gone now. He tried to focus but his mind flashed with confusion: this was getting in the way of their marriage? *This*?

Then she got to the part about Ibrahim Zahrani and his illicit lover and her attempts to help him find her.

'I was going to tell you,' she said quickly, seeing the shocked expression on his face. He tried to reassemble it and found that he couldn't. 'But it's dangerous information. And honestly, I wasn't sure how I felt about it myself. I know it's wrong. It's very wrong what he did. But this woman is missing and he needed a woman's help to find her and, well, we work together. So he turned to me.'

Then she explained the rest – that he'd been charged with adultery and was now under a very strict house arrest, in which he wasn't even allowed to use a mobile phone. That she'd gone to the prison to flush out Sabria's secrets and that she'd discovered the blackmail there.

He knew he was upset. It was upsetting. She had been hiding things from him and acting inappropriately. But the only thing he could really feel in that moment was a spurt of anger that everything they'd been trying to build, the whole delicate structure, might come crashing down because of the depravity of a total stranger. It bothered him to think of her keeping all of this hidden, but what bothered him more was the realisation that she didn't trust him. That she had been concealing her activities at work. That she feared his judgement.

She was looking at him now.

'I'm glad you told me,' he said. 'I don't like that you're working in secret with an adulterer. But a woman is missing and you want to help her. That's brave of you.'

'Yes, I want to help,' she said. 'I also want to be *able* to help.'

They were quiet for a long time. She was saying: *I want to be able to do these things – to talk to strangers and keep secrets with adulterers and dash into prisons. I don't want you to think less of me for doing them.* He didn't know what to say.

They were both in shock. There was more to be said, but it was getting to the hour where it would be inappropriate to show up unannounced, so he pulled back into the traffic.

The smoke had become so heavy in the apartment that Saffanah's eyes were turning red. Out of respect for her condition, Ibrahim had moved his self-destruction to the balcony.

It had been decided that afternoon that Jamila's family would be pressing charges. He was going to be tried for adultery crimes. He had been suspended from the police force pending an investigation

233

into his activities. They had already cut off his balls, now they were gearing up to cut off his head. And for what? For his pheromones, his chemistry, his sense of smell. For the way his heart beat hard in his chest when Sabria walked into the room. All those years he had quietly pined for her, all those years he believed he would never stand a chance, that he'd been saddled with Jamila and there was no way out. Until the day before Sabria left Undercover when he had raised the nerve to ask her – *Do you want to take a walk? Just to the kiosk. Let's get a Pepsi.* And she had said yes.

He wished Zaki would come home. No one knew if the boy's absence was because of Saffanah or because he'd discovered what his father had done. Ibrahim suspected the former. He felt the need to explain himself, and somehow he wanted to explain to Zaki more than anyone else. Hamida was upstairs managing Jamila and her brother, but even she hadn't been able to stop them from calling in the lawyers.

He couldn't believe they were going to do it. They were actually going to take him to court. Surely Jamila was living in a fantasy believing that this would soothe her anger. She'd get over it eventually. But with her brother goading her, it was no longer just about her feelings. It was about her brother's honour. And the kids? What would this do to them? He feared that in the end they would blame him. Now that the frozen block of their marriage had thawed, a gushing antagonism would run down the mountain, pure and cold and roaring with deadly force.

He was still on the balcony when a Land Rover pulled up in front of his building and Katya and her husband got out. He whistled and they both looked up. He motioned for them to stay there while he went back inside, found paper and wrote a hasty note, then tossed it down to them. She caught it and read it.

Nayir wondered why she'd told him all of this now.

Just before they'd pulled onto Ibrahim's street, she'd said, 'I may need you to convey this information about the blackmail to Ibrahim. Everyone at the station is saying that he's being held in a room without access to a telephone. That sounds a little extreme to me, but I have no idea what's really going on. I also don't know how segregated his household is. I suspect it's not, but you never know. It may be

234

doubly awkward if an unescorted woman were to show up. And obviously, I can't tell his family what I know.' She looked at him uncertainly. 'I may need your help.'

Need. Nayir felt the weight of that word. She needed him. She was going to need him for quite a long time. And now, in the aftershock of the conversation in the car, he wasn't sure he was up for it.

The note Ibrahim had dropped from the balcony said: *Tell my brother I need to get out of the apartment for a while. He lives next door.* So they'd gone to Omar and introduced themselves and explained that they were there on police business. They didn't say what the business was, and Omar didn't want to know. Katya simply showed him the note and said, 'Your brother wants a break from the apartment, if possible.'

Omar had escorted them back to Ibrahim's house and led them to the roof. They waited in the stairwell. Omar went back downstairs. They heard him arguing with the guards to let Ibrahim sit on the roof. Just for an hour. He needed some air. Even prisoners got to walk in the open once a day.

After arguments and phone calls and tedious bureaucracy, Ibrahim came around the turn in the stairs with a young woman beside him. She was completely veiled.

'This is my daughter-in-law, Saffanah,' he said. 'She needs some air, too.'

When they opened the roof door, they were hit by the noise of thirty children – his grandchildren, their cousins and second cousins. All the children whose parents were downstairs comforting the wife and deciding Ibrahim's fate. The children briefly registered their arrival. The boys were furiously engaged in a game of football and the girls were playing with a skipping rope, squealing or clumped in secret corners.

The adults sat on a carpet by the southern wall. There were cushions and a dirty tea set and ashtrays stacked beside a cold hookah. Ibrahim sat with his back to the wall. Nayir and Katya sat across from him. Saffanah knelt, picked up the tea set, and carried it downstairs.

The children weren't curious about Ibrahim, but they were struck by his guests. The minute Nayir and Katya sat down, the girls began to sneak closer. There were four of them at first. Ibrahim invited the youngest one to sit on his lap. His other granddaughters sat beside him, ages two, three and four, staring up at Nayir. Ibrahim explained that their mother – his daughter Farrah – was staying at the house for a few weeks. Saffanah returned with a lit hookah and Ibrahim took it gratefully. She went back downstairs.

Nayir studied Ibrahim. It seemed impossible that a man with such bounty – this enormous extended family, all these wonderful grand-children, the joy of this scene – would turn his back on his wife and cheat with a woman from his work. Yes, perhaps the marriage had gone sour and he'd fallen for a younger beauty. But had it been worth committing one of the greatest sins – and one of the most serious crimes? Nayir chalked it up to selfishness, a foolish dissatisfaction with all that he had here, and not a little cruelty. And yet in Ibrahim, he sensed no foolishness or selfishness, just tragic despair.

Saffanah came back with tea for the adults and biscuits for the girls. Katya seemed uncomfortable. She wanted to talk to Ibrahim but couldn't bring herself to say anything important in front of the children. While she attempted to make small talk, Nayir watched the kids play. It wasn't often that he could sit somewhere and stare at children without appearing creepy or improper, but children were all he thought about these days. He saw them everywhere, whole flocks racing through grocery stores, picnicking on the Corniche, piling into minivans and screeching at the funfairs. It had come to feel like God was inviting him into this world, saying, *This is what you shall have.*

The excitement and anticipation had been a glowing core inside him. He imagined his own children, how they would look, what their names would be, their personalities. And he wondered how they were going to raise those children. It had become clear to him over the past few days that he was going to have to do a lot of the work. Katya would be at the station all the time. He'd be the one to pick the kids up from school, cook their dinners and put them to bed. That was not the set-up God had intended, but it was going to be the thing that actually worked, and he suddenly wanted to tell her that: *I'll do whatever it takes, if you'll give me this.*

Ibrahim began to smoke. His granddaughters slipped around, fidg-eting, and one of the girls slid into Nayir's space. The others followed. The smoke from the hookah was blowing in their faces. Two planted themselves at Nayir's knees, one of them holding a

236

Barbie, the other holding a plastic toy phone, which she used to touch the sole of his sandal, probingly, to see if he would react. Finally, one plucked up the courage to slide into his lap. Ibrahim frowned at her, and she ducked her face in her hands. Then she looked up at Nayir, saw that he was fine, and settled in. He was afraid to touch her at first, but when she slid backward into his arm, he had no choice.

'Their father is in Dhahran,' Ibrahim said. Nayir understood what he meant: *They miss the comforts of a man.*

The night sky emerged, faintly, while beneath it the city shone. As the neighbourhood darkened and the hookah coals burned out, the children grew tired and began, finally, to listen to their mothers, who had come upstairs intermittently, stood inside the rooftop door and called to them: *Come in, it's time to leave.* The children had blithely ignored them, knowing the women wouldn't come out while Nayir was there (although Nayir suspected, from Ibrahim's disturbed face, that they were avoiding him as well).

The girls went down first, sliding out of his lap, saying goodnight, and nodding when their grandfather told them to listen to their mothers. The boys went with much more prodding. Finally, the rooftop was empty and Ibrahim put the hookah rope aside and said, 'Whatever you've come to tell me, you can say it.'

Katya glanced at Saffanah.

'She's fine,' Ibrahim said. 'I take it this isn't good news, or you would have spoken up before now.'

'It's not horrible news,' Katya said. She explained what she'd discovered at the women's prison. Ibrahim, who until then had seemed resigned to defeat, sat up with more interest.

'Did you go to the website and look at the videos?'

'Yes,' she said, glancing at Nayir. She hadn't given much detail about the videos in the car, and she seemed embarrassed now, from which he gathered that they were obscene. 'The problem is,' she went on, 'I don't recognise any of the men.'

'I need to see them.'

She took out her mobile phone. It had a touch screen and she fiddled with it for a moment before handing it to Ibrahim. He sat up, fumbled automatically for reading glasses that weren't in his pocket, then held the phone at a distance, squinting.

Horrible screams shot out of the little speaker. Katya leaned over to turn the volume down. Ibrahim barely noticed. His attention was riveted on the screen. Nayir couldn't help glancing at the screen himself, but the angle made it difficult for him to see, and anyway all he could think about was Katya watching the video. Katya seeing a woman being raped by a stranger. He understood then that *this* was the cold reality of her job.

Ibrahim set the phone on his lap. Saffanah, who had sat this whole time in the corner, so no one would be tempted to drag her into the conversation, was now staring intently at Ibrahim through a very narrow slit in her burqa.

'Do you recognise any of those men?' Katya asked.

'Yes,' Ibrahim said. His hands were shaking. He looked amazed. 'Yes, I do.'

34

Fouz Ubaid, the hypocrite who had spent so much time persecuting Inspector Zahrani, sat rigidly, his shoulders square, his hands folded neatly on the table in front of him. The interrogation room was quiet. He'd been alone since the guard had brought him in two hours ago.

They didn't have to charge him or give him access to a lawyer, but through the one-way mirror, Katya could see that he was already preparing his own defence. Something happened to a person's face when they began to justify their worst behaviour, a complex arrangement of righteousness and defiance, calculation and a tinge of fear. It wasn't impossible that he would defend himself. Yes, they had him on film raping a young housemaid. She'd been restrained with ropes. When she began screaming for help, he'd taped her mouth. It seemed obvious that the woman was not a willing participant.

Yet the first thing Ubaid had said when they'd brought him into the room was: 'She wanted me to do that. It was a mutual arrangement.'

That was all it had taken to stop the legal machinery.

The woman's complicity was a crucial question. If he was telling the truth, and this had been a consensual, if violent, act, then the toughest sentence Ubaid faced was ten years in prison and a thousand lashes. He wasn't married, so it wasn't a matter of adultery. He would only be charged with the crime of 'illegal sex'.

But if it could be shown that he had forced himself on this woman, then he'd be facing a charge of rape, which would be punished by public beheading.

It was going to take a lot to prove rape, especially after the notorious Qatif case. The woman who had been gang raped in the city of Qatif had been punished along with her rapists because a judge had decided that she'd gone willingly to meet the men who had raped her and had thereby broken one of the tenets of civilized society: that women do not interact with strange men. All of them had been punished for illegal sex, although the men had not been prosecuted for rape. Because of the exposure that case had brought, it was easier for men to feel confident in claiming consensual sex, knowing how hard it would be to prove rape – and how difficult it was for a woman claiming she'd been raped to avoid punishment herself.

The burden was now on the investigators to prove that Ubaid had been actively stalking his victim with the intent of raping her. Katya's first thought was that it would be possible to do this by proving that someone had used the tapes to blackmail him, *and that he had paid the blackmailer*. It suggested an acknowledgement of his own guilt. But looking at him now, she saw how squirrelly he was. He could claim that he'd paid a blackmailer merely because the footage was embarrassing, because it might have interfered with his career, and because it was, after all, illegal sex. It still didn't mean he had committed rape.

Anyway, the case wasn't going to be handled by Homicide. They were far too busy with the Angel murders to spend time searching for an unidentified Filipina girl while trying to build a rape case against a senior officer from Undercover. Even if they did find the girl, and she had the nerve to say that Ubaid had raped her, she would still have to justify what she had been doing alone with him in the first place. If she claimed that he had abducted her, she would have to prove it – with tangible evidence. And that was nearly impossible to do. With no evidence, it would come down to her word against his.

Perhaps Ubaid had thought this through already, but it didn't appear so. He looked to be working it out. So Katya was here now, watching expectantly, hoping that for the short while that Homicide still had possession of him, they might be able to squeeze out a little agony.

A few minutes later the door opened and Inspector Mu'tazz came into the room.

The women in Katya's lab always said that Detective Khouri, the one they called Abu-Haitham, was the most devout man in the department. He had earned the designation after repeatedly refusing to get into a squad car as long as any woman was inside, no matter how veiled and proper she was. He also had a preference for carrying a short camel whip like some of the more fanatical religious police used. The whip hung from his belt next to his holster, and had actually become so fashionable that a few of the other officers, including Mu'tazz, had taken to wearing one as well, a silent pledge of allegiance to Abu-Haitham's strict beliefs.

Mu'tazz was just as determined to prove that he was the purest of Muslim men, but unlike Abu-Haitham, he had a nasty edge. He had never spoken to Katya. She only knew what she had picked up from the gossip in the lab. Watching him now, she felt a quiet repulsion. He had a broad, square face, eyes that were jammed too tightly to his brow, and a large mouth that lacked all delicacy. When he opened his mouth, he could not avoid revealing a prominent set of teeth. They were ugly, yellow, widely spaced with black around their edges. He wore a trimmed beard around his lips and jaw line but it only served to highlight the bare cavity at its centre.

He set a folder on the table and looked down at Ubaid.

'No matter what the judges eventually decide about the rape charges,' Mu'tazz said, 'they're going to give you a lighter sentence if it looks like you've been cooperating with us.

'We know you were linked to a woman named Sabria Gampon. We know she was blackmailing you. She's been missing for over three weeks and, as you know, Undercover is anxious to find her.'

Ubaid was staring stubbornly at the one-way mirror.

'We think you might have some idea what happened to her.' Mu'tazz was now circling Ubaid's seat, studying him from every angle. 'If you know anything, we'd appreciate hearing it now.'

'I know nothing.'

With a speed that startled Katya, Mu'tazz smacked Ubaid on the back of the head. It humiliated him, you could tell from the fierce blush creeping up his cheeks. Mu'tazz continued pacing behind him. 'What did you say?'

'I know nothing,' Ubaid said.

Mu'tazz smacked him again, harder this time. It knocked Ubaid's head halfway down to the table.

'What did you say?'

Ubaid was quiet.

Smack! Mu'tazz hit him harder. *Smack!* Each time Ubaid raised his head, he looked more humiliated. There were tears in his eyes from the sting of each blow.

'Did you say you know where to find Sabria Gampon?'

'No, I—' *SMACK!*

'I don't know!'

Mu'tazz's face was expressionless. He even looked a little bored, as if he'd done this before, knew how it would evolve, and didn't much care what came of it.

Smack-smack!

Katya suddenly felt scared. Why had no one else come into the viewing room? People must have known what was going to happen. She probably shouldn't have been there herself, just in case anyone started asking questions later. This was how it happened: the torture of men was surrounded by complicit silence. And she found that, as much as she wanted to see Ubaid suffer, in reality she was horrified by it, and by the cold apathy on Mu'tazz's face.

Mu'tazz liberated the camel whip. He took a step back from his victim and said, 'What do you have to say about Sabria Gampon?'

Ubaid shook his head in despair.

CRACK! The whip tore across his back. Ubaid cried out in pain. His face was horrible to see.

'What do you have to say?'

'Nothing!'

CRACK! CRACK! CRACK!

'Please stop! I don't know anything about her!' Those were the final words Katya heard before rushing out of the room.

Katya spent the rest of the morning working quietly in the lab, riddled with feelings of fear and guilt. She kept telling herself that Ubaid deserved to be punished. That Mu'tazz had punished him – under a general conspiracy of silence, including her own – because everyone knew that the law was never going to do so properly. But she couldn't stop seeing the apathy on Mu'tazz's face as he struck another blow. She had seen men strike each other before. She had even been struck herself in that same interrogation room during an interview. But Mu'tazz's expression had suggested an utter lack of feeling, and, frankly, it had opened a pit of fear inside her. The Angel case was his now, and as much as she wanted to find this killer, she did not want to interact with Mu'tazz.

It was obvious that Mu'tazz was trying to keep her out of the case. He had not only moved her out of the situation room, but he had also taken back all of the solved case files. What was left was useless: two small boxes of unsolved cases from the mid 1990s. Another blow was struck when her boss, Zainab, came into the lab and cautioned Katya about the new situation.

'They're really cracking down,' she said. 'So we can't let anything get behind schedule. They've threatened to fire some of the lab workers if we do, and I have the feeling that you're at the top of their list.'

Katya wanted to say how ridiculous it was. They were still waiting for DNA test results, but most of the evidence from the Angel case had been processed already, or was being handled by the men downstairs. The work in the lab had trickled to barely nothing and they'd started working on their backlog of evidence from other cases.

In frustration, she went downstairs to the forensics lab, where she found Majdi and Osama going over some evidence. She had worked with Osama on a previous case and knew him to be the sort of liberal-minded man who wouldn't find it inappropriate that she was working on the Angel killings.

'Hello,' Majdi said, making an effort to smile. It relieved her. For the past three weeks he'd been so stressed he could barely look up from his work when she entered the room.

Osama looked disheartened. 'What's going on?' he asked.

'I just came to see what was happening with the Angel case,' she said.

Both men sighed in frustration. '*Nothing*,' Osama said. 'Nothing is going on.'

'What happened to the suspect?'

Majdi shook his head. 'It turns out that the blood and hair we found on the inside of his Red Crescent van was from a male. Then we discovered that the van had been sold because it had been in an accident. One of the paramedics had hit his head on the wall when the van turned over, and apparently Hajar had just never bothered to clean it.'

Osama leaned against the desk. 'There was nothing in the van that connected Hajar to any of the murders.'

'Or in the taxi,' Majdi went on. 'We went over every inch of his cab. The problem with taxis is that they have too many hairs and samples. So far not a single strand matches any of the victims. And it doesn't look like Hajar cleaned it – he doesn't clean anything.'

'Did they let him go?' Katya asked.

'No, not yet,' Osama said. 'Mu'tazz hasn't made the decision. He's in charge now.'

'I know,' Katya said. 'What do you think he'll do next?'

'I'm pretty sure he'll do what he usually does,' Osama replied. 'He'll think about it for a while. He's a pretty slow mover.'

Majdi said rather defensively, 'Some people are like that.'

'You're not,' Osama said.

'No, but I respect people who take the time to think about what's right. Sometimes it's not obvious.'

'Well, I think you're wrong,' Osama said. 'He needs to face the fact that we've reached a dead end. And the sooner he realises that, the sooner this case will move forward.'

On Wednesday, a man came into the lab and introduced himself as Jalal Taleb, the lawyer representing Ibrahim Zahrani. Because of the curious looks she got from her lab mates, Katya took him into the hallway to talk.

'Ibrahim asked me to come here today,' Taleb said, 'to look for some files that he had left in his office. I couldn't find them. I've been told by the Chief of Homicide that Ibrahim's office was cleaned out when he was arrested, and that all of his files were put into boxes and sent down to Records for sorting. I went down to Records and they were unable to give me any information about the files.'

'Which files does he want?' Katya asked.

'They were old case files from Undercover that all had some relation to Sabria Gampon. Ibrahim thinks it's possible she may have known the other two men on the videotapes – or at least learned about them – from her work in Undercover. He was eager to look at the cases again.'

244

'Has he talked to his brother about this?'

'Yes, it was his brother who had sent him the files in the first place and who told him yesterday that the files had not yet been returned to Undercover.'

'So they're still here,' Katya said.

'Apparently so.'

'And why are you telling me this?'

'Ibrahim said that if I was unable to track down the files in his office, I ought to come to you and explain the situation. It's possible that the records were turned over to another inspector in the department by accident. Ibrahim said he'd put them in the same drawer as the files he was keeping on the serial killer case. So perhaps those files are hiding in someone's office here in Homicide.'

Before Katya could ask her next question, Taleb raised his hand and said, 'What do you know about Ibrahim's case so far?'

'You mean the charges of adultery?'

'Yes.'

'Very little,' she said. 'Why?'

Taleb sighed. 'Things have taken a bad turn.' He proceeded to explain that, thanks to a court order, Ibrahim had been forced to clarify his relationship to Sabria. And he had done the only thing he could do in light of the evidence being presented against him: he had declared that he was officially, although secretly, married to her. He said they had signed a legal certificate called a *misyar*, a marriage document that was pre-signed by a sheikh. Inappropriate though it was, it was not illegal.

Ibrahim had also stated in court that they had married quietly, so that his wife wouldn't find out. If that could be shown to be true, then the worst he'd face was a lawsuit from his in-laws. His wife would file for divorce because he had married someone else without telling her. (Although their own marriage contract, written up twenty-odd years ago, had said nothing about whether or not he was required to notify her of his plans to take a second wife.) Unfortunately, Ibrahim was unable to procure the paperwork to prove that he was actually married to Sabria. She had had the paperwork in her bag when she went missing, he said, and he had no idea what had become of it.

'But at that point,' Taleb said, 'someone in Undercover pointed out that Sabria was already married to a man by the name of Halifi and that the two of them had never divorced. As you know, the law is pretty flexible about divorce – for example, sometimes it's done privately and not made official – so this investigator found Halifi, who told them that yes, he was still married to Sabria, as far as he knew. We have tried to discredit his statement on the grounds that the police found him high on heroin, but his testimony was taken by the court nonetheless.'

'This is horrible,' Katya said.

'Yes, and it gets worse. At my suggestion, Ibrahim then countered that Sabria had been forced into the marriage, and it had been abusive. After leaving, she hadn't seen Halifi in five years. The judge seemed to think this didn't matter. A marriage is a marriage. As long as they hadn't got divorced, she was still Halifi's wife, thus making Ibrahim an adulterer, even if he was genuinely married to her.'

'So let me guess,' Katya said, 'everyone's saying that Sabria lied to both of them.'

'Exactly,' Taleb replied. 'The judge assumed that Halifi and Ibrahim might be telling the truth, and that Sabria lied to both of them. In other words, she married Ibrahim without telling him about Halifi. Now I've let the situation stand, because it serves my client, but he's absolutely panicked about it. He has been since the beginning. It took quite a bit of work to convince him that this was the only way he could save his own neck, and that Sabria, who is missing, has a lot less to worry about than he does. But he's more afraid than ever that the police are going to find her and charge her with adultery. No matter how the situation plays out, she's going to be found guilty of one crime or another.'

'And that's why he wanted you to come to me,' Katya said. 'We have to find her before the police do.'

'That's one way of looking at it,' Taleb said. 'He trusts you more than anyone else in the department. You've done a great deal to help find Sabria, and you seem to care what happens to her. He feels very strongly that one of the men from the videos had something to do with her disappearance. His brother has kept him updated on the situation with Ubaid, and at this point, the police aren't ruling him out, but they're not inclined to think that Ibrahim was the cause of her disappearance, since he was actively looking for her.'

'I agree that we should look for those other men,' Katya said. 'But

246

what exactly does Ibrahim expect me to do? Go pry in the Chief's office?'

Taleb pursed his lips. 'I don't know that he had any specific plan in mind, just the idea that, when you want something, you often manage to get it.'

Katya's first decision was a spontaneous one. She took a taxi back to the Briman women's prison. If anyone would know more about the men on the tape, it would be Carmelita Rizal.

Miss Rizal was once again kind enough to meet with her. They sat in the same meeting room, this time without Rizal's son, who was playing in the nursery. Rizal was supposed to be in a ceramics class. Her tunic was spotted with paint and she smelled like wet clay.

When Katya explained Ibrahim's legal decisions and the fact that the police were now searching for Sabria so that they could charge her with adultery, Rizal became tense.

'Have you seen the videos yourself?' Katya asked.

Rizal shook her head. 'No. Sabria asked me to keep the password to the site, for exactly this kind of situation. But I never saw the footage. She wasn't going to bring it into a prison, believe me!'

'I need you to tell me everything you know about the people involved,' Katya said. 'It's really important that I find Sabria before the police do.'

'I don't see how I can help you,' Rizal replied.

'Would you mind looking at the videos now, to see if you recognise anyone?'

Rizal shuddered and shut her eyes.

'It may be our only way to find Sabria,' Katya said.

Reluctantly, Rizal held out her hand. Katya gave her the mobile phone and waited, watching as Rizal's face grew red, the muscles in her jaw tensing under the strain of clenched teeth. During the second segment, she blurted: 'Oh my God, that's Jessica!'

'Jessica?'

'Yes.' Rizal looked stunned. 'Jessica Camerone. She was a friend of ours.'

Katya took notes. 'Was?'

'Well, we lost track of her a while ago. I did, at least.'

'Did Sabria not mention her in relation to this?'

'No, not about this.'

'And you're sure it's her?' Katya asked.

'Yes, absolutely.'

'How did you know her?'

'We all worked for the same employer. Halifi.'

'Jessica was also abused by him?'

Rizal nodded. 'She disappeared before Sabria did. We were all so messed up back then. It was only later that Sabria found her. She'd been telling me all about Jessica's new life. I didn't know she was part of this.'

'What about the men?' Katya said. 'Do you recognise any of them?'

'No, not at all.'

'I need to find their names. Do you think Sabria kept that information somewhere?'

Rizal shook her head. 'I know she kept *nothing* that would tie her to the blackmail. She was extremely careful. She never wrote anything down. Everything she kept was on that website.'

'There was only video on the site,' Katya said.

'I know!' Rizal was beginning to sound stressed. 'I wish I could do something, but I don't know anything!'

'All right,' Katya said firmly. 'Maybe you don't know their names, but I bet you know other things. Sabria must have talked about the men at some point. Even if she didn't tell you the particulars, she might have mentioned some generalities. Try to relax and think back. Did she ever mention how she found out about the men in the first place? For example, did she know them personally?'

'No, no, she never met them. She only knew the women involved.'

'And aside from Jessica, how did she meet the women?'

'At Sitteen, like I said before.'

'What did she tell you about them?'

Rizal looked up at the ceiling with a pained expression. 'She talked about the fact that they'd been raped. That they were *being* raped on a regular basis by their employers, and that's why they'd run away to Sitteen.'

'How did she get the videos from the women if they'd already run away?'

'She found the employers and ...' Rizal took a breath, shut her eyes and crossed herself. 'I guess you could say she sent in an under-cover operative.'

Katya was stunned into a moment of silence. 'You mean that she sent women *back* to these employers, and these women knew up front that they were going to be raped?'

'No,' Rizal said. 'She sent a *new* woman into a household where an employer was known to be a rapist. I know it's horrible anyway. They went in just to get the video footage.'

'OK,' Katya said. 'So Jessica was one of those operatives.'

'I didn't know that,' Rizal said breathlessly. 'But yes, I guess so.'

'These women – what did they get out of it?'

'Sabria paid them. She gave each of them one payment – a big chunk of money from the blackmail. I don't know how much exactly. She also promised to help them get out of the country, and in most cases that was better than the money. But these women, I think they also did it to help other women. To punish the men. All of the money Sabria was making from the blackmail went to help other girls get out of the country.'

'How?'

'They bought forged documents. They bribed officials ...'

Katya nodded. 'So Sabria knew where the men lived, and she knew how to get a housemaid into each of their homes. She must have had some connections to do that.'

'I don't know all the details,' Rizal said. 'She worked with a company that places housemaids, but I don't know what it was called and I'm pretty sure the company didn't have any idea what she was doing. I just know Sabria could do any damn thing she set her mind to. She was like that.'

'Do you remember any details about the men?'

Rizal shook her head.

'Think back. There must have been something. It doesn't have to be specific, maybe just a vague memory ...?'

'Yeah, OK,' Rizal said in a shaky voice. 'I remember something about a holiday home. One of the guys had a home in Egypt. I don't know if he was the same one who also went hunting. One of them was big on hunting. He kept guns.'

'Do you remember what he hunted?'

'No. I think he went bird hunting.'

'OK.' Katya sat back. 'This is helpful, and you know more than you think.'

'It's all vague,' Rizal said. 'I don't know the details. When she was telling me this, all I really cared about was getting out of here – I wasn't really paying attention. And she didn't tell me names. God, she didn't even tell me about Jessica's being involved. She probably thought it would upset me.'

'This Jessica—' Katya said.

'Houbara!' Rizal said suddenly. 'That was the kind of bird that guy used to hunt.' Katya wrote this down. 'I'm sorry I can't tell you more than that.'

'That's fine. This Jessica, where is she now?'

Rizal let out a shaky breath and gave her directions to a house in Andalus. 'The house has a big garden in the front, that's how you can tell which one it is. Sabria talked about going there. I almost died when she told me. I promised myself that one of the first things I'm going to do when I get out of here is go to that house and find Jessica.' She handed Katya her phone and smiled a little. 'She's going to cry when she sees my son.'

35

Al Saqr al Jazeera was a falconry supply shop at the southern end of
Falasteen Street. The large store glowed a sandy desert brown in the
streetlights. It was Wednesday evening. Katya and Nayir sat talking in
the Land Rover, gazing at the windowless building and waiting for
Isha' prayer to end. A local mosque's loudspeaker was just calling out
the *adhan*, so it would be a good fifteen minutes before the shop was
allowed to reopen. They weren't sure that it would. No sign was posted
about the hours and it was possible it had closed for the weekend.

Rise up for prayer. Rise up for Salvation. God is great.

They had already gone to the apartment of Sabria's friend, Jessica.
If anyone could help them identify the men from the rape videos, it
would be her. But she wasn't at home. They had waited for an hour
and no one had come or gone from the apartment. Katya felt bad
making Nayir wait longer.

It had been his idea to come here. While sitting in the car, she had
told him about the houbara bustard. She knew it was illegal to hunt
the birds, but according to Rizal, one of their suspects had been doing
just that. Nayir said the falconry supply shop might be able to help
them track down a poacher.

He pointed out that it was still quite common, among a certain
well-to-do crowd, to hunt bustard the old-fashioned way: with a
falcon. It was the prey of choice for any falconer, and although the
bustard population had been decimated by overhunting, he knew of
wealthy sheikhs and businessmen who imported bustards to be
released on private hunting ground for the purpose of practising

251

traditional falconry. It was not technically illegal, since they imported the quarry themselves from Pakistan and disposed of it on private property. The royal family, who hunted their own bustards in Pakistan on holiday every year, certainly weren't going to punish those few privileged citizens who were practising one of the country's most ancient traditions. In their view, falconry was a revered, almost holy activity whose extinction would be as much a disaster as that of the bustard.

Katya suspected that the men they were looking for were wealthy. They wouldn't have been worth blackmailing if they weren't. She had brought still shots of the two unidentified men from the videos, hoping to show them to Jessica. But perhaps Nayir was right and someone at the local falconry shop would recognise them.

'They even have their own passports,' Nayir was saying.

'Falcons?'

'Yes. Some of them are worth more than half a million riyals. Their owners travel with them and want them to be safe.'

'That's crazy. Don't all those princes have their own jets? It's not like they're sending their birds through customs.'

'I suppose some of them do.' Nayir's eyes were gleaming with an amusement she rarely saw, and she was struck again with the jealous thought that the things that really pleased him were all part of a man's world.

'In fact, a good friend of mine makes monthly trips to Abu Dhabi,' he went on. 'They have the best falcon hospital in the world there, and even a four-star hotel for the birds.'

She let out a snort. 'Well, why hunt bustard when you can have caviar and champagne?'

'Bustard flesh is considered an extraordinary aphrodisiac. Men have hunted it for that explicit purpose for six thousand years.'

The jealousy was shape-shifting into a kind of yearning. She couldn't believe how casually he'd used the word 'aphrodisiac' and she imagined that, in conversation with men, Nayir became a very different person. She wished she could see him totally at ease more often.

'Don't you think they hunted the bustard for so long because it is one of the only birds that can survive in the desert?' she asked. 'It's not like they have a hundred birds to choose from.'

He smiled. 'Well,' he said slowly, 'my personal feeling is that the bustard is mostly prized for its behaviour.'

'What is that?'

'It has an arsenal of keen self-defence manoeuvres.'

'Such as?'

'When it sees the falcon coming, the first thing it does is spread its wings and raise its tail. It's a pretty big bird – probably three times as big as a falcon – and with its wings out, it's even more intimidating. If the falcon still comes at it, the bustard takes off and flies straight into the sun, so the falcon gets blinded. If that still doesn't work, the bustard ejects the contents of its intestines, which is an immediate deterrent.'

Katya smiled. 'So the hunters like watching the spectacle, then?'

'Yes. In fact, they'll always give the bustard a head start. It's more interesting that way.'

'Have you done it?'

'Yes, I've been hunting.' The amusement left his face, and for the first time he seemed sad. 'It's a beautiful thing, and too bad we can't do it the way it's supposed to be done any more.'

A car pulled into the parking bay beside them and two men got out. One of them opened the shop. The other was carrying a hooded falcon in a cage. They noticed Nayir and greeted him. Both men spared a quick glance for Katya.

The shop owner was a man in his forties whom Nayir did not introduce to Katya. He looked Asian, perhaps Pakistani. He was too gruff for formalities. 'Come in,' he said, 'we've got to get this bird a new feather.'

The bird was hooded and calm as he was carried into the shop. Katya followed Nayir inside.

The interior was large, and the items on offer were too sparse to fill even a quarter of the space. There were hoods, perches and gloves, a few expensive cages and travel carriers. Behind the counter, a large assortment of telemetry equipment was hanging from the wall. The rest of the shop was empty space. It took Katya a moment to notice that the area was sectioned off. Behind a cordon, two rows of perches faced one another. It was an aviary.

The men quickly but gently took the bird out of its cage, removed its hood and laid it on one end of the sales counter. The bird didn't seem to mind. The owner pulled a bucket labelled 'brown and white' from a shelf. It held a dozen feathers. He fished through them until he found one that matched.

'What's he doing?' Katya whispered.

'The falcon needs all of his feathers to fly correctly. He lost one, so they're replacing it. I think they're gluing it on.'

It was clear the men had done this before. The owner talked to Nayir casually while he worked. 'What can I do for you this evening, Mr Sharqi?'

Nayir slid the photos of the two suspects across the counter. 'I'm wondering if you recognise these men?'

The owner, who had been leaning over the hawk, straightened up and squinted at the photographs. 'Yes, I do know one of them. Why?'

'They may be able to help us find a killer,' Nayir said. Katya was quietly surprised that he had lied, but she could see that he was uncomfortable doing it. The owner seemed not to notice.

'Well, I only recognise one. This man's name is Hakim al-Adnan,' he said. 'He's a very rich man. Works for the General Investment Authority but lives here in Jeddah. He's one of these guys who has his own private jet. Not the kind you want to mess with.'

He pointed to the photograph of the man who had raped Jessica.

'I work with the police,' Katya said. The Pakistani gave her a dour look, which made her think he was yet another righteous stickler, but he seemed to be listening. 'This visit is off the record,' she went on. 'I could always go down to the station, but we're in a bit of a rush. Do you happen to have an address for Mr al-Adnan? We just need to ask him some questions.'

The Pakistani blinked a few times and nodded. He turned back to the falcon and finished setting in the new feather. Then he wiped his hands before disappearing into a back room. Katya checked Nayir's expression. It was neutral.

The owner emerged a few minutes later. 'He doesn't keep a credit card on file with us, and he's never requested a mail order, so I have no address for him.'

'Does he hunt often?' Katya asked.

'Oh yes, every winter.'

'Do you have any idea where he hunts?'

'I know he owns a place up near Taïf. I went up there once. I could probably draw you a map if you like. Otherwise, you can probably find him online.'

Back in the Land Rover, Nayir was thoughtful.

'How far is Taïf?' Katya asked.

'You want to go there now?'

'Maybe,' she said.

He looked surprised. 'It's nighttime. I'm not sure how much we'll be able to see. And won't your father—'

'I'll tell him it's work-related.'

'Won't he think that's odd – you staying out so late?'

She gave him a direct look. 'We're getting married, remember? He trusts you.'

Nayir turned to look out of the window but shook his head. 'The Taïf Expressway is a dangerous road. We shouldn't drive it at night. But I'd be happy to take you tomorrow.' He turned back to her. 'Right now I think we should see if Jessica is home yet.'

'The man the falconer just identified is the man who raped Jessica. It might not be worth going back there. We already know who the guy . . . ' She trailed off.

'What is it?' he asked.

It had been bothering Katya: it seemed likely that Sabria had been kidnapped at her apartment, but how could one of the blackmail victims have found out where she lived? She wasn't listed anywhere. Her visa had expired and the address was outdated. According to both Ibrahim and Rizal, she had protected her identity with paranoia. Jessica was the only one who seemed close enough to Sabria to know where she lived. And Jessica had been raped by al-Adnan.

'You're right,' she said. 'Let's go to Jessica.'

Rizal hadn't given Katya an address – apparently there wasn't one – only directions. About three blocks east of al-Andalus Street was a small supermarket with a bougainvillea painted on its window. Halfway down that street was an abandoned Hyundai missing its wheels. Somewhere nearby was a two-storey apartment building with a garden at the front. Rizal had memorised the location because she was determined to go there when she got out.

Lights were on in the apartment now. Katya and Nayir crossed the garden and were surprised by a dog. It hadn't been there the first time. A small black schnauzer trundled out to meet them, barked raggedly for half a minute, and then wandered back between two potted plants.

'I guess someone's at home,' Katya said.

They rang the bell for the apartment on the left and a young woman opened the door. Katya recognised her immediately from the tape.

'Jessica Camerone?' Katya said.

The woman nodded nervously. Like Sabria and Rizal, she had a beautiful face, but it looked tired.

'I'm sorry to bother you,' Katya said. 'I'm with the police, and I'd like to ask you a few questions about a friend of yours.'

'Which friend?'

'Sabria Gampon.'

Jessica's hand tensed on the doorframe.

'May I come in?' Katya asked.

Jessica glanced nervously at Nayir. He moved back and said, 'I'll wait outside.'

Katya stepped into the apartment.

'What's this about?' Jessica asked, motioning her to take a seat at the kitchen table. Katya sat, and Jessica sat across from her. She was shaking, but her face had taken on a look of suspicion.

'Sabria is missing,' Katya said. 'She's been gone for almost a month. Do you have any idea where she might be?'

'Oh my God.' Jessica clapped a hand to her mouth and shook her head. Katya waited a moment before repeating her question.

'I don't know,' Jessica said, sounding a bit defiant. 'Why are you asking me this?'

'I know about the videos,' Katya said. 'I know you were raped by a man named Hakim al-Adnan.'

'That's all over now,' Jessica said firmly. 'I've put it behind me.'

'How close were you to Sabria?' Katya asked.

'Oh, I don't know. I've known Sabria for a long time.' Jessica stood up and went to the counter. 'Are you accusing me of something?'

'I have reason to believe that Mr al-Adnan had something to do with her disappearance. But Sabria was living quietly. It would have been hard for him to find out where she was.'

256

'So you think I told him?' Jessica's voice shot up a few notes.

'There are two options here,' Katya said. 'You can tell me the truth and help me find out what happened to Sabria, and possibly put this man away, or I can arrest you and take you down to the station and they can force you to tell the truth. I think we both know that if they arrest you, they're also going to charge you with inappropriate behaviour.'

'I was raped!' she cried.

'It would be extremely hard to prove that in court,' Katya said. 'I won't arrest you as long as you tell me the truth about what happened.'

'No,' Jessica said. 'You'll still arrest me. Any information I give you is going to be used in court, right? And they're going to want to talk to me again to verify it. And then I'm going to have to admit to a judge that I was raped? No.'

'You don't have to go to court,' Katya said. 'I just need information. This is the only way we're going to find Sabria.'

Jessica stood at the counter, arms rigid at her sides.

'When Sabria sent you in to make the tape,' Katya said, 'she paid you a lump sum. Was it a lot of money?'

'Not really. I knew what she was doing. She kept extorting money from those men. She said she was giving it to all these women who needed help, but then I started noticing that she wasn't doing so badly herself. She wasn't working, and she was living in a nice apartment. She was doing just fine, and meanwhile I'm working two jobs just to be able to pay the rent for a room. There are four other women living here. It's kind of tight, if you know what I mean.'

'So you asked her for more money?'

'She said no.'

'And then what?'

'You know, it was *me* he raped.'

'It's reasonable that you felt you deserved some of the money,' Katya said. 'Did you contact al-Adnan yourself?'

Jessica took a moment to reply. 'I did a deal with him. I told him I'd ask for less than Sabria did.'

'How did you contact him?'

'I followed Sabria to the Chamelle Centre and kept a tail on the women she sent for pick-ups.'

'Explain that.'

'She met these other women there. They would do pick-ups for her: getting the money from the men she was blackmailing and bringing it to her.'

'How did the women get the money?'

'The men were instructed to give it to their wives' drivers. Most of these guys were married, and they employed drivers for their wives. The drivers would give the money packets to the women, who would bring them to Sabria at the Chamelle Centre. That was also where she gave out the money to women who needed it.'

'So you followed her one day.'

'Actually it took a week,' Jessica said. 'I kept following the girls to their pick-up locations and then following the drivers back to their residences until I found al-Adnan. He'd moved since he raped me, so I had no idea where he was living. Anyway, I stopped his driver and gave him a note for al-Adnan explaining what I wanted. A few days later, al-Adnan got back to me. He said he would take my offer.'

'But in order to assure him that Sabria wouldn't reveal him to the police, you had to destroy her copies of the tape, or do a deal with her,' Katya said.

'No, I just told her that if she didn't stop blackmailing him, I'd give him her address. But I didn't actually do that! You have to believe me. I was angry about the money, but there was no way I was going to throw her to the dogs like that. She was my friend.'

'How much did al-Adnan pay you?'

Jessica grimaced. 'He didn't.' She sat down at the table again.

Katya knew she was lying. It didn't make sense. 'Why would al-Adnan go after Sabria and not you?' Katya asked. 'You must have made a deal with him and given him Sabria's address.'

'No!' Jessica said.

'Then how did the drivers not find out where these women who took their employers' money were going? They could have come after Sabria at any time.'

'I don't know,' Jessica said nervously. 'The women were careful, I guess.'

'Were you careful?'

Jessica was quiet.

'Here's what I think,' Katya said. 'You met with al-Adnan. You made a deal with him. He gave you some money and you told him where to find Sabria.'

'No, no! You're wrong. He didn't give me any money, and I never told him where to find her. I went to meet him, all right? And that's when I realised that I'd made a mistake. I wasn't going to take his money. I saw him across a car park and decided I was never going to speak to him again. So I left. I was in a taxi, and I told the driver to leave. I didn't talk to al-Adnan at all.'

'Where did you go after that?'

Jessica exhaled and looked down at her hands. 'I went to Chamelle.' Her voice cracked. 'I knew Sabria would be there.'

'So you went straight back to Chamelle. And his men could have been following you.'

'I didn't think about it,' Jessica said. A tear rolled down her cheek. 'I don't know if they even saw me. I mean ... I don't know. I didn't talk to them.'

'Why did you go back to Chamelle?'

'When I first went to Sabria about this, she offered me more money. But I was too angry to take it. After the whole thing with al-Adnan happened, I was angry and afraid. I just realised I'd rather take money from her than have to deal with him.'

Katya nodded. 'What about Sabria? Did you see her at Chamelle?'

'Yes.' Jessica gave a trembling exhalation. 'She said she would get me the money a week later. I called her then, and she didn't answer. I assumed she was avoiding me. I didn't really think ...'

'So that meeting at the Chamelle Centre was the last time you actually saw her?'

'Yeah. It was about a month ago.'

'Al-Adnan's men probably followed you from that car park back to the mall.'

'But it's a women's-only shopping mall,' Jessica said.

'All they had to do was put on a burqa,' Katya replied. 'Did you and Sabria leave the mall together?'

Jessica nodded, and the tears fell more freely now. She bowed her head. Katya watched the teardrops soak into her shirt.

36

Katya went to the lab early on Thursday morning. It was the week-end and the building was empty but she switched on her computer and ran a search for Hakim al-Adnan. The Pakistani falconer was right: in the government database, there was a photograph of al-Adnan that matched the still shot from the video. He used to be an accountant for the Ministry of the Interior before his current position at the Investment Authority. His home address was listed in Jeddah.

Later that morning, Katya and Nayir stood in front of a pair of elaborately carved wooden doors. They were old and quite strikingly out of place on the front of the new stucco villa.

A servant answered. He was wearing a butler's uniform, a white shirt with cufflinks, a black jacket and tie, and even a pair of white gloves. His hair was short and neatly trimmed and when he spoke, his voice was unpleasantly affected.

'May I help you?'

Katya smiled politely. 'Yes,' she said. 'I'm a reporter with the *Arab News*. I'm finishing up a story about Mr Hakim al-Adnan and his role in the revival of historic falconry, and I wanted to follow up with some fact-checking questions.'

The butler looked askance at Nayir and said, 'Yes, well, I'm afraid Mr al-Adnan is not here.'

'I'm so sorry to bother you,' Katya said. 'He told me to drop in any time. I just haven't had a chance until now.'

The butler didn't reply.

'Do you know when he'll be back?' she asked.

'Not for another month, I'm afraid.'

'Ah, I see,' Katya said, trying to ignore Nayir, who was growing more tense beside her. She didn't like lying so blatantly in front of him, and apparently he didn't like it either. 'I first interviewed him about a month ago. He said he was going up to the house in Taïf, but I forgot to ask him when he was leaving. I'm so sorry.'

'He left for Taïf one month ago,' the butler said.

Katya thought back. It had been almost exactly a month since Sabria had disappeared.

'It's rather odd,' the butler said with a wry look, 'that he didn't invite you up there. After all, that's where he does his falconry.'

'Oh, he did invite me, actually,' Katya said quickly. 'I just didn't understand his schedule and that he would be up there so long.'

The butler pursed his lips. 'He spends more time up there than he does here.'

'Ah. Well, I'm sorry to bother you. Thank you for your help.'

The butler nodded.

Back in the car, Katya was certain that her cheeks were flushed.

'He knew you were lying,' Nayir said.

'At least I got the information I needed,' she said. 'Al-Adnan went up to Taïf the same week Sabria disappeared. If he did kidnap her, he might have taken her up there.'

Nayir nodded and cast her a questioning glance. 'I wouldn't mind going to find out.'

Nayir was right: the Taïf escarpment road was deadly. Just past al-Hada, the highway began to undulate. It lifted them over 6,500 feet in the short space of thirteen miles and with the daring use of more than ninety S-curves. By then, they were up in the mountains with baboons darting into the crevices on one side of the road and the landscape stretching out beside them on the other, a vast scenery of sand-coloured, rocky mountains. The other drivers seemed to think it was a race course, taking the turns at reckless speeds and passing the Land Rover wantonly on the two-lane road. The views were spectacular, the cliff drops alarming. Katya held tightly to the arm rest and prayed silently while Nayir steered them safely to the city.

261

The map the falconer had drawn led them to a paved road just outside the city. That road led them higher into the mountains and abruptly turned to dirt before pitching them back down into a valley. Below, nestled in a wadi and sheltered by the mountains, was a succulent strip of green earth, governed by a single white stucco villa. As they descended, the scent of roses filled the air.

The road ended at a gate, where they were met by a security guard. He asked no questions but simply waved them through with a friendly nod. Mountain hospitality, Katya supposed.

She was beginning to feel nervous. She wasn't sure how they would confront a wealthy, powerful man like al-Adnan. She should have told someone at work about identifying him. She could have mentioned it to Ibrahim at the least. But she wanted to find Sabria without the police knowing.

They stopped in front of the villa and waited.

A few minutes later, a young man in a brown robe came walking around the side of the building. He smiled and welcomed them with a wave. He had short hair, sun-darkened skin and enormous hands, which he used to greet both of them, shaking Katya's hand as easily as Nayir's and introducing himself as Yusuf, the caretaker of the rose farm.

'We are always happy to have guests,' he said. 'Where are you from?'

'Jeddah,' Nayir replied.

'Ah, that's a lovely drive.' Beyond that he wanted nothing more from them than their names and to know whether they'd like to stay in the villa that evening, since the past few nights had been cold and the campsite was not as hospitable as it was in spring.

'Actually,' Katya said, 'we came here looking for Hakim al-Adnan. We're with the Jeddah police and we'd like to ask him a few questions.' Yusuf immediately looked stricken. 'He may be able to help us with an investigation,' Katya added.

'Mr Adnan is not here,' Yusuf said. 'He's away on business and won't be back until next week. I'm so sorry.'

'I'm sorry too,' Katya replied.

'And you came all this way!' Yusuf said. 'Please sit for tea. Please.' He motioned them onto the villa's front terrace, where a small table and chairs waited in the shade of an arbour. 'If you can spare the time, I'd be glad to give you a tour of the gardens, since you drove all the way from Jeddah.'

Once they'd had tea, Katya and Nayir allowed themselves to be led on a tour of the villa and the gardens. Taïf was famous for its rose oils, which were used in luxury perfumes all over the world. With boyish enthusiasm, Yusuf narrated the details of his precious plants and the great war he waged to protect them from a family of malevolent porcupine.

'You know Mr Adnan well?' Katya finally said as they strolled through the garden.

'Yes,' Yusuf said uncertainly. 'He is the finest employer I could hope to have. I am lucky to work here doing something I love.'

'You said he was away on business?'

'Yes.'

'Delivering rose oil to the rest of the world?' She smiled and Yusuf returned a grin.

'As a matter of fact,' he replied, 'he's just taken a shipment to Mecca. He goes twice a year – in April and October – to donate attar to the Holy Ka'aba.'

It had been a few years since Katya had performed the Hajj, but she remembered that attar was used to perfume the large vertical stone in the southern corner of the Ka'aba. According to the Hadith, touching that stone would erase all sins.

'That's very good of him.' She checked Nayir and saw that he was not impressed by Adnan's apparent generosity.

They had reached the end of the garden. A row of bushes had recently been cleared away, leaving the topsoil exposed. It was a rich, black, loamy earth shaded from the sun by a thin fabric awning tied to a scaffold.

To the far right, three rows of young bushes were reaching for the sun.

Katya was struck with a sudden memory of a dream, of blood and petals and evil *efreet* burying her body in the earth. The recollection came sharp and fast, and she turned to Nayir, who seemed to understand that something was wrong but had no idea what.

'How long ago were these bushes planted?' she asked.

'Well, we put them in at the beginning of the summer. A few of them aren't doing so well.'

She went to the ones that seemed to be floundering.

'Please don't walk too close to them,' Yusuf said.

Katya kept moving.

'Excuse me, *Sa'eeda*,' Yusuf said more snappishly.

'Were these bushes recently dug up and then replanted?'

Yusuf looked annoyed. 'No, we didn't do that.'

'I'll need a shovel.'

'*What?*' He marched towards her now. Nayir came after him.

Katya was surprised that her heart was pounding in her ears. She felt a cold panic. Her voice shook as she asked: 'Exactly how long ago did the problems start?'

'*Sa'eeda*, I'm sorry, I'm going to have to ask you to step away.'

'*Exactly how long ago?*' Katya asked.

Yusuf turned away and began shouting at the house, calling for the head gardener.

'There may be a body buried under these bushes.'

Yusuf spun back to her in amazement.

The head gardener came striding along the path from the house, followed by two young men. One of them was carrying a shovel. It took fifteen minutes and a lot of discussion before they began to turn the earth, rolling it gently away from the plants and mounding it carefully at the edge of the plot. They drew the first rose bush out of the ground with the kind of reverence Katya had seen men use in documentaries about archaeology. The Pakistani falconer had been less careful with the injured hawk.

They set the first bush in a wheelbarrow filled with soil and water and went to work digging deeper. Katya paced. She wanted to get down on her knees and start shovelling earth with her hands. Was this just a dream, this certainty? A remnant fear seeded in her mind by the Devil? Her arms were shaking so she clutched her waist.

The shovel hit an obstacle. Soft but firm. Suddenly two men were down on their knees, pushing away the soil with their hands. Before she knew what she was doing, she was kneeling beside them. 'Be careful. Let me.' The earth was cool and damp, a soil like none she had ever seen, and when her fingers dug into the obstacle, she felt skin and clothing fibre and the stillness of death. She quickly brushed the last of the soil away. '*Ya Allah, na'uzhu bi Allah.*'

It was a woman's foot, her bright red toenails poking up through the earth.

37

It was just after noon and the Friday *Dhuhr* prayers were finishing. Ibrahim had become so bored with watching TV, so frustrated with Saffanah sitting on the opposite end of the couch, watching TV but not really watching and getting up only to pray, that he'd finally turned to her and said, 'Where is the father?'

She'd known at once what he was talking about and she didn't reply. Not even a shrug.

'I'd just like to know how you met him.'

They were alone. Constance was upstairs, acting as their eyes and ears to the situation with Jamila. Aqmar had gone to work and Zaki was still avoiding him.

'Look,' he said, 'there's nothing you can tell me that will shock me. And I promise you it won't leave this room.'

Saffanah didn't seem inclined to answer, so he went back to watching TV. After a few minutes, just as the commercial break was beginning, she said, 'The doctor's office.'

'Pardon me?'

'I met him at the doctor's office. He worked there.'

Ibrahim tried not to look at her. He was certain she would clam up if he did. 'What were you doing at the doctor's office?'

'Getting checked for marriage.'

He took that to mean that her mother had dragged her to the gynaecologist to be sure that her hymen was still intact. As if Zaki would have cared one whit whether or not his wife bled on the honeymoon sheets.

'Was he a doctor?' Ibrahim asked.

'No. A secretary.'

'Does he know about your situation now?'

She shook her head and went back to watching TV, lifting the tail of her head scarf and wrapping it over her nose and mouth. It was a casual gesture he'd seen her do often, but now it made her look scared.

So she'd fallen for a boy at the doctor's office and somehow they'd had sex. He thought it was interesting that it had happened after she'd agreed to marry Zaki.

'Where did you . . . ?' The minute he said it, he could tell he'd gone too far. She froze and sat there as unmoving as the wall behind her.

The news was still covering the recent story of another abused housemaid, this one in Dubai. He tried not to think about Sabria and how much stories like this angered her. When the news report showed the housemaid's photo, he stood up and went onto the balcony for a cigarette.

When he returned, they watched the news for another half-hour before Saffanah said in a small voice, 'At the mall. In a toilet.'

He turned to her. 'The men's toilet?'

She nodded.

'Did he make any promises?'

She didn't reply, but the rest unfurled in his mind like a giant tapestry woven with scenes of the lives of young women who dared to stray from the path of virtue. The heart-stopping excitement of talking to a boy. The fear and nervousness of lying to your mother and stealing off to the mall. The excitement of following him into the boys' toilets, into a stall. And then, after so many years of covering up, the terror of being uncovered, mixed with the agony of being a teenager and being half-naked with a stranger who was probably clumsy and thoughtless and urgent to satisfy no one but himself.

'He said he was going to marry me,' she said.

Ibrahim found that he was holding his breath. 'And then?'

She was staring at the television now, her hands tucked deep into her lap. 'We had another date. But he didn't turn up.'

He sat back against the sofa and stared up at the ceiling. There was nothing to say. She already knew that people were cruel. That there was no hope of getting this guy to take responsibility.

'You know you were lucky in one regard,' he said. 'Don't hate me for saying this, but at least you didn't get stuck with the guy.'

Now her determined chin said that the conversation was over.

It hit him suddenly: she was at least four months pregnant. He couldn't tell from looking at her. Even in the house she wore the long black *abaaya* that obscured her figure. It had been almost a month since he'd found out. She must have been at least three months pregnant then, because she'd had sex with the baby's father before she'd married Zaki. He realised what should have been obvious before: it was too late. She couldn't pretend any more that this baby was Zaki's.

He thought about Sabria but could not see anything lucky in her leaving.

Ten minutes later, there was a knock on the door and it swung open. Omar came in and shut the door behind him. Ibrahim stood up. He saw at once that something was wrong.

'What is it?' he asked.

'Sit down,' Omar said. 'We need to talk.'

'What's going on?'

'Sit down.'

Ibrahim refused. On the sofa, Saffanah sat up straighter.

Omar let out a heavy sigh. 'They found her.'

'Who?'

'Sabria.'

'Oh my God. Where is she?'

Omar's face said it all. Ibrahim dropped to the couch. Saffanah turned to him.

'Oh God, no,' Ibrahim said.

'I'm sorry,' Omar said.

Ibrahim felt a great violent rip, as if everything inside him were being turned inside out. The next half-hour was a dream. His consciousness registered everything in snapshots: him clutching his knees, having trouble breathing. Blackness, muffled voices. Saffanah leaning over him, holding his hand. Omar on the telephone. Constance crying, her thin white hand held over her mouth. And through it all, the great, wide knowledge that Sabria was dead, that although it had been building in the night sky for weeks, the supernova had finally exploded. She was never coming back, and everything he'd loved and sacrificed for, everything that had ever given him hope, had come to an end.

38

Katya lifted her ear muffs long enough to ask, 'Whose gun is this?'

'Ubaid's police weapon,' Majdi said.

Katya watched him point the gun into the clearing box and pull off three careful rounds. On the other side of the box, Inspector Osama Ibrahim stood with his arms crossed over his chest, looking as if he'd had a very bad weekend.

'Surely he isn't stupid enough to have used his police weapon,' she said.

'You never know,' Osama said.

'You can hear me through your ear muffs?'

He nodded.

'I must be getting old,' she muttered. She replaced her muffs while Majdi tested the second gun. There were four guns on the table. The first belonged to Ubaid, the other three came from Hakim al-Adnan's bodyguards.

'Have you talked to al-Adnan yet?' Katya asked.

'No,' Osama said. 'It's best to do this first.'

They had found al-Adnan in Mecca, making a circumambulation of the Ka'aba. The police had waited respectfully until he'd finished and then approached him, saying they'd like to ask him some questions. He was in the interrogation room now.

His three bodyguards were also being held. They were the only ones close to al-Adnan who carried weapons. Adara had pulled a bullet from Sabria's chest, and Katya had found two shell casings at the rose farm, in the same area that Sabria was buried. She'd been killed at close range by a .22 handgun. One shot to the head, one to the heart.

Technically, Undercover had been in charge of the case. Now that they had a body it was a Homicide investigation. Chief Riyadh had turned it over to Osama.

It seemed obvious that one of al-Adnan's men had killed Sabria. She was found on his property. Majdi finished test firing the fourth gun before taking off his goggles and ear muffs. 'I'll analyse the shell casings now,' he said.

'When will you have an answer?' Osama asked.

'Give me half an hour.'

Carmelita Rizal had already cried, now she was wet-faced and shaky, with a pile of tissues on her lap and the gaudy tissue box sitting on the sofa beside her. Katya felt the simmering discomfort that she imagined most police officers felt watching people fall to pieces over the death of a loved one. She wondered what Nayir's reaction would be if someone came to him to break the news of her death. She couldn't imagine him crying. His pain, like so many other things about him, would get bundled up and shoved deep inside.

Katya had explained that Majdi had matched bullets fired from the gun of one of al-Adnan's bodyguards to the shell casings found with Sabria's body. So al-Adnan's bodyguard had killed her. She told Rizal about the rose farm and her disturbing intuition that Sabria might be buried in the garden. It still felt odd to remember the cold sweat and inexplicable sense of urgency. The worst part had been explaining Jessica's involvement, however unwitting it was. Katya suspected that it had effectively robbed Rizal of two good friends in one swoop.

'I know one thing,' Rizal said now, wiping her face. 'When I get out of here, I'm going back to the Philippines. Even if I starve. I have no one here except my son.'

'If you need help getting an exit visa, let me know.'

'Yes, thanks. I think I might need that,' Rizal said. 'You know, one of the things Sabria did was procure fake exit visas. I probably shouldn't be telling you that either, but it doesn't matter any more, does it?'

Katya shook her head.

'I can't help feeling that everything she was doing was so brave and stupid. It was not the answer. I think for her, it was exciting. She felt like a heroine. But it was only ever going to be a temporary solution. Things are never going to change entirely until the law changes. They say they don't have to protect us, we're not Saudis, but there are as many of us as there are Saudis and we do more work.' She was quiet for a moment, folding up a wet tissue. 'So I'm going to leave. I don't care if I starve to death in Manila. At least I'll starve at home.'

39

Sunday at noon, Katya was sitting at her computer when the door opened and Charlie Becker poked her head in. Seeing Katya, she smiled.

'Glad you're here,' she said. She came in carrying two paper bags full of folders. Katya stood up in surprise. 'I finally managed to convince Riyadh that we still had work to do. These are all of their unsolved cases with female victims from the past five years – with photographs!'

Katya was amazed. 'Does Mu'tazz know about this?'

'I have no idea and I don't care,' Charlie said briskly. 'I keep telling these guys that they should be looking for patterns because this killer is obviously in love with his little structures and secret messages, but you know what?' She looked up, her face red from the effort of carrying so many files. 'I don't think they really want to hear what I have to say. So I say screw it, we can do this ourselves.'

Katya smiled at her stubbornness. 'I'm glad you're here. Sit down.'

Charlie pulled up a swivel chair and sat at the side of Katya's desk. The other women in the office cast a few curious glances their way, but Katya ignored them.

Charlie was right, all of the files contained photographs. The problem now was that there were so many of them, and each one could be viewed as one letter of the alphabet or another.

An hour later, Katya opened her file drawer and took out the familiar packed lunch. Charlie laughed. 'Let me guess – hummus, carrots, pretzels and cheese sticks?'

Katya laid the contents on the desk with a certain defensive pride.

'And don't forget the apple and the Diet Coke,' Charlie said.

Katya handed her the apple. 'Since we never share it, I want you to eat it today.'

'I can't, remember? I feel guilty that *you're* not eating it.'

'Oh yes, I forgot.'

So the apple sat between them and they split the rest.

The desk was too small and cluttered for Katya to lay out the maps of the crime scenes, so she had taped them to the side of her computer and to the narrow slice of wall space just beside it. The city map showed the location of the body parts from the Osiris case. The desert map showing the mass gravesite was a simple hexagon near a road in the wilderness. She had drawn a third hexagon on a transparency and placed it over another city map with a giant question mark printed on top. The only mark on it belonged to Amina al-Fouad's hand.

'I wonder what the men really think of this,' Katya said, motioning to the folders that were open on the desk.

'They're probably glad we're doing all the grunt work,' Charlie replied, then more seriously, 'I get the feeling they think it's possible that Amina is part of a bigger series of murders, but they don't think it's likely, so they can't afford to waste their time on it right now.'

'Amina al-Fouad has to be connected.'

'Now don't lose faith yourself,' Charlie said. 'Riyadh isn't saying that she's not connected. The severed hands make that obvious. He's just saying that she was a one-off, you know? He thinks there's no bigger pattern.' Charlie motioned to the maps. 'But I think you may be right, and that's why I'm here, helping you look for that third apple.' She motioned to the maps.

'It's a hexagon,' Katya said.

'Yes, well, if it had a stem, it would be an apple.'

Katya gave a half-smile and went back to eating but something flitted at the edges of her consciousness. *Apple*. She looked at the maps hanging there. They did look like apples. Three apples.

She set down her carrot.

'What is it?' Charlie asked.

'*Ya majnoun.* I . . .' She spun to the computer, opened the browser, and ran a search. 'The Tale of Three Apples' popped up immediately. '*Al'hamdulillah!*' she cried. The internet censors weren't fast enough to catch every version that appeared on the web.

It was one of the stories from *One Thousand and One Nights.* She had read it as a child. It was complicated, but she remembered the beginning well enough. The Caliph, Harun al-Rashid, who suffered from the worst insomnia known to man, was travelling the streets one night when he stumbled up on a fisherman who caught his fancy. He told the fisherman that he'd give him two hundred dinars in exchange for whatever he happened to catch that night. The fisherman gleefully agreed and threw out his net and came up with a monstrously large trunk. The Caliph brought it back to his palace. When he opened it, he discovered the body of a woman.

As far as she remembered, the story stood alone among all of the Tales. It was the only one in which a woman was killed and someone actually went out to look for her killer.

She read the story while Charlie watched with impatience. A few paragraphs into it, Katya clapped a hand to her mouth.

'What *is* it?' Charlie asked.

Katya explained about the story. 'I will show you what the Caliph finds in his box. Just a moment.' She turned back to the computer and found the story in English. She scanned through it until she'd found the right part. 'Somewhere here.'

Charlie leaned over and read: *They found therein a basket of palm leaves corded with red worsted. This they cut open and saw within it a piece of carpet, which they lifted out, and under it was a woman's mantilla folded in four, which they pulled out, and at the bottom of the chest they came upon a young lady, fair as a silver ingot, slain and cut into nineteen pieces.*

Charlie gasped. 'Are you kidding me?' She read the passage again. 'They cut her into nineteen pieces?'

'Yes,' Katya said. 'I can't believe I didn't think of this.'

Charlie slumped back into her chair. 'This changes everything.'

'What do you mean?'

'I mean, he's not just a religious fanatic any more. We thought that nineteen meant some magic number from the Quran, remember?'

'Yes, you're right.'

'Now it means something else. Nineteen could be a reference to this story. I mean, how many women get chopped into nineteen pieces in your folk tales around here? Is this common?'

'No. I can't think of any. In fact, this is the only murder case in the *One Thousand and One Nights*. Yes, people die, but in this story, it is due to a crime. And there is an investigator. I think it is the only story in the book like that.'

'Good Lord.' Charlie looked dumbfounded.

'This is the reference to the Osiris case,' Katya said.

'Yes.'

'I think it means that there are three apples. And we have only found two.'

Charlie nodded. 'What else happens in the story?'

Each read it in her own language. It was, as Katya remembered, a bit winding and archaic. Essentially a man travels for thirty days to find three apples to please his sickly, beloved wife. After a long saga, he kills her in jealousy and then discovers tragically that his wife had been faithful, Desdemona-like, and that he had been misled by a deceitful slave.

Katya and Charlie sat in silence for a while.

'I don't think we should ignore the religious component completely,' Charlie said finally.

'I agree. In both of the two cases, the killer left a religious quote.'

'This just changes how we think about him,' Charlie said. 'Let me ask you: is it acceptable to read the *Arabian Nights* here? I mean, how do religious people feel about this book? It is kind of racy, isn't it?'

'Yes, it has been forbidden here.'

'It's banned?'

Katya nodded. 'We are not allowed to read it, but we do anyway. Many people are proud of it. It is part of our history. Like Shakespeare for you.'

'The religious authorities have banned it, then?'

'Yes.'

'So it doesn't make sense that our killer would be a religious fanatic but also someone who reads the *Arabian Nights*,' Charlie said.

'No,' Katya said. 'It doesn't make sense.'

'OK, here's an idea,' Charlie said. 'We don't know who the Osiris victim was – and chances are that the Angel killer wasn't the one who killed her. He just placed her body parts around the city. It was probably satisfying for him, it fulfilled some urge. He only started killing later. He killed the nineteen women.

'If he was in his teens or early twenties back in nineteen eighty-nine, then he would have been about thirty when he started killing the desert victims, which fits the classic profile of a serial killer. They start in their thirties. Over the past ten years he's been killing women. We can assume he'd be about forty now. That's one piece of information we didn't have yesterday.'

'OK,' Katya said.

'What was the quote from the Osiris case?' Charlie asked.

'It said, "And We have created all things in order."'

Charlie nodded. 'That is his fundamental preoccupation – order. I think it's a way of controlling himself and justifying his actions. Tell me, is there anything about Islam that encourages structure?'

Katya shrugged. 'It is not . . . it is not preoccupied with it.'

'OK,' Charlie said. 'What about all your artwork? I'm thinking of elaborate mosaics and stuff. That's very geometrical.'

'Yes, you're right. There is also a structure to the day with the five prayers based on the movement of the sun.'

'Right,' Charlie said. 'Let's assume that he scattered the Osiris body parts because he recognised the box as a reference to the *One Thousand and One Nights*. That just means he's relatively well-educated. He knew the story. He thought he was being clever spreading the parts in an apple pattern. God, he's probably been waiting for decades for someone to spot it. Anyway, later, when he starts his own killings, he repeats the pattern with the victims in the desert. Only now he is really expressing himself. He's trying to impose a certain order on the world. Not just on his victims and the way they're buried. I think he may also be trying to impose some kind of moral order – and that's where the religious component comes in.'

'What do you mean?'

'He's targeting mostly foreign women. If you view them through the eyes of a strict Muslim, you might argue that these women are acting inappropriately. They are living in houses, living intimately with strange men. Most of them aren't Muslims, right? They're from the Philippines and Sri Lanka.'

'Some of them may be Muslim,' Katya said. 'But most are probably not.'

'They probably even help raise children here, don't they? They're having some influence on Muslim children, but they're not Muslims and they probably don't follow the rules of society as well as Saudi women would.'

'Yes,' Katya nodded. 'I see what you mean.'

'Are there any organisations here that protest the use of all these foreigners in menial labour positions? I'm thinking that in America we have the Ku Klux Klan, which is a group of people who want society to be a certain way and who are often willing to commit racist acts to achieve their goals. These sorts of secret societies might draw people like our killer. Do you have anything like that here?'

'No,' Katya frowned. 'Most people feel that these workers should be here. Saudis don't think of work as necessary for them. It is for someone else to do.'

Charlie sighed. 'Right. I think I knew that.'

'Then what about Amina?' Katya asked.

Charlie sat back. 'I think we both believe the killer is writing a new message. We just don't know what it is.'

Katya was trying to imagine what it would be. He was a madman, driven by his own perverse sense of meaning. He was an executioner. An Angel guarding hell. The only thing that all of his murders and the Osiris case had in common was that he was writing messages. He wasn't just obsessed with order, his madness found its expression in words and letters. He was obviously literary – perhaps even a calligrapher. But what did it mean? That they should hunt down every artist and writer in Jeddah?

She was exasperated. The case was growing more bloated by the day, always dangling a new lead that would mean weeks of tedious work.

'Don't give up,' Charlie said. 'We'll find him. We just need to narrow down who had access to the Osiris box the day it was stolen.'

'Yeah,' Katya said. 'But it could have been anyone who was at the marina.'

'Yes.' Charlie gave a grim smile. 'But chances are, it was one of the boys who were on the boat with Colonel Sa'ud.'

40

Katya was wretchedly tired. Three hours of sleep the night before and even that had been broken by worries. When she did sleep, it was no reprieve, only a dark space in which her fears were allowed to proliferate. She got up before the first call to prayer and drank coffee in the car with Ayman while they were stuck in traffic, choking on the fumes of a diesel truck that they couldn't seem to pass. She was grateful that he was quiet.

She was sitting at her desk, staring dumbly at her computer, when Zainab came in. Her boss was a severe and commanding woman, the sort who would never cover her face at work. The other women in the lab sometimes whispered that, with a face like that, her husband didn't have to worry that another man might snatch her away. Katya hated that they were probably right. This morning, her expression was darker than usual, furrowing her already prominent brow so that her small eyes were almost lost in the folds of skin.

Two of Katya's lab mates had just arrived and were hanging their bags at the back of the large room and discussing their work. Zainab approached Katya's desk.

'The department is cutting its budget,' she said in a quiet voice, 'and I'm afraid they're going to have to let you go.'

Katya stared at her. She was having trouble absorbing this news.

'I've managed to convince them to make this temporary, so it's only a suspension—'

'Why?' Katya asked, her voice angrier than she'd expected.

'It's just until they can sort out the budget.'

'That's ridiculous,' Katya said. Her hands felt cold and she could hear her voice shaking. Inside she felt a strange numbness about it all, but her body was reacting. 'I'm the head pathologist in this lab. I have seniority. Are they letting everybody go?'

Zainab frowned at her. *Please don't make me reprimand you.* 'As I said, this is just until the budget gets sorted out. Please don't take it personally.'

But it was personal. Deeply. She watched Zainab talking, details about the shifting of workloads. The continued discussion at the back of the room told her that her lab mates hadn't heard anything. But Katya was certain they would see it on her face. She stood up, pushed past Zainab, and left.

A march down the hall. The women's toilets. No paper towels. She wiped her face on her cloak and went straight to Chief Riyadh's office. The door was closed, the light off. Even his secretary's desk was abandoned. It was probably too early, but the building was alive with voices laughing and lifts dinging. She went straight down to the first floor to find Majdi. Coming out of the lift, she bumped into Adara.

'There you are,' Adara said. 'I heard about the suspension.' She pulled Katya into a nook beside the water fountains. 'Abu-Musa told me.'

'How does he know about it?' Katya asked. She was aware that she sounded contemptuous, but she didn't care.

'I don't know, but he used it to warn me. If I don't stay in line, as he put it, I may be next.'

'Bastard.'

Adara raised an eyebrow. *Obviously.* 'I suspect this wasn't Chief Riyadh's doing. It was probably Mu'tazz. He knows about your involvement with the Zahrani affair and he's dismissing you, politely, for improper behaviour.'

'I'm not letting this happen,' Katya said.

Adara glanced down the hall at Mu'tazz's office door. It was shut but a light was glowing inside. 'Just put on your burqa,' she said.

Katya pushed past her. Marched off down the hall. She didn't put on her burqa and she didn't bother to knock on the door. She simply opened it and walked in.

Mu'tazz was sitting at his desk, writing a report with a long, elegant pen. His attention to the task, his careful posture and the apparent enjoyment he took from the work all collapsed in an instant when he looked up and saw Katya. He laid the pen down.

'I want to know why I'm being suspended,' she said.

'You're going to have to talk to Chief Riyadh,' he replied. His voice was even. His gaze remained pinned to her face.

'No,' she replied. 'He's not here and I want to know now. This was your doing.'

He blinked and looked down at the desk. 'We know you've been overstepping your bounds,' he said, 'and not doing the work you were actually hired to do.'

'That's bullshit.'

A faint smile was on his lips.

'I was the one who found the first pattern,' she said. 'I am the one who has been looking through all the files, night and day, to find another pattern. I found out about the Osiris case when you hadn't told Inspector Zahrani anything about it, and I now believe that the cases are connected.'

His cool expression began to slip. She explained about the connection to 'The Tale of the Three Apples'.

'I don't think the Angel killer killed the woman in the box,' she said, 'but he was probably the one who dispersed her body parts in a hexagon pattern throughout the city. He was educated enough to recognise the tale from the forbidden book, and he decided, at some later point, to make two more apples to fit the story. It shouldn't be too hard to narrow down the suspects who were on the boat with Colonel Sa'ud that day. I know you've interviewed them already.'

'Last time I checked,' Mu'tazz said coldly, 'you were not an investigator.'

'I would like some more time to look through all the files,' she went on. 'I want to find out if there's a third hexagon of city killings. It may have been going on for some time now, and those files are our only clue. I think working out this pattern is our best chance of finding Amina al-Fouad.'

'I'm sorry,' Mu'tazz said, picking up his pen. 'You're going to have to talk to Chief Riyadh.'

'I'm not leaving until we catch this killer.'

What was that look on his face? Was he grudgingly impressed? Catlike, he said, 'You have two days to clear your desk.'

Katya went upstairs with a violent, shuddering feeling in her chest. She took refuge in the women's toilets and locked the door. She sat on a toilet, which flushed automatically every time she moved, and put her face in her hands. Breathe.

A pounding headache was forming. She went to the sink and splashed water on her face, wiped her face on her cloak and marched into the hallway. She went back into the lab, sat at her desk. Opened a report on her computer. Stared at the screen. It took a few minutes for the decision to arrive, but when it did, she grabbed her bag from its hook and strode out of the door.

41

The security guard at the front desk had an annoying habit of spooling out an entire formal greeting every time Mu'tazz went past. *Salaam aleikum wa rahmatullahi wa barakatu.* 'Good to see you're back from lunch, Lieutenant Colonel.'

Yasser Mu'tazz did not like greetings any more than he liked all the other fluff of language: please, thank you, thanks be to God. He didn't bother replying to the guard, he simply strode into his office and shut the door.

He had long ago realised that he worked best alone, quietly, researching away on a computer, or in a library, or pawing through old files in forgotten corners of records rooms. He had never liked the human component of his job. It was surprising what you could find out from a small sheaf of papers. He had become quite good at drawing conclusions about people from the barest facts. It was extremely satisfying, almost artistic.

In a similar way, you could sum up the entire emotional content of a word in the shape of the letters that formed it. Just last night he had spent two whole hours drawing the word *fitna*. It used to be a metallurgic term referring to the removal of dross, but now it meant chaos, tribulation. At some point it had evolved into a description of the destructive charms of a woman. It was one of those words that didn't have spaces, where one single line flowed together, its bumps and grooves uniform. All of the dots that indicated letters were clustered on top like sprinkles on a cupcake. It was so easy to make words like that look elegant. But it wanted destruction. He had drawn a thick, ugly word in blackest ink on white parchment. The dots looked like smallpox, the line itself a scar. He'd cut into the paper and let the ink bleed onto the desk, staining the rest of the parchment and a nearby book. And he'd left the whole thing there. His only dissatisfaction was that there was no one to appreciate his art.

After talking to Colonel Sa'ud that day three weeks ago, Mu'tazz had gone looking for the boys from the boat. He had found and interviewed all but two of them: Ali Dossari and Mohammed Wissam.

The ones he had interviewed had solid alibis for the day that Amina al-Fouad disappeared, so he had ruled them out. But it seemed Dossari and Wissam didn't exist any more. There was nothing on either man since the early nineties. No passports, no IDs, no drivers' licences (of course, the latter was not exactly a requirement in this country). No marriage or death certificates. The last known photos of the boys were from juvenile detention – Wissam with a small rat-like face, and Dossari with a strange melon-shaped head and a pair of flapping ears. According to the visa office, employment records showed that Wissam, who was Egyptian, had worked in Jeddah as an assistant chef in a small restaurant for three years back in the late eighties. Mu'tazz managed to track down the restaurant owner and discover that Wissam had gone back to Alexandria fifteen years ago. The owner had never seen him again.

Dossari was different. He was a citizen, and although it was possible that he had also left the country, it would have shown up on police records. But there was no record of him ever applying for a passport. Mu'tazz had even called the Ministry of the Interior's secret service, to beg some information. The Mabahith kept tabs on people, and maybe they had something on Dossari. Dossari could even have become a Mabahith or a Makhabarat agent himself. But Mu'tazz's contact at the agency came back with a frank explanation that they had no record of the guy and that he didn't work for them. From all of this, Mu'tazz had concluded that Dossari had gone underground and changed his name.

So he tried a different tack. He still believed that Dossari had stolen the box from the marina warehouse back in 1989. When body parts began showing up around the city, the police had gone straight

282

for Dossari. He had been arrested in the Osiris case, but the confession seemed to have been coerced and they had not come up with enough evidence to convict him. He was eighteen at the time. Eventually, they'd let him go. Technically, they hadn't had to, but the Chief had been a merciful man.

Mu'tazz's own research into serial killers had taught him that they showed early signs of cruelty and lack of empathy and were often noted in schools and sometimes on police records for crimes like pyromania and animal abuse. And indeed, that's why Dossari had been on the boat that day: he'd been found guilty of killing a neighbour's donkey. But he hadn't just killed it; he had burned half its backside with cigarettes, then cut out its eyes, cut off its ears and tail, and skinned it – all while it was still alive. Back in the eighties, most parents would have taken a boy like that straight to an exorcist. Of course he had to be purified, but he also needed a good doctor, which only the police rehabilitation programme had provided. He was assigned to a counsellor, one Dr Saleh.

Mu'tazz had looked for Saleh and found that he had died in a house fire in 1992.

He didn't report any of this to Ibrahim because it wasn't going to help anyone. He had quietly notified one of the younger men, Shaya, that he had his own ideas about the investigation and that he was searching for a kid from a twenty-year-old case. Shaya promised to keep an eye out for the name Dossari, but he hadn't been that interested in hearing about him. Apparently the name had never come up, since Shaya hadn't got back to him. Mu'tazz had no idea what Ibrahim was actually doing with his time – aside from ordering shakedowns of Sitteen and cavorting not-so-privately with the girls in forensics.

Ever since he'd been put in charge of the case, he'd been miserable. Now all the work of coordinating the team – and keeping fires lit under a hundred bureaucratic arses all over the city – had become his responsibility. There was no more time for thinking creatively. That was someone else's job. They would bring their creative ideas to him, and he'd get to tell them how sharp they were and then make sure that the ideas were executed. It was all a bunch of grunt work, really. Not to mention that being at the centre of attention went against all his instincts of modesty.

Riyadh had assured him that it was only temporary, so he'd agreed. He tried not to complain to anyone. He tried not to lose his temper or start secretly hating the whole office. He kept his mind focused on getting things done. If there was one thing he believed in, it was that, when you set yourself on the path of righteousness, God would help. You just had to pay attention to His signs.

Majdi had devised a large photo giving an aerial view of the desert site with the women's bodies posed in the shapes of the letters. The photo took up his entire desk, leaving only a little room for the lamp and the telephone. After Miss Hijazi's discovery, Mu'tazz had been furious with himself. He'd spent enough time thinking about the case, looking at photographs, reading reports, that he should have noticed the pattern himself. That's what he excelled at – seeing things on paper. But he'd missed it, dumb fool. He finally decided that the sheer depravity of such a thing would not normally have occurred to him, and he forgave himself. Then he got down to the business of studying the photos.

Two things were obvious. First, the killer thought he was an artist. One of those modern guys like Baldaccini who couldn't just stick to canvas and ink but had to impose his artistic vision on public spaces, like roundabouts or buildings, or that fountain in the Red Sea, the one they jokingly called 'the King's bidet'. In this case, it was the desert. It put the killer in that class of self-important pricks who, unfettered, would someday start manipulating clouds to resemble phalluses, or tear down whole forests to draw women's naked bodies. Thank God the government kept a handle on those guys.

Second, even though the message was religious, and people kept saying he was a religious fanatic, clearly he was nothing of the sort. He was the opposite: an apostate. Mu'tazz would bet a whole month's salary on the fact that this killer had given up on religion long ago. Never mind the obvious cruelty and evil of the murders, if the desert site was his canvas, then it was blasphemous for one big reason: it depicted the human form. Any rendering of the human body was treacherously close to idolatry, and therefore forbidden. It had been that way since the inception of Islam.

So they were looking for a blasphemous artist, nothing else.

A week ago he'd started making phone calls to art institutes, galleries, metalsmiths. There were no doubt plenty of blasphemous artists hiding in various crannies in the city, but there wouldn't be that many who were self-important and twisted enough to do something blatant like this. People like that tended to want to be noticed, and he was counting on that flaw. He was trusting in God. A prayer ran through his head all hours of the day: *Praise be to Allah. He will show you His signs and you will recognise them.*

Sighing, he opened a folder and got to work.

42

Amina al-Fouad's house was a testimony to the determination of its housemaids. It was spotless, its polished stone floors and clean white furniture showing no trace at all of the children who lived there.

A housemaid met her at the door. Her face was drawn with grief, and when Katya explained that she was with the police, the woman's eyes began to well with tears. She invited her in and took her into the main room before she excused herself for a moment.

Katya stood in the quiet space and tried to gather her thoughts before being assaulted by every last detail of Amina's world. The killer targeted immigrant women. Amina was the exception. She was a Saudi housewife with six children and an over-protective husband who claimed that she never left the house without his permission, and that when she did leave the house, she went to women-only shopping malls. If shopping for her niece's birthday was the only time she had gone to a mall that was open to men and women, it seemed improbable that she just happened to walk right into the killer, and that he had kidnapped her on the spot. Malls were crowded places. Someone would have noticed.

The killer liked everything organised. Planned. Maybe he was angry that the police had found his secret graveyard, but whatever anger he felt about the way the world worked was always turned into a structured response. He had probably seen Amina before he'd kidnapped her, and although she wasn't his previous type, something about her had attracted him. What was it?

The housemaid returned with an apology and introduced herself as Joy. No one was at home except the other housemaid, Maria, who was preparing dinner. The children were out or at school and the father was at work. They were all, she said, making an effort to keep their hope alive. It's what Amina would have wanted.

'I was wondering if I could ask you some questions,' Katya said.

'The police have already talked to Abu-Jamal,' Joy replied, referring to Amina's husband.

'I'm thinking there may be things that Abu-Jamal couldn't tell them about his wife,' Katya said in a carefully neutral tone.

'Oh no,' Joy replied. 'Amina was a good mother and wife. She would never have kept secrets from her husband.'

They were standing in the living room, and Katya was beginning to wonder if she would be invited to sit down and have a drink. That, she thought, is probably what Amina would have done.

'This isn't information that's going to go into the official report,' she said. 'You understand. As a woman, I don't have an obligation to tell the investigators everything.'

Joy's expression seemed to loosen a little.

'I'm sure Abu-Jamal has told us everything he possibly can that will help us find his wife,' Katya went on, 'but was there something he couldn't tell us, perhaps because he didn't know?'

Joy pressed her lips together. It was surprising how quickly she capitulated. 'Come into the bedroom.'

They went down a hallway and entered the master bedroom. The bed was covered in a floral quilt, a pair of expensive pillows, and a chenille throw. Various dressers and wall hangings exhibited the same shades of pink and pale green. Joy went through a doorway and into a closet and came back with a duster. 'I brought you in here because I don't want Maria to overhear this,' she whispered. 'She's been here longer than me, and she's *really* devoted to the family, if you know what I mean.'

Katya came to the dresser and watched as Joy dusted.

'I don't know if this can help you,' Joy said, 'but I'll just tell you. Amina went out a lot. Her kids are all in school now, and she hated being at home alone all day. She usually went to visit her sister or her cousin, but she didn't do that all the time. Some days she would just go to the mall. She even went to that big one by herself – what's it called? Red Sea Mall?'

'Did she usually tell you where she went?' Katya asked.

'Yes,' Joy said. 'You see, Maria keeps tabs on her and reports things to Abu-Jamal. I don't do that.'

'Can you tell me where she went before she disappeared? Anywhere she might have come into contact with men?'

Joy rolled her eyes. 'Well, she got into taxis if she needed to, but only when Maria had a day off. I know the police were asking about that. She would never tell her husband about going to the malls, and I don't think he would have minded that, except that she had to get into a taxi to get there because her son was at school and couldn't give her a ride.'

There was a noise from down the hall and Joy dropped the duster. 'Stay here,' she whispered, heading out of the door.

Katya looked around. Amina's wardrobe was sparse, but the items in it were expensive. Not difficult to imagine why. An upper-middle-class woman with children in private school. A ball gown for weddings. A pair of designer jeans. Her taste was a bit conservative. Katya moved out of the wardrobe and walked around the room.

A bookcase in the corner contained no books, just a few mother-ing magazines and a heart-shaped box full of glass beads that looked like it belonged to some abandoned craft project. The rest of the shelves contained photos of her family in expensive gold and silver frames. On the opposite side of the room, her husband's wardrobe was small and well-organised. Black suits. Pinstripes. Yves Saint Laurent. One half of the wardrobe was filled with white robes and neatly pressed head scarves. A row of shoes.

The housemaids kept it clean, but Amina had kept it sterile. Katya felt an ache. What sort of person felt comfortable living without at least an item of clothing discarded on the carpet? Come on. An old box on the wardrobe floor? She was so annoyed by the orderliness of the whole apartment that she might have suspected the husband of being the killer if he hadn't had a solid alibi.

What happens to a woman who is made to sit at home all day while her kids are all in school, who has one housemaid who reports to the husband about her behaviour, and another one who kowtows to the senior servant? When everything is made uniform, down to the match-ing blinds, doesn't a sense of emptiness open up in your chest? It had hit Katya within minutes of arriving. She had an instinct to flee. Shake

288

it off. Mess up her hair, dirty her shoes. How did Amina respond to the false austerity?

Katya studied the items on the dresser. A hairbrush. A picture of Amina's children in their school uniforms. Another picture of Amina and her husband. Behind a little screen stood a wooden jewellery box lined with velvet and filled to the brim with gold and baubles. The items had been tidied – probably by Joy – but the sheer volume of jewellery and the fact that the box was open suggested a kind of reaction to the sterility.

Joy returned, vastly annoyed and shaking her head.

'Can I ask you something?' Katya said. 'Did Amina ever have any artwork commissioned?'

'No.'

'What about calligraphy?'

'No, not really. Ah, but one thing!' Setting down the duster, she opened the top drawer of the dresser, revealing a few dozen gift boxes, the kinds you could buy at most jewellery shops. Each box was about the size of a large purse.

'Are those full?' Katya asked.

'Yes.' Joy let out a laugh. 'This was her latest.' She took out a red box and prised it open. Inside was a rather traditional display: half a dozen rings, six sets of earrings, a bracelet with charms. From the top half of the box hung a few necklaces in different lengths. In boxes like these, all of the items would be in a matching style and usually set with the same gemstones. This one was plain gold, and each piece was decorated with the name 'Amina' written in a beautiful script.

Every woman had a box like this. If the jewellery inside didn't show her name, it showed at least the first letter of it. But this one was unusual. The name was not simply written, it was curved into shapes – a bird, a fleur-de-lis. The object was different on every piece. Even on one of the tiny rings, the artist had shaped her name into a perfect circle. The necklace at the centre was the only thing that showed a simple 'A'.

Something was racing through Katya's mind, and she had to still herself to see it. The script. Calligraphy. *Amina.* The letter 'A'.

The first letter, she thought. *He's doing a calligraphic primer. An alphabet.*

'Where did she get this?' Katya asked.

'It's beautiful, isn't it? I don't remember. Let me think ... '

'May I?' Katya took the box and prised back the velvet lining. There, at the bottom, was a small square of fabric stamped with the name of the store. *Rayhan Jeweller's.*

'Rayhan Jeweller's. Where is that?' She did a search on her phone and discovered that it was at the Jamjoom Centre. Her stomach dropped.

'How long ago did she buy this?'

'It's been over a month now ... '

Katya was out the door before saying goodbye.

43

The Jamjoom Centre near the King's Fountain on Falasteen Street was a beige concrete monstrosity that sat in the shadow of a dark blue, glass-and-chrome tower block. The whole complex took up four city blocks and was owned and operated by the Jamjoom family, whose patriarch, Sheikh Ahmad, had served as everything from Commerce Minister to Director General of the national airlines in his eighty years of life. The shopping centre had been fashionable in the eighties, when it was the biggest such structure in the country. Now, compared to Jeddah's modern super malls, Jamjoom seemed dated. Recently, the Carrefour supermarket had moved out, and the number of shoppers had dropped drastically, leaving the place feeling even more depressed.

Just before evening prayer, Katya and Nayir entered the main hall and stopped at a building map that was posted in a glass case. The tile floors of the hall had recently been polished and the overhead lights reflected from every surface, a gaudy display. Rayhan Jeweller's was tucked between a perfumerie and a video game centre, where children were running about in packs, screeching and howling, while cloaked mothers struggled to keep an eye on them all.

They stopped in front of the jeweller's and looked inside. It was a modest place, a bit shabby and small, but tidy, with two display windows at the front of the shop and a single long counter stretching in a U-shape along the walls. There were no smiling young sales-women, just a single man standing at the counter talking to a female customer.

Pretending to look at the window display, Katya moved closer to the doorway and watched the shop owner. He was a tall man, thin and gaunt, with a broken nose and a large round head. He was leaning with one arm on the display case. He looked tired, bored. The woman said something and he reached into the case, extracted a small ring, and laid it on the counter. She picked it up.

The shop owner glanced over at Katya and she quickly looked away. Nayir was studying the jewellery in the window.

'Do you like any of these rings?' he asked.

'Not really.' She went back to watching the owner. The woman set the ring on the counter and he replaced it in the case. As the woman thanked him and turned to leave, he pushed himself up. Katya heard a *clunk*. It had come from his wrist. Now that he was upright, she could see that he had a prosthetic hand. It had hit the glass counter when he pushed himself up.

She spun around, feeling a painful shot of adrenalin.

'What is it?' Nayir asked.

'Let's go.'

They began walking back towards the mall's entrance. She regretted not having explained to Nayir what she was doing here. She hadn't had the energy and she didn't want him to ask questions. When she'd said 'jewellery shop', he'd assumed it was for the wedding. She reached into her bag for her phone and it fell to the ground. Nayir picked it up. She glanced back at the shop, saw the shop owner standing in the doorway now. He was watching them. There was something feral and suspicious in his eyes. He turned and went back inside.

She snatched the phone from Nayir and called the station.

'Put me through to Mu'tazz.'

It took a minute to do this. In that time, she saw the owner pulling down the metal grille, shutting his store for prayer time. He was locked inside.

'This is Mu'tazz.'

'This is Katya Hijazi. I think I've found the killer.'

She couldn't tell if his silence was opprobrium or interest.

'On what basis do you make this claim, Miss Hijazi?'

'He works at Rayhan Jeweller's at the Jamjoom Centre. He made a set of jewellery for Amina al-Fouad that she purchased shortly before her disappearance. I'm at the centre right now. The owner is about

1.9 metres tall, balding. He has a strangely shaped head and big ears.'

'How big?' Mu'tazz sounded interested now.

'They really stick out. He's also missing a hand. He wears a prosthetic.'

'We have a team nearby,' he said.

She was frankly surprised at Mu'tazz's compliance.

'I'll send them to Jamjoom immediately.'

'He just shut his shop for prayer time,' she said, 'but there may be a back entrance.'

'Don't do anything,' Mu'tazz said harshly, 'until the police arrive.'

She heard sirens immediately. It couldn't be them.

The phone went dead. She stuffed it back into her bag and saw Nayir staring at her in frank amazement.

'I'm sorry I didn't tell you.'

'You stay here where people can see you,' he said. 'I'll go check for a back entrance.' And he was gone.

She stood, too scared to move. But she had to get closer. She had to see if he was there. She moved forward slowly, saw that the lights behind the counter were out. Only the display lights were on. The shop was empty.

On instinct, she started walking towards the far entrance. Nayir had left the building. She would exit through the east entry, swing back, and meet him coming the opposite way.

Outside it was dusk, but lights filled the car park. She saw Nayir at once. He was moving along the front side of the mall at a slow jog. She walked towards him, scanning the car park and the various private entrances to the building. It was busy. There were crowds of young men loafing around their cars, listening to music and looking bored. A large family was climbing into a minivan. Some mall workers were gathered around an ashtray stand.

Suddenly, movement.

Nayir had spotted him and was running across the car park. She hitched up her *abaaya* and took off. The jeweller saw Nayir chasing him and began to run. He was faster than them both, his long legs pumping, unencumbered by a robe. He headed east across the car park, two hundred yards from Katya, further from Nayir. Even sprinting, she wouldn't be able to cut him off.

She ran anyway, gave it everything she had, dropping her bag and yanking her skirts well above her knees. Halfway between her and her quarry was a group of young men.

'Thief!' she shrieked.

The boys needed no prodding, they saw where she was pointing and took off after him.

'The one in the green shirt!' she screamed.

Shouts echoed around the car park.

'Thief!'

'Stop him!'

One of the young men caught him. Katya realised too late that the jeweller might have a weapon. There was a tussle. A young man went down. Blood on his shirt. But there was another man behind him. Three more coming from the other side. All these boys, their young lives wasting in mall car parks, were waiting for an opportunity to prove themselves. To take down a thief who was also a killer. To save a woman from shame. To civilise society when the police could not. They took him like a pack of wild dogs, throwing him to the ground, falling on him, tearing at his limbs. It was savage and beautiful. She'd forgotten what it felt like to see human justice, to see a man who preyed on innocents being taken down.

44

Tawfiq Zhouri had worked the Red Crescent night shift for five years and was always grateful when the first call of the night didn't involve the usual traffic fatality. This one took him to the area around Jamjoom, to an old, regal-looking home, somewhat shoddy on the outside and easy to miss, tucked away as it was between all the apartment buildings.

They'd arrived in eight minutes and found six police cars waiting at the scene. Two officers hustled them into the house, and Tawfiq, the back half of a stretcher team, felt an immediate sense of unease.

From what he could see from the entrance hall, the house was normal enough. A bit sparsely decorated but clean and neat. He was led almost immediately to a basement door. The air coming up the stairs smelled of bleach and hospital cleansers, which was probably why he felt sick as they made their way down into a subterranean room.

It was stark and brightly lit. A concrete floor, white stone walls, a bank of stainless-steel cabinets, and an enormous freezer at the far end of the room. That, combined with the smell and the fluorescent lighting, reminded him of a hospital morgue.

In the furthest corner was a smaller room made completely of Perspex. The police officers were gathered there, and as Tawfiq drew closer he saw a woman inside. She was unconscious, lying on the metal floor of the Perspex chamber. Beside her head was a drain, and from that came the unmistakable odour of blood. There was a chair beside the woman that had been welded to the metal flooring. It looked as if she had been in the chair and the officers had released her. From each arm rest hung a broken handcuff. There was still a metal cord around her legs. They were cutting it away now.

'She's alive,' an officer said.

Tawfiq and his partner put her on the stretcher and rushed her to the van, driven as much by their own need to escape as by the urgency of her condition.

Tawfiq climbed into the back to assist the other responder and began covering her with blankets. She was in shock. He wondered wildly what had happened – his sick, involuntary visions merging horribly with the smell of bleach left over from the basement. He had the sense of touching an evil he'd never encountered before, and he began to whisper a prayer against dark magic. *O Allah, I surrender myself to You, I direct myself towards You, I entrust my affairs to You, so keep me safe, with the preservation of belief, from in front of me, from behind me, from my right side, from my left side, from above me, from below me, and repel evil from me with Your strength and power, because, verily, there is no strength and no power save with You . . .*

45

Ali Dossari was doling out information. One piece of the puzzle came every day, usually after about nine hours of frustrated interrogation. The detectives were getting fed up, but Katya suspected that Dossari would continue playing this game even if Mu'tazz decided to use the whip. He had nothing to lose.

They had already gathered a serviceable picture of the man from files they'd found in his house, from his medical history and legal documents. They'd also interviewed jewellery shop customers and Dossari's neighbours. But what they wanted was a confession: *Yes, I killed those women*.

In the disgusted silence of the observation room, the men talked about his missing hand. Funny that a jeweller was missing a hand. Had he stolen his own goods? No, he'd told his customers, it only meant that he knew how to spot a thief. People respected him at Jamjoom. He was a bit off, never speaking above a whisper. An accident with nitrates when he was a child had damaged his larynx. It made him seem soft and kind.

They had found a white GMC sport utility vehicle in his garage. In the boot were two large magnetic strips, the kind you could adhere to a car door, both imprinted with a false taxi company logo. They also found a broken taxi meter and a placard identifying him as an employee of the fictitious company.

Yesterday, they had been able to squeeze one vital fact from him: he had used the SUV – in the guise of a taxi – to pick up women from beneath the Sitteen Bridge. He liked Filipina girls, he said. They

297

climbed so eagerly into his cab when he offered a discount. If he got sick of Sitteen, he went to Asian restaurants in different parts of the city. When they pressed him about May Lozano, he gave a smug little smile and said, 'She needed convincing.'

They weren't sure how he had managed to 'convince' her on a crowded street without anyone noticing, but the minute they started asking questions, he clammed up and gave them nothing else.

The woman in his basement was not Amina al-Fouad. Amina was dead, he said, and he wouldn't say where she was. The room had been cleaned, but they found her other hand in a freezer. It had been cut off *post mortem*. Traces of her blood had been found in the drainpipe of the small Perspex room where she had probably also been held.

The woman who was in the basement when the police arrived was named Bassma Gilani. Her hands were still intact. She was a Saudi, and young – only seventeen. Her parents had been notified and a search of her bedroom had produced a jewellery box much like the one Amina had purchased. Bassma's first name fit with Katya's alphabet theory: that Dossari's new project was to kill women based on their first names, in alphabetical order. Katya suspected that he had already buried Amina somewhere after posing her body in a straight line – the shape of an 'A'.

There were two large freezers sitting in his basement. The investigators had found Amina's other hand in one of them. In the other, they had found eighteen hands. Although not all the lab work was finished yet, there was little doubt in Katya's mind that the DNA from those hands would match the DNA of the desert victims. The killer had kept one hand as a totem from each of his kills – except for one. Both of May Lozano's hands had been found at the gravesite. In the freezer where her hand ought to have been, they found only a small ring. Dossari had needed both of Lozano's hands to form the diacritic marks beneath the second-to-last letter in his desert message, so he had kept the ring as a totem instead.

Lieutenant Daher had brought the ring to Lozano's employers, who had identified it as something she had bought a month before she disappeared. They remembered the ring because it held her birthstone, a peridot. She hadn't known anything about birthstones before she bought it, but green was her favourite colour, and she'd been delighted with the discovery. She'd bought it from a jeweller at Jamjoom.

Katya suspected that there had been something else unusual about Lozano's killing. She was the only victim from the desert whom Dossari had found at his jewellery shop. And she was one of the last victims from that group. Perhaps killing her had given him the idea to begin choosing victims from among his customers instead. Once he realised that Lozano's disappearance had not got him into trouble, he began to plan his next series of kills with an even bolder stroke. He would choose women from a place that could be tied directly back to him. That was certainly more risky than picking them up off the street. It would also explain why his type of victim had changed. Instead of killing immigrants, he had turned to killing Saudi women. It was probably more common to see the wealthier Saudis in his shop.

But no matter how much evidence they had against him, no matter what DNA and fingerprints they found, no matter the woman imprisoned in his basement, the detectives still strove to get a confession. The system prioritised it. And Dossari was making it hard for them.

Anybody who entered the observation room and stood for five minutes to stare at the man felt that no judge in Jeddah could fail to sentence him. Judges were more gentle to those who repented. It might mean they allowed the prisoner a Valium before the beheading, to calm him in his final moments. But Dossari didn't seem to care about that. He was enjoying the dual benefits of exasperating the interrogators and building up suspense and interest about his crimes. Charlie Becker, who spent some time with Katya in the observation room, said grimly that Dossari seemed proud of his work.

Back in 1996, he had opened a silversmith shop at the Souq al-Bado under the name Zeddy al-Munir. Three years later, he had stolen a body from the city morgue and was caught with it in the boot of his car. The body had been that of a nine-year-old girl who'd died of leukaemia. The victim's family was powerful. Appalled by what he had done, they arranged to have him punished severely for the theft, and the city executioner had removed his hand.

Because of the stigma that goes along with such a punishment, he had changed his name to Asif Dakheel and started afresh. Using the new alias, he had leased a property in the Jamjoom Centre and opened a jewellery shop, which was not as lucrative but much more reliable.

Ten years ago had been a busy time for him, Katya mused. He'd opened Rayhan Jeweller's, killed his first victim, Amelia Cortez, and realised how easy it was to make an immigrant disappear. The police were less inclined to follow up on immigrants' cases, given the sheer number of them and the difficulty of keeping track of visa infractions and Hajj overstayers. Dossari's escapade of killing had gone unnoticed for a decade.

Watching him now, Katya felt a violent disgust filling every part of her body. She prayed to God with a slow-burning, silent thought: *If you're listening to me, grant me this wish. Remove this sick person from the world and cast him into the furthest reaches of Jahannam.*

She left the observation room when Mu'tazz came in to talk to Dossari. She didn't want to watch another beating, didn't want to risk feeling any pity for the killer. But as she was exiting, Mu'tazz left the interrogation room again. He was riffling through his folders as if he had forgotten something.

Mu'tazz saw her in the hallway and stopped. They hadn't spoken since the phone conversation at the mall.

'Thank you, Miss Hijazi, for your work.'

She regarded him steadily. He wouldn't meet her eyes so he talked to an invisible spot above her head.

'Your suspension has been revoked,' he said, 'pending a full investigation.'

She still didn't like him, but if she wanted to keep working in Homicide, she was going to have to come to terms with him.

'Thank you,' she said.

Mu'tazz turned and went off down the hall.

Ibrahim and Saffanah were sitting in front of the TV when the guard opened the door and Osama came in.

'*Salaam aleikum*,' Osama said. He wore the kind of look Ibrahim had seen on his brother's face a few days before. Ibrahim stood up. 'I've come to take you to court,' Osama said. 'Your lawyer wants you to make a formal statement in front of the judge. This might take a few hours.'

Now that Sabria was dead, it was going to be difficult for Jamila's family to win their adultery case against him, but they were going ahead anyway. Ibrahim's lawyer had assured him that he didn't need to worry; he wouldn't get the death penalty without eyewitnesses to his sexual liaisons with Sabria. But the process was going to humiliate him nonetheless, which was just what Jamila and her family wanted.

Saffanah got to her feet at once. Ever since they'd had the discussion about the father of her child, she hadn't gone far from his side. They even slept in the living room on opposite sofas. He'd wake at night and see her face in the flickering lights of the TV. She would always open her eyes then, as if somehow by sitting together in the same room for so many hours, their rhythms had intertwined and she could sense when he woke. She would regard him silently for a moment. Her gaze had a message in it, but he could never tell if it was a fearful plea not to reveal her secret or a silent exhortation for him to be strong, to go back to sleep and store up his energy for the approaching battle. Then she'd turn over and go back to sleep.

In those dark, sacred hours of night, he remembered Sabria, the way he used to wake and find her staring at him, waiting patiently for him to open his eyes so she could wrap herself around him in a different way, adjusting their bodies for another round of sleep. Even now, he could smell the fruity tang of her skin. He spoke to God, the one he believed in, and asked for information, clarity, advice. God answered him with tortured dreams of dark places that filled him with an even deeper sadness.

Ibrahim slid into his shoes and grabbed his jacket from the back of the door. Saffanah came over and stood defiantly beside Osama as if daring him to make her stay.

'Maybe you shouldn't—' Ibrahim began.

'I'm coming,' she said.

Osama made no response so Ibrahim followed the detective to the car and Saffanah followed them. Lieutenant Shaya was there, looking quietly pleased to see his old boss. He waved through the window and shot a curious glance at Saffanah before they took off.

Ibrahim was surprised when they turned south on Medina Road, heading in the wrong direction. He said nothing. If Osama didn't know his way around, then he wasn't going to correct him. Beside him, Saffanah was quiet, staring out the window.

Looking out at the sprawling suburbs, the jumble of apartment buildings, office blocks and warehouses, he was surprised by how beautiful it suddenly seemed, how messy and unstructured and neglected, a whole city of concrete growing as rapidly as weeds but taking some quiet dignity in its own chaos. Surely, he thought, there were a thousand other men like him who'd made mistakes enough to ruin their lives, their careers and their families, and yet surely those men had carried on, as had their families. There was room for everything in this vast, disordered place.

'What's happening with Ubaid?' Ibrahim asked.

Osama glanced at him in the rear-view mirror. 'He didn't kill anyone.'

'I know,' Ibrahim said. 'I know he didn't kill her. It was the other guy, al-Adnan. But Ubaid must have *known* about her. This whole time I thought he was going after me, but he wasn't. He was going after her.'

'Maybe.'

'There's no *maybe*,' Ibrahim said. 'From the first moment he heard about her disappearance, he was trying to find her guilty of something. I could feel it. He had to have known. You're telling me it was just a coincidence that the man she was blackmailing got put in charge of finding her?'

'They think Ubaid and al-Adnan may have known each other,' Osama admitted. 'They belonged to the same falconry club. They may even have gone hunting together. But we don't have any proof that they ever talked about the blackmail together. It's still a very thin connection.'

'Oh, come on!'

'Would you tell someone you were being blackmailed?'

'Sure. Maybe. Look, Miss Hijazi told me that Sabria found these men through her connections at Sitteen. She went looking for women who'd been abused by their employers, and that's how she found her blackmail victims. But Ubaid was the exception. He had to be. She worked with him in Undercover. That's probably how she found out about his tendencies in the first place.'

'Maybe,' Osama said. 'But it doesn't mean that *he* knew she was the blackmailer.'

Ibrahim sat back. 'So back to my question: what's happening with Ubaid?'

Osama gritted his teeth. 'He's still claiming that it wasn't rape, it was consensual. And until we find the woman on the tape, we can't disprove his claim. You know how these things work.'

'I want to kill him myself.'

'Well, don't go ruining your career now,' Osama said.

They turned onto a side street that ran parallel with Makhzoumi and which took them into Television Street in Ghulail, the notorious car-washing blocks, where African men stood poised on every corner with buckets and cloths, waving at passers-by. They ignored the police car, unmarked though it was. Most of the workers were illegal; they had sharp eyes for the law. Some men slid into alleys but most simply went about their business. The area seemed chaotic, but the men were all governed by a few bosses, a veritable car-washing mafia, although its leaders were good enough to pay *zakat* by donating ten per cent of their earnings to the people even poorer than those working for them.

When the car reached Mahjar Street, Ibrahim saw that they were headed for the King Abdul Aziz Hospital.

'What's going on?' he called up to Osama.

'Just making a quick stop,' Osama replied.

They drove up the quiet street beneath the shade of palm trees, went through a car park surrounded by lush, green shrubbery, and stopped in front of the hospital's stone façade. Osama left Shaya in charge of the car and motioned Ibrahim and Saffanah out.

With some surprise and a growing dread, Ibrahim got out, Saffanah on his tail. The hospital was for members and families of the National Guard. He couldn't imagine what he and Saffanah were doing there. They followed Osama to a side door, past a security desk and down a long hallway.

Osama wound them through a labyrinth that ended at a small room. A cloaked and veiled woman stood beside the door. She swung it open.

They went inside. The room was empty.

From his pocket, Osama removed a folded sheet of paper and a set of keys. 'Take these.'

'What are they?'

'A set of keys to a car parked around the side of the building and a map of where you're supposed to be going.'

'Are you kidding me?'

Osama shook his head. 'In the car's glove compartment you'll find an envelope with some money in it, a fake passport and a credit card. You'll be driving to the marina. There's a boat there that will take you out of the country. You'll find a change of clothes on the boat.'

'You could lose your job over this.'

'Not if they don't catch you.'

'I'm coming with you.' Saffanah's voice was small but it stopped them.

'No.' Ibrahim turned to her. 'I'm not going anywhere. *We* are not going anywhere. We're going back to the house.'

'I have to go,' she said.

'You can't—' He stopped himself and realised how stupid he was going to sound. Of course she had to go. She was carrying her proof of adultery, and soon it was going to show.

'She can go with you,' Osama said. 'Tell them she's your wife. She won't need a passport.'

'I'll tell you what,' Ibrahim said to Saffanah. 'I'll take you to the marina, and I'll make sure you get on the boat.'

'What?' Her voice was sharp now. 'I can't go on my own.'

'She's right,' Osama said.

'You stay out of this.' He turned back to Saffanah and suddenly didn't know what to say. *You should stay here? Face the accusations and punishments that are coming your way?*

She glanced at Osama. 'Where is the boat going?'

'Egypt,' he said.

She turned to Ibrahim without a moment's hesitation. 'I have to go.'

'Saffanah . . .'

'It's the only place I can go.' She looked at Osama, and then again at Ibrahim.

Osama must have noticed him capitulate. He motioned them to the window. 'Let's go before we're caught.'

Saffanah went first and Ibrahim followed, both making the short leap into the shrubbery below. He told himself he was only going to take her to the boat. His heart was racing, his senses hyper-focused and he scanned for the slightest signs of movement in the bushes. When he turned back to the window, Osama was gone.

They crept along the side of the building until they reached a parked car, half-hidden by hedges. He handed Saffanah the map.

He had to struggle to focus on the road. Information filtered in. Saffanah was talking in nervous spasms. Take a left here. Go right. She had put on her seat belt.

They arrived at the marina and Katya's husband was there, standing on a boat marked plainly with Coast Guard insignia. It all became clear to him then. Of course he couldn't let Saffanah go alone. He had to escort her out of the country, at least make sure she got set up on her own somewhere. Nayir rushed them on board and down into the hold where they wouldn't be seen, and Saffanah led the way without a moment's hesitation.

They sat on a small couch built into the hull. When the boat hit choppy waters, Saffanah ran to the bathroom to throw up and he gripped the seat cushion, swallowed his own nausea, and tried very hard not to think of all he was leaving behind.

Ali Dossari was beheaded in the car park of Jeddah's Juffali mosque. Because of the exposure that the criminal trial had brought to the case, the police and the Ministry arranged to conduct the execution on a Friday after noon prayers, when everyone was expecting it. The Ministry of the Interior also decided that his punishment should be a special one.

Once the executioner had chopped off Dossari's head, the doctor who attended all executions – typically to determine if the beheading had in fact killed the criminal – was instructed to sew Dossari's head back onto his body. The doctor had some practice with this, as certain families requested the procedure before burying their dead. Once the head was sewn back on, the body was strung up on a pole that was affixed to the centre of the car park. The body remained there for the rest of the day, under police guard, so that people would see just what happened to those whose crimes were especially heinous.

Such 'crucifixions' were rare, and this was perhaps only the second one in thirty years, but the Ministry had openly sanctioned it. And while the human rights groups cried foul, anyone who read the Quran would know the justification.

The punishment of those who wage war against Allah and His Messenger, and strive with might and main for mischief through the land is: execution, or crucifixion, or the cutting off of hands and feet from opposite sides . . . that is their disgrace in this world, and a heavy punishment is theirs in the Hereafter.

At the end of the evening, they took down Dossari's body. They gave him his last rituals, the proper washing and recitations, and buried him in the city graveyard. Even though there were people who said that his actions had perverted Islam and that he did not deserve to be considered a Muslim, and so did not deserve an Islamic funeral, the country stuck by its policy that even murderers should be treated as Muslims and given a certain dignity in death.

46

In the end, Katya's wedding was the biggest one she'd ever been to. After her father had called his sister in Lebanon and mentioned, mildly, that he was worried that 'only one hundred people' would show up, Aunt Nour gave a battle cry and summoned an army of Hijazis from up and down the Levant. Cousins Katya had never heard of came from as far as Gaza, and the ones she did know brought their entire families, including in-laws. How they all paid for their trips to Jeddah, she had no idea, but it touched her deeply that they had made the effort simply to make sure that her wedding was suitably crowded with happy guests.

For the first half of the banquet she sat in a small corner of the hall, on what appeared to be a Royal Family Throne, meeting the women and receiving their good wishes. It seemed that every third person she met was so-and-so, my friend from Facebook. It became clear that in their efforts to fill the room, people had dragged in as many Jeddawis as possible, even if they were only internet friends. But the women were joyful and seemed to be having a wonderful time.

It was only when she got off her throne and began to wander through the room, escorted by a small battalion of young cousins, that she began to realise that the guests were looking at her with a certain not-too-flattering awe. There was something like disbelief in their faces, and Katya overheard enough whispering to understand their marvel: that a woman of her age had managed to arrange a union with such a wealthy fellow – for that's all that was being whispered about Nayir. His uncle had paid for everything. It naturally followed that Nayir himself was as filthy rich as a prince, and that Katya, being neither exceptionally beautiful nor of an age that was considered desirable, had probably used up a lifetime of luck to win a man of Nayir's status. She did not disabuse anyone of their notions.

She wondered how Nayir was faring. The men's banquet hall was just across the street. According to Aunt Nour, who kept a tab on events there by calling Abu on his mobile phone every hour, the men's hall had already been raided twice by a certain faction of the religious police who were devoted to assuring that weddings remained segregated. Abu's opinion was that the *mutaween* were simply making a bid for free food and a portion of the cake.

Four hours into it, Aunt Nour found Katya in the crowd and told her it was time for the groom to come in, so three hundred women could sit in their seats and take a good look at the husband-to-be. Katya was escorted to a corner of a large stage that had a catwalk and flashing pink and purple lights. Aunt Nour looked out at the crowd with a sigh.

'They're nice people,' she said, 'but in the end, Katya dear, you shouldn't give a damn what they think.'

Nayir stood facing a large black curtain that was thick and heavy and stubbornly unmoved by the circulating air. It hung from a ceiling thirty feet above him and felt both protective and ominous. Beyond the curtain, invisible and muffled, was a room full of women, all moving to their seats and slowly falling silent as they waited for him to step onto the stage. He would walk like a ridiculous fashion model past the rows of seats, so that he could show them his face and convince them, *insha'allah*, that he was a good man, healthy and solid and honest and strong, someone worthy of Katya's love.

These male-model catwalks had been known to go wrong. He'd heard tales of women heckling and hooting lasciviously. He'd heard about booing. He'd heard about men stumbling and falling. But what scared him the most was simply knowing that in a few short minutes, three hundred women were going to be scrutinising his terrified face.

He heard rustling near the curtain's edge. They were coming for him now and every single atom in his body felt the urge to turn and run away. Was this really necessary? He could simply go out the back door and no one would come after him. He would come back later, in an hour or two, when his face and palms had stopped leaking like taps. It would be easy to do, except that he couldn't move. His feet were made of stone, his body like boulders piled atop one another. Any movement would send everything tumbling down. Then the curtain parted and Katya appeared.

She was radiant. Even the nervousness in her eyes couldn't dim the smile lighting up her face. She took his hand and squeezed it.

'Are you ready for this?'

They'd been officially married the day before but they hadn't spent the night together. The wedding wasn't over yet. This was the last step, and it surprised him that it should prove the most difficult one of all.

'You don't want to do this,' she said.

Was he crazy? He'd spent so many years wanting to be married, wanting a wife of his own, children, in-laws, a bigger immediate family than his bachelor uncle could provide. This was a doorway to the world he had never been allowed to enter until now, the world of a woman's voice, her body, her touch. A world of kitchens and bedrooms and shouting children, and now, after so many years, the door was opening.

'No,' he said. 'I'm ready.'

'It's only for a few minutes,' she said.

'OK.'

He was going to do something he'd never done before, and would probably never do again, and he told himself that this was what he wanted, what he had always wanted, even if he didn't believe it right now. Without another word, he pulled the curtain aside.

They met a sheer wall of sound, an audience exploding in joyous ululations and applause. Nayir stepped onto the stage, holding Katya's hand. She laughed nervously. He squeezed her fingers. They let the sound wash over them as they stood staring, happy and frightened, blinded by the glittering lights.

GLOSSARY

abaaya – a long, loose black cloak worn by women in Saudi Arabia.

adhan – the Islamic call to prayer recited by a muezzin.

ahlan biik – 'and welcome to you'.

ahlan wa'sahlan – 'welcome' (hard to translate – loosely it's something like 'family and familiar comforts').

al-Balad – a historical neighbourhood in downtown Jeddah.

al'hamdulillah – 'Thanks be to God'.

ar-ruqyah ash-shar'eeya – a type of spiritual healing, similar to exorcism. ('An incantation of Sharia.')

bism'allah, ar-rahman, ar-rahim – 'In the name of Allah, most gracious, most merciful', the opening phrase of a Muslim prayer.

boofiya – a small café and bodega.

burqa (also *niqab*) – in the Gulf countries, burqa or *niqab* refers to a veil that covers a woman's face. Not to be confused with the enveloping outer garment, also called a burqa, worn by women in other Muslim countries.

Dhuhr – the second of the five daily Muslim prayers, occurs just after noon.

djinn – the collective genie.

djinni – a single genie.

du'a – an invocation or prayer to express submission to God or to ask for assistance.

efreet – a supernatural creature similar to a *djinni*, usually malicious.

Fajr – the first of the five daily Muslim prayers, occurs just before sunrise.

311

fatwa – a religious opinion or edict issued by a Muslim cleric.

ghutra – a cotton head scarf made of a large square of fabric and worn by men.

Hadith – the collected narratives about the prophet Mohammed.

Hajj – the pilgrimage to Mecca.

halal – kosher, permissible by Islamic law.

halala – a small unit of currency in Saudi Arabia, one hundredth of a Saudi riyal.

halawa, also halva – various types of confections, commonly a tahini-based, crumbly paste made with pistachios.

hookah (also *shisha*) – a water pipe used for smoking tobacco.

insha'allah – 'God willing'.

'iqal – a loop of black cord used to fix the male head scarf (*ghutra*) onto the head.

Isha' – the fifth of the five daily Muslim prayers.

istiqara – a type of prayer that asks for guidance in difficult matters.

Jahannam – the Islamic concept of Hell.

jihad – a war or battle waged in the name of religious duty, also a personal struggle in the name of spiritual development.

Ka'aba – the black monument in the centre of the holy mosque, the Masjid al-Haram, in Mecca.

karkadé – dried hibiscus flower, used for dyeing things a bright purplish red.

la hawla walla kuwata illa billa – 'There is no strength or power but Allah'.

Mabahith – the secret police in Saudi's Ministry of the Interior.

Maghreb – the fourth of the five Muslim daily prayers, occurring just after sunset.

majlis – lit. 'a place of sitting'. Any gathering place, typically a living room or an assembly hall.

masa' al-khayr – 'Good evening'.

mash'allah – a phrase that serves to express praise or happiness for someone or something. ('God has willed it.')

mehram – a man with whom a woman is allowed to associate in strict interpretations of Islam, i.e., her father, brother, husband or son.

misyar – a marriage institution in Islam whereby a man can have a wife without financial responsibility.

muezzin – a man who leads the call to prayer at a mosque.

mujahideen – freedom fighters.

Mukhabarat – the primary intelligence agency of Saudi Arabia.

mutaween – plural of *mutawwa*, religious policemen from the Committee for the Protection of Virtue and the Prevention of Vice in Saudi Arabia. (Also called *hay'ah*, or the 'commission'.)

na'uzhu bi Allah – 'We seek refuge in God'.

niqab – (also burqa) a black veil that covers the face, worn by women.

sabah al-khayr – 'Good morning'.

sa'eeda – 'madame'.

salaam aleikum – a greeting, literally 'peace be with you'.

salaam aleikum wa rahmatullahi wa barakatu – 'May the peace, mercy and blessings of God be with you'.

Sambooli – a type of sandwich usually consisting of eggs and shrimp.

shaytan – a kind of evil genie (plural: *shayateen*).

shisha – can refer to a hookah pipe or to the molasses-based tobacco that is smoked in it.

souq – an outdoor market, any commercial marketplace.

subhan'allah – 'glory be to God'.

zakat – the practice of giving a donation to charity based on a portion of your wealth.